DAUGHTER
OF THE
DEEP

Series by Rick Riordan

PERCY JACKSON AND THE OLYMPIANS

THE KANE CHRONICLES

THE HEROES OF OLYMPUS

MAGNUS CHASE AND THE GODS OF ASGARD

THE TRIALS OF APOLLO

DAUGHTER
OF THE
DEEP

BY RICK RIORDAN

DISNEY • HYPERION

LOS ANGELES   NEW YORK

Text copyright © 2021 by Rick Riordan
Illustrations copyright © 2021 by Lavanya Naidu

First Hardcover Edition, October 2021
First Paperback Edition, April 2023
10 9 8 7 6 5 4 3 2 1
FAC-029261-23048
Printed in the United States of America

This book is set in Sabon LT Pro/Monotype
Designed by Joann Hill

Library of Congress Cataloging-in-Publication Control Number for
Hardcover Edition: 2021009225
ISBN 978-1-368-07793-4

Follow @ReadRiordan
Visit www.DisneyBooks.com

SUSTAINABLE
FORESTRY
INITIATIVE

Certified Sourcing

www.sfiprogram.org
SFI-01054
The SFI label applies to the text stock

Nature's creative power
is far beyond man's
instinct of destruction.

–Jules Verne,
20,000 Leagues Under the Sea

FOREWORD
Don't Pick Up a Starfish by Its Arm

Did you know more than 80 percent of the ocean remains unexplored? EIGHTY, PEOPLE! It is very possible that at this moment a mermaid and a giant squid are munching on macro-algae macaroni and wondering when we're going to catch up and discover that Atlantis was just a theme park that went terribly wrong. Who knows?

No one can say for certain, because so much of the ocean is unknown. And I am terrified of the unknown, so it goes without saying that I am absolutely terrified of the ocean. Perhaps it started when, at the age of ten, I picked up a starfish by one of its arms . . . and soon found myself holding a single wiggling appendage. At the time, I didn't know that starfish arms could regenerate. I believed I was a murderer. I fell to my knees and bellowed with horror. (CURSE YE, FORMIDABLE MIGHT! SUCH INNOCENCE . . . DESTROYED! DOES THIS MEAN I CAN PERMANENTLY SKIP GYM?)

But the more that something terrifies me, the more I tend to obsess over it. And ever since that fateful starfish encounter, the ocean, with its strange inhabitants—that's right, I'm looking at you, various *echinoderms* and *ophiuroids*—has loomed large in my mind as a place of unknowable power, unimaginable beauty, and untapped potential.

Rick Riordan's *Daughter of the Deep* captures every single facet of that awe and terror.

If you have ever craved a story that will leave your heart racing, your lungs gasping from numerous twists and turns, your soul heaving from the effort of carrying around an ensemble cast that includes smol, ingenious, and possibly bloodthirsty cinnamon rolls (oh, and a humongous creature of the deep who, truly, just wants love), you will find all that and more in the pages ahead. Our story begins with two warring schools and a cataclysmic event that sends the freshman class of the elite Harding-Pencroft Academy on a deadly mission to unearth a secret about the kind of technological power that can remake the world. I was on the edge of my seat the whole time as the crew navigated high-tech high jinks, deep-sea riddles, and the sort of military tactics that somehow make *me* feel smarter despite the fact that I have been ensconced in a soft blankie for the better part of the day.

I cannot think of a better captain to helm this watery adventure than the formidable Ana Dakkar. Ana is everything I wished I could be at fifteen. Fearless, brilliant, a linguistic whiz, friends with a dolphin named Socrates, and—most importantly to a daydreaming adolescent Rosh—burdened with an ancestral legacy that is the stuff of legends.

You see, Ana is one of the last descendants of Captain Nemo, and that's where things get complicated. As the last of the Dakkars, Ana not only finds herself grappling with an inheritance that could change the entire world's understanding of technology, but she's also struggling with larger questions, like what are we owed, and what do we owe others? It's easy to make the right decisions when all the world is watching, but when you're deep underwater, where the sun can't see you, you might just end up doing something you never expected. . . .

To me, this story is a lot like the ocean. Equal parts thrilling and terrifying, and, no matter which way you look at it, downright cool. Enjoy! And don't eat too many cinnamon rolls.

Roshani Chokshi

INTRODUCTION

My journey under the sea started in landlocked Bologna, Italy, in 2008. I was there for a children's book fair, right before *The Battle of the Labyrinth* and *The 39 Clues: The Maze of Bones* were scheduled for release. I was having dinner in the basement of a restaurant with about fourteen of the top brass from Disney Publishing when the president of the division turned to me and said, "Rick, is there any existing Disney intellectual property you'd love to write about?" I didn't hesitate in saying, "*20,000 Leagues Under the Sea.*" It took me another twelve years before I was ready to write it, but my version of that story is now in your hands.

Who is Captain Nemo? (No, not the cartoon fish.)
If you're not familiar with the original Captain Nemo, he's a character created by the French author Jules Verne in the nineteenth century. Verne wrote about him in two novels, *20,000 Leagues Under the Sea* (1870) and *The Mysterious Island* (1875), in which Nemo commands the world's most advanced submarine, the *Nautilus*.

Captain Nemo was smart, well-educated, courteous, and massively wealthy. He was also angry, bitter, and dangerous. Imagine a combination of Bruce Wayne, Tony Stark, and Lex Luthor. Formerly known as Prince Dakkar, Nemo had fought the British colonial government in India. In retaliation, the British killed his wife and children. This was Dakkar's supervillain/superhero origin story. He renamed himself Nemo, which is

Latin for *no one*. (Greek myth fans: This was an Easter egg about/shout-out to Odysseus, who told the Cyclops Polyphemus that his name was Nobody.) Nemo dedicated the rest of his life to terrorizing the colonial European powers on the high seas, sinking and plundering their ships and making them fear the unstoppable "sea monster" that was the *Nautilus*.

Who wouldn't want to have that kind of power? As a kid, every time I jumped in a lake or even a swimming pool, I liked to pretend I was Captain Nemo. I could sink enemy ships with impunity, go all over the world undetected, explore depths no one had ever visited, and uncover fabulous ruins and priceless treasures. I could submerge into my own secret realm and never return to the surface world (which was kind of horrible anyway). When I eventually wrote about Percy Jackson, the son of Poseidon, you can bet that my old daydreams about Captain Nemo and the *Nautilus* were a big reason I chose to make Percy a demigod of the sea.

Now, I'll be honest, I found Verne's novels slow going when I was a kid. But I *did* enjoy my uncle's old Classics Illustrated editions, and I loved watching the Disney film version of *20,000 Leagues Under the Sea*—even the cheesy bits like Kirk Douglas dancing and singing, and the giant rubber squid attacking the ship. Only when I was older did I realize how rich and complex the original stories were. Nemo was even more interesting than I had imagined. And I began to see little openings in the narrative where Verne had left room for a possible sequel. . . .

Why does Captain Nemo still matter?
Verne was one of the first writers of science fiction. Looking back from the twenty-first century, it can be difficult for us to appreciate just how revolutionary his ideas were, but Verne imagined technology that would not exist for hundreds of years

to come. A self-powered submarine that could circle the globe continuously and never have to dock for supplies? Impossible! In 1870, submarines were still newfangled inventions—dangerous tin cans that were more likely to blow up and kill everyone on board than to complete a trip around the world. Verne also wrote *Around the World in 80 Days* at a time when making the trip that quickly was unthinkable, and *Journey to the Center of the Earth*, a feat that is still far beyond human technology, though someday, who knows?

The best science fiction can shape how humans see their own future. Jules Verne did that better than anyone. Way back in the 1800s, he suggested what *could* be possible, and humans rose to the challenge. When people talk about how fast a plane or a ship can circle the world, they still use *Around the World in 80 Days* as a benchmark. At one time, eighty days was an incredibly short trip for circumnavigating the globe. Now we can do it in less than eighty hours by plane, and less than forty days by sea.

Verne's *Journey to the Center of the Earth* inspired generations of spelunkers to explore the earth's cave systems and spurred geoengineers to figure out how the layers of the earth function.

Captain Nemo, on the other hand, raised awareness of the importance the oceans would have for the future of the planet. We know most of the Earth is covered with water, and 80 percent of the oceans are *still* unexplored. Figuring out how to tap the power of the sea, and to live *with* the power of the sea as our climate changes, may be key to human survival. Verne envisioned all of that in his books.

Nemo and his crew are able to live self-sufficiently without ever touching dry land. The sea provides all their needs. In *20,000 Leagues*, Nemo tells Aronnax that the *Nautilus* is entirely electric, and draws all its power from the ocean. In *The Mysterious Island*, Cyrus Harding speculates that when coal runs out, humans will learn to draw energy from the abundant hydrogen of the ocean. That is *still* a goal people are trying to achieve today, and one of the reasons I decided that Nemo must have unlocked the secret of cold fusion.

In *20,000 Leagues*, Nemo's crew uses electrical Leyden guns that are more effective and elegant than standard arms. They have almost limitless wealth thanks to the many shipwrecks they've plundered. They've discovered the secrets of subaquatic agriculture, so food is never an issue. Most importantly, they have *freedom*. They are independent of any nation's laws and can come and go as they please. They answer to no one except Nemo. Whether that is good or bad . . . I guess that depends on what you think of Nemo!

The importance of the sea, the importance of imagining new technological advances—these are great reasons to still read Jules Verne. But there's one more critical thing to consider. Verne made Captain Nemo an Indian prince whose people suffered under European colonialism. His character explores themes that are just as critical now as they were in Victorian times. How do you find a voice and power when society denies you those privileges? How do you fight injustice? Who gets to write the history books and decide who were the "good guys" and the "bad guys"? Nemo is an outlaw, a rebel, a genius, a scientist, an explorer, a pirate, a gentleman, an "archangel of vengeance." He's a complicated guy, which makes him a lot of fun to read about. I was fascinated by the idea of fast-forwarding his legacy into the twenty-first century and looking at what his descendants would be dealing with all these years later.

What would *you* do if you had the power of the *Nautilus* at your command? I hope *Daughter of the Deep* will inspire you to think about your own adventures, the way Jules Verne inspired me. Make ready to dive. We're going deep!

DAUGHTER
OF THE
DEEP

HARDING-PENCROFT ACADEMY

HOUSE DOLPHIN
communications, exploration, cryptography,
counterintelligence

HOUSE SHARK
command, combat, weapons systems, logistics

HOUSE CEPHALOPOD
engineering, applied mechanics, innovation,
defensive systems

HOUSE ORCA
medicine, psychology, education, marine biology,
communal memory

THE FRESHMAN CLASS
OF HARDING-PENCROFT

HOUSE DOLPHIN
Ana Dakkar, prefect
Lee-Ann Best
Virgil Esparza
Halimah Nasser
Jack Wu

HOUSE SHARK
Gemini Twain, prefect
Dru Cardenas
Cooper Dunne
Kiya Jensen
Eloise McManus

HOUSE CEPHALOPOD
Tia Romero, prefect
Robbie Barr
Nelinha da Silva
Meadow Newman
Kay Ramsay

HOUSE ORCA
Franklin Couch, prefect
Ester Harding
Linzi Huang
Rhys Morrow
Brigid Salter

CHAPTER ONE

Here's the thing about life-shattering days.

They start just like any other. You don't realize your world is about to explode into a million smoking pieces of awfulness until it's too late.

The last Friday of my freshman year, I wake in my dorm room at five a.m. as usual. I get up quietly so as not to disturb my roommates, change into my bikini, and head for the ocean.

I love the campus in the early morning. The white concrete facades of the buildings are turning pink and turquoise in the sunrise. The quad's grassy lawn is empty except for seagulls and squirrels waging their eternal war for the snack crumbs we students have left behind. The air smells of sea salt, eucalyptus, and fresh cinnamon rolls baking in the cafeteria. The cool Southern California breeze raises goose bumps on my arms and legs. It's times like this I can't believe I'm lucky enough to go to school at Harding-Pencroft Academy.

Assuming I survive this weekend's trials, of course. I might wash out in disgrace, or die tangled in a net at the bottom of some underwater obstacle course. . . . But hey, it's still better than ending the term doing five jillion multiple-choice problems on some state standardized test.

I follow the gravel footpath that leads to the ocean.

A hundred yards past the naval-warfare building, the cliffs drop into the Pacific. Far below, white surf ribs the steel-blue sea. Waves rumble and reverberate around the curve of the bay like the snores of a giant.

My brother, Dev, is waiting for me at the edge of the cliff. "You're late, Ana Banana."

He knows I hate it when he calls me that.

"I *will* push you off," I warn.

"Well, you could try." When Dev grins, he does this lopsided squint, like he can't equalize the pressure in one ear. The other girls tell me it's adorable. I'm not convinced. His dark hair is spiky in front, like a sea urchin. He claims it's his "style." I think it's just because he sleeps with a pillow over his face.

As usual, he's wearing his standard black HP wetsuit with the silver Shark logo on the front, indicating his house. Dev thinks I'm crazy to make the dive in a bikini. In most ways, he's a tough guy. When it comes to cold temperatures, though, he's kind of a baby.

We do our predive stretches. This spot is one of the few places along the California coast where you can free dive without getting smashed to pieces against the rocks below. The cliffs are sheer, plunging straight into the depths of the bay.

It's quiet and peaceful this time of morning. Despite Dev's responsibilities as a house captain, he is never too busy for our morning ritual. I love him for that.

"What did you bring for Socrates today?" I ask.

Dev gestures nearby. Two dead squid lie glistening in the grass. As a senior, Dev has access to the aquarium's feeding supplies. This means he can sneak little treats for our friend under the bay. The squid are about a foot long from tail to tentacles—slimy, silver and brown like oxidized aluminum.

Loligo opalescens. California market squid. Life span six to nine months.

I can't turn off the data stream. Our marine biology professor, Dr. Farez, has trained us too well. You learn to remember the details because everything, literally *everything*, will be on her quizzes.

Socrates has another name for *Loligo opalescens.* He calls them breakfast.

"Nice." I pick up the squid, still cold from the freezer, and hand one to Dev. "You ready?"

"Hey, before we dive . . ." His expression turns serious. "I have something I want to give you. . . ."

I don't know if he's telling the truth or not, but I always fall for his distractions. As soon as he has my attention, he turns and jumps off the cliff.

I curse. "Oh, you little—"

Whoever jumps in first has a better chance of finding Socrates first.

I take a deep breath and leap after him.

Cliff-diving is the ultimate rush. I free-fall ten stories, wind and adrenaline screaming in my ears, then punch through the icy water.

I relish the shock to my system: the sudden cold, the sting of the brine on my cuts and scrapes. (If you don't have cuts and scrapes as a student at HP, you haven't been doing your combat exercises right.)

I plunge straight through a school of copper rockfish—dozens of frilly orange-and-white bruisers who look like punk-rock koi. But their tough looks are just for show, since they scatter with a massive burst of YIKES! Ten meters below me, I spot the shimmering whirlwind of Dev's bubble trail. I follow it down.

My static apnea record is five minutes. Obviously, I can't

hold my breath that long when I'm exerting myself, but still, this is my environment. On the surface, Dev has the advantage of strength and speed. Underwater, I've got the endurance and agility. At least, that's what I tell myself.

My brother floats above the sandy seabed, his legs crossed like he's been meditating there for hours. He's keeping the squid behind his back, because Socrates has arrived and is nuzzling Dev's chest as if to say, *C'mon, I know what you've got for me.*

Socrates is a gorgeous animal. And I don't say that just because my house is Dolphin. He's a young male bottlenose, nine feet long, with bluish-gray skin and a prominent dark streak across his dorsal fin. I know he isn't *actually* smiling. His long-beaked mouth is just shaped that way. Still, I find it unbelievably cute.

Dev produces his squid. Socrates snaps it up and swallows it whole. Dev grins at me, a bubble escaping from his lips. His expression says *Ha-ha, the dolphin likes me best.*

I offer Socrates my squid. He's only too happy to have seconds. He lets me scratch his head, which is as smooth and taut as a water balloon, then rub his pectoral fins. (Dolphins are suckers for pectoral-fin rubs.)

Then he does something I'm not expecting. He bucks, pushing my hand up with his rostrum in a gesture I've come to read as *Let's go!* or *Hurry!* He veers and swims off, the wake from his tail buffeting my face.

I watch until he disappears into the gloom. I wait for him to circle back. He doesn't.

I don't understand.

Usually he doesn't eat and run. He likes to hang out. Dolphins are naturally social. Most days, he'll follow us to the surface and leap over our heads, or play hide-and-seek, or pepper us with squeaks and clicks that sound like questions. That's why we call him Socrates. He never gives answers—just asks questions.

But today he seemed agitated . . . almost worried.

At the edge of my vision, the blue lights of the security grid stretch across the mouth of the bay—a glowing diamond pattern I've grown used to over the last two years. As I watch, the lights wink out, then flicker back on. I've never seen them do that before.

I glance at Dev. He doesn't appear to have noticed the change in the grid. He points up. *Race you.*

He kicks for the surface, leaving me in a cloud of sand.

I want to stay under longer. I'm curious to see if the lights go out again, or if Socrates comes back. But my lungs are burning. Reluctantly, I follow Dev.

After I join him on the surface and catch my breath, I ask if he saw the grid flicker off.

He squints at me. "Are you sure you weren't just blacking out?"

I splash his face. "I'm serious. We should tell somebody."

Dev wipes the water from his eyes. He still looks skeptical.

To be honest, I've never understood why we have a state-of-the-art electronic underwater barrier across the mouth of the bay. I know it's supposed to keep the sea life safe by keeping out everything else, like poachers, recreational divers, and pranksters from our rival high school, Land Institute. But it seems like overkill, even for a school that produces the world's best marine scientists and naval cadets. I don't know exactly how the grid works. I *do* know it isn't supposed to flicker, though.

Dev must see that I'm genuinely worried. "Fine," he says. "I'll report it."

"Also, Socrates was acting weird."

"A dolphin acting weird. Okay, I'll report that, too."

"I could do it, but like you always say, I'm just a lowly freshman. You're the big, powerful house captain of the Sharks, so—"

He splashes me back. "If you're done being paranoid, I really *do* have something for you." He pulls a glittering chain from the pouch of his dive belt. "Happy early birthday, Ana."

He hands me the necklace: a single black pearl set in gold. It takes me a second to understand what he's given me. My chest tightens.

"Mom's?" I can barely say the word.

The pearl was the centerpiece of Mom's mangalsutra, her wedding necklace. It's also the only thing we have left of her.

Dev smiles, though his eyes get that familiar melancholy drift. "I got the pearl reset. You'll be fifteen next week. She'd want you to wear it."

This is the sweetest thing he's ever done for me. I'm going to start weeping. "But . . . why not wait until next week?"

"You're leaving for your freshman trials today. I wanted you to have the pearl for luck—just in case, you know, you fail spectacularly or something."

He really knows how to ruin a moment.

"Oh, shut up," I say.

He laughs. "I'm kidding, of course. You're going to do great. You always do great, Ana. Just be careful, okay?"

I feel myself flush. I'm not sure what to do with all this warmth and affection. "Well . . . the necklace is beautiful. Thank you."

" 'Course." He stares at the horizon, a flicker of worry in his dark brown eyes. Maybe he's thinking about the security grid, or he really *is* nervous about my weekend trials. Or maybe he's thinking about what happened two years ago, when our parents flew over that horizon for the last time.

"Come on." He musters another reassuring smile, as he has done so often for my sake. "We'll be late for breakfast."

Always hungry, my brother, and always moving—the perfect Shark captain.

He swims for shore.

I look at my mother's black pearl—her talisman that was supposed to bring long life and protection from evil. Unfortunately for her and my father, it did neither. I scan the horizon, wondering where Socrates has gone, and what he was trying to tell me.

Then I swim after my brother, because suddenly I don't want to be alone in the water.

CHAPTER TWO

In the cafeteria, I wolf down a plate of tofu-nori scramble—delicious as usual. Then I rush to the dorms to grab my go bag.

We freshmen live on the second floor of Shackleton Hall, above the eighth-graders. Our rooms aren't as spacious as the sophomore and junior digs in Cousteau Hall. And they're *definitely* not as nice as the senior suites in Zheng He, but they're light-years better than the cramped barracks we shared as eighth-graders during our "chum year" at HP.

I suppose I should get this out of the way. Harding-Pencroft is a five-year high school. We're divided into four houses, based on the results of our aptitude tests. We call the academy HP for short. And, yes, we've heard all the Harry Potter jokes. Thanks anyway.

When I get to my room, my roommates are freaking out.

Nelinha is stuffing tools, extra outfits, and cosmetics into her pack. Ester is frantically sorting index cards. She has, like, twelve stacks, all color coded, labeled, and highlighted. Her dog, Top, barks and jumps up and down like a furry pogo stick.

It's the usual pandemonium, but I can't help but smile. I love my crew. Thankfully, rooms aren't assigned by house, or I would never feel like I could be off duty and relax with my besties.

"Babe, don't over-pack," Nelinha tells Ester, while stuffing more socket wrenches and mascara into her own bag. (Nelinha calls everybody *babe*. It's just her thing.)

"I *need* my index cards," Ester says. "And treats for Top."

Yap! Top barks in agreement, trying his best to touch his nose to the ceiling.

Nelinha shrugs at me. *What can you do?*

She's rocking a sort of Rosie the Riveter look today. Her lush brown hair is tied back in a green bandana. The tails of her short-sleeved denim work shirt are knotted over her dark midriff. Her calf-length khakis are permanently stained with machine grease, but her makeup, as usual, is perfect. I swear, Nelinha could be crawling through the aquarium's pump system or fixing a boat engine and she'd *still* manage to look fashionable.

Her eyes widen when she sees the black pearl at the base of my throat. "Pretty! Where'd *that* come from?"

"Early birthday present from Dev," I say. "It, uh . . . belonged to our mom."

Her lips form an O. My roommates have heard all the tragic stories about my family. Between Nelinha, Ester, and me, our dorm room is one of the world's largest producers of tragic stories.

"Well," she says, "I've got the perfect skirt and blouse to go with that."

Nelinha's great for sharing clothes and makeup. We're more or less the same size, and we have the same skin tone—she's Brasileira parda; my ancestry is Bundeli Indian—so she can usually fix me up nicely for a school dance or a Saturday furlough in town. But today is not that kind of day.

"Nelinha, we're going to be living on a boat for the weekend," I remind her.

"I know, I know," says the girl who's made herself up just for the bus ride to the boat. "But when we get back. Maybe for the end-of-year party!"

Ester stuffs one last bag of dog biscuits into her duffel.

"OKAY," she announces. She turns in a circle, examining the room to see if she's forgotten anything. She's wearing her blue HOUSE ORCA T-shirt and flower-patterned shorts over a one-piece swimsuit. Her face is flushed. Her frizzy blond hair has been blown in three different directions. I've seen pictures of her as a baby: pinchable plump cheeks, wide blue eyes, a startled expression, like *What am I doing in this universe?* She hasn't really changed much.

"I'M READY!" she decides.

"Volume, babe," Nelinha says.

"Sorry," Ester says. "Let's go! We'll miss the bus!"

Ester hates being late. It's one of the anxieties Top is supposed to help her manage. How Top could make anybody feel *less* anxious, I've never understood, but he's the cutest emotional-support animal you'll ever meet. Part Jack Russell, part Yorkie, part tornado.

He sniffs my hand as he follows Ester out. Maybe I didn't clean all the squid juice from under my fingernails.

I grab the go bag I packed last night. I'm not taking much: Change of clothes. Wetsuit. Dive knife. Dive watch. None of us knows what the weekend trials will be like. They'll be mostly underwater (duh), but the upperclassmen won't tell us anything specific. Even Dev. They take their vows of secrecy *very* seriously. It's annoying.

I rush to catch up with my friends.

To get to the quad, we have to go downstairs and pass through the eighth-grade wing. For a long time, I thought this was an annoying interior-design flaw. Then I realized the dorms must have been arranged like this on purpose. It means the chum have to get out of our way several times a day, looking at us freshmen with expressions of fear and awe. For our part, every time we pass through, we can think *As lowly as we are, at least we're not* these *poor schmucks.* They all seem so small, young, and frightened. I wonder if we looked like that last year. Maybe we *still* look like that to the upperclassmen. I imagine Dev laughing.

Outside, the beautiful day is heating up. As we hurry across campus, I think about all the classes I'll be missing because of our trip.

The gymnasium: six climbing walls; two rope courses; hot and cold yoga rooms; courts for basketball, racquetball, volleyball, and bungee ball (my favorite). But Fridays are for martial arts. I'd be spending my morning getting thrown into a wall during malaa yuddha matches. I can't say I'll miss that.

The aquarium: the largest private research facility in the world, I'm told, with a better variety of marine life than Monterey Bay, Chimelong, or Atlanta. We operate rescue-and-rehabilitation units for leatherback turtles, otters, and sea lions (all of whom are my precious babies), but today would be my day to scrub the eel tanks, so see ya!

The natatorium: three swimming pools, including the Blue Hole, big and deep enough to run submarine simulations. The only larger swimming pool in the world is at NASA. As much as I love my indoor dive classes, I'll take the open ocean any day.

Finally we pass Verne Hall, the "gold-level" research wing. What goes on in there, I have no idea. We won't be allowed entry until we're juniors. Verne's gilded metal facade stands out among the campus's white buildings like a gold-crowned tooth. Its dark glass doors always seem to taunt me. *If you were cool enough, like your brother, you might be able to come inside. HA-HA-HA-HA.*

You'd think out of forty upperclassmen, *somebody* would be willing to drop a little juicy gossip about gold-level classes, but nope. Like I said, their commitment to secrecy is absolute and annoying. Honestly, I don't know if I'll be able to stay so tight-lipped if I get to be an upperclassman, but that's a problem for another year.

In the main quad, seniors are lazing on the grass. They're all done now except for finals and graduation, the lucky bums. Then they're off to top universities and promising careers. I don't see Dev, but his girlfriend, Amelia Leahy, my house captain, gives me a wave from across the lawn. She signs, *Good luck.*

I sign back, *Thanks.*

I tell myself, *I'll need it.*

I shouldn't be too worried. Our class is already down to twenty people—the max number allowed to advance. We lost ten students during our chum year. Another four so far this year. Theoretically, the rest of us could all survive the cut. Also, my family has attended HP for generations. And I'm the freshman prefect for House Dolphin. I'd have to screw up really badly to get kicked out. . . .

Ester, Nelinha, and I are almost the first ones to the bus. But, of course, Gemini Twain has gotten there before us. He's standing at the door with his clipboard, ready to take names and kick whatever needs kicking.

The Shark prefect is tall, dark, and lanky. Behind his back, everybody calls him Spider-Man, because he looks like Miles Morales from *Into the Spider-Verse*. He's not nearly that cool, though. We've come to a truce since last year, but I still don't like him.

"Nelinha da Silva." He checks off her name but won't meet her eyes. "Ester Harding. Prefect Ana Dakkar. Welcome aboard."

He says this like our shuttle bus is a battleship.

I give him a little bow. "Thank you, Prefect."

His eye twitches. Everything I do seems to bother him. That's okay with me. During our chum year, the guy made Nelinha cry. I will never forgive him for that.

Bernie is our driver today. He's a nice old dude, retired navy. He's got a coffee-stained smile, silver hair, and gnarled hands like tree roots.

Dr. Hewett sits next to him, going over the day's schedule. As usual, Hewett is pallid, sweaty, and disheveled. He smells like mothballs. He teaches my least-favorite class, Theoretical Marine Science, or TMS. Most of us call it "too much stuff." Sometimes we use a different word that begins with *s*.

Hewett is really strict, so this doesn't bode well for the trials. My friends and I sit at the back of the bus, as far away from him as possible.

As soon as all twenty freshmen are on board, the bus gets underway.

At the main gate, the heavily armed paramilitary dudes wave and smile as we leave, like, *Have a nice day, kids! Don't die!* I guess most high schools don't have this level of security or the fleet of tiny surveillance drones that constantly circle the campus. It's weird how quickly you get used to it, though.

As we turn onto Highway 1, I look back at campus—a dazzling collection of sugar-cube buildings perched on the cliff top above the bay.

A familiar feeling washes over me: *I can't believe I go to school here.* Then I remember I have no *choice* but to go to school here. After what happened to our parents, it's the only home Dev and I have in the world.

I wonder why I didn't see Dev at breakfast. What had security said when he reported that flicker of light along the security grid? It was probably nothing, like he thought.

Still, I clutch the black pearl at the base of my throat.

I remember the last words my mother ever said to me: *We'll be back before you know it.* Then she and my father disappeared forever.

CHAPTER THREE

"Freshmen." Dr. Hewett says the word like an insult.

He stands in the aisle, bracing himself with one hand on the seatback. He breathes heavily into the bus's microphone. "This weekend's trials will be very different from what you might be expecting."

This gets our attention. Everybody fixes their eyes on Hewett.

The professor is shaped like a diving bell—narrow shoulders tapering down to a wide waist, where his rumpled dress shirt is half untucked from his slacks. His frazzled gray hair and sad, watery eyes make him look like Albert Einstein after a night of running failed calculations.

Next to me, Ester shuffles through her index cards. Top rests his head in her lap. His tail thumps softly against my thigh.

"In thirty minutes," Hewett continues, "we will arrive in San Alejandro."

He waits for our whispering to die down. We associate San Alejandro with shopping, movies, and Saturday-night karaoke, not end-of-year trials. But I suppose it makes sense we would start there. The school's boat is usually moored in the harbor.

"We will proceed directly to the docks," Hewett continues.

"No detours, no side trips to buy refreshments. You will keep your phones *off*."

A few kids grumble. Harding-Pencroft strictly controls all communication through the school intranet. The campus is a cellular dead zone. You want to look up the breeding habits of jellyfish? No problem. You want to watch YouTube? Good luck with that.

The teachers say this is to keep us focused on our work. I suspect it's yet another security precaution, like the underwater grid, or the armed guards, or the drone surveillance. I don't understand it, but it's a fact of life.

Typically, when we get into town, we're like dehydrated cattle at a watering hole. We stampede to the first place with free Wi-Fi and drink it in.

"I will have further instructions once we're at sea," Hewett says. "Suffice to say, today you'll find out what the academy is truly about. And the academy will find out whether you can survive its requirements."

I want to think Hewett is just trying to scare us. The problem is, he never makes idle threats. If he says we'll have extra weekend homework, we do. If he predicts 90 percent of us will fail his next exam, we do.

Theoretical Marine Science *should* be a fun fluff class. We spend most of our time contemplating what ocean technology might look like in one or two hundred years. Or if science had taken a different course, what might have happened? What if Leonardo da Vinci had done more to develop sonar when he discovered it in 1490? What if the plans for Drebbel's "diving boat" hadn't been lost in the 1600s, or if Monturiol's anaerobic steam-powered submarine hadn't been scrapped for lack of funding in 1867? Would our technology today be more advanced?

It's cool stuff to think about, but also . . . not so practical?

Hewett acts as if his questions have right answers. Like, it's *theoretical*. How can you give somebody a B minus on their essay just because their guess is different than yours?

Anyway, I wish Colonel Apesh, our military-tactics professor, were chaperoning this trip. Or Dr. Kind, our physical-fitness teacher. Hewett can barely shuffle a few feet without getting winded. I don't see how he's going to judge what I imagine will be intensely physical underwater trials.

He turns over the microphone to Gemini Twain. Gem has made our group assignments for the weekend. We'll be divided into five teams of four, one member from each house. But first, he has a few rules to tell us about.

Of course he does. He is *such* a Shark. You could put him in charge of a toddler soccer team and he'd get delusions of grandeur. He'd have the kids marching in perfect unison within a week. Then he'd declare war on a neighboring toddler team.

He rattles off a list of his favorite regulations. My attention wanders. I look out the window.

The highway winds from switchback to switchback, hugging the cliffs. One moment, you can't see anything but trees. The next, you can trace the entire coastline all the way back to HP. When the school is in full view, I spot something strange in the bay. A thin line of wake heads toward the base of the cliffs, just where Dev and I were diving this morning. I can't see what's making it. There's no boat. It's moving too fast and too straight to be a sea animal. Something underwater, under propulsion.

The pit of my stomach feels like I'm free-falling again.

The wake line splits into three segments. It looks like a trident, its prongs racing to jab the coastline beneath the school.

"Hey!" I tell my friends. "Hey, look!"

By the time Ester and Nelinha get to the window, the view has disappeared behind trees and cliffs.

"What was it?" Nelinha asks.

Then the shock wave hits us. The bus shudders. Boulders topple into the road.

"Earthquake!" Gem drops the mic, literally, grabbing the nearest seatback to steady himself. Dr. Hewett is thrown hard against the window.

Cracks splinter the asphalt as we skid toward the guardrail. All twenty of us, well-trained freshmen, scream like kindergarteners.

Somehow, Bernie regains control of the bus.

He slows, looking for a place to pull over. We round another bend, and HP comes into view, except now . . .

Ester screams, which starts Top whimpering in her lap. Nelinha presses her hands against the glass. "No. No way. No."

I yell, "Bernie, stop! Stop here!"

Bernie pulls into a turnout—one of the scenic overlooks where tourists can snap pictures of the Pacific. The view is clear all the way back to HP, but there's nothing scenic about it now.

Kids are crying. Their faces press against the windows. My insides twist with disbelief.

A second shock wave hits us. We watch in horror as another massive wedge of earth calves into the bay, taking the last of those beautiful sugar cubes with it.

I shove my way down the aisle. I hammer on the doors until Bernie opens them. I run to the edge of the cliff and grip the cold steel guardrail.

I find myself mumbling desperate prayers. "Three-Eyed One, Lord Shiva, who nourishes all beings, may He liberate us from death. . . ."

But there is no liberation.

My brother was on that campus. So were 150 other people and an aquarium full of marine animals. A square mile of the California coast has crumbled into the ocean.

Harding-Pencroft Academy is gone.

CHAPTER FOUR

Some of my classmates stand at the guardrail and cry. Others hug one another. Others desperately search for a phone signal, trying to text friends or call for help. Eloise McManus howls and throws rocks at the ocean. Cooper Dunne paces like a captive lion, kicking the bus's front tires, then the back ones.

Mascara traces down Nelinha's cheeks like dirty rain. She stands protectively over Ester, who sits cross-legged on the gravel, sobbing into Top's brown-and-white fur.

Gemini Twain says what we're all thinking: "This is impossible."

He waves his arms, pointing to where our school used to be. *"Impossible!"*

I'm not really present. I'm floating about six inches above my body. I can feel my heart hammering in my chest, but it's a dull, distant beat, like music coming from a stereo system in the dorm room below mine. My emotions are wrapped in gauze. My vision flickers around the edges.

I realize I'm dissociating. I've talked with the school counselor, Dr. Francis, about this. It's happened before, when I got the news about my parents. Now Dev is gone. Dr. Francis is gone. My house captain, Amelia. Dr. Farez. Colonel Apesh. Dr. Kind.

The baby otters I nursed just yesterday in the aquarium. The nice cafeteria lady, Saanvi, who always smiled at me and sometimes made coconut-filled gujiya pastries almost as good as my mom's. Everyone at HP . . . This can't be happening.

I try to control my breathing. I try to anchor myself in my body, but I feel like I'm going to drift away and evaporate.

Dr. Hewett lumbers off the bus. He mops his face with a handkerchief. Bernie follows, lugging a big black supply case. The two men have a hushed conversation.

I read Hewett's lips. I can't help it. I'm a Dolphin. My training is all about communication. Gathering intelligence. Codebreaking. I make out the words *land* and *attack*.

Bernie responds: *Inside help.*

I must have misread. Hewett couldn't have meant Land Institute. Our high schools have been rivals forever, but this isn't some prank like them egging our yacht or us stealing their great white shark. This is annihilation. And what did Bernie mean by *inside help?*

I breathe. I gather my shock and compress it into my diaphragm, the way I do with oxygen before a free dive.

"I saw the attack," I say.

Everybody is too distracted to hear me.

I say it again, louder. "I SAW THE ATTACK."

The group falls silent. Dr. Hewett peers at me.

Gem stops pacing, and I don't like the way he's glaring at me. He clenches his fists. "What do you mean *attack?*"

"It was some kind of torpedo," I say. "At least, I think it was."

I describe the wake line I saw heading toward the cliffs, the way it split into three parts just before impact.

"Can't be," says Kiya Jensen, another Shark. "The grid was up. Anything coming through would've been neutralized."

My legs tremble. "This morning, Dev and I . . ."

Grief bubbles up in my throat, threatening to choke me.

Oh, god, Dev. His lopsided, squinty grin. His rascally brown eyes. His ridiculous pillow-flattened hair. Seeing him every day, I could hold on to the memory of what our father looked like. I could tell myself that our parents weren't completely gone. But now . . .

Everyone is staring at me. They're waiting, desperate for understanding. I force myself to continue. I describe the strange flicker I saw in the lights of the grid.

"Dev was going to report it," I say. "He was probably in the security office right when . . ."

I gesture north. I don't make myself look again, but I can feel the gaping hole in the landscape where Harding-Pencroft used to be. It's like a dull ache in my jaw where a tooth has been pulled.

"One torpedo?" Tia Romero, the House Cephalopod prefect, shakes her head. "Even with multiple warheads, there's no way a single missile could do that kind of damage. To trigger a landslide of that magnitude . . ."

She looks at her Cephalopod housemates. They start whispering among themselves. Cephalopods are problem-solvers. It's what they do, like me reading lips. Dump a box of Legos in front of them, tell them to construct a working supercomputer out of the pieces, and they won't rest until they've figured out a way. Only Nelinha stands apart, keeping silent watch over Ester.

"It doesn't matter *how* it happened," Gem decides. "We need to go back and search for survivors."

"Agreed," I say.

On any other day, this would be headline news. Gem and I haven't agreed on anything since we started at HP almost two years ago.

He nods grimly. "Everybody, back on the—"

"No." Dr. Hewett hobbles forward, cradling his tablet

computer in one arm. Sweat patches have soaked through his shirt. His complexion is the color of frozen custard.

Behind him, Bernie kneels and opens the supply case. Inside, nested in foam, are a dozen silver drones the size of hummingbirds.

Hewett taps the screen of his control pad. The drones buzz to life. They rise from their foam cradles, gather overhead in a swarm of blue lights and tiny propellers, then zip along the coastline, heading toward HP.

"The drones will run surveillance." Hewett's voice shakes with anger, or grief, or both. "But I warn you not to expect survivors. Land Institute has launched a preemptive strike. They mean to eliminate us. I have been fearing an attack like this for two years."

I touch the black pearl at my throat.

Why is Hewett talking about LI and HP as if they're sovereign nations? Land Institute couldn't just destroy a chunk of the California coastline and *kill* over a hundred people.

Top's tail *whop*s against my leg. He buries his head in Ester's lap, demanding affection, trying to get her out of her dark place.

"Dr. Hewett . . ." Franklin Couch, House Orca prefect, looks ready to crawl out of his skin. "We might have wounded friends back there. People buried in rubble. We have a duty—"

"Do NOT speak!" Hewett roars.

Suddenly, I am back in my first day of TMS, when Daniel Lekowski—who washed out later in the year—dared to ask what good theoretical marine science was. I remember how terrifying Hewett can be when he gets angry.

Bernie stands behind the professor. He doesn't say anything, but his presence seems to bring Hewett's rage down to DEFCON 5.

"We continue to San Alejandro," Hewett says in a more even tone. "All of you, listen to me carefully. You may be all that remains of Harding-Pencroft. We must not fail. Trials are canceled. Instead, you will learn what you must know on active duty. As of this moment, we are at war."

Twenty freshmen stare back at him. They look just as scared as I feel. We have been trained in military tactics, yes. A lot of HP graduates go on to the best naval colleges in the world: Annapolis, Kuznetsov, Dalian, Ezhimala. But we aren't marines or Navy SEALs. Not yet, anyway. We're not even graduates. We're kids.

"We will continue to the docks," Hewett says. "Once we are safely at sea, I will give you further instructions. In the meantime, Gemini Twain?"

"Sir." Gem steps forward. He's ready for orders, ready to be put in charge of our class. Military command is what Sharks train for.

"Standard weapons are stored in the bus's hold?" Hewett asks.

"Yes, sir."

"Arm your team," Hewett says. "Weapons hot until further notice."

Gem snaps his fingers. The four other Sharks run to get their gun cases.

A cold sense of reality starts to pull me back into my body. When the Sharks are allowed to arm themselves, I know we are in serious, serious trouble.

"Prefect Twain," Hewett continues. "You have a new standing order."

Gem's eyes gleam. "I understand, sir."

"No," Hewett says. "I'm not sure you do. As of this moment, you are responsible for one life above all others. You will not leave her side. You will protect her with your dying breath. You will make *sure* she stays alive, no matter what happens."

Gem looks confused. "I . . . Sir?"

Hewett points at me. "Ana Dakkar must survive."

CHAPTER FIVE

I don't need this.

My school has been destroyed. My brother is probably dead. Now we're back on the bus, heading toward San Alejandro as if nothing has happened. And on top of everything, I have Gemini Twain as a personal bodyguard.

Why me?

I'm not Ester, who's descended from one of the school's founders. My family isn't rich or powerful or famous. The Dakkars have been at HP for generations, yes, but so have a lot of families. I'm not the only one in the group who may have lost a sibling in the attack, either. Brigid Salter's brother is—*was* a junior. Kay Ramsay had a sister a year older than us. Brigid and Kay look like a gentle breeze would be enough to make them both topple right now, but neither of them has a bodyguard.

Dr. Hewett sits in the front row, staring at his control pad. The sweat blotches on his dress shirt have expanded into alien continents.

I can only hope his drones find survivors at HP.

I had no luck texting Dev. That doesn't surprise me. The whole area is still a cellular black hole, but I had to try. Now Hewett has confiscated our phones and locked them in a strongbox, which makes me feel like I'm trying to function with one arm duct-taped behind my back.

Hewett assures us his drones will alert local emergency services. I keep waiting for ambulances, police cars, and fire trucks to scream past us on the way to HP. This is the only road they could take. So far, nothing. The school is so isolated that unless Hewett calls the authorities, it could be hours before anyone notices a giant chunk of the countryside has disappeared into the sea.

I have been fearing an attack like this for two years.

Then why didn't he *warn* us?

Maybe it's a coincidence that two years ago, my parents died on a scientific expedition for Harding-Pencroft. A tragic accident, the administrators told us. Whenever I asked for details—why Tarun and Sita Dakkar were on that expedition for HP, what they were looking for—the faculty at HP seemed to get selective amnesia. I assumed they were trying to spare my feelings, letting me work through my grief with Dr. Francis.

Now I'm not so sure.

I have a sudden image of Amelia Leahy, my house captain, Dev's girlfriend, lounging in the sunlit quad this morning. She smiled and wished me good luck.

Amelia was so excited about graduating. She had big plans: the US Marine Corps, fast-track to comm school at Twentynine Palms. In her five years at HP, she'd learned twelve languages. She could break linguistic codes that stumped our professors. Her goal was to become the youngest intelligence commander in corps history. Now she's gone.

I try to keep the oxygen going in and out of my lungs. I'm not doing a great job with it.

I start to cry. I'm shaking with anger. Why is it that I can keep myself together when thinking about Dev, but I break down at the thought of his girlfriend dying? What is wrong with me?

"Hey, babe . . ." Nelinha rests a hand on my shoulder. She doesn't seem sure of what else to say. She just hands me a pack of tissues.

Yeah . . . one tissue is not going to do it today. And I'm not the only person having trouble.

By the window, Ester is still puffy-eyed and sniffling. She's furiously writing notes on a new index card, trying to process all this awfulness. Top, sensing who needs him most, pads over and pushes his nose between my knees. *Hi, I'm cute. Love me.*

Gem sits across the aisle. His jaw is set like a bear trap. SIG Sauer P226s are holstered on either side of his belt, Wild West gunslinger–style. These are his "twins," which is how he got the nickname Gemini. Resting on his knee is an M4A1 assault rifle.

Another one of those oddities I don't think about much: Harding-Pencroft has a dispensation to use military-grade equipment for our training. I suppose that's fortunate, seeing as we're apparently now at war with another high school.

The bus is strangely silent. Everyone seems lost in their own dismal thoughts.

Finally, Gem asks me, "Do you have any idea what's going on?"

His brown eyes reflect the landscape racing past. I've never seen him show much sign of stress. Now a single bead of sweat trickles down the side of his face.

I don't blame him for wanting answers. I'm grateful he doesn't sound bitter or angry at me. I know he doesn't want to be my babysitter any more than I want him to be.

I shake my head. "Honestly, no idea."

I *am* telling the truth. Yet I feel like I'm lying. I can hear the guilt in my voice. I hate that feeling.

Gem taps his thumb against the stock of his rifle. "I'm going to need your help. All of you." He nods to include Ester and Nelinha. "I know we haven't always gotten along—"

Nelinha snorts.

"—but you know what I'm going to say is true." Gem glances up the aisle, then lowers his voice. "The four of us are the best in our houses. No disrespect to Tia and Franklin. They're great at what they do. But if we're going to war, you guys are my top picks, even if you're not all prefects."

"How flattering," Nelinha grumbles.

"I'm just saying—"

"Badly," Nelinha suggests.

"He's right." Ester keeps her attention on her note card, now almost filled with tiny words. "Maria's our top theorist, but Nelinha's scores in applied mechanics and combat engineering are higher. Franklin's got more advanced medical skills than me, but . . ." She shrugs.

Gem gives her a dry smile. "But you're Ester Harding."

"I was going to say I'm better at everything else," Ester says. "Except that would probably be rude. Is that rude?"

None of us bother to answer. Ester is Ester. We all know she would hate being a prefect. We also know she is the quintessential Orca. Her note cards are really just an emotional-support tool, like Top, because her mind holds more information about Harding-Pencroft, natural history, and marine ecosystems than all the books in our recently destroyed library. She isn't fond of humans, with the exception of Nelinha and me, and would much rather spend her time with animals. She's a genius empath when it comes to nonverbal communication with other species. Ester can tell what animals—sometimes people, though she finds that harder—are thinking and feeling. She can predict their actions with uncanny accuracy . . . assuming her own raw nerves don't overwhelm her.

Gem forges on. "We're going to have to work together to figure out what happened. And what we're going to do next. You know Hewett isn't telling us everything."

"He isn't telling us *anything*," Nelinha says.

"But if I'm going to protect Ana—"

"Which I didn't ask for," I say.

Gemini looks like he wants to make an angry comment. He never curses. He's super straitlaced. But I think he *wants* to.

"None of us asked for this." He keeps his voice even. "We have to formulate a response. To do that, we have to know what we're dealing with. How could Land Institute destroy our entire school?"

Ester shudders. Top immediately abandons me and jumps in her lap, forcing her to cuddle. I've never been so grateful that Ester, and all of us, has this fluff tornado drama king.

"Seismic detonators," Nelinha theorizes. "One torpedo with three warheads. Simultaneous impacts at fracture points along the base of the cliffs—"

"Hold up," Gem says. "That's TMS. Pure science fiction. The technology doesn't exist."

"Six warheads," Ester says. "You'd need six. Ana probably didn't see the others because they were too deep. The attack would only work if they could hack the school's security systems. Not just the grid. They'd need to fool the drones, the long-range sonar, the interceptor missiles—"

"We have *interceptor* missiles?" Nelinha demands.

Strawberries bloom on Ester's cheeks. "I wasn't supposed to say that."

I make a note to grill Ester about that later. I'm curious to know what else she, as a Harding, might know that she isn't supposed to say. At the moment, we have more immediate problems.

"All the HP security systems are self-contained," I say. "The firewalls have firewalls. There's no way anyone could hack their way in without being detected."

"Unless . . ." Nelinha says.

My mouth turns dry. "Right. I overheard Bernie and Hewett talking when we got off the bus."

" 'Overheard'?" Gem makes air quotes around the word.

"Okay, I read their lips."

Gem's eyes narrow. The particulars of Dolphin training aren't common knowledge outside our house. I imagine he is rewinding the last two years, wondering what else I might have *overheard.* "And what did they say?"

I glance at Dr. Hewett, still fiddling with his control pad. Whatever he sees in his readouts, he clearly doesn't like it.

"Bernie mentioned 'inside help,' " I say. "Which means—"

"Someone at HP sabotaged us." Gem is definitely biting back a curse now. "And if that person didn't want to die in the attack—"

"They would be on this bus."

CHAPTER SIX

Half an hour later, we arrive at the docks where our training vessel, the *Varuna*, is moored.

While the other students unload the bus's cargo bay, I pull the Dolphins aside in the parking lot: Lee-Ann, Virgil, Jack, and Halimah.

"Tá fealltóir againn," I tell them.

Literally, this translates as *There is a betrayer at us*, which seems appropriate.

We've been using Irish as our internal code since the beginning of the year. Irish is so rare, the chance of anyone understanding a word we say is remote. Each class of Dolphins chooses their own language. Amelia's learned Coptic. The juniors had Maltese. The sophomores chose Latin because they had no imagination. If you don't have a talent for languages, you wash out of House Dolphin pretty quick.

I tell my housemates what I suspect. Sabotage. Treachery. Cold-blooded murder.

It's a lot to take in.

Telling them is a risk. I have no idea who betrayed the school. Any of them could have done it. But I can't start mistrusting everyone. I need their help.

Dolphins focus on communication and exploration, but we also train in espionage. I want my housemates on high alert.

Halimah Nasser looks so angry I imagine steam bubbling under her hijab. "How do we find the traitor? And what do we do with them?"

"For now," I say, "just watch and listen."

In Irish, this is "Bígí ag faire agus ag éisteacht." *Be at your watching and listening.* Again, that sums things up pretty well.

Lee-Ann Best's face is brick red. She's our best at counter-espionage. She probably takes this news as a personal insult. She scans the faces of our classmates, no doubt assessing each of them for the potential of betrayal. "I had friends in the other grades."

"We all did," Jack Wu says. He lifts one eyebrow toward Dr. Hewett. "Ana, you have any idea why the professor assigned a Shark to you?"

The Shark in question, Gemini Twain, stands just out of earshot. He's surveying the wharf for any sign of threats. I wish he didn't take his bodyguard duties quite so seriously.

The docks aren't crowded, but Gem gets some strange looks from the local fishermen. I guess it's not every day they see a fourteen-year-old standing sentry with a military-grade assault rifle and two sidearms. Gem just nods at them politely and tells them good morning. They give him a wide berth.

"No clue," I say. "Hopefully we'll find out once we're at sea."

Virgil Esparza has been quietly staring at the crushed-shell pavement. Now he says, "He used to teach at Land Institute, you know."

My shoulders tighten. "Who?"

He nods toward Dr. Hewett.

I'm so stunned I can't remember the Irish for *Are you kidding me?*

"Freshmen!" Hewett calls out. "Gather up!"

I give my Dolphins one last order in ASL, tapping my temple with all four fingertips: *Be alert.*

We take our places. Fifteen of us make a semicircle facing Dr. Hewett: Dolphins, Cephalopods, Orcas. The Sharks stand around the perimeter, weapons ready. Gemini Twain moves to Dr. Hewett's side, where he can both keep an eye on me and make clear that he is the dominant freshman.

Ester scratches Top's ears. He sits next to her patiently, his brown eyes locked on Hewett as if to say, *See? I can be a good boy.*

To my surprise, Nelinha has managed to wash her face and reapply her makeup. How did she do that so quickly? She gives me a wink, a gesture of solidarity.

My heart hurts. I love my friends so much. I love this entire class, even the individuals I don't like that much. I hate whoever tore our world apart.

Hewett wraps up his conversation with three HP security guards who have walked over from the pier. I guess they were on board the *Varuna*, keeping an eye on it until we arrived. They all look shaken. Hewett must have told them about the attack.

For a moment, I'm relieved. At least we'll have more adult backup.

Then Hewett gives them an order. I lip-read the words *Buy us time.*

The guards nod grimly. They jog over to the shuttle bus. Bernie sits behind the wheel, the engine idling. As soon as the guards are on board, Bernie closes the doors. He gives me a listless wave, his expression part concern, part apology. Then he drives away, shells crunching under the wheels.

Why would Hewett dismiss three perfectly good guards? Why would he send Bernie away, along with our bus?

There's no longer any school for them to return to. *Buy us time* sounds disturbingly like a command you'd give a suicide squad.

This whole situation is wrong. I don't want Hewett as our only adult supervisor. I remember what Virgil said: *He used to teach at Land Institute.*

Not to mention his less-than-robust physical condition. The professor's face is almost as colorless as his droopy mop of hair. I try to guess how old he is. Sixty? Seventy? It's hard to tell.

I wonder when he taught at Land Institute, and how he ended up here. I don't know much about our rival school. They follow the same basic curriculum as HP—marine sciences, naval warfare. Maybe LI is slightly more on the warfare side, while HP leans slightly more toward scientific research, but our grads often end up working side by side in the world's best navies and maritime institutes. The way the upperclassmen talk about LI, you'd think its students are all sociopaths and their teachers have devil horns and pointy tails. I always assumed the upperclassmen were exaggerating. After this morning, I understand.

Hewett gives his tablet a sour look. Then he regards us as if he can't decide which is the bigger disappointment. "Freshmen, you need to understand that this is no longer a weekend trip. This is an indefinite assignment. All of you are in danger, not just Ana Dakkar."

The others glance at me. Awkward.

"Yes, yes," Hewett says, acknowledging their concern. "I will explain once we are out of range."

He doesn't say out of range of *what.*

I look past him. The school's 120-foot training vessel waits at the end of pier six. The *Varuna* is the biggest yacht in the harbor by far. I love that it's named after the Hindu sea god. Usually, when I see its gleaming white hull, I feel proud and excited. Painted on the prow is the HP logo with the four house icons— shark, dolphin, cephalopod, orca—inside the quadrants of an old-fashioned nautical wheel. The words HARDING-PENCROFT ACADEMY scroll below. Today, the sight makes me blink back a fresh swell of tears. The ship is all we have of the academy now.

Hewett continues, "I know you have questions. . . ."

"I do," says Rhys Morrow, one of the bolder Orcas. "Sir, our families will think we're dead. We have to contact them—"

"*No,*" Hewett snaps. "Miss Morrow, I know this is hard to hear. But for now, your families are safer, *you* are safer, if the world thinks you are dead. We must hope that Land Institute doesn't yet realize this class escaped the attack. If we can disappear before they . . ."

He glances at his control pad. Whatever blood remains in his face seems to drain away. Gem catches his arm before he can fall sideways.

Gem frowns at the screen. He mutters a question I can hear just fine without lip-reading: "Sir, what *is* that?"

Hewett's eyes have more life in them than the entire rest of his body. They're incandescent with fear.

"Everyone on board," he says. "We need to leave *NOW.*"

CHAPTER SEVEN

It's not that simple.

With a 120-foot yacht, you can't just turn on the ignition and speed away. Supplies have to be stowed, systems checked, moorings cleared. Over the past two years, we've worked on the *Varuna* half a dozen times. We know the ship, and we know our jobs. Still, it takes time to get ready.

It doesn't help that we find ourselves stumbling over equipment we've never seen on board before. On deck, several metal crates the size of washing machines have been lashed down and covered with tarps. Belowdecks, the corridors are lined with smaller boxes that look like foot lockers—each fitted with a biometric fingerprint pad and labeled GOLD-LEVEL CLEARANCE.

I've seen boxes like these at school, but only from a distance. Usually they're being transported to and from Verne Hall under armed guard. Whatever is inside is top secret. Only faculty and upperclassmen are allowed to work with them.

Suddenly, we're surrounded by the containers. It's like we've spent two years being told not to touch the artwork and now we're tripping over Picassos. It's unnerving that Hewett moved so much valuable school property to the *Varuna*, especially right *before* HP was wiped off the map. . . .

It might be easier to guess what Hewett was thinking if I knew what was in the boxes. Dev never gave me the slightest hint. Whenever I pestered him, he'd say, *You'll find out soon enough.*

Don't think about Dev, I chide myself.

But that's impossible. Simply getting through the day is like swimming through an underwater minefield. Tomorrow will be just as hard. And the next day. You might think the horror of losing my parents would have given me some coping strategies for dealing with this kind of tragedy. It hasn't. If anything, it makes the stab to the chest even more painful.

I try to lock those feelings away in a gold box of my own. I have work to do. I check the comm-system batteries, the satellite dish, the VHF aerial, and 3-D sonar transducer. Gemini tags along behind me, alternately giving orders to his Sharks and making sure I am not being accosted by any ninja sea lions.

We've barely pulled away from the pier when Hewett's voice comes over the loudspeaker. "Prefects, report to the bridge."

Franklin and Tia are already there when Gem and I arrive.

Tia is piloting. Franklin hovers fretfully over Dr. Hewett, who's sprawled in the captain's chair, wheezing like he's just run a 10K.

"Sir," Franklin says, "at least let me take your blood pressure."

What's wrong with the professor? I wonder. This seems like more than a stress reaction. . . .

"I'm fine." Hewett waves him aside. Then the professor struggles to his feet and hobbles to the chart table. "Gather round, you four."

Tia Romero looks uneasy about this, since she's officer of the watch. She checks the autopilot and the ECDIS one more time before joining us at the table. I wish she could stay at the helm. I want her pushing the boat to maximum speed so we can get away from whatever Dr. Hewett saw on his control pad.

It's driving me crazy to not know what we're running from.

On the laminated surface of the table sits a gold-level box. If Gemini Twain keeps breathing down my neck, I'm thinking the box might be large enough for me to stuff his body into if I can fold him over enough times.

"Normally," says Dr. Hewett, "the information I'm about to give you would be revealed in stages. This weekend's trials were meant to be your first exposure to Harding-Pencroft's true mission."

"True mission?" Franklin brushes his streak of blue hair behind his left ear. He's always struck me as a bit of a follower, but I *do* like that one rebellious gesture against our dress code. "Isn't the school mission to prepare us for careers at sea?"

"Partially," Hewett says. "Having our graduates in positions of power helps us in many ways. But we intend to prepare you for much more than that." He scowls at me in particular. "You are meant to become the custodians of Harding-Pencroft's secrets, the agents of its great agenda. It is a heavy responsibility. Not every student succeeds."

This talk of secrets and agendas makes the hair stand up on the nape of my neck. I don't know what he means, but I can't shake the feeling that when he says not every student succeeds, he means *survives*. I wonder what Dev thought of this "great agenda."

I glance at the other prefects. They look just as confused as I am.

Hewett sighs, the way he does when he passes back our graded essays. "And now you require a crash course. Dakkar, open the case."

My lower back muscles clench. I've been warned for two years: Try opening a gold-level case as an underclassman and you'll get expelled, assuming the attempt doesn't kill you. I guess Hewett wouldn't order Gem to protect my life at all costs if he was just going to kill me with a booby trap. Still . . .

I press my hand against the biometric pad. The lid pops open like it's been waiting.

Inside, nested in black foam, are four of the strangest-looking guns I've ever seen.

"Oh, wow!" Gem says. This is the strongest exclamation I've ever heard from him. His eyes gleam like a kid in front of a Christmas tree. He glances at Dr. Hewett. "May I—?"

Hewett nods.

Carefully, Gem extracts one of the guns. The weapon is too big to be a pistol, too small to be a shotgun. Some kind of miniature grenade launcher? An oversize flare gun? Whatever it is, it's been meticulously handcrafted. Its leather grip is tooled with a wave design. The golden barrel looks electroplated with some kind of copper alloy. Wires run along the outside like braided vines. The stock-loaded magazine is too short and thick for any sort of ammunition I can think of. It's plated with the same alloy, which someone has gone to the trouble of engraving with the HP logo.

There's no way these guns can be functional. They're too ornate, like nineteenth-century officers' swords or dueling pistols—works of art not meant to be used. I've never said this about any kind of firearm before, but they're strangely beautiful.

"This is a Leyden gun," Gem marvels.

The name doesn't ring any bells. I look at Franklin, our Orca rep. House Orca knows all the obscure historical facts and weird bits of trivia. Their members could destroy anyone on *Jeopardy!* They excel at other things, too, but we jokingly call them House Wikipedia.

Franklin nods. "Jules Verne."

Hewett curls his lip, like the author's name is an unpleasant but necessary fact of life. "Yes. Well. Shockingly, he reported a few things correctly."

I remember now. The summer before our chum year, we had to read Verne's *20,000 Leagues Under the Sea* and *The Mysterious Island*, the first science fiction novels about marine technology. I'd assumed the point of the assignment was *Let's expand our minds with some "fun" (air quotes) reading about the sea!* Honestly, I found the books an annoying slog. The plots were slow. The language was super dated. The characters were a bunch of harrumphing Victorian-era gentlemen I didn't care about.

Two of the main characters in *The Mysterious Island* were Harding and Pencroft, men with the same surnames as the founders of our school. At the time I'd thought, *Okay, that's a little weird.* Later in the book, when the crazy sci-fi submarine commander Captain Nemo revealed that his real name was Prince Dakkar, I admit I got a shiver down my back. But the books were just fiction. Seeing as the most important building at HP was Verne Hall, I supposed the school's founders must have been hard-core Jules Verne fanboys. Maybe they recruited my family generations ago as an elaborate inside joke, because they liked our surname.

Beyond that, I had two main takeaways from Jules Verne. First, the title *20,000 Leagues Under the Sea* didn't mean what I thought it did. Old Captain Nemo hadn't dived to a *depth* of 20,000 leagues. That's 60,000 nautical miles, which would have plunged his sub through the earth and a quarter of the way to the moon. Instead, the book title meant he'd traveled a *distance* of 60,000 nautical miles underwater, which was still crazy by nineteenth-century standards. It meant he circled the world seven and a half times in that old rusty can, the *Nautilus*.

The other thing I'd taken away from the book: Verne had come up with some cool ideas that would never work. One of those was Leyden guns. I think the name came from some electrical research Dutch scientists did in the city of Leyden in the

1700s. I'm also pretty sure I got that question wrong on Dr. Hewett's midterm.

"It can't be real." Tia Romero picks up another gun and removes the magazine.

"Careful, Prefect," Hewett warns her.

I'm losing my patience.

Our school has been destroyed for I-don't-know-what-reason. My brother may be dead. We're on the run from Land Institute, going I-don't-know-where. Now it turns out our big gold-level secret is that Dr. Hewett enjoys live-action role-playing.

He's brought along boxes of handcrafted Jules Verne ray guns so we can run around the boat all weekend pretending to shoot one another while yelling *Pew-pew!* I'm starting to doubt his sanity. And I'm starting to doubt *my* sanity for following his orders.

"Sir." I struggle to keep the anger out of my voice. "Maybe you can tell us what's going on. Then we can play with your toys later?"

I expect him to yell at me. I'm prepared for that. I really don't care anymore. Instead, he studies me with a sad, heavy expression—the kind I got from HP faculty whenever they mentioned my parents.

"Prefect Twain, may I?" Hewett holds out his hand.

Reluctantly, Gem surrenders the Leyden gun.

Dr. Hewett looks it over, maybe checking the settings. He gives Gem a weary smile. "I hope you'll forgive me, Prefect. This will be faster than explaining."

"Sir?" Gem asks.

Hewett shoots him. The only sound is a high-pressure hiss. For a millisecond, Gem is wrapped in flickering white tendrils of electricity.

Then his eyes cross, and he collapses in a heap.

CHAPTER EIGHT

"You killed him!" Franklin rushes to Gem's side.

Hewett turns a dial on the stock of his weapon and nonchalantly says, "Did I?"

Tia looks at me with alarm, silently asking what we should do.

I'm paralyzed between the desire to help Gem and the urge to tackle our teacher.

Franklin presses two fingers against Gem's neck. "N-no. He's got a strong pulse." He scowls at Dr. Hewett. "You can't just go around *electrocuting* people!"

"There will be no permanent damage," Hewett assures us.

"That's kind of not the point," I say, at the risk of getting shot.

Having heard that Gem won't die, Tia turns her attention to her own Leyden gun. Like any good Cephalopod, she sets it down and starts to disassemble it. Her mass of bronze corkscrew hair sways and bounces around her face like the coils of a complicated machine. She extracts a projectile from the top of the magazine and holds it up for inspection. It's a shiny white lozenge about the size and shape of . . . Well, honestly, the first thing it reminds me of is a tampon.

"Some kind of glass?" Tia asks.

"Not exactly," says Hewett. "Each projectile is based on a Leyden jar. It stores an electrical charge that is released upon impact. But the casing is constructed from a special type of secreted calcium carbonate."

"Like abalone shell," I say.

Hewett looks pleased. "Precisely, Prefect Dakkar."

I try not to feel gratified about giving him a correct response. We're not in class anymore. Also, he just shot my bodyguard.

"If the casing is secreted," I say, "what is it secreted *from*?"

Hewett just smiles. Suddenly I don't want to know.

"Upon discharge," he says, "every trace of the projectile is destroyed. The stun effect lasts anywhere from a few minutes to an hour, depending on the target's constitution."

As if on cue, Gem wakes with a snort. He sits up, shaking his head. "What happened?"

"Hewett shot you," Franklin says.

Gem looks at Hewett with awe, as if he didn't know the old man was capable of being so cool.

"You're fine," Hewett tells him. "On your feet, Prefect. I was just about to explain. In the event of another attack by Land Institute, you will use these weapons. You'll find them more reliable than conventional guns."

Gem's expression changes to disbelief. "More reliable than my SIG Sauers?"

"I'm not doubting your skills, Mr. Twain," Hewett says. "I'm aware that you have the highest marksmanship scores in the school's history. But our enemies will have body armor that is quite effective against standard firearms."

"Kevlar isn't perfect—"

"I'm not talking about Kevlar." Hewett's expression hardens. "Besides, we will shoot to incapacitate, not to kill. We are not Land Institute. We are better than that."

His tone is so bitter I wonder if I was wrong to suspect

him. He sounds genuinely disgusted with his former employer. I just wish I understood why he left them and graced us with his presence.

"The range of the Leyden guns is limited," he continues. "However, any contact with the target's body will release the charge. You will find the guns accurate to a hundred feet."

"One-third the range of my regular handguns," Gem mutters.

"Let us hope you do not have to test your skills with either type of weapon," Hewett says dryly. "But we must be prepared. There are three more boxes like this one in the armory. I've set the locks to open to the handprint of any prefect. Mr. Twain, arm your Sharks first. Then the rest of the crew."

Tia is shaking her head. "Sir . . . how do these things even *work*? They shouldn't be possible."

Hewett grimaces—his famous *Lord, give me patience* expression. "Prefect Romero, the impossible is merely the possible for which we don't yet know the science."

"But—"

"I understand it is a lot to absorb," he says. "Normally during freshman trials, I would introduce the Leyden gun and leave it at that for the day. I'd save the more outlandish alt-tech for Saturday and Sunday."

"Alt-tech?" Franklin asks.

"*More* outlandish?" Gem sounds excited, like he's volunteering for further target practice.

"Unfortunately," Hewett says, ignoring both questions, "we don't have the luxury of time. To survive, we will need everything we have. Miss Romero, you see that case against the far wall? You remember my lecture on opto-electric camouflage, I hope."

Tia blinks. "Like the skin of an octopus."

"Exactly. That case contains projection modules. They must

be installed around the exterior of the hull, just above the water-line at one-meter intervals. Do you understand?"

"I . . . Um, yes?"

"Good." Hewett glances out the window. He looks frustrated to see how close we still are to shore. "Mr. Couch, there's another case on the bench just behind you. Inside is a pulse-dispersion unit. Please install it on the forward deck. It should jam any radar or sonar."

"Uh . . ." Franklin's face is turning almost as blue as the streak in his hair, like he's forgotten to breathe for the last several minutes. "Okay, sir."

"Now, Miss Dakkar—"

"Alt-tech," I blurt out.

I feel like I'm emerging from a trance, or maybe going into one. At this point, I'm not sure I'd know the difference. I don't even correct Hewett on the *Miss Dakkar* thing, which I find incredibly patronizing.

"Your class," I say. "Theoretical Marine Science. All the bizarre, dangerous tech you talked about. It isn't theoretical at all, is it?"

He gives me that sad expression again. "Oh, my dear, I am so sorry."

This apology scares me worse than anything he could have said. And *my dear*? He's only ever called me Prefect Dakkar (my correct title), or Miss Dakkar (which I hate), or sometimes *hey, you* if he's feeling particularly perky.

It seems dangerous to keep asking questions. It feels like I'm standing on the highest cliff I've ever dived from. I take the plunge anyway. "You said Jules Verne *reported* a few things correctly. You didn't say he *foresaw* or *imagined*. Are you telling us the events in those novels actually happened?"

Hewett sets down his Leyden gun. His fingertips linger over

the elaborate wiring on the barrel. "The age-old question: Where do authors get their ideas? In the case of Verne, the answer was personal interviews. He heard rumors. He sought eyewitnesses. Those witnesses lied to him about certain details to protect themselves. Verne changed other facts to make his stories read like, well, *stories*. But yes, my dear, the bulk of those tales is true."

A fragile silence descends on the bridge. The only sounds are the hum of the engines and the thump of waves breaking on the prow. The other prefects look dazed. When Hewett talks again, they lean in, as if trying to hear a voice from a century-old phonograph.

"Since the school's founding," he says, "we have been able to reproduce some of Nemo's alt-tech. Much of it we still do not understand. The mission of Harding-Pencroft is to safeguard his legacy, keep his technology out of the hands of human society, and thwart Land Institute, which would use alt-tech to dominate the world. I'm afraid, as of today, the balance of power that has existed between our schools for nearly a hundred and fifty years has been broken. Land Institute is on the verge of final victory."

I study Dr. Hewett's aggrieved expression. My nerves feel like a shoal of herring all swimming frantically in different directions. Finally, I can't contain the chaos anymore. I burst out laughing.

I must look like I've gone crazy. I can't help it. My life has been upended *again*. I've lost my brother, my school, my future. I've been running on adrenaline for hours. And we're talking about Captain Nemo!

I hug my ribs. I wheeze and blink away the tears. I'm pretty sure that when I stop laughing, I'll cry myself to death. Franklin steps toward me. He must sense I'm near a breakdown. Even Gem and Tia look worried.

Hewett's eyes remain as dark as squid ink. "I'm sorry, Miss Dakkar."

"*Prefect,*" I correct him, though it's hard to come across as serious when I'm wheezing hysterically.

Hewett frowns. "I wish we had more time. We spent almost a year slowly orienting your brother. He was being trained to lead, to take over where your parents left off. As much promise as he showed, the pressure nearly destroyed him. Now, I'm afraid I have to ask even *more* of you. I wish—"

He's interrupted by a *ding* from his tablet computer. I've never heard it make any sound before, and despite the cheerful noise, I can tell from Hewett's expression it isn't good news.

"They've found us," he announces.

Gem's hands gravitate to his sidearms. "Is it the thing I saw on your screen before? What *was* that?"

"No time," Hewett says. "Alert the crew. We're under attack!"

CHAPTER NINE

They literally erupt from the sea.

I have time to yell "Incoming!" before scuba divers rocket to the surface on our starboard side, all on kickboard-size DPVs—diver propulsion vehicles—moving at twelve knots or more, faster than any I've ever seen. I register eight hostiles, some carrying strange silvery weapons that look like harpoon guns, others brandishing . . . Wait, are those *grenade launchers*?

Two fist-size metal canisters plunk onto our gangway and roll hissing and steaming across the deck.

"Flash-bangs!" Gem yells.

I shut my eyes and cover my ears, but the explosions still leave my head ringing. For a moment, I can only stagger in a daze through plumes of blue smoke. By the time my crewmates and I have recovered from our confusion, our enemies have fastened grappling hooks to the starboard rail, discarded their DPVs and oxygen tanks, and begun climbing over our gunwale like they've been practicing this assault for months.

Eloise and Cooper are the first to return fire. They spray our attackers with their M4A1s, but it's like they're shooting wax bullets. The rounds make smoking white impact points against our enemies' wetsuits, making them flinch but causing no visible damage.

Two hostiles fire their silver weapons. Miniature harpoons impale Eloise's shoulder and Cooper's leg. White arcs of electricity blossom from the projectiles, and both Sharks crumple.

I scream in rage. My friends closest to starboard, most still unarmed, charge the intruders. It's a desperate move, but a melee with armed opponents is better than getting shot down one by one, and we seem to have numbers on our side. I want to join them—I want to take apart these attackers with my bare hands for the destruction of my school, for Dev—but Gem holds me back.

"Fire if you see an opening." He hands me a Leyden gun. "But *stay behind me*, please." I bristle at his demeaning orders but obey as he yells to his remaining housemates. "Dru, Kiya!"

He tosses them each a gun from his gold-level case like he's Militia Santa Claus. "Point and shoot!"

Perfect instructions for a Shark.

Two more attackers are just climbing over the rail. Gem makes them pay for their late arrival by shooting both of them center mass. They topple backward, flickering like defective Christmas lights until they hit the water. Maybe their wetsuits will keep them afloat. Maybe they'll come to before they drown. At the moment, that's not my biggest concern.

Dru Cardenas shoots another intruder. Unfortunately, the electricity also arcs to Nelinha, who had been in the process of pummeling said intruder with a socket wrench. Both of them go down.

Five enemies left, scuffling with about ten of our crew who happened to be on deck at the time. Why would they attack us with so few? And where is Dr. Hewett? He hasn't yet followed us out from the bridge. Just as I was starting to believe he might not be a traitor, my trust pendulum swings back toward *extreme doubt*.

I can't tell much about our attackers. Dive masks and full hoods obscure their faces. Nevertheless, the Land Institute insignia is clearly emblazoned on the breast of each wetsuit: an old-fashioned harpoon in silver, its rope making a circle around the letters LI.

Our attackers must be upperclassmen—they look taller and older than us, but not like adults. Land Institute surely has faculty trained in combat, armed security, adult alumni. If catching us is so important, why are they sending students? And as nasty as those harpoon guns look, they don't appear designed to kill. After destroying our entire school, why hesitate to use lethal force?

I wonder if this could be a ruse . . . some sort of training exercise. No. The destruction of HP was real enough.

But this whole thing smells fishy. . . .

My hands are sweaty on the stock of the Leyden gun. I can't get a clear shot. After what happened to Nelinha, I'm not going to fire randomly into the crowd with a weapon I don't fully understand.

One attacker shoots Meadow Newman point-blank with a mini-harpoon Leyden pistol. She falls, electric sparks popping around her. Ester gets revenge by body-slamming the guy— Ester is an excellent defensive lineman—and the attacker goes down flailing. Top joins the party, clamping his jaws around the guy's throat, which is absolutely a form of emotional support. If not for the strange bulletproof fabric of the dive hood, the guy would be Top's lunch. As it is, he crab-walks backward, screaming and trying to shake off the furious twenty-pound fluff demon attached to his windpipe.

This is too easy, I mutter to myself, though I doubt my

unconscious classmates would agree. Six are now out of commission, some bleeding from nasty harpoon barbs.

Still, I feel like I'm missing something. . . .

Perhaps Land Institute wasn't expecting opposition. After destroying our school, maybe they thought they'd find a bunch of terrified freshmen who would plead for their lives. The four remaining attackers are holding their own, kicking, jabbing, using their greater size and strength, but it's only a matter of time before we overwhelm them. Gem, Dru, and Kiya keep their guns trained on the chaos, though I can tell from their postures even they are starting to relax. They think we've almost won.

LI planned this assault carefully. Their movements were synchronized. They made as flashy an entrance as they could on our starboard side. Why would they botch it? Unless . . .

"Gem!" I call.

He doesn't seem to hear me. Between the gunfire, the ship's engines, and the residual ringing from the flash-bangs, I'm not surprised. It's enough noise to cover up almost anything. All three Sharks have eyes forward, keeping me behind them and facing the obvious threat.

Think like a Dolphin, I tell myself. *Espionage, not frontal assault.*

A thousand tiny crabs scuttle down my back. *It's a feint.*

"GEM!" I yell again.

I start to turn, to check the port side of the boat, but I'm too slow. Maybe I'm still in shock from grief, or maybe I'm dazed from the grenades. I've only made it ninety degrees when someone behind me locks his forearm across my throat. I feel a sharp pain like a wasp sting in the side of my neck.

Terror washes through my veins along with whatever they've injected me with. The Leyden gun slips from my numb fingers.

I've been trained in a dozen ways to get out of a chokehold, but my knees turn to putty. My arms hang uselessly at my side. I can't feel anything except the panic building in my chest. Off the port side of the *Varuna*, I can now see the pontoon my captor came in on. Another LI commando mans the outboard motor.

The Sharks are shouting now. At least I got their attention. Dru and Gem flank my captor, their guns raised. Kiya reaches the port rail first, notices the pontoon, and immediately shoots at the guy on board. She hits the motor instead. The guy fires back, and Kiya collapses in a shimmering Tesla cage.

"HOLD YOUR FIRE!" my captor roars. "Or Ana Dakkar dies!"

He twists so his back is to the rail and I'm between him and the Sharks. He knows my name. Of course . . . I was the target all along. I don't understand the motive, but this whole attack has been about capturing me.

Gem and Dru keep their Leyden guns trained on us. On the starboard side of the deck, the last LI commando goes down when Tia Romero smashes him in the groin with a fire extinguisher.

I lock eyes with Gemini Twain. I try to say *Just shoot us both*, but my voice won't work.

"I wouldn't," my captor warns Gem. "Maybe you didn't notice the needle I've got at your friend's neck. Nasty what you can make from sea-snake venom. She'll survive, unless you freshmen get stupid with those Leyden guns. Shock me, you shock her. That *really* wouldn't be good for her nervous system right now."

Slowly, Gem sets down his Leyden gun. Then, just as slowly, he draws his twin SIG Sauers. "How about I shoot you in the mouth instead?" he suggests—calm and polite, as if he's offering our guest a moist towelette. "Unless your face is bulletproof, too."

Gem is an excellent marksman, but that doesn't decrease

my level of panic. My captor's face happens to be right next to mine.

"I don't care how good a shot you are, Twain," my captor snarls. He knows Gem, too. He's done his homework. "This needle *will* go into her neck. A second dose of sea-snake venom? Definitely fatal. I'm going over the side now, with Dakkar. And you're going to let me."

"You're just going to leave your friends behind?" Gem flicks one of his gun barrels toward the pile of unconscious LI commandos now decorating our starboard deck. "How about we make a trade?"

My captor snorts. "Keep them. They did their job. This one, though?" He tightens his grip on my throat. "None of us can afford to see *her* get killed, can we?"

My captor and I tumble backward—free-falling from the side of the *Varuna*. I get a glimpse of blue sky. I feel the *thunk* of our impact as we crash into the water. Then the cold sea closes over my face like the folds of a burial shroud.

CHAPTER TEN

When we surface, I'm choking and spluttering. I have a blurry view of my classmates gathered above, their grim faces lining the port rail of the *Varuna*. Dr. Hewett is there too now, looking seasick. Gemini Twain has switched to his M4A1, the rifle's sight fixed on my captor.

The *Varuna* has cut her engines. The world is quiet except for the slosh of waves against the hull and my captor's ragged breathing in my ear. It must be hard work pulling me along, using me as a human shield while swimming backward toward his pontoon. I hope he drowns.

Above us, Gem says grimly, "I've got the shot, sir."

I don't think he meant for us to hear this comment, but voices carry at sea. The idea of him firing makes my stomach twist. With the ocean swells, and the movements of the ship and my captor, it would be a tough shot even for Gem. Besides, I assume my captor still has his little hypodermic needle somewhere at hand. I hope he sticks himself with it.

"Stand down, Mr. Twain," Hewett orders.

Really? I think. *That's all you've got, Hewett?*

"That's right," my captor mocks. "Stand down, Mr. Twain."

Hewett narrows his eyes. "Caleb South, I know your voice. Don't do this."

Caleb curses. Apparently, he doesn't love Hewett any more than I do.

We reach the pontoon. Another set of rough hands grabs me. The guy at the motor hauls me aboard.

"Dave," my captor snaps, still in the water. "Keep a needle on her while I get aboard."

Great. I've been abducted by two evildoers named Caleb and Dave. I wonder if the Land Institute yearbook voted them most likely to open a family restaurant or maybe a gardening center.

My limbs still aren't working, but I can feel some tingling in my toes. The toxin is wearing off. I try to speak. All that comes out is a gurgle.

Caleb South climbs into the boat. He pulls me over him so I'm once again blocking Gem's line of sight. Dave scoots astern and starts messing with the outboard engine.

"Dave, hurry," Caleb barks.

"I'm trying," Dave mutters. "That stupid girl shot the motor."

This makes me happy. I hope the engine explodes in Dave's face.

Dr. Hewett calls down from the deck, "Caleb, listen to me. This is madness."

"Yeah, I remember your lectures." Caleb's tone is as toxic as his syringe of venom. "Our plans are madness, blah-blah. But the *Aronnax* is operational now and Harding-Pencroft is gone, so maybe you were the crazy one to leave us, huh?"

I don't know what the *Aronnax* is. The name alone makes me shiver. It sounds sharp and heavy like a cleaver's blade. On the other hand, the fact that I'm able to shiver is good news. I try to move my head. It lolls to one side. Any hour now, I'll be ready for combat.

"Your new toy is nothing," Hewett tells Caleb. "Dakkar is everything."

"*Toy?!*" Caleb shouts.

"After what you did this morning," Hewett continues, "to the academy, to Ana's brother? She's irreplaceable."

I don't like the way Hewett is talking about me—as if I'm a valuable commodity rather than a person. I wonder if he'll start bargaining, maybe offer to split me in half so they can share the profits.

I can feel Caleb's fingers trembling on my throat. He's getting agitated, and he's holding a needle against my carotid artery. I don't like that combination.

In the stern of the pontoon, Dave lets out a triumphant "Ha!"

The outboard motor sputters to life.

"Good-bye, Dr. Hewett," Caleb calls as the pontoon pulls away. "You sucked as a teacher anyway."

Well, Hewett may not be aiding and abetting the LI students, but he isn't much help to me, either. I can think of only one thing to do. I gurgle loud enough to get Caleb's attention.

He tightens his grip on my neck. "What's that, Dakkar?"

I babble like I'm trying to tell him something important. I sense him leaning in. It's human nature—he wants to know what I'm saying. I judge my timing and angle. Then I use the only weapon I have. I snap my head backward and hear the satisfying crunch of Caleb's nose breaking.

He screams and loosens his grip—just for a moment, but it's enough. His wet fingers lose their traction on my throat as I twist away from his poison palm and limply topple out of the boat.

I take a gulp of air before my head goes under. My limbs are soggy noodles, but I manage to keep my chest upright for buoyancy. I bob to the surface long enough to hear the hiss of a Leyden gun from the *Varuna*. Dave yelps.

Caleb growls and dives into the water after me. Two shots from Gem's M4A1 zing off the back of his wetsuit. Caleb grabs me by the hair and starts dragging me after the pontoon, which is rapidly getting away from us.

"They told me to bring you back alive," he says. "But if I can't do that . . ."

Out of the corner of my eye, I see him raise his free hand. The injector needle protrudes from the inside of a ring slipped on his middle finger. It reminds me of the gag handshake buzzer Dev used to torment me with when we were little. I don't want that to be my last thought.

Gem fires another shot. It ricochets off Caleb's hooded forehead and splashes a few inches from my ear. Hewett yells, "Stop firing!"

I try to struggle. My body won't obey me. Caleb sneers. The blood from his nostrils makes him look like he's got walrus tusks.

"You're more trouble than you're worth," he decides.

He pulls back his hand to slap me with his poison buzzer ring—but help comes from an unexpected direction. Right next to us, a mass of sleek blue-gray flesh explodes out of the sea, and Caleb is body-slammed into oblivion under the weight of a six-hundred-pound bottlenose dolphin.

The resulting waves push me under. My sinuses fill with salt water. I'm sinking, flailing my weak limbs.

Then the dolphin slides underneath me, gently nudging me to the surface. I wrap my arms around his dorsal fin, which is marked with a prominent dark streak.

We break the surface. My first word is a cross between a choke and a sob. "Socrates?"

I have no idea how he found me, or how he knew I needed help, but his familiar clicks and squeaks leave me no doubt what he is saying. *I tried to warn you, silly human.*

I lay my face against his smooth, warm forehead and start to weep.

CHAPTER ELEVEN

We don't let Caleb drown.

If we'd put it to a vote, I'm not sure he would've had enough support, but Dr. Hewett insists we fish him out of the water. Then Kiya and Dru haul him off for interrogation.

The rest of the LI attackers we strip of their weapons, constrain with zip ties, and set adrift in the pontoon. Dr. Hewett assures us they'll get picked up soon enough—by the Coast Guard if they're lucky, by their schoolmates if they're not.

"Land Institute doesn't reward failure," he says. "We must get underway."

Tia Romero stares at him in disbelief. "Sir, we've been attacked. We have wounded. We should call the Coast Guard ourselves."

Hewett gives her a pitying look. "The authorities can't help us, Prefect. We would just put them in danger, too. Finish your modifications and start the engines. The *Aronnax* will not be far behind."

Tia doesn't look happy about it, but she hurries off to comply.

House Orca has their healing work cut out for them. Meadow, Eloise, Cooper, and Robbie Barr all suffered flesh wounds from miniature harpoons. Franklin thinks they'll be okay, but they'll need stitches.

"Completely unnecessary," he complains, holding up one of the six-inch hooked projectiles. "If you're going to shock somebody unconscious, why spear them, too?"

I don't have an answer. The fact that Land Institute would develop a Leyden gun that causes unnecessary pain doesn't surprise me, though.

The rest of our crew suffered only minor injuries. Franklin urges me to go to the sick bay so he can run some tests, make sure the poison is really out of my system. I assure him I'm fine.

He doesn't believe me. Neither do Nelinha and Ester, but the last thing I want is to be confined in a small room belowdecks, attached to a bunch of monitors. I need open air and the sea. I need to watch Socrates swimming alongside our boat, happily chattering at me. After everything else that has happened today, my abduction has left me trembling with shock, terror, shame, and rage. Sea-snake venom isn't the only poison I'm trying to flush out of my system.

The Cephalopods run around finishing Dr. Hewett's alt-tech modifications. The pulse-dispersion unit is installed to block radar and sonar. Projection modules are fixed around the hull for dynamic camouflage. From the rail where I'm standing, I can't see any difference in the ship's appearance, but the Cephalopods look excited. They talk to one another breathlessly about specs and parameters like they're discussing magic spells.

"Can you believe this?" Nelinha grins at me as she passes by. Getting zapped by Dru's gun hasn't slowed her down at all. If anything, it seems to have charged her batteries. Her smile fades, however, when I don't respond. She rests a hand briefly on my shoulder. "You sure you're okay, babe?"

Then her housemate Kay calls, "Oh, no way. Look at these phased-optics reaction times!"

And Nelinha is off.

She is the most caring friend you could ever want, but you have to accept that sometimes you'll take a back seat to shiny new tech.

In a matter of minutes, the *Varuna* is underway.

We head due west. Socrates keeps pace with us easily. He and I talk as best we can, but as usual, it's all questions and no answers.

I wish I knew how he found me, and whether he understands that Dev is gone. He can't tell me these things.

No, that's not correct. I know enough about dolphin intelligence and communication to know he is absolutely capable of telling me. Dolphin language is infinitely more complex and nuanced than human languages. It's just that I can't understand him well enough.

"Thank you," I say to him, also using ASL to make my point more visual. "I wish I could repay you."

He gives me his sideways dolphin smile. I imagine he's saying, *Yes, you owe me all the squid.*

A voice behind me says, "I got upstaged by a dolphin."

Gemini Twain leans against a capstan. His arms are crossed, his expression glum. His dark hair is flecked with sea salt.

"My one job was to protect you," he tells me. "I'm sorry."

I'm tempted to snap *I don't need a protector.* But he looks so depressed I don't have the heart for it.

"Don't beat yourself up, Miles Morales," I say.

Gem laughs under his breath. "Easier said than done."

He pulls at his collar like he's wearing a tie that's too tight.

I don't know much about him. After his altercation with Nelinha during our chum year, I decided I didn't want to deal with him any more than I had to. I guess Harding-Pencroft hasn't always been easy for him, either. He's the only Latter-day Saint at HP, as far as I know. How does a Black Mormon kid from landlocked Utah get interested in a career at sea? I've never asked. Now I hope we'll get more chances to talk—not because I like him, or because I feel like I *have* to like him, but because he's a classmate. Today I was reminded that anyone in my life can be taken away in the span of a heartbeat.

"What did you see," I ask him, "when you looked at Dr. Hewett's tablet?"

He frowns. "A dark shape under the water. Like a massive arrowhead."

"The *Aronnax*," I guess. "Some kind of submarine?"

Gem scans the horizon. "Not like any I've ever heard of. If that's what attacked HP, and it's after us . . ."

He leaves the thought unfinished. Any vessel that can destroy a square mile of the California coast is not something we can fight in the *Varuna*, even with assault rifles, zappy guns, and a luchador dolphin. If we can't go to the authorities, which Hewett seems adamant about, then our only hope is to run and hide. That leads me to an uneasy question: Run and hide *where?*

Ester strolls over with Top at her heels and a dead squid in her hand. Without preamble, she hands me the squid, which is both warm and icy—and extremely gross.

"I found it in the freezer," she says. "I put it in the microwave for sixty-five seconds. I didn't do it any longer because I didn't want it to get too squishy. I mean, it's a squid, so it's already squishy."

She says all this without a pause and without meeting my eyes. Of course, she's just trying to make me feel better. She knew I would want to give Socrates a treat, and she found just the thing.

I've heard "experts" say that autistic people have trouble with empathy, but sometimes I wonder if these experts have ever actually sat down and talked to autistic people. When we first met, I didn't understand why Ester wouldn't say something comforting when one of us was upset. I found her behavior a complex code, like jumbled words and signals. But once I cracked that code, I realized that she just does things a little differently. She's more likely to *do* something nice, or offer an explanation, as a way of helping me feel better. She is, in fact, one of the most empathetic people I've ever met.

Top sits at my feet and wags his tail. He gives me his most soulful stare. *I'm a very good boy. I almost killed someone earlier.*

"He's already had tons of treats," Ester assures me. "The squid is for Socrates."

"As long as it's not for me," Gem says.

"That was a joke," Ester says, her expression deadly serious. "I get it."

"This is wonderful," I tell Ester. "Thank you."

I throw the squid to Socrates, who snaps it up eagerly. I wish I could bring it down to him and feed him by hand, but we're moving at a fast clip now, and so is he. I know he can easily keep pace with our boat, but I'm not sure whether he'll follow us or not. Dolphins have their own priorities.

"He can rest on board if he gets tired," Ester tells me.

It takes me a second to process that sentence. "What do you mean *on board*?"

"Have you seen the captain's room?" she asks. "Harding-Pencroft has always had dolphin friends. It's like Top." She scratches his ear. "There's always been a Top at Harding-Pencroft. I mean, before Harding-Pencroft was destroyed."

I don't quite understand what she means about Top and the dolphins always being at HP, but when she mentions the school's destruction, she gets agitated again. She starts tapping her fingertips on her thighs. The volume of her voice goes up several notches.

"ANYWAY, I CAME TO GET YOU," she says.

"I— Okay. What's up?"

I'm not sure I want to know. It has been a very long day already.

"Dr. Hewett wants to see you two on the forward deck," Ester tells us. "He's not well. I'm not an expert, but I would say he has diabetes and probably an additional underlying condition."

Gem and I glance at each other uneasily. The idea that Hewett is ill doesn't surprise me. He has looked awful since . . . well, always. Ester doesn't have much of a bedside manner, but I trust her instincts. She once announced loudly in the middle of lunch that my monthly cramps might not be so horrible if I increased my intake of vitamin B1. For the record, she was right.

"Okay," I say. "Is that why he wants to see us? Because he's ill?"

"No," Ester says. "I just thought about it, so I said it. He wants to see you because the prisoner is starting to talk." She looks at her palms. "Also, I have squid slime on me. I'm going to go wash my hands because that seems like the right thing to do."

CHAPTER TWELVE

Caleb South is zip-tied to a metal folding chair. His wrists are bound behind him, his ankles fastened to the chair legs.

When I see him, my anger tries to harden into a suit of armor, but I'm so exhausted it's more like a worn-out sleep shirt. It keeps falling away, stretching into an amorphous mass of grief and shock.

Caleb is still in his wetsuit. His mask and hood have been removed, revealing close-set brown eyes and a wedge of blond hair tinged green from chlorine. His broken nose is swelling up nicely. Blood has crusted on his upper lip.

He's been positioned facing west, so he has to squint into the sun whenever he looks up at Dr. Hewett. Dru and Kiya, brandishing their new Leyden guns, stand to either side of the captive. Kiya still looks grumpy from getting electrocuted. Behind Dr. Hewett stands Linzi Huang, one of the Orcas.

I'm relieved to see Linzi. It means Dr. Hewett is still following standard procedures. An Orca is supposed to be present at all important negotiations. Aside from being the school's medics, they're our recorders and witnesses, our school conscience. Having them around tends to keep everybody else on good behavior.

I don't really think any of my classmates would do something like beat up a prisoner to get information, but after what we've been through, nerves are frayed. Tempers are high.

Considering Caleb's broken nose and the fact that he was recently body-slammed by a dolphin, he looks pretty good. The only torture he's endured is Harding-Pencroft's trademark form of humiliation. Around his biceps are children's inflatable water wings, bright yellow with pink duckies. A matching inner tube circles his waist. This is how upperclassmen treat chum-year kids who prove inept at their assignments. They're forced to wear pink duckies for an entire day. Many kids never get over the shame. Why we had some inflatables on board, I'm not sure, but I'm also not surprised.

Caleb scowls when he sees me, but he offers no snide comments. The duckies must have broken his spirit.

Hewett leans toward the prisoner. "Mr. South, tell Miss— tell Prefect Dakkar what you told me."

Caleb curls his lip. "This boat is going to end up at the bottom of the sea."

"Not that part," Hewett says wearily. "The *other* part."

"The *Aronnax* is coming."

"Your submarine," I say, remembering my conversation with Gem.

Caleb lets out a broken laugh. "The *Aronnax* is a submarine the way a Lamborghini is an economy car. But yes, genius, it's our ship. You've got maybe an hour if you're lucky. They sent us to take you alive. . . ." He spits a flake of dried blood from his lip. "Since we failed and never reported in, they'll follow. They'll torpedo this hunk of junk and confirm the kill afterward."

Confirm the kill.

I feel a coldness in my belly that's as sharp as the edge of a fillet knife. I wonder if the *Aronnax* crew talked about Dev and me this way before they destroyed our school, as if we were nothing more than impersonal targets.

I want to slap him. I hold back the urge. Linzi's presence is a calming reminder: *That is not who we are. We don't stoop to their level.*

"Why the attack?" I ask Caleb. "Why me? And why did they send a bunch of students who couldn't do the job?"

He shakes his head in disgust. "You just got lucky with that stupid dolphin. LI doesn't *coddle* their students the way HP does. Destroying HP . . ." He gives me a bloodstained grin. "That was our senior project, and I'd say we aced it."

Dru steps forward, raising the butt of his Leyden gun, but Gem stops him with a stern look.

Caleb watches the exchange with obvious amusement. "As for *why you*, Ana Dakkar . . . You *really* don't know anything, do you?" He glances at Dr. Hewett. "I guess the professor hasn't told you the truth about HP. Were you even trained in Leyden guns until today? Did you even know they exist?"

An uncomfortable ripple goes through our group.

"That's what I thought," Caleb says. "At LI, we aren't afraid to *use* our knowledge. How many world problems could you cowards have solved if you just *shared*?"

Behind me, Gem says, "Shared what, exactly?"

"You had *two years*." Caleb sounds bitter, even regretful. "You could have cooperated with us. You could have negotiated."

I can't tell if the ship is pitching or if it's my own lack of equilibrium. *Two years* since my parents' death. Two years Hewett has been fearing an attack. Two years in which Caleb says Harding-Pencroft could have negotiated.

I fix my eyes on Dr. Hewett. "What happened two years ago?"

His gaze is sadder than Top's when he begs for dog biscuits. "We will have that conversation soon, my dear. I promise."

Caleb snorts. "You aren't really stupid enough to believe Hewett's promises, are you? He promised us a bunch of stuff, too, when he was at LI."

Hewett's knuckles whiten as he clenches his fists. "That's enough, Mr. South."

"Professor, how about you tell them what you were working on for LI back when I was a freshman?" Caleb suggests. "Before you lost your nerve. Tell them who had the idea for the *Aronnax*."

He might as well have thrown another flash-bang grenade. My skull rings like a struck bell.

Gem takes a sharp breath. "Professor, what is he talking about?"

Hewett looks more annoyed than ashamed. "I did many things I wasn't proud of at LI, Prefect Twain, before I knew what they were capable of." He returns his glare to our prisoner. "And today, Mr. South, Land Institute proved why they can *never* be trusted with advanced technology. You destroyed a noble institution."

"Noble institution? You were protecting the legacy of an outlaw." Caleb squirms in his pink-ducky inner tube. "If you're going to kill me, go ahead and do it. This thing is uncomfortable."

Dru and Kiya stare coldly at Dr. Hewett. Even Linzi looks shaken. Maybe, like me, they didn't know before today that Hewett once worked at Land Institute. But it's worse than that. Dr. Hewett had the idea for the *Aronnax*. He helped create the weapon that destroyed our school and killed my brother.

"We don't execute prisoners," Hewett announces. "Dru, Kiya, throw him overboard."

Caleb's arrogant expression crumbles. "Hold on—"

"Sir," Linzi protests.

"He'll be fine," Hewett assures her. "He has his buoyancy-control vest, his wetsuit, his water wings. Guards, proceed."

Dru and Kiya look like they're tempted to dump the professor instead, but after a glance at Gemini Twain, the Sharks follow orders. They untie Caleb from his chair, then drag him thrashing and cursing to the port side and chuck him into the sea.

My last glimpse of my ex-abductor is his blond head bobbing up and down in our wake, spluttering and yelling unkind things about Harding-Pencroft. I imagine he'll be picked up by someone soon enough. He's loud. Also, his pink-ducky floaties make him easily the most colorful thing off the San Alejandro coast.

"Miss Huang," Hewett says, "report to the bridge. Maintain our course due west at maximum speed."

Linzi stirs. "Sir, we deserve—"

"You'll get your explanations," Hewett promises. "But first things first. Double-check the camouflage projectors and pulse-dispersion unit. Have the Orcas sweep the ship for any tracking devices. We *must* get away from the *Aronnax*." He turns toward me. "As for you, Ana Dakkar, you're coming with me. I think it's about time you gave us a course heading."

CHAPTER THIRTEEN

On the way, I grab Nelinha and drag her along.

I need a friend at my side, even if she has to coexist with Gem for a while. I'm still reeling from . . . well, everything. I didn't like Caleb's warnings. I don't understand why Dr. Hewett thinks I'm the one who should decide our course heading. Why does he keep singling me out like this? *He's* the one with all the secrets. And I'm still not sure I trust Gemini Twain to have my back.

At the end of the corridor, Hewett opens the door to the captain's cabin. I've never been inside before. The place is massive: a full-size bed against the port wall, windows overlooking the bow, a big conference table, and on the starboard side . . .

I gasp. *"Socrates!"*

The entire starboard side of the room is an open saltwater tank. The Plexiglas wall is maybe twelve feet long, five feet high, curved inward at the top to prevent the water from sloshing out when the ship moves. The tank isn't big enough for the dolphin to live in, but there's enough room for him to splash around, turn, and float comfortably. On either side is an underwater metal flap that reminds me of a giant pet door. I don't quite understand how the tank was engineered, but the chutes must connect to the open sea, allowing Socrates to come and go as he pleases.

Socrates pokes his head over the lip of the Plexiglas. This puts him at eye level with me. He chatters happily. I give him a hug and kiss him right on the beak. I realize I'm smiling for the first time since the school's destruction.

"I don't understand," I say. "How did you even find us?"

Hewett answers for him. "Your dolphin friend knows this boat well. HP has cultivated friendships with many of his family over the years. Socrates, did you call him?"

"I . . . Yes." I was about to explain that Dev and I dive with Socrates every morning, but remembering that ritual is like walking barefoot over broken glass.

"An appropriate name," says Hewett. "Well, Socrates knows he always has a berth on the *Varuna* if he wants to travel with us. Now come here, Miss Dakkar. Look at this."

Again with the *Miss*. This is how they wear you down: They just keep making the same "oopsie," hoping that you'll eventually get tired of calling them on it.

"Prefect," I grumble, but Hewett has already turned his attention to the conference table, where Gem and Nelinha have joined him.

I guess they don't consider the bottlenose dolphin in the stateroom a big deal. Reluctantly, I go and sit down with my fellow humans.

Spread across the table is a nautical map of the Pacific. In some respects, it's old-fashioned. The names are in fancy calligraphy. The compass rose is elaborately colored. Illustrated sea monsters writhe in the corners.

However, the map is made of a material I've never seen before. It's light gray, almost translucent, and perfectly smooth like it's never been folded. The ink shimmers. If I look at it sideways, all the markings seem to disappear. I don't want to think this with Socrates in the room, but the map reminds me of dolphin skin. Maybe, like the calcium carbonate of the Leyden projectiles, it has been organically "secreted" in a lab somehow.

Oh, great. My thought process is spiraling down the alt-tech rabbit hole.

Sitting on top of the map is a coppery dome-shaped paperweight thingy. At least, in a normal world, it would be a paperweight. Its curved surface is laced with intricate wires. At the apex is a smooth, round indentation. It looks like the eye of a steampunk robot. I really hope it doesn't open and stare at me.

Hewett eases himself into the chair across the table. He mops his brow with a handkerchief. I remember what Ester said: *Diabetes. Underlying condition.* Hewett has never been my favorite teacher. I don't trust him. Still, I'm worried about his health. He is literally the only adult in the room, and the only one who might be able to give me answers.

Nelinha stands on my right, Gem on my left. They studiously avoid looking at each other. Socrates chatters and splashes in his tank.

Hewett picks up the paperweight. He leans across the table and sets it in the center of the map, like he's calling my bet in a poker game.

"I won't ask you to do this until you feel comfortable," he says. "But it is the only way forward."

I look more closely at the object. That indentation at the top . . .

"It's a thumbprint reader," I guess. "I put my thumb on it and . . . what? It shows us a location on the map?"

Hewett smiles faintly. "It's a genetic reader, actually. Keyed to your family's DNA. But yes, you have deduced its purpose."

I'm starting to deduce *my* purpose, too—why Hewett and Caleb South both talk about me like a commodity. I'm putting together the broken pieces of this horrible day, and I don't like what it's showing me.

I try to pick around the edges of my real question. "So, Jules Verne . . . You say he interviewed actual people."

Hewett nods. "*20,000 Leagues Under the Sea. The Mysterious Island*. The foundational texts are based on real events."

A weight grows in my stomach. "Foundational texts . . . You make them sound sacred."

"Hardly," Hewett scoffs. "They are novelizations. Misrepresentations. But at their core, they contain truths. Ned Land was a real Canadian master harpooner. Professor Pierre Aronnax was a French marine biologist."

"Ned Land . . . Land Institute," Nelinha says.

"And *Aronnax*," Gem chimes in. "That's the name of the sub."

Hewett is silent long enough to tap each of his fingertips against the map. "Yes. Land and Aronnax, along with the professor's manservant, Consiel, were the only survivors of a doomed naval expedition. In the 1860s, they joined the search for a supposed sea monster . . . a creature that was sinking ships across the globe. Their expeditionary vessel, the *Abraham Lincoln*, was lost somewhere in the Pacific. Over a year later, Land, Aronnax, and Consiel were found, inexplicably, in a small lifeboat off the coast of Norway."

I find myself leaning forward. I know the plot of *20,000 Leagues Under the Sea*. But now it seems more like a prophecy . . . one that predicts an apocalypse. I don't like apocalypses.

"No one believed the story they told about their lost year," Hewett continues. "They were dismissed as madmen. I doubt even Jules Verne believed them, but he *did* listen. Several years later, after Verne's novel became famous, he was approached by a different group of men. These were former castaways who had survived on a desert island in the Pacific. They claimed they'd had an encounter similar to the one described in *20,000 Leagues*. They wanted to correct what they called inaccuracies in Verne's account. Verne's subsequent novel, *The Mysterious Island*, was based on his interviews with *those* men."

"Cyrus Harding and Bonaventure Pencroft." My mind is racing, connecting dots I do not want connected. "The founders of our school. Just like Ned Land founded Land Institute."

Nelinha raises one eyebrow at Hewett. It's the same expression she uses when she wants to tell the mean sophomore girls to back off or they'll get a butt-kicking.

"If all that's true," she says, "you're telling us the main dude was real, too. Nemo."

"That's correct, Miss da Silva."

"And we're not talking about the cartoon fish," she adds.

Somebody had to say it.

Hewett rubs his face. "No, Miss da Silva. The *main dude* was not a cartoon fish. Nor was he the fictional character from Jules Verne's books after whom that fish was named. Captain Nemo was a real nineteenth-century person—a genius who created marine technologies generations ahead of their time. The most important and powerful advances were keyed to Nemo's own body chemistry . . . what we today call *DNA*. He and his descendants were the only ones who could operate his greatest inventions."

That's it. I sit down. I don't trust my legs to hold me any longer.

"Ester is descended from Cyrus Harding," I say.

Hewett stares at me, waiting. His expression is a mixture of sympathy and cold analytical interest, like a TV-show cop in a morgue, about to uncover the murder victim for the next-of-kin to identify.

"And Captain Nemo . . ." I say. "That wasn't his real name. It was Prince Dakkar. An Indian noble. From Bundelkhand."

"Yes, Miss Dakkar," Hewett agrees. "As of today, you are his only surviving direct descendant. This makes you quite literally the most important person in the world."

CHAPTER FOURTEEN

"Nope."

Honestly, it's the only answer I can muster. "You are *not* telling me that our school was destroyed, my brother was killed, and Land Institute tried to kidnap me because I am descended from a fictional character."

"Not fictional," Hewett says again, his voice strained. "Prince Dakkar was your fourth great-grandfather."

"I agree with Ana," Nelinha says. "This is crazy."

Gem sets his Leyden gun on the table. "We've got evidence."

Nelinha waves off the gun, or maybe she's just waving off Gem. "Your electroplated zapper is cool. That doesn't mean Jules Verne wrote nonfiction. I could reverse-engineer a Leyden gun if I had enough time."

"Which is exactly what Harding-Pencroft did," Dr. Hewett says. "And Land Institute, unfortunately. But Nemo's greatest innovations—"

"Wait." I raise my hands like I'm trying to hold all of this new information together, but I'm failing badly. "You've reverse-engineered super Taser-guns. You've got dynamic camouflage and radar blocking that's better than military-grade. This is all from a guy who lived a hundred and fifty years ago."

Hewett gives me the sort of expectant nod he uses in his classroom, as if telling me *Go on. You are not entirely stupid.*

"Then what do you need me for?"

Hewett winces. I get the feeling he wishes he *didn't* need me.

"Miss—Prefect Dakkar," he says, seeing the intensity of my scowl, "in the last one hundred and fifty years, we have succeeded in re-creating only a few of your ancestor's scientific advances. We have been like children playing dress-up in the great man's clothes. Most of his work, I'm sorry to say, is still beyond our reach."

"And you think I can change that?" I laugh, though there is nothing funny about it. Behind me, Socrates chatters in response. "Professor, I don't have any family secrets."

"No," he agrees. "That was part of Nemo's plan."

Gem sits down next to me. His hand curls around the barrel of the Leyden gun. "Nemo's plan?"

Hewett inhales, as if preparing himself for his final lecture. "Only two times did outsiders meet Captain Nemo and live to tell the tale. The first time—"

"Was Land and Aronnax," Nelinha says. "The bad guys."

Hewett musters a weary smile. "Yes, Miss da Silva. They would not, of course, call themselves *bad guys.* They fled from Nemo's sub, the *Nautilus,* convinced that they had barely escaped the world's most dangerous madman."

"An outlaw," I remember. "Caleb said we were protecting the legacy of an outlaw."

"Yes," Hewett says. "And Nemo *was* a bitter, dangerous outlaw. He hated the great colonial powers. He sank their ships across the globe, hoping to wreck their trade and bring them to their knees."

Gem frowns. "So . . . nice guy."

"A brilliant scientist," Hewett counters, "who had personal reasons to hate imperialism." He hesitates, as if weighing whether or not he wants to tell me about yet another family tragedy. "During the Indian Rebellion of 1857, Prince Dakkar stood up against the British. In response, the British destroyed his principality and killed his wife and elder son. After that, Dakkar went into hiding, eventually becoming Captain Nemo. You, Ana, are descended from his younger son, his only living heir."

Nobody says anything for a minute. Even though the tragedy happened generations ago, I feel a familiar aching emptiness inside me, as if Nemo's wife and child were two more people I lost when HP crumbled into the sea.

Finally Nelinha mutters an unkind comment in Portuguese about what imperialists can do with their national flags.

As far as I know, Dr. Hewett doesn't speak Portuguese, but he seems to understand the sentiment. He nods in sympathy.

"At any rate," he says, "when Ned Land and Pierre Aronnax escaped the *Nautilus*, they were terrified by the captain's rage and power. They made it their lives' work to save the reigning world order from his agenda. They decided they could only do that by re-creating or stealing Nemo's technology by whatever means necessary, claiming his power for themselves."

Nelinha studies her nails, chipped from a hard day's work braining enemies with her socket wrench. "So that's where Land Institute came from. Like I said, the *bad guys*. They want to save the world order. What does that make us—the good-guy outlaws?" She arches her eyebrows. "For the record, I'm okay with that."

"I'm so glad," Hewett says dryly. "As Prefect Dakkar deduced, our school was founded by the second group who encountered Nemo—the one led by Cyrus Harding and Bonaventure Pencroft. They had the good fortune of becoming stranded on an island that happened to be one of the captain's secret bases. He helped them survive and eventually escape."

"He had a lot of secret bases?" Gem asks, like he's always wanted one.

"A dozen that we know of," Hewett says. "Perhaps more. Anyway, by the time Harding and Pencroft met Nemo, he was a different man. His personal tragedies had left him broken and disillusioned. Despite being a genius, despite possessing the most powerful submarine ever built, he had failed to make any real change in the world. . . . Or so he believed."

"He died in his sub." I didn't realize how much I remembered about *The Mysterious Island*. I guess it feels different now, knowing that this guy shared my blood as well as my name. "Nemo helped the castaways escape. Then he sank the *Nautilus* in a subterranean lagoon or something, right before the island went up in a big volcanic explosion. The sub was his tomb."

I can see the goose bumps ripple across Nelinha's arms. For a genius engineer, she is pretty superstitious. Ghosts, dead people, tombs—that stuff totally freaks her out. "There wasn't anything in that book about Harding and Pencroft starting a school," she says.

"Of course not," Hewett says. "The only reason Harding and Pencroft spoke to Jules Verne was to change the public narrative. For our purposes, if anyone *did* begin to suspect that Captain Nemo was real, it was much better if they never saw him as a threat. By the end of his life, Nemo had given up his quest for vengeance. And yes, he did die aboard the *Nautilus*, which was supposedly demolished in the destruction of his island."

"*Our purposes,*" Gem says. "What are those?"

Hewett gestures at the map. "Just before Nemo died, he pulled Cyrus Harding aside and had some final words with him. It says that much in Verne's book. What it does *not* say is that Nemo gave Harding a treasure chest of pearls and also entrusted him with a mission: to make sure his technology was never used by the world powers or stolen by Land Institute. We were to safeguard Nemo's legacy, to reveal his advances only a little at a time, when we decided the world was ready for them. Most importantly"—he looks at me—"we were to safeguard his descendants until the time was right."

I don't want to ask, but I do anyway. "Right for what?"

Again, Dr. Hewett simply watches me, waiting for the hints to fall into place.

"This map leads to one of Nemo's bases," I say, getting goose bumps worse than Nelinha's. "Not just any base. The island where Nemo died. It wasn't completely destroyed in the eruption, was it?"

Hewett gives me his rarest classroom gesture. He simply points at me to say *Correct*. "Ana, two years ago, your parents gave their lives to find this island. Your brother was being prepared to take charge of operations there once he graduated college. Since we discovered it, the island has become a field lab and underwater archaeology site staffed by HP faculty. It holds our most advanced technology. And . . . artifacts."

Gem rubs his forehead. "That's what Land Institute wants. Access to this island. And you . . . you used to work for LI." He sounds personally hurt, as if Hewett has broken a promise.

Hewett stares at the nautical map. "That's true, Mr. Twain. When I was younger, I graduated from HP—House Shark, like you and Dev Dakkar. Nevertheless, I always had a grudging admiration for Land Institute. They favor action over caution, offense over defense. That was alluring to me. In some ways, they are a school made entirely of Sharks. That's why I accepted a job there, and why I spent years designing specs for a submarine that could rival the *Nautilus*. It took me a long time to see the ugly, brutal side of LI, to realize what they would do with such power. . . ."

He gives me a mournful glance. "I don't expect you to trust me. But my past with LI is one reason I wanted to be Dev's advisor. I tried to guide his progress, to teach him why HP's approach is the only responsible way forward. Dev reminded me so much of myself at his age. . . ."

If I wasn't so shocked, I might be tempted to laugh. I can't imagine two people *less* alike than Dev and Dr. Hewett. It's hard to envision Hewett as a Shark, or young, or anything other than our professor. But it makes me wonder what Dev might have accomplished when he got older. Would he have gone on to command his own ship and then his own fleet as he'd always dreamed? Or is it possible he would have ended up a frustrated, dejected teacher like Hewett? That idea is almost as sad as knowing that, now, Dev will never get the chance to have any future at all.

Hewett sighs, as if thinking the same thoughts. "At any rate . . . when your parents found Nemo's base, Land Institute feared it would give HP an unstoppable advantage. As I said, Nemo's most important work could only be operated by his descendants. And, unlike Land Institute, we have . . . good relations with the Dakkar family."

I get the uncomfortable sense that Hewett almost said *we have control of the Dakkar family*. He doesn't seem to notice the cold look I'm giving him.

"The island is completely off the grid," he says, some color coming back into his face. "It is cut off from all outside communication. Its location is unknown even to me. The only way to find it—"

"Is me." I look at the coppery paperweight thing.

"Exactly, my dear. The base is our only hope. The staff there won't know about HP's destruction. We must warn them. We can regroup there, rearm ourselves, protect—"

"We could just go to the authorities," I say. "We *have* been attacked. Our school has been destroyed. We tell—"

"Who?" Hewett demands. "The police? The FBI? The military? Best-case scenario, they write us off as lunatics. Worst-case scenario, they *believe* us. Are you prepared to be whisked off to a secret government site and spend the rest of your days being interrogated? Land Institute and Harding-Pencroft agree on almost nothing. But we *do* agree on one thing. Turning Nemo's technology over to the world's governments, or worse, the world's corporations, would be disastrous. We must—"

He slumps forward like he's been punched.

Gem shoots to his feet. "Professor?"

"I'm fine," he wheezes. "Just overtaxed myself."

I exchange a glance with Nelinha. *Yeah, that's a total lie.*

"Prefect Twain," Hewett gasps, "some assistance, please."

Gem seems relieved to have something to do. He grabs Hewett's arm and helps him up.

"I'll leave you for now, Prefect Dakkar," Hewett says. "Take some time to think. Our course of action will be up to you. We will follow your orders."

I stare at him. *Follow my orders?* The idea terrifies me.

"But . . . you're leaving?" I stammer. "This is your cabin."

"Oh, no," Hewett says. "It's yours. I *did* say you're the most important person on the planet, so suffice it to say you're also the most important person on this ship. We will talk again in the morning. Mr. Twain, if you will help me to the bridge . . ."

Before they reach the door, I call, "Sir."

Hewett turns.

"You mentioned artifacts . . ." I don't want to continue, but I force myself to. "You said Nemo's sub was *supposedly* demolished. What my parents died trying to find—"

"They succeeded, Ana," he tells me, his voice wistful, like he's talking about Santa Claus. "After four generations of fruitless searching, your parents succeeded. They discovered the wreck of the *Nautilus*."

CHAPTER FIFTEEN

What do you do with that information?

You're now the most important person in the world. You have to decide the fate of your friends and classmates. By the way, your parents died during the discovery of a make-believe super sub from the 1800s.

Me . . . I call for a slumber party.

I ask Ester and Nelinha if they'll bunk with me in the captain's cabin. I don't want to be alone in that huge room, even if I do have my teddy dolphin, Socrates. I want Ester's reassuring *puff-puff-snore* nearby, and the rustle of Nelinha's satin hair bonnet whenever she turns her head on her pillow. I want Top's warm doggy smell and his contented sighs as he curls up at Ester's feet.

Once we've settled in for the night, Gemini Twain checks on me one last time. He tells me that the bridge is maintaining a general westerly course until I say otherwise. He will check back with us in the morning.

"Okay," I say. "Thanks. Good night."

Gem gives me an uneasy look. Maybe he sees me differently now that he knows I'm related to a famous outlaw/madman/genius/submarine captain. Or maybe he's contemplating sleeping outside our door all night in case someone else tries to kidnap me. I hope it's the former.

Nelinha and Ester insist that I take the bed. They are happy with their bedrolls. I figure we'll stay up talking for hours. This day has been a smoking crater of misery. My mind is racing, and I have so many emotions to process. How could I possibly sleep? But as soon as I lie down on that comfy full-size mattress, exhaustion kicks in. My body says, *Nope, you're done, girl.* And I pass out.

I always sleep well at sea.

That night I have vivid, fragmented dreams, mostly about smells. After temple, sandalwood incense clings to my mother's sari as she hugs me close, laughing at some silly joke I've made. We stand together in the kitchen during Holi, watching pastries bake in the oven. My mouth waters from the maddeningly delicious scents of cardamom, khoya, and coconut. Then my father is carrying a very small me. I pretend to remain asleep so I can enjoy the feel of my cheek pressed against the warm crook of his neck. His clove-scented aftershave makes me think of pumpkin pie. Then my brother is holding my hand as he walks me home after a fistfight in elementary school. He's really not much older than me, but he seems so mature. Dev's voice is soothing but also deeply offended. He tells me other people are stupid not to respect me. I am brilliant and powerful and deserve the world. My busted mouth tastes of copper. We walk past the honeysuckle blooming at the end of our block. From then on, the sweet smell of honeysuckle will always make me happy. It makes me want to hit Maddy White on the playground all over again, just so my brother will compliment me and walk me home.

I wake to the sound of voices. Ester and Nelinha are standing over me, having a hushed argument. Somehow, I've slept through them getting up, hitting the showers, and getting dressed. Outside, it's daylight. Socrates's giant aquatic hamster tube is empty. He must be out hunting for breakfast. I can't remember the last time I slept past dawn.

Nelinha notices my eyes are open. "Hey, babe. How are you feeling?"

I prop myself up on my elbows.

Top rests his chin on my leg and gives me his *Get up!* grunt. Everybody's a critic.

I guess yesterday really happened. Harding-Pencroft is gone. Dev is gone. I'm at sea . . . literally and emotionally. How do I feel?

"I—I'm awake," I decide. "What's going on?"

Nelinha gives Ester a cautionary look, like, *Remember what we talked about.*

"The good news is he's not dead," Ester says.

Nelinha throws her hands in the air. "Ester . . ."

"Well, you told me to start with the good news," Ester protests. "That's the good news. He isn't dead. Not yet."

"Who . . . ?" A spark of hope flickers through my still-groggy mind. For half a second, I wonder if she could mean Dev. But Ester doesn't let me dream.

"Dr. Hewett," she blurts out. "Franklin found him unresponsive in his cabin."

Dread washes through me.

"Show me." My body somehow manages to find more adrenaline. I'm still in my cotton shorts and sleep shirt, but I don't care. My heart pounds as we hurry down the corridor.

Gemini Twain guards the door to the sick bay. He looks as if he hasn't slept all night. Inside, Franklin Couch and Linzi Huang stand on either side of Dr. Hewett, who lies unconscious on a hospital bed. He's hooked to an IV and several monitors. The straps of his oxygen mask make his gray hair bristle like the fins of a lionfish. I'm no medic, but his vitals don't look good on the displays. Top finds the sick bay smells very interesting . . . until Linzi shoos him away.

Linzi's eyes are bloodshot, and a surgical mask hangs from her right ear. "We ran the most comprehensive blood panel we could with our onboard equipment. His liver function and complete blood count are both off. Blood sugar is high. Our best guess is late-stage cancer, maybe pancreatic, with type-two diabetes, but we're not set up for advanced diagnostics, much less treatment. He needs immediate medical help."

"Except *Gemini* here," Franklin growls, "won't let us put out an SOS."

"The professor's orders." Gemini's voice cracks on the word *professor.* "Complete radio silence no matter what. If Land Institute finds us . . ."

He doesn't need to remind me of Caleb South's warning. The *Aronnax* will send us all to the bottom of the sea. In the last twenty-four hours, I've heard a lot of things I had trouble believing. Caleb's threat wasn't one of them.

Hewett's face is a map of pale blue veins and liver spots. I want to curse him for having medical issues *now.* He should have taken better care of himself. But, of course, that isn't fair of me to think.

What would Hewett want me to do? I know the answer. Keep going. Find this secret base. But how far would that be? And is it worth him dying?

"Can you keep him alive?" I ask Linzi and Franklin.

Franklin shrugs helplessly. "We're *freshmen*, Ana. We've had medical training, but—"

"IF IT'S LATE-STAGE PANCREATIC CANCER," Ester breaks in, making everyone except Hewett jump, "his survival odds are bad no matter what. Even a state-of-the-art hospital won't be able to do much for him."

Her blunt bedside manner makes Linzi's jaw drop. "Ester, we're Orcas. We can't just—"

"She's not wrong, though," Franklin says.

"I don't believe this," Linzi says. "We have to turn back!"

"The base," Gem says. "Hewett mentioned it has our most advanced tech. They might have medical supplies. Stuff that's *better* than state-of-the-art."

Nelinha clicks her tongue. "That's a huge long shot."

"What base?" Franklin demands, hope kindling in his eyes. "How far is it?"

Everyone looks at me for guidance. I wonder if Gem has shared the news that I am now an Important Person. I don't have any guidance to offer. I don't even have shoes on.

But there's a map in the captain's cabin that might help.

"Do your best to keep Hewett stable," I tell Franklin and Linzi. "Gem, Ester, Nelinha—come with me. Let's see if we can find some answers."

CHAPTER SIXTEEN

Since when do my classmates follow my orders?

Without further protest, Franklin and Linzi go back to monitoring their patient. Ester and Nelinha fall in behind me like an honor guard. Even Gem seems content to join the parade as we head down the corridor to the captain's cabin.

I still can't call it *my* cabin. That feels wrong and scary. . . .

I make Gem wait outside while I change into proper clothes.

Socrates has returned to his tank. He chatters at me as if to say, *Hey, human, where's my squid?* I make a mental note to find him one soon.

Top stands on his hind legs and sniffs the dolphin. He doesn't seem terribly concerned about our new roommate, though I get the feeling he'd prefer to sniff Socrates's tail for a formal introduction. I'm glad he can't do that.

Once I'm dressed, we bring in Gem. We gather around the conference table.

Ester twists her fingers like she's playing itsy-bitsy spider. "I just want to point out that I am not a prefect, and neither is Nelinha. We don't have seniority. Tia and Franklin should be here instead."

"It's fine, babe," Nelinha says. "I told Tia I'd keep her in the loop. And you saw Franklin. He's kinda busy."

Ester doesn't look reassured. "Okay . . . I guess that's okay."

Gem eyes the robot-eyeball paperweight as if it might attack us. "Do you know how to work that thing?"

"Hey," Nelinha chides him. "Don't question my friend's abilities." She squints at me. "*Do* you know how?"

"Only one way to find out." I grip the paperweight.

The metal is warm, like a phone that's been recharging. I press my thumb against the impression at the top. A mild electric tingle goes up to my elbow, but I resist the urge to pull away.

The map ripples. The paperweight rises, hovering just over the gray surface, and begins to move around. I'm reminded of the time we tried a Ouija board in our dorm room. Nelinha screamed as soon as the pointer started drifting. I got an attack of the giggles. Ester launched into a long lecture about ideomotor effects and involuntary muscle impulses. We never did find out what the Ouija board predicted for our futures.

This time, nobody screams or giggles. The paperweight shifts to a point off the California coast. Our current position? How the robot-eye thing can know this, I'm not sure.

A glowing line extends from the base of the paperweight like a sunbeam, stretching across the surface of the map, past latitude and longitude lines, numbers for sounding depths, and gentle curves indicating the ocean current patterns and underwater topography. The line stops at a point in the middle of the Pacific Ocean where nothing is marked, just open water.

The thumbprint reader starts to hurt. The electric charge is building.

"Ester," I say with a clenched jaw, "can you memorize those coordinates?"

"I ALREADY HAVE," she says. She's excited. I get that.

I release the paperweight. The glowing line winks out of existence.

Nelinha whistles. "Okay, what we just saw? I can only *guess* how it might work. DNA activation releases some kind of encoded electric signal into the paper—or not-paper, whatever that material is. It shows you the encrypted route. Leaves absolutely no trace afterward. Like, wow."

"Electric eels communicate with low-energy pulses," Ester says. "The parchment could be eel skin, or probably a lab-grown organic material derived from eel skin, because killing eels would be cruel. Nemo wouldn't do that, would he?" She looks at me for confirmation, then decides for herself. "No. That's impossible."

"Whatever the case . . ." Nelinha shakes her head in amazement. "My god."

"Please don't blaspheme," Gem says.

"Who are you, my mother?"

"I'm just asking politely. . . ."

"Both of you, knock it off," I say.

Surprisingly, they do.

"Ester," I say, "how far are those coordinates from our current position?"

I'm pretty sure I know the answer. Dolphins excel at navigation. I can read nautical maps just fine. But Ester's command of hard math is better than mine. She can juggle more variables.

"Maintaining top cruising speed," she says, "in a straight line? Seventy-two hours. That's assuming favorable weather, no mechanical problems, and no more attacks by LI's varsity commandos. Also, there's nothing marked on the chart at that location. Nothing even close. If we don't find a base, we'll be in the middle of nowhere with no supplies. We'll die."

Well . . . no sugarcoating.

But three days is not as bad as I feared. We're provisioned for a weekend. If we ration carefully, we might make it with the supplies we have on board. My suspicious mind wonders if Hewett planned it this way. He *said* he didn't know the location of the base. Nevertheless, we have exactly three days of supplies for a three-day trip. That's quite a coincidence.

On the other hand, I don't think Hewett is faking his coma. I doubt he would knowingly risk his life to lure us to a secret base and betray its location to LI.

Also . . . I hate to admit it, but I love treasure hunts. Secret maps. X marks the spot. Nobody at Harding-Pencroft *doesn't* love that stuff, and all I've ever wanted to do with my life is explore the world, solving its puzzles. Whether this is a trap or not, it's hard to resist.

A lot of things could go wrong. We're only twelve hours out from San Alejandro. The responsible thing would be to turn around, but who on the mainland could help us?

Our class has trained, suffered, and worked for two years. The goal has been to graduate from Harding-Pencroft as the best marine scientists, naval warriors, navigators, and under-water explorers in the world.

We owe it to our lost schoolmates to find out what's at the other end of that glowing line. I want to know why my parents sacrificed their lives, and why Dev is . . . gone, too. But I can't make this call on my own, no matter what Hewett said about following my orders.

"Assemble the crew," I tell my friends. "We'll make this decision together."

CHAPTER SEVENTEEN

I've never liked oral reports.

Put me in a group project, and I will volunteer to do the research. I will draw the maps. I will write the essay and create the multimedia slides. I prefer to leave the presenting to somebody else.

This time, though, it has to be me who delivers the news.

Everyone assembles on the main deck. They line up by house, the way we did yesterday at the docks in San Alejandro. I don't tell them to do this, it's just our custom. The only people absent are Linzi, who is attending to Dr. Hewett in the sick bay, and my fellow Dolphin Virgil Esparza, who has the bridge. I've already filled them in personally.

It's midmorning. The ocean is ash gray with light swells. Clouds hang low and heavy, promising rain. Not the most auspicious weather for making a major decision.

Gemini Twain stands on my right. I guess I appreciate the backup, but I'm still not used to having a heavily armed Shark breathing down my neck. I half expect him to push me out of the way and say, *So, now that I'm in charge* . . .

The worst part is, I'm not sure I would object. I didn't ask for leadership. I don't like everyone staring at me, waiting for answers.

"Here's the situation," I begin.

I know there may be spies among us. Somebody betrayed our school to LI and sabotaged our security from the inside. That somebody may be on this deck. But I can't let that paralyze me. My classmates and I have been through a lot together over the last two years, and the last twenty-four hours. I'll keep trusting them until one of them gives me a solid reason not to.

Besides, we're observing radio silence now. Hewett confiscated all our cell phones after Tia checked them for tracking chips, and even if the phones *weren't* locked in a box in the captain's quarters, there's no way anyone could get a signal this far out at sea. We've activated sonar and radar blocking and dynamic camouflage. We've swept the ship for secret transmitters. No one on board should be able to share our location or our plans with the outside world. At least in theory . . .

I tell the crew everything. Surprise, I'm descended from Captain Nemo. No, not the cartoon fish. Our zappy guns and other gold-level toys are based on Nemo's tech. Land Institute and Harding-Pencroft have been fighting a cold war over said tech for 150 years. Now that cold war has been turned up to a full boil. The mother lode of alt-tech, including the wreck of Nemo's sub, is supposedly at a secret HP base three days from our current position. If LI's sub, the *Aronnax*, finds us in the meantime, we're fish food. Oh, and by the way, Dr. Hewett is in a coma in the sick bay and needs immediate treatment.

"The way I see it," I say, "we have two options. We find this base, warn our people there, and maybe get help against LI. That's what Hewett wanted. Or we turn back to California, report everything to the authorities, and hope they can handle it. Questions?"

The group shifts uncomfortably. Everybody looks at everybody else, wondering who's going to speak first.

Kiya Jensen raises her hand. "So, you're in charge now, Ana?" She glances at Gem. "And we're okay with that?"

I try not to take this personally. Sharks are trained for command. According to school tradition, Gem should be calling the shots, not me.

I wonder if he will call for a vote on the matter. I imagine he'd win, and honestly, I would be kind of relieved. Gemini Twain is competent and reliable. He's annoying that way.

He gives Kiya a curt nod. "The professor's orders were clear: Find this base, no matter what. Ana's got good intuition, and her Nemo genes let her operate things we can't touch. I agree with Dr. Hewett. She's our best shot."

I face our classmates with what I hope is a calm *I totally knew Gem would support me* expression.

Rhys Morrow holds up an index finger. "You're assuming the base even exists. If Hewett was lying, we'll find ourselves in the middle of the Pacific with no supplies. He worked at LI, right? He could be our spy, sending us to our deaths."

Always a sunbeam of optimism, that girl. But she raises valid points.

There's some uneasy murmuring in the group. Nobody looks shocked by Rhys's allegations. Rumors travel quickly.

"The base is there," Ester says.

She's kneeling next to Top, picking bits of crusted sea salt off his furry ears. Ester doesn't speak loudly, but she gets everyone's attention.

"You *know* this?" Franklin asks her.

"Not for sure." She's still addressing Top. "Not because I'm a Harding or anything. If Dr. Hewett wanted us dead, there are easier ways than sending us to a make-believe island in the middle of the ocean. If Dr. Hewett is a spy, it's more likely he was using us to find this base. He would need Ana for that. Then he could sell us out to LI. *Then* they could kill us."

That cheerful idea hangs in the warm, wet air. The sea churns under our feet. Again, everyone is looking at me for answers.

I want to kick an LI upperclassman. I'm a week shy of fifteen years old. Why do *I* have to be handling this crisis? I want to scream, *This isn't fair!* But I've been screaming that internally ever since my parents died, and it's done me no good. I've learned that the world doesn't care what is right for me. I have to *make* it care.

"Searching for the base is a risk," I admit. I'm amazed my voice doesn't break. "Our other option is to turn back. That's a risk, too. The *Aronnax* is somewhere in these waters, and we saw what it did to the school. We had a lot of . . . a lot of friends on campus."

More than friends. I think of Dev's crooked grin. His early birthday gift to me, my mother's black pearl, hangs heavily around my neck. I look at Kay Ramsay, whose sister was a sophomore. Kay's watery red eyes are glaring a hole in the deck boards. Brigid Salter, who had a brother in the junior class, trembles as she leans against her housemate Rhys for support.

Yesterday was about shock, uncertainty, fear. Our world was shattered. Today, we have to figure out how to reassemble ourselves from the broken pieces.

Some of us were *literally* shattered. Eloise McManus's left shoulder is wrapped in gauze, her arm in a sling so she can't hold a rifle. For a Shark, that must be infuriating. Meadow Newman stands stiff and pale. Her shirt hides her bandages, but I remember the silver barb that hit her in the shoulder.

Her fellow Cephalopod Robbie Barr leans on a crutch, his right leg in a gel cast from his encounter with a Leyden harpoon.

He wipes his nose with a cloth handkerchief. He's not crying, he's just famous for his many allergies. Even on the open sea, he can find something that makes him sneeze.

"This alt-tech . . ." Robbie squints sideways at me. "You're saying it was HP's mission all along to safeguard this stuff. And none of us were told. Not even you?"

"Not even me," I confirm. "Until yesterday, I knew nothing."

I try not to let my eyes drift to Ester. I'm pretty sure she knew more than she was allowed to say, but I don't want to put her on the spot in front of everybody.

Cooper Dunne hefts his new Leyden pistol. "And there are more surprises like this at the secret base?"

Cooper's leg is still bandaged from the harpoon wound yesterday, but he doesn't seem bothered by it. If anything, he sounds anxious for a rematch with LI—preferably with bigger guns on our side next time.

"Hewett said that Leyden weapons were the simple stuff," I recall. "He claimed Nemo's most complicated tech is still *way* beyond our best science. Our trials this weekend were supposed to be our first introduction."

More grumbling in the ranks. Ah, yes, the good old days of twenty-four hours ago, when our biggest worry was passing the trials and staying at HP.

Tia Romero tugs at her corkscrew hair. "So the upperclassmen, even the sophomores . . . they knew all about this stuff, and they never breathed a word."

I can tell nobody likes the idea that the sophomores had important inside information. The tenth-graders were the worst.

On the other hand, the secret of alt-tech does explain why they always looked at us so smugly. A lot of things make sense now. The tight security around Verne Hall. The armed guards. The gold-level crates.

I still can't believe Dev kept all these secrets from me . . . about our family heritage, and especially about the circumstances of our parents' death. The more I think about it, though, the less angry I am. It just makes me sad that Dev had to carry that weight alone. I wish I could have helped him. Now he's gone. . . .

"We can't let them have it." Brigid Salter's voice draws me out of my thoughts. She still looks shaky, like she's emerged from a three-day bout with the flu, but her expression is hard as iron. "This base. It might be all we have left of HP. We can't let Land Institute take it. Or you, Ana . . . We can't let them have you, either."

I get a lump in my throat. It would be so easy for Brigid, for *all* my classmates, to blame me for what has happened, given the fact that *I'm* the one Land Institute is after. Instead, I can sense the anger rippling through the group, and that anger isn't directed at me.

"I call for a vote," Gem announces. "I say we give Ana command. We follow her orders, work together, and find this base. Then we make Land Institute pay for what they've done. All in favor?"

The vote is unanimous. Everybody raises a hand except Top, and I like to think I have his moral support.

I swallow the metallic taste of fear. I've just been made acting captain of a ship with a crew of twenty freshmen, a dog, a dolphin, and one comatose adult.

I do not want that responsibility. Just because I'm descended from Nemo does not mean I'm captain material. But my classmates need someone to rally behind, someone who will bring them better fortunes. God help them, they've decided that someone is me. For them, for our lost friends, and especially for Dev, I have to try.

"I won't let you down."

As soon as those words are out of my mouth, I think, *How can I promise that?*

"Prefects, to the bridge with me," I say, my legs shaking. "Everyone else, to your assigned stations. We've got work to do!"

It's only seventy-two more hours, I tell myself.

Then we'll either find help at this secret base . . . or we'll most likely die.

CHAPTER EIGHTEEN

Turns out running a ship is hard work.

I guess I should've known this. I've been on the *Varuna* enough times before. But I've never been in charge of an entire crew, especially not one trying to figure out crates full of Nemo-based alt-tech.

My meeting with the prefects goes well enough. We organize our assignment schedule and daily shifts. One Dolphin and one Shark will be on the bridge at all times as quartermaster and officer of the deck. Orcas and Cephalopods will conduct a careful unpacking and analysis of our gold-level tech. Linzi and Franklin will alternate in the sick bay looking after Dr. Hewett. Everyone will take turns preparing meals, keeping an inventory of supplies, monitoring the critical systems, and cleaning the *Varuna*. (Ships get dirty quickly with twenty-one people and a dog on board.) Meanwhile, Top will follow Ester around and look cute. Socrates will come and go as he pleases, eating fish and playing in the ocean. Why do the animals get the best jobs?

Once all that's decided, I set our course. I figure we'll have to risk traveling in a straight line to the island. We don't have enough time or supplies to be tricky and zigzag around the ocean, hoping to throw off any pursuers. Hewett's advanced camouflage and anti-sonar tech had better work.

I leave Virgil Esparza and Dru Cardenas in command for the first watch. Tia Romero stays on the bridge, too. She's been working on Dr. Hewett's control pad, trying to get access and route the encrypted data to the onboard computer. I wish her luck, though I'm not sure I can handle any more mind-blowing secrets that Dr. Hewett might have been waiting to spring on us.

I spend the first part of the day making the rounds. I check on the crew. I give them encouragement. I try not to trip over the many open gold-level boxes now scattered around the ship. I get a lot of questions from excited Cephalopods and Orcas: What is this? How does it work? Most of the time, I don't have a clue what I'm looking at. I might have Nemo's DNA, but it did not come with any latent knowledge or a handy user's manual.

By noon, rain is hammering down. Swells have risen to five feet. It's nothing we haven't handled before, but it's not great for morale. If you're stuck working belowdecks and can't get fresh air or see the horizon, even those with the strongest stomachs can get seasick.

I find Nelinha in the engine room. She's sitting on the corrugated steel floor, her legs in a V with a gold-level crate open in front of her. Today, she has refreshed her Rosie the Riveter look with a red top and red polka-dotted bandana. She seems completely engrossed in sorting through wires and metal plates. I have a flashback to Dev in sixth grade, building Lego robots.

I turn to Gem, who's been following me around all morning. "Why don't you get some lunch? I'll be fine."

He looks torn between his duty as bodyguard and his discomfort at being around Nelinha. Finally, he nods and lopes off. This is a relief. He's been standing behind me so long, I'm starting to think his breath is leaving an impression on my shoulder.

"How's *that* going?" Nelinha waves her screwdriver at the spot where Gem was standing.

I'm tempted to say that Gem isn't so bad, but that's not for me to tell Nelinha, given their history. I just shrug.

"Hmph." Nelinha turns her attention back to the half-disassembled device in her hand.

I think back to that infamous day in September of our chum year. We were brand-new, trying to survive the meat grinder of orientation month. Two of our classmates had already dropped out and gone home in tears.

Nelinha was struggling more than most. Her English was excellent, but it was still her second language. She was relieved to sit next to me in the cafeteria because I knew some Portuguese. Then, one night at dinner, Gem's shadow fell across our table. He stood over us, gawking at Nelinha like she was a unicorn.

"Are you the scholarship kid?" he asked. "From Brazil?"

There was no malice in his voice, but his words carried. We'd just finished a hard day of physical training. Nobody had much energy left for chatting. Our classmates turned to see who Gem was talking about.

The scholarship kid.

Nelinha's face hardened. My fingers curled around the handle of my fork. I was tempted to stab Gemini Twain in the thigh. He'd just reduced my new friend's identity to three words that would cling to her for the rest of the year.

Gem seemed oblivious. He started rambling about his brother who was an LDS missionary in Rocinha. Did Nelinha know him? Had she met any of the missionaries? How was life in the favela?

Eventually I would realize that being a straight shooter was just an extension of Gem's personality. When he saw a target, he aimed and shot. He did not think about collateral damage.

Nelinha put down her utensils. She gave Gem a sour smile. "I don't know your brother. Ana, you finished?"

She stormed off. I gave Gem a withering look, then abandoned my dinner and rushed to follow her out of the cafeteria.

Later in the eighth-grade barracks, after lights-out, I heard Nelinha sobbing in her bunk. At first, I assumed it was Ester. But Ester was fast asleep and snoring. Nelinha was curled up and miserable, shivering under her blankets. I crawled in next to her and held her while she wept, until finally she fell asleep.

Nelinha had gone through a lot in her thirteen years. She grew up an orphan—no family, no opportunities, no money. Then, thanks to an elementary-school teacher who saw something special in her, Nelinha was recommended for the HP entry tests in Rio. She blew the tops off all the mechanical-aptitude scores. She deserved to be known as more than *the scholarship kid.*

Since that day in the cafeteria, I've stayed angry at Gemini Twain for almost two years. I guess that wasn't fair or justified. But I don't like anyone making my friends hurt.

Now, HP has been destroyed. Nelinha's future is once again a giant question mark. Like me, she doesn't have any family or home to return to. All we have is this boat ride to the middle of nowhere. . . .

"This is crazy." Her voice breaks me out of my trance. I wonder how long I've been standing there watching her work.

"What's crazy?"

She holds up her gadget, which looks like a bespoke metal tennis ball that had a head-on collision with a Slinky. "If I'm right, this is a LOCUS."

I try to place the name. The memory of Dr. Hewett's dry voice comes back to me from some long-ago theoretical marine sciences lecture. "An electrolocation sensor?"

"Correct!" Nelinha wriggles her immaculately groomed eyebrows. "Imagine a more effective, undetectable alternative to radar and sonar, based on aquatic mammals' senses. Whales. Dolphins. Platypuses. If I can figure it out, it could allow us to check for incoming hostiles without giving away our position."

"Or it could make us light up on sonar screens," I speculate.

"Maybe," Nelinha agrees cheerfully. "Where's your sense of adventure?"

I shake my head in amazement. "How can you take all this so calmly? Stuff like that shouldn't be scientifically possible."

She tosses the LOCUS into the air and catches it again. "Babe, our understanding of the laws of science changes all the time. We've only got so many senses. We have such a narrow perspective on reality—"

"Uh-oh." I realize I've blundered right into a #NelinhaLecture.

"That's right, *uh-oh*. This LOCUS . . . it's like something dolphins might engineer if they wanted to augment their natural senses. Or squid, if they had a few more millennia of evolution. Your ancestor was a genius. It's like everybody was looking at the world in three dimensions, and somehow, he was able to step back and see it in *five*. Everything is the same, but everything is different. If we could replicate—"

I'm saved from the rest of the lecture when Ester stumbles in breathlessly, Top at her heels.

"COME WITH ME—YOU NEED TO SEE THIS." Her eyes are red from crying. "YOU DON'T WANT TO, BUT YOU NEED TO."

CHAPTER NINETEEN

What I hate the most?

None of us will ever be able to get these images out of our heads. The feed recorded at HP by Dr. Hewett's drones is playing on six monitors on the bridge. We will be reliving this trauma in full color for the rest of our lives.

Tia stands back from the console, her hands tented over her mouth. Virgil and Dru seem paralyzed at their stations. When we walk in, Nelinha grunts like she's been punched in the chest.

The drones show us our former campus from six different angles. The bay churns white and brown, frothy with debris. The cliff has been sheared away in a near-perfect crescent, like some god took an ice-cream scooper and helped himself to a giant serving of California. Nothing remains of Harding-Pencroft except the buckled asphalt of the main driveway leading to the now-abandoned gatehouse. None of the videos show any people. I can't decide if that's a blessing or a curse.

What happened to the guards at the gate? Is it possible some of the students got out before the buildings collapsed?

My gut tells me no. There wasn't time. There probably wasn't any warning, either. Everyone at HP is now at the bottom of the bay. Given what I've learned about marine decomposition, it may be a long time before any evidence comes to the surface.

Evidence. Oh, god. How can I think of my schoolmates as *evidence?*

I remember Dev smiling at me. *You're leaving for your freshman trials today. I wanted you to have the pearl for luck—just in case, you know, you fail spectacularly or something.*

My mother's black pearl feels like an anchor around my neck.

"There's—there's this, too." Tia hits a button on the keyboard. All six screens switch to the same image: a dark triangular shape, floating underwater just inside the entrance of the bay. It's hard to judge the object's depth or relative size, but it looks massive, like a sunken stealth bomber. As we watch, it ripples and vanishes.

"The *Aronnax,*" I say.

"It has dynamic camouflage," Nelinha notes.

Pressure builds in my throat. I need to howl. I need to throw things at the monitors. *This is so wrong. And it's way too much for me to handle.* Somehow, I manage to push down my rage.

"Anything else?" I ask Tia.

"Um . . ." Her fingers tremble over the keyboard. "Yeah. Dr. Hewett was recording satellite newsfeeds for a couple of hours after the attack. We made international headlines."

The monitors switch to television reports from around the Pacific Rim: California, Oregon, Japan, China, Russia, Guam, the Philippines. On Seattle local news, a grim-faced reporter talks over the tagline MASSIVE LANDSLIDE CLAIMS SECONDARY SCHOOL IN CA: OVER 100 FEARED DEAD. On China's state network, the news ticker reads in Mandarin CRUMBLING AMERICAN INFRASTRUCTURE CAUSES ANOTHER TRAGEDY. The anchor quotes "unnamed sources" who believe faulty foundation work and lax building regulations may have led to the tragedy. None of the stories call the incident an attack.

"How can they not *see* it?" Virgil demands. "A landslide doesn't leave a perfect semicircle!"

But the images on the news are different from the feeds recorded by Dr. Hewett's drones. By the time the media helicopters got to the scene, apparently hours after the attack, the edges of the landslide had crumbled and turned ragged, making it look more like a natural disaster.

Some of the news programs cut to faces of weeping parents.

"Turn it off," I say. "Please."

The monitors go dark.

The bridge is silent for the space of two swells. The *Varuna* surges and plunges as we forge through the storm, leaving my heart at the crest of each wave. Looking out the bridge's windows, I can see the crew staggering around in rain gear, lines on, making sure our water collectors are open to harvest the downpour.

I look at Tia. "The others don't need to see this footage right now. Everyone is already upset enough. I'm not saying we hide the information, but seeing those images . . ."

Tia nods. "It's just . . . None of the reports mention our field trip. That means everybody probably assumes we're dead. Our parents. Friends. Relatives."

I know she's thinking of her own family back in Michigan. She goes by Tia because she has three baby nephews and two nieces she adores. Her mom and dad, her aunts and uncles, her brothers and sisters . . . they all will be going out of their minds.

"I get it," I say, though that's kind of a lie. I have no one back home waiting for me, worrying about me. "The thing is, Land Institute knows we're alive. The *Aronnax* is hunting us. If we break radio silence—"

"We might *be* dead," Dru says.

A typical point-and-shoot Shark comment, but he's right.

Virgil rubs his chin. "Bernie, our bus driver—he knows we're alive, right? And those guards from the docks in San Alejandro. They'll tell everybody we weren't on campus when it collapsed, won't they?"

"If they're still alive," Dru offers.

I remember Hewett's orders to the guards. *Buy us time.*

"For now," I say, "we keep going. We just have to hope . . ."

I'm not sure how to finish that thought. There are too many things we have to hope for. Right now, our supply of hope feels as limited as our food and water.

Top bumps against Ester's leg. He makes a little whimper, looking up at her with his mournful *Pet me* eyes. That's when I realize Ester has been silently crying. Top is really earning his dog biscuits.

"Hey," I tell Ester. "We'll get through this—"

She makes a noise somewhere between a sniffle and a hiccup. Then she rushes out of the bridge, Top right behind her.

"I'll go after her," Nelinha offers.

"No, I'll do it," I say. "Nelinha, show Tia your LOCUS thingy. If it works, I want it installed right away."

"LOCUS thingy?" Tia asks.

Nelinha holds up her metal tennis ball/Slinky catastrophe.

"Cool," Tia says. As I'm turning to leave, she calls, "Ana, I want to try one more thing with Hewett's control pad. When his drones flew over the campus, they would've tried to sync with the school's intranet."

I suppress a shiver. "But the school had already been destroyed."

Tia hesitates. "The computer systems were designed to withstand a lot. Like the black boxes on airplanes. It's possible the drones retrieved some data before the intranet died completely."

I don't feel confident about this plan. More data will mean more pain, more reminders of what we've lost, but I manage a nod. "Sounds fine. Keep up the good work."

Then I jog after Ester and Top.

CHAPTER TWENTY

I find Ester in the ship's library.

On past trips, it's been one of our favorite spots. The walls are lined floor-to-ceiling with books: everything from physics manuals to recent best sellers. Wooden crossbars secure the shelves to keep volumes from flying around when the ship moves. The mahogany study table has armchairs for six. Against the back wall is a comfy old corduroy sofa that we always fight over when we have free time. When we *had* free time. There won't be much of that for the foreseeable future. Ester is curled up at one end, clutching a leather-bound book in her lap. Top lies next to her, wagging his tail.

"Hey . . ." I sit cross-legged on the rug at Ester's feet. This gets me a sloppy wet kiss from Top.

"It's my fault." Ester sniffles. "I needed to . . . They have to let me rebuild. They will, won't they? I didn't bring extra index cards. I'm so stupid. It's all my fault."

I don't follow everything she's saying. Sometimes when Ester talks, you just have to go along for the ride and enjoy the scenery. But one thing I *do* understand.

"None of this is your fault, Ester."

"It is. I'm a Harding."

I would give her a hug right now, but she isn't like Nelinha. Unexpected physical contact with anyone other than Top, especially when she's feeling upset, makes her uncomfortable. Exceptions are hugs she asks for and the occasional tackle in combat training.

"Just because your family started the school . . ." I falter. I realize for the first time that our fourth great-grandfathers knew each other. Their meeting set in motion everything now affecting our lives. It's enough to give me vertigo. "You couldn't have known what would happen."

As usual, her frizzy hair makes her look like she recently stuck her finger in a light socket. Her pink blouse accentuates her strawberries-and-milk complexion. Nelinha has advised her many times to wear another color—dark blue or green— but Ester likes pink. The fact that Ester is stubborn about that makes me appreciate her even more.

"I *did* know," she says miserably. "And I know what's going to happen to you."

One moment, I feel like I'm holding up my friend. The next, I feel like she's dangling me off a cliff.

My mind races. I'm dying to yell *WHAT DO YOU MEAN?* and pull the information out of her. But I don't want to make things worse.

"Tell me about it?" I suggest.

Ester wipes her nose. The gilded title of the book in her lap reads *The Mysterious Island*. Of course we would have a copy on board. I wonder if it's a first edition signed by Captain Nemo. Prince Dakkar. Fourth Great-Grandpa. I don't even know what to call him.

"Harding and Pencroft," she starts. "Nemo asked them to safeguard his legacy."

I nod. I'd learned as much from Hewett. I just have to wait and see where Ester takes me on this ride.

"Since Nemo couldn't destroy the *Nautilus*," she continues, "he wanted Harding and Pencroft to make sure no one discovered its final resting place until the time was right."

"Why couldn't he destroy his sub?" I ask, though the very question seems wrong. It's like asking why Botticelli didn't burn *The Birth of Venus* before he died.

Ester traces her finger over the gold lettering on the book's cover. "I don't know. The best Nemo could do was sink the *Nautilus* under that island. He knew Aronnax and Land were searching for him. He was alone, dying. I guess he had no choice. He decided to trust Harding and Pencroft with his secrets and his treasure."

Nemo, I think. *Harding and Pencroft.*

Ester and I were bound together centuries before we were born. It makes me wonder about reincarnation and karma, and whether our souls might have met at another time.

"So how were they supposed to know?" I ask. "I mean . . . how would Harding and Pencroft know when the time was right to find the sub again?"

Ester tucks in her knees. "That gray map in the captain's cabin. The genetic reader. They would only work for Nemo's direct descendants. Only after a certain number of generations had passed. I don't know how Nemo decided. We didn't . . . My ancestors didn't know exactly how long the wait would be. Your dad tried it when he was a student at HP. No luck. Then he tried it again, two years ago, just to see, I guess. For whatever reason, it worked. He was the first."

A clinch knot tightens in my throat.

I remember the electric sensation traveling up my arm when I had gripped that weird robotic paperweight. My father had done the same thing before me. I can almost feel his warm, callused hand slipping into mine.

"I knew about alt-tech." Ester shivers, which makes Top

cuddle closer. "The board of trustees—they briefed me last fall. Not all the details, but about your family. And *my* family. I wanted to tell you. Keeping those secrets felt wrong . . . and *dangerous*. But the trustees control my inheritance, and the school. They made me sign a bunch of papers. If I said anything to anyone, even you . . . I'm so sorry, Ana. Maybe if I'd talked to you earlier, we could have saved HP."

I want to reassure her, but my voice won't work. Too many facts are swirling around in my head.

"I'm the last of the Hardings," she says. "The Pencrofts died off a generation ago. The trustees don't like me. After my aunt died when I was six . . . She was the last of the really *great* Hardings. I'm just . . . just me."

The sadness in her voice makes my heart ache. "Oh, Ester—"

"When I turn eighteen," she forges on, "they're supposed to give me some control. But . . . you know, they might never. They doubt I'm capable. Now the school is gone. I need to rebuild HP. I don't know how. I'm sorry if you hate me now, Ana. I don't want you to hate me."

I think about poor Ester living at HP since she was six years old. I knew about her aunt's death. I knew she had no living family, just legal guardians, but I'd never appreciated how much pressure and responsibility went along with the Harding name. All her life, instead of being loved and nurtured, Ester had been watched over by a council of lawyers who loved and nurtured her money while monitoring her for signs of incompetence. At least I'd known my parents. I'd had them in my life.

"Ester, I don't hate you," I promise. "Of course I don't. You weren't allowed to say anything."

Her lip quivers. "The others will hate me, though."

"No. And if anybody does, I will put pink-ducky water wings on them and throw them overboard."

She sniffles some more. "That was a joke, right?"

"No. But no one will hate you."

"What about the trustees? I told you what I know. They'll disinherit me."

"If the trustees give you any problems, I will personally kick each and every one of them in the groin."

Ester considers this. She doesn't ask if I'm joking. "Okay. That's good. I love you."

She says it with such a flat tone that anyone else could have missed it, or taken it as a polite, meaningless phrase, like *How you doing?* But I know she means it.

"I love you, too," I say. "Can I ask you one more thing?"

She nods. As she strokes Top's ear, I notice how badly she's chewed up her cuticles.

I'm not sure I want to know the answer, but I ask anyway. "You said you knew what was going to happen to me. What did you mean?"

She frowns at the picture on the front of the book. A dark, jagged volcano rises from the churning sea. In the foreground, a drenched dog that looks very much like Top trembles alone on a tiny outcropping of rock.

"When your parents found the *Nautilus*," she says, "they tried to open it. They tried to go inside. Your dad should have been able to do it. He was a direct descendant of Nemo. I don't know exactly what happened, but something went wrong. That's why HP was so careful with Dev. They didn't want him to go near the sub until they understood—"

"Wait," I say, my head spinning. "My parents' death was an accident."

"I don't think so." For a rare moment, Ester actually meets my eyes. "The *Nautilus* is dangerous, Ana. I think it killed your parents. I don't want it to kill you, too."

CHAPTER TWENTY-ONE

Over the next two days, I try not to obsess too much about Ester's words.

I don't succeed. At night, I lie awake thinking about my parents' deaths. I imagine them diving into the creepy rusted-out wreck of a sub, only to get trapped inside, or killed by some ancient booby trap. I think about Dev, and how it must have torn him up to keep so many secrets. I have nightmares about the dark arrowhead shape of the *Aronnax* hurtling toward us underwater, cracking the *Varuna*'s hull in two.

During the day, I'm too busy stressing about immediate problems to worry about problems that might kill me later. Thank goodness for small favors.

Among the low points: We're running short of food. We've needed a lot more than I thought we would, and we weren't as good about rationing as I'd hoped. This makes me feel guilty that I sneaked an extra chocolate-chip cookie after dinner the first night. (What I really wanted was a fresh-baked gujiya dipped in hot chai, but desperate times call for desperate comfort foods.)

Also, I had to break up a fistfight between Cooper and Virgil. They got into it after one of them made a comment about—actually, I didn't even care. I pushed them apart and did some yelling. This felt better than it probably should have. I was tempted to confine them to their quarters, but I need everybody working. Their fight made one thing clear: Nerves are starting to fray.

Also, Dr. Hewett's condition continues to deteriorate. Franklin and Linzi have worked themselves to exhaustion keeping him alive, but they can't say for sure whether he'll make it another day. His blood pressure is low. His heartbeat is weak. His urine . . . I may have blanked out when they told me about his urine.

The trip's high points are notably fewer.

For one, Nelinha has gotten the LOCUS working. Gem, Ester, Tia, and I join her on the bridge for the big reveal. We're not sure what to expect. The metal tennis-ball thingy has been mounted on top of the navigation console. Its Slinky-esque coils run in all directions like the tentacles of an octopus, attached to various points of the console with seemingly no rhyme or reason. Do they work like antennae? Grounding wires?

"Here we go." Nelinha turns a copper dial on the side of the orb.

The room fills with floating green patches of light, like we're inside an aquarium that desperately needs cleaning.

Ester says, "This seems wrong."

"Hold on," Nelinha says. "Let me recalibrate the display resolution. . . ."

She twists another knob. The green lights shrink into a glowing sphere the size of a basketball, hovering over the base of the LOCUS.

I realize immediately what we're seeing. Our boat is the tiny white dot hovering in the center. The sphere's upper half is a swirl of faint green lines: wind patterns, rain, and clouds in real time. The lower hemisphere shows conditions underwater in a darker emerald light: currents, depth readings, and a whole host of dots and blobs of various sizes moving beneath us.

"Marine life," I guess. "That's got to be a school of fish. What's that, a whale?"

Nelinha beams. "We are electrolocating, gang."

I'm enthralled by the three-dimensional readout. It should be too much information, too complicated to read, but I understand it instinctively. I can *feel* the ship's position, how it relates to the currents and the winds, how it affects the movements of the creatures around us.

"This is so much better than sonar or ECDIS," I murmur. "How is this possible?"

Nelinha looks pleased, like she's just baked a batch of cookies everybody loves. "I told you, babe—a different perspective on the laws of science. What we're seeing is a visual representation of the way marine mammals sense their environment. And yeah, it's *way* better than puny land-animal tech."

"Nice work, da Silva." Tia Romero squints at the controls around the base of the LOCUS. "You're sure this isn't making us light up on the radar screens of every ship within a thousand miles?"

"Pretty sure. Like ninety percent. Eighty-five percent."

"What if the *Aronnax* has similar tech?" I ask. "Will dynamic camouflage fool a LOCUS?"

Nelinha's smile turns to a grimace. "Maybe?"

It's an unsettling thought. There are no signs of other vessels on the LOCUS readout—submarine or otherwise. But is it possible the *Aronnax* is out there, as invisible to us as we're (hopefully) invisible to them?

"If they *do* show themselves," Gem says, "we'll test our other new toy."

He points out the window. On the forward deck, the Sharks

have assembled their favorite discovery from the gold-level boxes: a Leyden cannon the size of a Jet Ski. Its coppery barrel is laced with wires and intricate gear work. Its mounted pedestal swivels 270 degrees. I don't know what it might do to an enemy ship, especially one like the *Aronnax*, but Gem and his housemates are raring for target practice. I have already warned them they are *not* allowed to electrocute whales or fishing boats.

The other high point of our trip: The *Varuna*'s engines freeze up.

I know that sounds like a bad thing. Getting stranded in the middle of the ocean and starving to death would typically fall into that category. However, the Cephalopods are confident that they can make repairs. In the meantime, Halimah Nasser suggests that somebody use this opportunity to do a visual inspection of the hull's exterior. I volunteer so fast I make her jump.

I get on my buoyancy control vest and scuba tank. I grab my mask, fins, and a dead squid (for obvious reasons). The water is warm enough that I don't need a wetsuit. I topple backward into the sea. As soon as my cloud of bubbles dissipates, I spot Socrates swimming toward me, delighted to have a playmate.

He chatters and nudges me cheerfully. I give him the squid, but that doesn't seem to satisfy him. As I start to inspect the hull, he gooses me to get my attention.

"Rude!" I mumble through my breather.

This makes no impression on him. Dolphins are shameless goosers.

He nudges me again, and I realize he wants to show me something.

I follow him to the forward starboard side of the hull. Just below the water line, there's a fist-size grappling hook embedded in the wooden knockdown rail. A frayed cord trails from it into the gloom. I guess this is a souvenir left by our uninvited guests from Land Institute. They must have fastened a line to the *Varuna* just before they surfaced.

The damage is probably superficial, but I don't want to take chances. I also don't want *anything* from LI on my ship. I tug the hook free and let it sink into the depths.

I thank Socrates with a pat on the head. Then I surface to request repair supplies.

By the time I've patched the damage and inspected the rest of the hull—which looks fine—I still have thirty minutes of air in my tank.

Socrates and I go for a quick dive. Fifteen feet under, we dance together. I hold his flippers and continue my year-long campaign to teach him the Hokey Pokey. Humming through my breather, I lead him through the moves. *You put your right flipper in, you put your right flipper out.* Socrates clearly doesn't understand this strange human ritual, but judging from his laughing face, he finds it (and me) very amusing.

At one point, a sunfish cruises by that's bigger than either of us. It's a wonderfully weird-looking thing, like somebody fused a shark, a cauliflower, and a chunk of iron pyrite and flattened it until it's almost two-dimensional. Socrates ignores our visitor, since it's neither dangerous nor edible. I wave and invite the sunfish to dance with us. It glides on by. I remember a humor column by Dave Barry that my dad read to me when I was little, about how fish only have two thoughts, *Food?* and *Yikes!* But there is a third fish thought, which this sunfish's expression relays perfectly: *Y'all humans are weird.*

I wish I could stay underwater with Socrates forever, dancing in the silver swirls of bubbles with sunlight rippling through the green.

I guess I lose track of time.

I hear the sharp *clink, clink, clink* of a metal object being tapped against the hull. Someone is telling me to surface.

I give Socrates a high five for good work. Then I start my ascent.

Back on board, I feel much better. The sea always refreshes me. I secure my tank and rinse my gear as we get underway. The repaired engines hum smoothly. The weather has cleared, leaving us with smooth seas and a rich burgundy sunset. By the end of the day tomorrow, if we're lucky, we should arrive at HP's secret base. We might find help, safety, answers. And, who knows, maybe even a new supply of chocolate-chip cookies.

My good mood lasts until Gemini Twain pokes his head out of the bridge. "We need you." His tone makes it clear there is more bad news.

I find Tia Romero hunched over the comm station, clutching headphones to her ears. She frowns when she sees me.

"We retrieved some audio from the school's intranet," she says. "You'd better sit down."

CHAPTER TWENTY-TWO

I think I'm prepared for anything.

I'm wrong.

When Dev's voice comes through the headphones, I choke back a sob.

"*—major threat. Need everyone to EVACUATE. I—*"

The recording breaks into static.

I pull off the headphones and throw them down. I back away from them as if they're a tarantula.

"I'm so sorry," Tia says. "There's nothing else. Just feedback."

My legs shake. I'm wearing only my bikini. Salt water runs down my legs, dripping on the rubberized floor around my feet. I'm not sure if I'm shivering more from cold or from shock.

"Dev warned them," I murmur. "They might have gotten out. He might still be alive?"

Lee-Ann Best is the navigator on duty. Her ears turn red, a "tell" that she is about to lie. Lee-Ann knows this about herself. Given her interest in counterespionage, you'd think she would grow her hair long to hide her lie-detector ears. Instead, she keeps her black locks shaved on the sides.

"Maybe," she says. "I mean, it's possible, right?"

Gem frowns. "I don't think there was time. Ana, the noise at the end of the recording . . ."

I know he's right.

That jumble of static was most likely the sound of our school collapsing into the ocean. I imagine Dev was speaking over the school intercom. He was probably down in the security room, under the administration building. He wouldn't have left until he was sure people were evacuating.

The drones captured no footage of anyone alive. None of the news reports mentioned survivors. Dev is really gone.

All I have left is a garbled recording of his last desperate moments.

I try to say something. I realize that if I don't leave now, I will fall to pieces in front of everyone. I turn and exit the bridge.

I don't remember making it to my cabin.

I curl up in my bed. I stare at the water sloshing around in Socrates's empty tank.

I try to recapture the feeling of serenity I had in the sea, dancing with my dolphin friend. It's gone. Guilt has clamped its metal claws on my gut.

I should have been there for Dev. Maybe if I'd been more insistent about what I saw: that strange reset of the grid's lights . . . Maybe if I'd gone straight to the security team myself instead of taking time to eat breakfast . . . my brother might still be alive.

I never got to say good-bye to my parents. Not properly. They said they were going off on another expedition and they'd be back in a month or so. They told me to be good. I let them leave with nothing but a hug, a kiss, and a roll of my eyes. *Of course I'll be good. You guys should worry about Dev!* My mom said, *We'll be back before you know it.* And I believed her. They always came back.

Now I've lost Dev, too. Why do I keep missing my chances to say good-bye?

The pain in my gut is getting worse. It takes me a moment to realize it's not just from grief. My period has started.

Great. Like I don't have enough going on.

I stagger to my feet and rummage through my bag for toiletries and some clothes.

When I open the cabin door, Nelinha and Ester are both standing there. They look sheepish, like they were just debating whether or not to knock. They register my pained expression, the box of maxi-pads clutched in my hand. They get out of my way, understanding that I need to reach the bathroom.

"I'll get the Midol," Ester says.

"I'll fill the hot-water bottle," says Nelinha.

I mumble my thanks as I stumble past. They know the routine. Even with the B1 supplements, constant exercise, and a good diet, my monthly cramps are torturous. I understand why periods were historically called a "curse." Two and a half years I've been dealing with this now. Without my friends, I don't know how I would have coped.

Once I'm dressed and back in the cabin, I curl up in my bunk again. I gulp down some Midol and press the hot-water bottle against my abdomen.

Yellow spots of pain dance before my eyes. What feels like metal grabber arms continue to clamp my gut.

Top trots over and kisses me on the nose. He wants to help.

"YOU'RE NOT GOING TO DIE," Ester tells me.

I laugh, which hurts. "Thanks, Ester. I always get through this."

"NOT YOUR PERIOD," she says. "I MEAN ON THE ISLAND."

"Volume, babe," Nelinha says.

"Sorry." Ester sits at the table and begins flipping through index cards. "I've been writing down all the secrets I can remember. All the stuff I wasn't supposed to tell you. It's here somewhere."

"Ester has been busy," Nelinha tells me. "We're just going to be sure to keep these cards safe from now on, right, Ester? We won't leave top secret notes lying around where anyone can find them?"

"I put them down in the kitchen for a minute," Ester confesses. "While I snuck a cookie. It's fine. Nobody saw."

Aha. So I'm not the only chocolate-chip cookie thief. If the crew mutinies, Ester and I will both have to walk the plank.

When I first realized Ester had such a great memory, I asked her why she needed the note cards. She explained it like this: She can remember an entire symphony orchestra, a hundred musicians playing at once. But if you ask her what the oboe was doing in the second bar of the third movement, she can't immediately unravel that information from all the other sounds she absorbed. The cards help her make sense of the music. She can color-code the brass section, so to speak, and keep it separate from the strings and the percussion. She can unwrap the symphony and study it instrument by instrument, line by line.

Without her index cards, the world is a scary, overwhelming place.

"Here." She holds up a bright-blue card, covered front and back with her neat handwriting. "Tomorrow, when we get close to the secret base, there's going to be a challenge."

I try to concentrate. The hot-water bottle is slowly doing its work, relaxing the knots in my belly, but the pain is still blinding. Dev's voice crackles in my head. *Major threat. Need everyone to EVACUATE.*

"A challenge?" I manage.

Ester nods. "Standard protocol when someone approaches

a base. It says so right here. I don't know what kind of challenge. Something to make sure we are legitimate. If we're not, the island will probably destroy us with alt-tech weapons."

"But that won't happen," Nelinha says.

"No," Ester agrees. "Because . . ." She looks at Nelinha. "Why won't it happen?"

"Because we're going to figure out how to pass the challenge," she says gently. "We'll do that while Ana gets some sleep. Remember?"

"That's right," Ester agrees. "Ana, that's why you're not going to die. Get some sleep."

She says this like it's as simple as switching off a radio.

Maybe it is.

I want to join them at the table. I should help them figure out this challenge. But my body is shutting down. Hearing Dev's voice was too much. The medicine and the heat and the cramps are fighting for dominance, turning my nervous system into a choppy sea. I cling to the sound of my friends' voices like a life raft.

I close my eyes and drift into the painless depths.

CHAPTER TWENTY-THREE

In my dream, it's the Fourth of July. I'm ten years old. I'm sprawled on a blanket in the San Alejandro Botanical Gardens, waiting for the fireworks to start.

Dev dances around our family's picnic spot, waving a sparkler. My mother sits next to me, her face swallowed by the shadow of her broad-brimmed straw hat. Her black pearl gleams at the base of her throat. She wriggles her bare toes (she always hated shoes) in time with the John Philip Sousa music being piped over the loudspeakers.

She reclines against my father's chest. His arm circles her waist. Their show of affection makes me vaguely embarrassed. Are parents *allowed* to cuddle in public?

My father's white shirt, white linen slacks, and glass of white wine all seem to glow in the dusk. His slick black hair is perfectly combed. His *Mona Lisa*–like smile makes him look like he's just woken from a beautiful reverie.

My mother gazes out over the field of poppies, sunflowers, and baby blue eyes that lead down to the lake. She sighs contentedly. "When I die, sprinkle my ashes in the water here. I like the view."

"Mom!" I say.

She laughs gently. "My dear, dying is nothing to be embarrassed about. It happens to everyone."

"Okay, but can we not talk about it now?"

She gives me a playful pinch on the arm. "Ana, it's good to be honest about such things. Besides, I'm just saying . . . this would be a nice place to rest in peace."

"But you're not dying!"

"What?" Dev stops his sparkler dance and marches over, on high alert for scandal. "Who's dying?"

The sparkler sheds a cascade of golden starbursts across his bare arm. He doesn't seem to notice.

"No one is dying," my father assures us. "At least, not until after I've finished my chardonnay." His eyes gleam with humor. They're deep brown like the centers of the sunflowers. "I'm with your mother, though. When the time comes, sprinkle my ashes here, too, will you?"

I'm about to protest that they are being impossibly morbid, when the fireworks explode overhead. . . .

I wake in my bunk. Judging from the angle of the sunlight through the windows, I've slept through the whole evening and night.

My whole body aches, and my skull is throbbing. Ester and Nelinha are nowhere to be seen. They must have wanted to give me the chance to sleep in.

Dying is nothing to be embarrassed about. It happens to everyone.

Oh, Mom . . .

I couldn't even honor her wish. We had no ashes to sprinkle in any lake. Now I have nothing but my mother's pearl. Even getting *that* back was a miracle. It was delivered to us by the school, with deepest condolences—the only thing they could retrieve after the "accident."

I'm tempted to lie in my bed and wallow in misery, but I

know that would only make things worse. I've found out the hard way that with grief, like with menstrual cramps, I just need to keep moving. And today's the day we're supposed to reach the secret base. If there is such a thing . . .

I get myself cleaned up and dressed. No shower. We're rationing water. Breakfast is a seaweed protein bar. We're rationing food, too.

Finally, I arrive on the bridge.

Nobody gives me a hard time for showing up late. Still, I feel guilty. With our supplies dwindling, the tension on board is as charged as a Leyden gun. For the sake of the crew, I need to be operating at 100 percent. Or at least to *pretend* that I am.

Our challenge arrives at 10:00 a.m., sharp.

The LOCUS display lights up with a swarm of purple splotches.

"Aircraft!" yells Jack Wu. "Wait. No . . . What *are* those?"

The purple blobs flicker in and out, changing shape and intensity. On the LOCUS, they appear to be aerial objects, hovering directly in front of the *Varuna*, but when I look out the forward windows, there's nothing but open water all the way to the horizon.

Jack senses the answer before I do. He's the best in House Dolphin at this kind of thing.

"Those aren't physical objects," he realizes. "See how the blobs are flattening into waves?"

I nod. "Clever."

"What?" Dru Cardenas demands, his voice jumpy. "Are we under attack?"

He looks like he desperately wants to shoot something with his shiny new Leyden cannon. Even by Shark standards, Dru is trigger-happy. I decide I should give him a task that does not involve weapons.

"There's no attack," I assure him. "At least, not yet. Would you round up the other Dolphins and bring them to the bridge, please? We've got a code to break."

A few minutes later, Virgil stumbles in, groggy and squinting from working the graveyard shift. Lee-Ann and Halimah follow on his heels. By the time all five of us are together, Jack and I have identified the break where the pattern starts repeating. We have also discovered how to feed the LOCUS's electrical impulses into the bridge's speakers, converting the glowing purple squiggles into sounds.

Halimah tilts her head. "Blue whale?"

"Partly," I say. "But it's more complicated than that. Keep listening."

HP has used blue-whale song as a code for years. The pitches, sweeps, and lengths of tone can be pegged to components of human languages, making a multilayered form of encryption that is almost impossible to break if you don't know the key.

But this code is more complicated still.

After a few seconds, the pattern changes. A series of clicks like a dolphin coda overlays the whale song. Two seconds later, the clicks and song are replaced by tones like wind through a conch horn.

Then the pattern repeats.

"The sender knows HP encryption methods," Jack ventures. "They must assume we have a LOCUS to receive their transmission."

"That's good, right?" Lee-Ann says. "It must be from our base."

"Unless it's a trap," Virgil says. "If this is from the *Aronnax*, and we reply . . ."

That's a fun thought.

I find myself shaking my head. "No. This must be the base. We were expecting a challenge—"

"We were?" asks Halimah.

I tell them about Ester's warning from last night. "So if this is the challenge, and we *don't* respond, that will not be good. Either way, we need to decipher the code. Then we can decide what to do."

My housemates visibly relax. Deciphering a code . . . *that* is a challenge we can tackle. It's what Dolphins train for.

"Let's assume the first part is blue whale." Jack whips out his pencil and notepad. He starts sketching the purple blobs and waves. He says he thinks better when he's working by hand, and since he's our best codebreaker, I never argue. "That second part, with the clicks . . . Can we slow that down?"

"Uh . . ." I'm no Cephalopod, but after a few minutes of tinkering, I manage to replay the transmission at one-quarter speed, which makes the pattern clear. "That's five by five."

I don't realize Gem is standing behind me until he asks, "What's five by five?"

I almost jump out of my socks. Seriously, I'm going to have to put bells on his holsters so he can't sneak up on me like that.

"It's like Morse code," I explain. "But different. In the Vietnam War, prisoners of war used it to tap out messages to one another."

"And the third section," Halimah says. "What is that?"

We gather around the map table and play the recording over and over at different speeds. Jack fills his notebook with sketches and mathematical equations. Halimah and Virgil argue about phonetic versus alphabetic symbology. Lee-Ann lectures us on the relationship between acoustics and fluid dynamics. It's basically a giant Dolphin nerd fest.

I don't realize how much time has passed until Gem sets a tray of sandwiches in front of us. "Lunch."

While the others eat, I take a bathroom break. I freshen up, splash water on my face, take more medicine. My gut pain is now competing with back pain from being hunched over for so long, looking at codes. I consider throwing up but suppress the impulse by sheer force of will. Once I give in to nausea, the vomit genie is not easy to put back in the bottle.

On the way to the bridge, I freeze in my tracks. Suddenly, all the pieces of code that have been swirling around in my brain fall into a perfect pattern. I live for these moments. They're as exhilarating as cliff-diving, and they're the main reason I love being a Dolphin. Jack's a better cryptographer. Halimah is more gifted at navigation. Lee-Ann has a stronger grasp of counter-espionage, and Virgil is our expert at electronic communications. But I'm the best at putting all the pieces together to make a bigger picture. That's why I was elected the freshman prefect.

With a grin on my face, I march back to the bridge. "I've got it."

I walk my housemates through the code. The first section, the blue-whale song, is an algorithm for decrypting the second section, which is the actual message. The third section provides phonetic clues that tell us the language used in that message: Bundeli, a derivation of Hindi, which happens to be my ancestral tongue and the native dialect of Captain Nemo.

"Wow." Halimah nods appreciatively. "Nice work, Ana."

"No kidding," Virgil says. "I thought I was going to go crazy if we listened to that recording one more time. I wish I had your ear."

I try not to feel too pleased with myself. "I just put together what you guys did. Jack, can you—?"

Jack's mouth is full of peanut-butter sandwich, but he starts scribbling, translating the coded message into English.

He hands the notepad to Lee-Ann to read.

She clears her throat dramatically. "And the winner is . . . 'This is Lincoln Base. Identify. Five hours.'"

Halimah frowns. "That was a lot of work for a really short message."

"Île Lincoln," Gem chimes in. "That's what Harding and Pencroft named the island where they were stranded."

The Dolphins turn and stare at him.

"What?" he asks. "I read *The Mysterious Island*, too."

I study the LOCUS display. It's still riddled with purple blotches like the pattern from a shotgun blast. My nerves tingle. Our situation finally starts to feel *real*. We're getting close to the island of Captain Nemo. . . . The place where my parents died.

"*Identify.*" Lee-Ann drums her fingers on the table. "That part is clear enough. They want to know who we are. *Five hours* . . . Is that our time to arrival?"

"It would be two hours now," Gem says. "You guys were working on that code for three hours."

That seems impossible. But according to the ship's chronometer, Gem is right. It's one in the afternoon. I remember the coordinates I got from the supersecret map in the captain's stateroom. I do some quick calculations based on our current course and speed.

"It's not our ETA," I decide. "We shouldn't arrive at the island until seven p.m. The *five-hour* thing is an ultimatum. We need to figure out how to answer this challenge. And we need to do it in the next two hours."

Virgil gulps. "And if we don't respond in time, or respond the right way?"

"Then," I say, "I imagine our own secret base will blow us out of the water."

CHAPTER TWENTY-FOUR

But no pressure.

It's one thing to decrypt a message. It's much harder to figure out the correct answer and say it back in the same code. And we have less than two hours to do it.

Maybe Lincoln Base—if it really *is* Lincoln Base—has a machine that generates messages in blue whale/five by five/ Bundeli. We do not. Nor do we have access to that superweapon of information, the internet, which might help us put together the pieces.

We have to trust our own training and best guesses.

That's terrifying.

"Virgil," I say, "do you still have that simulator app on your phone, the one that makes whale songs?"

He stares at me in surprise. "I— Yeah!"

"Will it work without an internet connection?"

"Of course." He sounds mildly offended. "I downloaded the whole library of whale songs."

This doesn't surprise me. I have spent years teasing Virgil about the number of useless apps on his phone. Now I owe him a huge apology.

"Virgil, you're amazing," I say. "Gem, go with him to open the lockbox. Just make sure that phone stays *offline*."

I doubt they could get a signal anyway, and neither Virgil nor Gem seems like the type to try sneaking a look at TikTok in the middle of the Pacific. But I feel I should remind them.

Gem nods, and off they go.

Meanwhile, Jack runs to get Nelinha. Once the two of them are back, they start puzzling out how to use the LOCUS to send messages rather than just receive.

Lee-Ann runs computations for a new encryption base. We can't simply send back the same whale-song algorithm. That would be too easy. If it *is* an HP base we're talking to, they'll expect us to keep the format but change the register, like modulating to a new key in the middle of a song.

Halimah and I brainstorm expressions in Bundeli that we might want to send. We start with *DO NOT FIRE*. We figure that will be important.

Virgil and Gem return with the phone. Virgil starts playing whale songs, which isn't annoying at all. Gem serves as our time-keeper, periodically letting us know how much longer we have until we are blown to bits. Again, not the least bit annoying.

After an hour and a half, my eyesight is starting to blur. A line of sweat trickles down my back and sticks my shirt to my skin like superglue. We put the finishing touches on our trans-mission, coding the phonetic components into the sweeps and pitches of whale song, as if blue whales sang in Bundeli.

The message says *VARUNA FROM HP. DO NOT FIRE. EMERGENCY SITUATION. ANA DAKKAR ON BOARD.*

At least, I hope that's what it says. At this point, my brain is so mushy the message could say *TOFU IS MY FAVORITE MAMMAL* and I wouldn't know the difference.

I feel self-conscious using my name as part of the response. The other Dolphins have convinced me it's necessary. They figure that if I'm really so valuable, my presence on board might keep anyone—friends or enemies—from torpedoing us with alt-tech death weapons.

"Unless we're talking to an automated relay," Virgil muses. "If it's looking for a specific code word, and we don't send it—"

"Then we've come a long way just to get killed," Halimah says.

"There's that can-do Dolphin spirit I love," I say.

It's a long-running joke among us. Combined, we're fluent in, like, two dozen languages, but we have no word for *optimism*.

Nobody smiles. The stakes are too high.

I turn to Nelinha. "Are we good to transmit?"

"As far as I can tell." She sounds cheerful. She's chosen a festive tangerine shade of lip gloss and eyeshadow to go with her green skirt and orange hoodie. I swear her go bag must be an extra-dimensional space to accommodate all her outfits. "Of course, the transmitter might not work. Or we might give away our position to the *Aronnax*. But we have to try new things, right?"

Gem coughs. He's wearing his usual commando black, standing next to Nelinha, so together the two of them look like a printer-ink test page. "Twenty minutes until the reply deadline," he says.

"Permission to send?" Lee-Ann asks.

I hesitate. "Not yet. Gather the crew. They deserve to know what's happening."

The afternoon sun beats down on the main deck. I tell the assembled crew about the challenge, the response we've prepared, and the 273 things that could possibly go wrong.

"When we send this signal," I say, "we'll be revealing our location. We have to gamble that this isn't a trap, and that we've evaded our enemies." It still feels strange referring to Land Institute as our *enemies*, but there's nothing else to call them.

We're way past toilet-papering each other's school buses now. "Also, if we send the message and it's not correct, we could be under attack in fifteen minutes."

"Eleven," Gem says.

"Thank you, Prefect Twain," I say dryly.

Some of our classmates crack a smile. I guess nervous humor is good.

"If, however," I continue, "we *are* communicating with an HP base, then we could be among friends by this evening."

An anxious murmur goes through the group. After three days at sea, our old lives seem far away. It's starting to feel unbelievable that anyone who's not on this boat could exist, much less be a "friend." Nevertheless, no one protests. No one asks questions. At this point, in the middle of the ocean with almost no supplies left, what choice do we have?

"Prefect Romero," I say.

"Captain."

I blink. This is the first time anyone has called me *captain*. I'm not sure how I feel about that. "All hands for general quarters. Nelinha?"

"Yes, babycakes?"

That gets some laughter. I silently thank Nelinha for having an insubordinate sense of humor. It's been a long time since any of us had a good laugh. Besides, *babycakes* doesn't sound any more ridiculous to me than *captain*.

"Send the message," I tell her. "If anyone needs to use the head, now would be a good time."

The crew disperses. All things considered, their spirits seem high. I hope I haven't led them astray.

I hit the bathroom. I change maxi-pads, take Midol, and throw up. Today is a great day.

I get back to the bridge just as Nelinha sends the message.

Ester and Top have joined us for the big moment.

Gem fidgets like he's got a jellyfish in his shirt. Like Ester, he's one of those people who thinks *on time* means *thirty minutes early*. It must be killing him that we're cutting things so close to the deadline.

We wait for a response.

I remind myself to breathe.

I imagine ballistic missiles hurtling over the horizon, zeroing in on our position. I remember the trident-shaped wake lines of the torpedoes that destroyed our school. I picture a full complement of alt-tech sonic fish burrowing through the water toward our hull.

Nothing happens.

Then, suddenly . . . still nothing happens.

Five more minutes pass. More nothing.

The minutes turn into an hour. Funny how that happens when you put sixty of them together.

The afternoon sun slants through the forward windows. This turns the bridge into an Easy-Bake Oven. Sweat trickles down my neck. Ester's face is the color of a boiled crab. Even Nelinha's perfect makeup is starting to melt. Top finishes his second bowl of water and continues panting like crazy. (I don't think he understands water rationing.)

Outside, Dru and Kiya man the Leyden cannon. They look miserable in their life vests and tactical gear.

The sea ahead remains flat and empty, except for Socrates, who leads the way like a pilot fish. Occasionally he leaps out of the water, turning as he breaches. He looks back at us with his sideways smile. I imagine him thinking, *Come on, guys! If you get blown up or whatever, it's fine! I'll be safe!*

"We're still alive," Ester notes. "That's good. Maybe we passed the test."

I hope she's right. I was sort of hoping for confirmation, though. A giant glowing smiley face on the LOCUS display would've been sufficient. Or confetti. The silence is unnerving.

The sun is just touching the horizon when I order engines to a full stop.

The weather is clear. If there was an island anywhere close to us, we should be able to see it. This was supposed to be our destination. There's nothing here.

My mouth feels like rice paper.

"Send the message again," I tell Nelinha.

This time, she doesn't call me *babycakes*. Everyone on the bridge wears a grim expression.

The second transmission has no obvious effect.

We float in the calm of the sunset. Out on the foredeck, Dru and Kiya stare to the west, their cannon forgotten.

I curse myself for believing in Dr. Hewett's pseudoscience map. I actually thought I could safely captain a 120-foot training yacht with a crew of freshmen into the middle of the Pacific and find a place that doesn't exist on any nautical chart.

I think about what to tell the crew. With no food or water, how long can we last? If we put out an SOS, will anyone hear us? Will anybody reach us in time?

I mentally kick myself for not preparing a Plan B. I've sentenced us all to death.

"Guys . . ." I'm not sure what to say to my bridge crew. How do you apologize for such a massive failure?

"LOOK!" Ester yells.

Directly off our bow, the air ripples. It's as if a mile-wide curtain of mirrors has been reflecting the sea. Now the curtain shatters.

The island takes my breath away.

The central volcanic peak rises three hundred feet, jagged and crumbly like a heap of burnt brown sugar. Surrounding it is a turquoise lagoon, ringed by an atoll maybe a mile in diameter, with sandy white beaches hugging a spine of thick vegetation. Off our starboard side, a break in the atoll forms a natural gateway into the lagoon.

No dynamic camouflage in the world should be good enough to render this island invisible at point-blank range. Yet here it is.

"We did it," Gem marvels.

A woman's voice crackles over our intercom. "*Varuna*, this is Lincoln Base."

She sounds a bit cranky. "Your visit was not scheduled. Stand by for harbor drone guidance. Make any sign of aggressive intent, and you will be destroyed. If we do not see Ana Dakkar aboard, safe and unharmed, you will be destroyed."

Okay. Maybe she sounds a *lot* cranky.

A garbled noise comes over the feed, as if someone else is speaking to her in the background.

"Fine," the woman growls slightly off mic. Then to us: "You will advise the drone how many will be joining us for dinner. Jupiter is baking lasagna. Lincoln Base out."

CHAPTER TWENTY-FIVE

Given the choice between destruction or lasagna, I will choose lasagna every time.

Whoever Jupiter is, I hope he can cook enough for twenty extra people. (Dr. Hewett makes twenty-one, but his diet is presently being administered through an IV.)

I scan the lagoon entrance for the pilot drone. I guess I'm expecting something large, like a tugboat. I don't even see the drone until it buzzes past my ear and settles on the navigation console.

An alt-tech dragonfly flutters its copper-and-crystal wings. Its segmented eyes gleam like tiny Fabergé eggs. I'm glad no one tried to swat it. I'm pretty sure that would count as a sign of aggressive intent.

Top barks.

The drone turns its head and makes a *pop* of static electricity between its front legs. Top whimpers and hides behind Ester.

"Hi, there," I tell the dragonfly. I try to sound calm, like I talk to mechanical bugs every day. "I'm Ana Dakkar. As you can see, I'm safe and unharmed. We have a crew of twenty for dinner, please. Also, we need urgent medical care for Dr. Hewett. He's comatose in the sick bay."

The dragonfly wriggles its antennae. A copper thread unspools from its mouth and snakes its way into our auto-nav console.

"Okay," Tia Romero mutters. "I'm sure that's fine."

The ship's engines rumble to life.

Pilot Bug steers us to starboard and guides us into the lagoon.

We have arrived in a heavily weaponized paradise.

Along the perimeter of the atoll, turret guns peek from the brambles. They swivel to follow our progress. Targeting lasers wink and flicker along our hull. Whatever projectors control the island's impressive camouflage system, I imagine they are also hidden in the vegetation.

I've spent the last three days struggling to believe this place could exist. Now that we're here, I still can't believe it.

Socrates, fearless as usual, leads the way into the lagoon. Two local dolphins swim over to meet him. Within moments, they are leaping around together, chattering happily. So much for my friend being a loner.

The water is so clear, I can see a labyrinth of jagged reefs below the surface. Schools of tropical fish swirl through the evening light like jets of colored paint. I want to dive in that lagoon so badly I can feel the ache in my teeth.

We cruise toward the central volcanic isle. It has no shore to speak of—just dark cliffs that plunge straight into the lagoon. The only sign of habitation is a single wooden dock, with a small shack anchored at the base of the rocks. The structure looks so flimsy, I imagine it would break off in the first strong storm. It certainly doesn't look big enough for twenty people.

Nevertheless, Pilot Bug guides us toward it. Twenty feet out, it cuts the engines.

"Tia, make ready the moorings," I say. "Pilot Bug, permission to come ashore?"

The drone retracts its wire tongue, spits another spark of electricity, and flies away. I decide to take that as a yes.

The crew ties off the *Varuna*. I'm the first one off the ship, followed by Gem, Ester, and Top.

On the pier, I have the same sense of disorientation I always get when I go ashore. My legs try to compensate for the lack of rolling and rocking. It's disconcerting. Solid land . . . I've never trusted it. I *definitely* don't after what happened to HP.

Gem's hands hover over his holsters. "What now?"

The shack's door flies open with a *bang!* I step in front of Gem to keep him from drawing his guns.

A tall, slender, dark-skinned man steps into the light. His white skinny jeans and vertically striped soccer shirt accentuate his spindly limbs, making him look like an anime character—maybe one of the pirates from *One Piece*. His close-cropped black hair is flecked with gray. His hands, sheathed in oven mitts, hold a steaming pan of bread that smells of butter and garlic.

My mouth starts watering.

"Ana Dakkar, yes?" He has a friendly smile. "You look just like your parents."

I've been told this a million times before, but after the stress of the last few days, and what happened with Dev, the comment hits me in the gut. It takes me a second to find my voice.

"I— Yes. This is the freshman class of Harding-Pencroft. We have some bad—"

"Freshman class?" The bread pirate laughs. "What in the world!" I can't quite place his accent until he says, "I'm Luca Barsanti."

I switch to Italian. "Piacere."

"Ah, parli la lingua del bell'paese!"

"Certo, sono un Delfino."

"Ottimo! Prego, entrate tutti! Anche povero Hewett, porta-telo. La mia prossima pagnotta di pane sta bruciando!"

He plunges back inside.

"Um . . . What just happened?" Gem asks.

"He says come on in, and bring Hewett," I translate. "His next loaf of garlic bread is burning."

CHAPTER TWENTY-SIX

I send the Orcas to get Dr. Hewett from the sick bay.

Moving him will be risky. I'm not sure what kind of medical facilities this secret base has, but Barsanti said to bring him. I hope their cutting-edge tech can do more than camouflage the island and bake garlic bread.

"No aggressive moves," I tell the rest of the crew.

The Sharks look at me like, *Who, us?*

It hits me that I just gave an order to my classmates, and they took me seriously. Three days ago, they would have laughed or ignored me, or at the very least teased me for acting like an authority figure. A lot has changed. I'm not sure if that's good.

I lead the way into the shack, which turns out to be nothing but a sort of foyer. The rubber welcome mat reads BLESS THIS MESS. Against the left wall is a stand-up shower. Against the right is a rack of dive masks, tanks, fins, and spearguns. A security camera peers down at us from the ceiling. At the back of the room, a tunnel has been bored straight through the volcanic rock, leading into the heart of the mountain.

I glimpse Barsanti's silhouette up ahead in the gloom. His

voice echoes back to us. "I have turned off the lasers, so they should not cut you in half! Please, come!"

At Ester's side, Top sniffs the air. He doesn't look worried—more like he's hoping for some of that bread. Top is usually a pretty good judge of danger. I forge onward, following the scent of garlic butter.

After about a hundred feet, the corridor opens into a large rectangular space like an artist's loft. More corridors branch off in different directions. How big *is* this place?

The ceiling is lined with ventilation ducts and big industrial light fixtures. The polished stone floor glistens like melted chocolate. Worktables overflow with bits of disassembled alt-tech.

In the left corner, a living-room area has been set up. Two cushy sofas make an L around a coffee table. A tire swing hangs from the ceiling. (Why?) A jumbo television, attached to half a dozen gaming consoles, is playing what looks like a cooking show. Stacks of Blu-rays are piled next to the screen. I guess the island doesn't get satellite or streaming services.

In the right corner of the room, a chandelier made of abalone shards glitters above a long metal dining table. Sitting alone at the far end is a diminutive woman with a magnificent mass of braided gray hair like a heap of barbed wire.

She's cross-legged and barefoot. Her thick steel-rimmed glasses glint in the light of her laptop computer. Steel bangles decorate her forearms. Her black leggings and yoga top don't look so much like athleisure wear as a diabolical-acrobat costume.

She gives Barsanti a guarded glance, as if she's ready to press a very dangerous button on her laptop. "Should I vaporize them?"

"No, no, they're friendly." Barsanti holds up his bread pan. "I must check the oven. Jupiter will kill me."

"Fine." The woman waves him away. She looks a bit disappointed.

Barsanti smiles at me. "This is Ophelia, mia moglie. Please, make yourselves at home."

He hurries off down one of the side corridors.

Ophelia rises. She is decidedly not tall. She pads over to us like the Steel Ninja Leprechaun of Death. She appears ready to say something—perhaps an explanation of how she will incinerate us if we misbehave—when our Orca team arrives with Dr. Hewett's stretcher.

Ophelia scowls at our comatose patient. After three days in the sick bay, he looks terrible. He smells even worse.

"Theodosius, you idiot," Ophelia grumbles. She snaps her fingers at the Orcas. "Come. No time to waste."

We all start to follow, but Ophelia clicks her tongue. "Just the medics, thank you. The rest of you, wait here."

Off they go down another corridor. Nelinha starts to drift toward one of the worktables until Ophelia yells back, "TOUCH NOTHING."

The rest of us stand there uneasily, looking at one another like, *Well, here we are. Now what?*

"Make yourself at home!" Nelinha says, mimicking Luca Barsanti. Then she switches to Ophelia's voice: *"But touch nothing!"*

Robbie Barr sneezes. "Well, she didn't say we couldn't *look*. I'm going to check out those game consoles."

"Me, too," Kay Ramsay says. "Whoa, is that a Nintendo 64?"

Gem gestures at his fellow Sharks. They fan out to examine the room. Nelinha and Meadow Newman conduct a purely visual inspection of the disassembled gadgets on the nearest table.

Halimah sidles up to me. "Cad a cheapann tú?"

The other Dolphins gather around.

"I'm not sure," I answer, also in Irish, though I doubt any language is safe, given the level of coding we had to do just to get in the front door. "They seem friendly enough. If they were with Land Institute . . ."

I let that thought drift away unanchored. How would we know if we had walked into a trap? I'm starting to wonder if I've made a terrible mistake bringing us here. . . .

Then Robbie Barr does the unthinkable. He stops the video playing on the TV.

I guess he assumed the *touch nothing* order didn't apply to entertainment options. As he rummages through the Blu-rays, an outraged howl erupts from one of the side corridors. A humanoid creature waddles into the room, flailing his furry orange arms. My god. It's an orangutan. And he's wearing a cooking apron decorated with smiley-face daisies.

The orangutan bares his fangs at Robbie, then says in perfectly clear American Sign Language, *NO TURN OFF MARY BERRY.*

CHAPTER TWENTY-SEVEN

The Sharks reach for their guns.

"Stand down!" I yell.

Thankfully, they listen.

"Robbie," I say, my heart pounding, "put down the remote control and back away."

Not being an idiot, Robbie does so. I gesture at my friends to give the orange newcomer some space.

The orangutan snatches up the remote control. He returns us to our regularly scheduled program, which appears to be a bunch of British people sweating over the creation of bread puddings.

I approach the orangutan slowly. My hands are out to show they're empty. The orangutan seems unconcerned about being surrounded by armed humans. He's no more than five feet tall, but he's still an impressive and scary-looking guy. He probably weighs as much as I do. He's definitely got bigger teeth. His face—flat and round with a wispy orange beard—reminds me of picture-book illustrations of the Man in the Moon. Fur cascades off of his limbs like orange fringe curtains. The name JUPITER is stitched onto his smiley-face daisy apron.

When he notices me, I sign, *We are sorry about the TV. I see you speak sign language.*

His eyes are a beautiful dark brown, full of quiet intelligence. He slips the remote control into the pocket of his apron. Then he signs back, *You speak Orangutan.*

I introduce myself as *A-N-A.* (I am fortunate to have an easy name to sign.) I'm trying to figure out which of several dozen questions I want to ask when Luca Barsanti hurries back into the room without his cooking mitts or bread pan.

"Oh, dear," he mutters. "I see you have met Jupiter. Please never turn off *The Great British Bake Off.* It is a religion for him, and Mary Berry is his goddess."

Jupiter climbs onto the couch. He stares at the screen intently as an older British woman with perfect blond helmet-hair holds forth on the perils of pie crusts.

"I remember this episode," Gem says. "Season three. They make fruit tarts."

I raise an eyebrow.

"What?" Gem demands. "It's good TV."

Jupiter must understand some English. He studies Gem with obvious approval, then pats the cushion next to him. Gem, not wanting to offend the chef with the large fangs, joins him on the couch.

Luca chuckles. "Made a friend already. Good! Jupiter has watched each episode at least twenty times. I suppose it would be annoying if he didn't re-create the recipes for us."

Nelinha points at the orangutan, then the screen, then the orangutan. "So this is your lasagna guy. . . ." Suddenly, she doesn't sound anxious for dinner.

"He's much more than the lasagna guy," Luca assures her. "He can make almost anything! He keeps trying to make me his sous chef, but I'm afraid the oven is one machine I cannot master."

"And . . . he's an orangutan." Nelinha mentions this delicately, as if Luca might not have noticed.

"Of course!" Luca agrees. "There has always been a Jupiter at Harding-Pencroft."

Luca's words are almost exactly what Ester said about Top. With a sudden shock, I remember that there was an orangutan in *The Mysterious Island*, too. Another Jupiter. This Jupiter must be his . . . What? Clone? Twentieth great-grand-monkey? Apparently, the Jupiters have evolved to the point where they can now communicate in fluent ASL and cook soufflés.

Luca turns to me, his brow furrowing with concern. "Now, my dear, perhaps you should tell us why you are here. We weren't expecting your brother for another four years. We weren't expecting you . . . well, *at all*. Something must have gone very wrong."

I'm sure he doesn't mean the words to hurt. They do anyway.

I grew up in Dev's shadow. Mostly I was okay with that. My parents were loving and accepting, but they had some very old-fashioned ideas about their firstborn son carrying on the family legacy. I was happy to let Dev be their Chosen One. It freed me to do whatever I wanted with my life—or so I thought.

Now there's a Dev-size void in the world and no way I can fill it. Luca and Ophelia weren't planning on me being here, maybe *ever*. My presence is a sign that something terrible has happened.

I need to tell Luca the bad news: Dev is dead. Harding-Pencroft is gone.

My vocal cords refuse to make a sound.

I'm saved from answering when Ophelia returns from the sick bay. She marches over to us with Ester, Top, and Rhys Morrow at her heels. Ester's face is puffy and red from crying. Rhys plays counselor, whispering to her in a reassuring tone.

"Pancreatic cancer," Ophelia tells me. Her gaze is as steely as her hair and her glasses. "Theodosius was a fool."

My rib cage tightens. "*Was?*"

"No, no, he's still alive. Your friend Franklin is administering one of our experimental treatments right now. I just meant Theodosius should've sought medical help months ago. What was he thinking, coming out here in his condition with a crew of freshmen?"

She scowls at me, waiting for answers I don't have.

Top pads over to the couch. He sniffs Jupiter's toes. Jupiter just looks down at the dog, pulls a cookie from the pocket of his apron, and gives it to Top. Another friendship secured.

"I . . ." My voice falters. I've been trying to hold myself together for three days. I can't break down now, not in front of my whole crew.

Gem gets up from the couch. He and Nelinha both gravitate to me, as if sensing that I need backup.

"How about we sit and talk?" Gem suggests to our hosts, gesturing to the dining table. His calm tone reminds me that Sharks are trained to be diplomats as well as soldiers.

"Good idea," Nelinha says. That makes twice this week she has publicly agreed with Gem, which probably means doomsday is nigh. "The rest of the crew can secure the *Varuna*, maybe get themselves cleaned up. Right, Ana?"

I nod, grateful for the help. It's better than me dissolving into ugly sobbing.

"You could all use showers," Ophelia concedes.

I guess after three days at sea, rationing our fresh water, the twenty of us don't smell so great.

Ophelia makes a clicking sound at the side of her mouth, like she's encouraging a horse. Two mechanical dragonflies buzz into the room and hover at her shoulders.

"The drones will show your crew the facilities," she says.

"They'll also keep any naughty children from straying into restricted areas and getting themselves killed."

"I'll get the espresso and biscotti." Luca's smile turns fragile, as if he suspects it might break under the weight of our story. "I have a feeling we might need a predinner pick-me-up."

CHAPTER TWENTY-EIGHT

It never gets easier, talking about what happened to Harding-Pencroft.

When I explain how my brother died, I feel like I'm collecting ashes from his funeral pyre, clawing through the hot cinders of his life with my bare hands.

Gem and Nelinha sit on either side of me. Ester, still quietly sniffling, sits on Nelinha's right. I don't know if Ester is crying because of Dr. Hewett's condition, or the loss of the school, or the scary new place and new people she is having to deal with. All are solid reasons.

As usual, the other two prefects should be in on this conversation, but they seem content to let Ester and Nelinha be their stand-ins. Franklin remains in the sick bay, tending to Dr. Hewett. Tia Romero, bless her, is playing aunt to everybody. She's herding the rest of the crew around, making sure they don't get zapped by lasers or mechanical dragonflies as they settle into the base.

When I'm done with my story, Luca and Ophelia give each other a long look. They don't seem surprised by anything I've told them. Their expressions convey grim vindication, as if they've been fearing this news for years.

Ophelia adjusts her steel-rimmed glasses. She sets her elbows on the table and laces her fingers, letting her bangles cascade down her forearms. "Ana, I'm so sorry. You deserved better from us."

Her tone surprises me almost as much as her apology. She sounds angry and bitter, which makes me realize how much of those emotions I've been holding inside for the past three days. I swallow back the taste of bile. I guess it's a welcome change from debilitating sorrow.

"What *did* I deserve?" I ask. "Maybe the truth?"

Luca frowns into his cup of espresso. "Certo. La veritá. Ma non è così semplice, cara mia."

"Why not?" I demand. "It seems pretty simple to me. Why did Dev have to keep silent about what he knew? Why did Ester have to live with her secrets?"

Ester blushes.

I realize maybe I should not have put her on the spot like that, which makes me scowl even harder at Ophelia. "And do *not* tell me the school was trying to protect me."

Ophelia shakes her head. "No, Ana. The school was trying to protect itself."

"And you went along with it."

Gem clears his throat, a subtle warning that my tone is getting aggressive. I'm not sure why I'm so angry at Luca and Ophelia. I barely know them. They've been kind to us so far, aside from the threats of annihilation.

With a sigh, Luca dips a biscotto in his espresso. "Ana, when your parents died . . . Ophelia and I were here with them. We were part of their team."

I look down at my own coffee and cookie. I want to smash the biscotto into a million pieces, but I'm pretty sure Jupiter baked it from scratch and I don't want to offend the orangutan.

"What happened?" I manage to ask.

Luca's jaw muscles ripple under his dark skin. "The truth? We are still not sure. We should have been more careful. You understand, after four generations of Dakkars searching, your father finally found this place. Your mother and he were determined to move forward."

"You mean to explore the wreck of the sub," I say.

Luca hesitates long enough for the coffee to soak halfway up his biscotto. "We tried to urge caution. Ophelia did, mostly. . . . But this was like telling someone who had just found the Holy Grail not to drink from it. Your parents were sure they could handle the dive. And after . . . after the accident . . ."

Luca lowers his head.

Nelinha understands before I do. "You blame yourselves," she says. "You were friends."

Ophelia puts her hand on her husband's shoulder. "The four of us graduated together from Harding-Pencroft." She turns to me. "When Tarun and Sita died, some of the faculty at HP wanted to bring you and your brother here immediately . . . for safekeeping. Theodosius Hewett was one of those."

"We did not agree," Luca says. "We thought it was too dangerous. It is *still* too dangerous. We wished you both to have more training, more years of life on the mainland before you had to face the legacy of Nemo. We didn't think Land Institute would ever risk such a brazen attack and put you and Dev at risk. You were simply too important. But now that your brother . . ." Luca's voice cracks. "It seems we were wrong. I am so sorry."

My head buzzes, and it's not just from the caffeine.

I try to imagine what it would have been like if Dev and I had spent the last two years on this island. I never would have met Nelinha or Ester. I wouldn't be a Dolphin prefect. I would've had more time with Dev, but we would have spent it in this subterranean base, in the middle of nowhere, where our parents died.

I can't blame Luca and Ophelia for not wanting that. Still, a fist-size lump of anger burns in my chest. Dev and I weren't given the choice. If this base is our family's inheritance, if the alt-tech is *ours*, what right did Harding-Pencroft have to hide it from us? Why do they get to control our lives?

I remember what Caleb South said about Harding-Pencroft keeping secrets: *How many world problems could you cowards have solved if you just* shared?

I wonder if Caleb had a point. Is Harding-Pencroft really so much better than Land Institute?

Ophelia seems to read my thoughts. "You have no reason to trust us, but we will trust you, Ana. You are the last Dakkar. Theodosius clearly thought you were capable, and you did manage to bring your crew safely to Lincoln Base."

Luca gives his wife a troubled glance. "Are you suggesting . . . ?"

"Yes," Ophelia says. "We will show Ana everything. Let her decide."

Gem's chair creaks as he sits forward. "What exactly is *everything*?"

He does a pretty good job keeping the excitement out of his voice. Still, like any good Shark, he is probably dreaming of shiny new weapons.

Ophelia's gaze stays on me. "You understand that the alt-tech devices you have seen so far—the Leyden guns, the dynamic camouflage—are only pale imitations of Nemo's technology. Over the last century and a half, both HP and Land Institute have tried to re-create what Nemo did. We've had a few other successes: the microwave, fiber-optics, lasers, nuclear fission."

"The microwave?" Nelinha looks stunned. I can't imagine her surviving without the microwave oven in our rec room at HP. She does love her popcorn.

Ophelia musters a faint smile. "Yes. One of Nemo's less dangerous inventions. By the late 1940s, we felt it was safe to leak that technology to the general public."

"Hold on," Gem says. "Nuclear fission? You're telling us Captain Nemo had atomic bombs?"

Ophelia smirks. "Of course not. He would never have created such crass, clumsy weapons. But he did pioneer nuclear physics. During World War II, Land Institute decided they could 'improve' the world by leaking some of Nemo's knowledge to help along the Manhattan Project. They still maintain they did a good thing, even though the subsequent Cold War arms race came close to destroying the world half a dozen times."

"Okay . . ." Gem says slowly. "But that tech also led to nuclear power, cancer treatments, and long-range space exploration, right? Tech can be good *and* bad."

Luca puts his hand over Ophelia's wrist, as if he's afraid she might jump over the table and strangle Gem.

"My boy," Luca says, "every time an alt-tech advance is leaked to the rest of the world, it is incredibly destabilizing. Nuclear fission is just one example. Can you imagine if we told the world that Nemo knew the secret to cold fusion?"

Nelinha takes a sharp breath.

I'm not as much of a hard-science expert, but even *I* understand how big a deal that would be. Fission breaks apart heavy atoms to make energy, but it also creates a bunch of nasty radioactive waste. Fusion is the opposite. It combines atoms. It's the force that powers the sun. If humans could learn to harness that process at room temperature, "cold" fusion, they could make unlimited energy and produce nothing but harmless gasses for exhaust.

"Why would you not share that information?" I ask. "It would revolutionize the world."

"Or *destroy* the world," Ophelia counters. "Imagine a world government monopolizing that power. Even worse, a corporation."

That sends a shiver down my back. "You're saying the secret to cold fusion is here on this base."

"That secret," Luca agrees, "and many others. But we cannot unlock them or study them, much less reproduce them, because Nemo keyed his masterpiece to his own family's blood—*your* blood."

The ball of anger in my chest begins to cool and shrink, creating its own little cold-fusion reaction. "Nemo's masterpiece . . ." I say. "You don't mean the base. You mean the *Nautilus*."

Luca and Ophelia remain silent.

I shake my head in disbelief. "But it's a wreck."

I think about photos I've seen from the resting place of the *Titanic*: a broken metal shell covered with rusticles, slowly crumbling to dust. And *that* ship went down something like fifty years after the *Nautilus*. "There can't be much left. It was sitting on the bottom of the ocean for a century and a half."

"No, my dear." Luca sounds melancholy, like this news is even worse than the destruction of Harding-Pencroft. "Your parents found the *Nautilus* intact. Tomorrow, we will introduce you."

CHAPTER TWENTY-NINE

How to make twenty freshmen hyperactive:

1. Give them access to an espresso machine.
2. Offer them a safe haven after seventy-two hours of running from death.
3. Feed them a home-cooked meal made by an orangutan.
4. Tell them that tomorrow, they will get to see a make-believe submarine from the 1800s that is actually not make-believe.

Luca insists that we will not talk any further about the *Nautilus* until the morning. Even though I am burning with questions, I suppose that's just as well. My head already feels like it is going to explode from too much impossibility.

How could a submarine survive intact underwater for over 150 years? And what does Luca mean by *intact*? The shell is recognizable? The inside wasn't completely flooded? Most of all, what does he mean about "introducing" me to the sub? He makes it sound almost like . . . No, I'm not going to follow that line of thinking. It's crazy.

During dinner, only ten of us can fit around the dining table.

The rest of the crew spreads out through the main room. They sit wherever they can, though nobody is brave enough to try Jupiter's tire swing.

The volume of conversation increases. I hear occasional laughter. My classmates joke with one another, looking as relaxed and happy as I've seen them since before our world was destroyed. If I close my eyes, I can almost believe I'm back in the Harding-Pencroft cafeteria on an average school night.

My melancholy starts spiraling out of control, until Jupiter places a steaming plate of lasagna in front of me. He's added a beautiful mixed salad on the side, along with two slightly burnt pieces of garlic bread.

He points at Luca. *The bread was his fault.*

Thank you, I sign.

Jupiter picks up my napkin and puts it in my lap. Because, like most higher primates, he knows more about dining etiquette than I do.

The smell of the lasagna makes my mouth water. Cheese and tomato sauce bubble between golden sheets of pasta.

I turn to Luca. "I don't want to insult Jupiter's cooking, but this doesn't have any beef, does it? You know, Hindu."

Luca chuckles good-naturedly. "No beef. In the early days of the *Nautilus*, Nemo and his crew hunted sea animals for meat, but as he got older, Nemo became what we would call a vegan. He realized that was better for the ocean. He cultivated his own hybrid crops in subaquatic gardens down in . . ." A momentary shadow passes over his face, as if he realizes he's said something he shouldn't. "In the water nearby. Many of those crops went wild. They're still flourishing today. Everything on your plate is from those gardens."

On his other side, Ester sniffs a piece of her garlic bread. "Even this?"

"Well, not the garlic itself," Luca concedes. "I keep my own aboveground garden on the atoll for herbs and spices that are difficult to simulate. But everything else, yes. White seaweed flour, sodium bicarbonate and acid for the yeast—"

"What about butter and cheese?" I ask.

"Specially processed macroalgae and carrageen-moss extract."

"Yum?" Nelinha says from across the table.

Ophelia nudges her arm. "Give it a try."

Nelinha nibbles the bread. Her eyes widen. "Actually, yum! It's a little burnt, but—"

"Okay, enough of that!" Luca says.

Ophelia grins, which makes her look less steely, more . . . I don't know, *silvery*. "Anything Jupiter sees on *The Great British Bake Off*, or any of his other cooking shows, we can simulate with sea-plant products. The orangutan keeps us on our toes."

I try the lasagna. It tastes even better than it smells. "You could feed the world with those crops."

Ophelia raises an index finger in warning. "Or we could feed the bottom line of multinational corporations who would want to exploit the food sources—or more likely strangle them—to keep their monopolies."

Suddenly, my dinner tastes a bit more like macroalgae.

Top sits patiently at Ester's feet. He doesn't beg—he's too clever for that. He just looks cute and sad, staring into the distance as if thinking, *Alas, my poor stomach!* Whenever someone slips him a scrap, which happens frequently, he looks surprised. *For me? Well, if you insist.*

He is part emotional-support animal, part con artist.

Meanwhile, Jupiter circulates among the Dolphins, chatting with them in sign language. He describes the culinary wonders they are enjoying. Some of his cooking lingo is hard to follow. I have never learned the ASL terms for *sauté* or *carrageen moss*. Still, the Dolphins know how to say *delicious* and *thank you.* That seems to please him.

Gem sops up the last of his lasagna with his garlic bread. "So, Dr. Barsanti—"

"Luca, please."

Gem shifts uncomfortably. He likes formalities. "Er, did you and Dr.—"

"My surname is Artemesia," says Ophelia, "but call me Ophelia."

Gem manages to process this without bursting a blood vessel. "Uh, Ophelia and Luca . . . you said you both went to Harding-Pencroft?"

Luca nods. "Like my father, and his father, and his father before him! In my senior year, I was Cephalopod captain."

A few of the Cephalopods mumble "Yesss!" and pump their fists in house pride.

"That same year," says Ophelia, "I was Orca captain. I also completed Shark coursework summa cum laude."

I look at her with newfound awe. Graduating from two houses is not unheard of, but it is *extremely* difficult. It nearly doubles your workload. To be house captain *and* complete coursework summa cum laude for another house . . . Unbelievable.

On top of that, Sharks and Orcas are generally considered diametric opposites. Sharks are frontline fighters, tacticians, weapons specialists, commanders. Orcas are medics, community builders, archivists, and support personnel. I can't even wrap my mind around how someone could be good at both.

Gem's forgotten bread hovers over his plate, dripping subaquatic simulated marinara sauce. "So . . . wow. Dr.—I mean Ophelia—you had Tarun Dakkar as your Shark captain?"

"Indeed I did. And Sita was my best friend. I taught her everything she knew about terrorizing our younger classmates."

"You also terrorized me," Luca says with a grin. "The way you stole my heart!"

"And I've been putting up with you ever since." Ophelia keeps a straight face, but she gives her husband a quick wink.

Luca laughs. "That much is true. By the way, Ana, your mother was a brilliant Dolphin captain. She would be very proud of you."

This isn't the first time I've heard someone talk about knowing my parents. But it's strange to think of Luca and Ophelia and my parents as teenagers—swaggering around Harding-Pencroft together during their senior year like they owned the place, just like Dev does today. . . . Or like he did before the attack . . .

I try to murmur *Thank you*. It comes out more like "Unk."

I set down my fork, hoping nobody notices my trembling fingers.

Of course Nelinha does. "SO, LUCA . . ." She draws his attention with a volume level worthy of Ester. "*How* many generations was your family at HP?"

His eyes gleam. "Since the beginning. We were recruited because of my ancestor's work on internal combustion."

Nelinha's expression of interest dials up a few notches. "Wait, your ancestor was Eugenio Barsanti? The guy who created the first internal-combustion engine?"

Luca spreads his hands. "Many famous families have been associated with HP for generations. The school needed the best minds to replicate Nemo's technology! But surely this is no surprise. Your class has a Harding, a Dakkar . . ." He glances at Gem. "Your surname is Twain, isn't it? Wasn't there a famous American author—?"

"No relation," Gem mutters. "Anyway, that guy's real name was Clemens."

"I see." Luca sounds vaguely disappointed, like he had wanted an autograph. "At any rate, each generation must prove its own worth at HP, as I'm sure you will!"

Around the table, my classmates' expressions turn glum. I imagine they're thinking the same thing I am. How can we prove our worth if HP no longer exists?

Maybe we would have made house captains someday. Maybe we would have found love among our peers, the way Luca and Ophelia did (though, frankly, I have a hard time imagining that). Maybe we would've had brilliant careers.

There's no way to know. Four days ago, our futures were blasted off the side of a cliff.

Ophelia picks up on the change of mood. She sighs in exasperation. "Ah, Barsanti."

Luca looks confused. "What did I do?"

I get the feeling Luca is the type of guy who would cheerfully skip through a minefield and somehow come out unharmed on the other side, while Ophelia would tear her hair out and chide him for being careless. I have no trouble imagining them being friends with my parents. They are just the right combination of caring, adventurous, brilliant, and eccentric.

"If we're done eating," Ophelia continues, "perhaps our guests can help us clean up. Jupiter does the cooking, but he does not do dishes."

She puts us to work. Nothing like scrubbing lasagna pans to put your problems in perspective. After the kitchen and dining area are spotless, most of the crew heads back to the *Varuna* for the night. The ship has been cleaned and resupplied, so my classmates will be comfortable enough. Besides, the base doesn't have enough beds for everyone. I'd prefer to go back with them, but Luca and Ophelia have asked me to stay in the base's guest room. It has two sets of bunk beds: enough space for Nelinha, Ester, and me. Nelinha brings my go bag ashore along with her own.

Gem looks torn, like he wants to take the fourth bunk so he can guard me.

Yeah . . . That's not going to happen.

"I'll be fine," I tell him. "Take care of the crew on the *Varuna*, okay? We'll see you for breakfast."

He hesitates. "Just be careful."

I'm not sure if he doesn't trust our hosts, or just doesn't trust life in general. After our recent experiences, I can't blame him either way.

Ophelia shows us to our room: a simple stone chamber with the bunk beds and not much else. I try not to dwell on how much it looks like a holding cell. For the first time since leaving HP, I sleep in a room that doesn't rock and sway.

This only makes my nightmares worse.

CHAPTER THIRTY

I dream of drowning, which isn't like me.

I'm trapped with Dev in the Harding-Pencroft security office, deep beneath the administration building. On multiple monitors, we watch torpedoes racing toward the base of the cliffs. Dev yells into the PA system, *"Major threat. Need everyone to EVACUATE. I—"*

The room crumbles around us. The floor breaks like a sheet of ice. Monitors and control panels explode. The ceiling collapses. We tumble into oblivion.

We sink beneath the bay, trapped in an air pocket amid a shifting tomb of wreckage. We scream and beat our fists against slabs of broken concrete. Salt water pours in. Dev reaches out to take my hand as my head goes under. My lungs fill with brine and sediment.

I wake in a cold sweat.

For a few shaky breaths, I don't know where I am.

I hear Ester's *puff-puff-snore* from the next bed over. In the bunk above me, Nelinha grumbles in her sleep. Maybe I'm back at Harding-Pencroft, and everything is fine. . . .

Then I remember. Lincoln Base. My old life is gone. There's a reason I'm dreaming about wreckage. . . .

I sit up, shivering. At least my period cramps have started to subside. That's a major blessing.

I check my dive watch: 5:30 a.m.

I know I'll never be able to get back to sleep. I slip out of bed as quietly as I can and grab a swimsuit from my bag. When you dream of drowning, there's only one thing to do: get in the water as soon as possible.

I encounter no one as I retrace my way through the main room and out to the pier. The *Varuna* rests dark and silent at her moorings.

As dawn breaks, the lagoon turns to turquoise-and-pink glass. I plunge into the warm clear water. Immediately, I'm surrounded by a tornado of angelfish. I free dive through the reefs. I wave good morning (from a safe distance) to a viper moray who's peeking out from his crevice. I admire a fourteen-foot nurse shark cruising through the sea grass.

After a while, Socrates finds me. He introduces me to his local dolphin friends. We swim together until the sky is full of light.

By the time I pad back into the base, I'm feeling refreshed. The smell of baking pastries raises my spirits even more. Jupiter waddles around the dining table, setting out baskets of croissants, muffins, and Danish in anticipation of the morning rush. I can't believe one orangutan baked so much in such a short amount of time.

That smells amazing, I tell him. *Can I help?*

He hands me a turnover. *Taste this.*

It melts in my mouth: butter that is not butter, perfect flaky crust that tastes nothing like seaweed, fruit filling that reminds me of pears and oranges but is probably from one of Nemo's botany projects harvested fifty feet below.

If I lived here all the time, my cholesterol levels would go through the roof. . . . Or did Nemo figure out a way around cholesterol, too?

Delicious, I say. *Mary Berry would be proud.*

Jupiter calmly signs, *I love you.* Then he waddles back to the kitchen. I nab a basket of pastries to take to my room—just for my friends, of course. I make a mental note to ask Jupiter if he can bake gujiyas. If not, I'll have to teach him. Surely Mary Berry would approve.

I find Ester and Nelinha showered and dressed. They don't seem worried about where I've been. They're used to my morning dives.

"Orangutan pastries?" I offer.

"Yes, please." Nelinha takes a turnover. She looks me up and down. "I'm glad you didn't get zapped by any underwater defenses in the lagoon."

Her comment makes me feel dumb, because I didn't even think of that.

Ester picks at the crust of a faux-apple tart. She's wearing her pink blouse and pink leggings today. I assume that means she's especially nervous, since pink is her comfort color. Her hair, combed back in wet blond coils, is already drying and puffing out in different directions. Like Ester's thought process, her hair always ends up doing what it wants.

"I was thinking last night." She stares at my feet. "You remember how I said the *Nautilus* is dangerous? How I think it killed your parents?"

I nod.

It's not like I could forget.

"I think I understand now," she says. "After listening to Luca and Ophelia talk last night, I don't think you should—"

Someone knocks on our door.

Ophelia pokes her head inside. "Ah, good. You're all up."

Her tone makes me suspect that she already knew this. There must be security monitors throughout the base, maybe even in this room.

Ester blushes and looks down. Top sits in front of her protectively, staring up at Ophelia as if to say, *My human.*

"Ready?" Ophelia asks me. "Are your friends coming?"

It takes my brain a moment to catch up. Of course. She means am I ready to see the *Nautilus.* Jupiter's turnover does a turnover in my stomach. "Uh . . ."

"Yes," Nelinha answers for me. "We're coming."

"I'd like them to." I look at Ester. "If that's okay."

Ester nods. Her ears turn the color of flame angelfish.

Behind her steel-framed glasses, Ophelia's eyes look sad. I wonder if she's remembering my parents. "Very well," she says. "This way."

Top trots along beside us. He's the only one who doesn't look nervous. Ophelia leads us down a corridor that is perfectly round, like it was bored into the heart of the volcano by a single massive drill bit.

"Is Luca coming?" I ask.

"He's already there," Ophelia says.

I'm tempted to ask where exactly *there* is, but I have a feeling I'll find out soon enough. I wonder if I should have waited for Gem to come with us. I imagine he'll give me a hard time about that later. Somehow, though, I'm not sure a hyperprotective, heavily armed bodyguard would make me any safer this morning.

At the far end of the corridor stands a metal hatch that reminds me of an old bank-vault door.

"Was—was this here before?" I ask. "I mean, in Nemo's time?"

Ophelia looks at me curiously. "What makes you ask?"

I have to think about this. The door's plating and gear work don't show any signs of wear or corrosion. The style is similar to other alt-tech devices I've seen, like the LOCUS and the Leyden cannon. But the vault door seems to radiate weight and power.

"It seems old," I decide. "Like, *really* old."

Ophelia gives me a dry smile. "Very astute, Ana. From this point forward, we will be entering Nemo's original base. This door was sealed by Cyrus Harding shortly after Nemo's death. It remained shut until we excavated it two years ago, when your father opened it."

Ester hugs her shivering arms. "But the volcanic eruption destroyed the island. It said that in *The Mysterious Island*."

"Yes, well . . ." Ophelia peers over the tops of her glasses. "Harding and Pencroft may have stretched the truth a bit when they spoke to Jules Verne. Adventurers and treasure hunters were less likely to search for the island if they believed it had been obliterated."

"So the book lied." Ester sounds offended, as if her meticulous note cards have betrayed her. "That explains . . ."

She stops herself. In the dim overhead light of the corridor, her skin looks like stressed coral, slowly losing its healthy pink.

"What *is* that metal?" Nelinha asks our host. "It isn't steel or brass. It doesn't seem to corrode."

"Ingenious, isn't it?" Ophelia agrees. "For lack of a better term, we call it nemonium. We still have not managed to re-create the alloy, though we can work with it and repurpose old pieces for our own alt-tech. As far as we can tell . . ."

She launches into a detailed analysis of nemonium's tensile strength, malleability, and density that I'm sure several people in the world could understand, one of them being Nelinha. Meanwhile, I turn to Ester and whisper, "You okay?"

She chews her thumb. I resist the urge to pull her hand away from her mouth.

"Just be careful inside," she says. "I think it would help if you talk to it first."

I'm not sure I understand her. One of the problems with being

RICK RIORDAN

multilingual is that sometimes you second-guess yourself about the meanings of words. Did Ester say *talk to it*? Isn't *it* a neutral pronoun in English? Isn't that the language we're speaking?

I start to say, "Talk to—?"

"Ana," Ophelia interrupts. "Would you do the honors?"

She gestures to the vault door. It has a massive round gear plate in the middle, with pistons radiating outward like the spokes of a ship's wheel. In the center of the gear plate, where the wheel's spindle hole would be, is a hemisphere of nemonium, the same size as the DNA-reader I used on Dr. Hewett's nautical map.

"Me?" I ask, as if she might be talking to some other Ana.

"Well, I *could* do it." From her pocket, Ophelia fishes what looks like a metal security card. "We were able to jury-rig the lock after your father first opened it. But since it's already keyed to your DNA . . ."

She waits. I don't know if she's testing me or letting me test myself. I think about the unpleasantly warm electrical current that went up my arm the last time I touched a Nemo DNA-reader. Then I think about my dream of drowning—the hopeless feeling of terror as Dev reached out for me and seawater filled my lungs. I am the last Dakkar.

I press my hand against the spindle-wheel lock. The metal doesn't shock me. The central plate rotates. Pistons retract. Air hisses around the edges of the door like I've broken a vacuum seal. The door itself doesn't move, but I suspect that if I pushed it now, it would swing open easily.

Ophelia raises her hand in caution. "Before we proceed . . . Please remain calm when we get inside. It's best to avoid sudden movements and loud noises. Especially you, Ana. Approaching the *Nautilus* should be quite safe. Luca and I are in and out of this cavern on a daily basis, and we've had no mishaps."

Mishaps. The term seems like quite an egregious understatement, considering my parents died because of the *Nautilus.*

"But you're still worried," I note. "Because I'm the first Dakkar to approach the sub since . . . since the accident."

Ophelia's barbed-wire braids glisten in the dim light. "We've been working for two years to clean and repair the submarine's systems as best we could."

"Hold on," Nelinha says. "You've been *on board?* It's still got systems left to *clean?*"

"It's easiest to show you," Ophelia says. "Most of the sub's higher functions are dormant because . . . well, operating them requires a living Dakkar. What happened with Tarun and Sita was most likely a malfunction, a misunderstanding. Still, we can't be sure—"

"A *misunderstanding?*" I don't mean to shout, but she's talking about my parents' deaths. I don't feel like remaining calm.

Ophelia grimaces. She faces Ester.

"Would you like to explain, my dear?" Ophelia says. "I can tell you've figured it out."

Ester picks at her blouse. "Ana, like I said, your parents' death wasn't an accident. The submarine killed them. I'm so sorry."

My legs turn wobbly. "You make it sound like it was on purpose."

"It must have been angry," Ester says. "It had been sitting at the bottom of the ocean for a hundred and fifty years. Nemo abandoned it."

"Nemo died inside it," Ophelia says grimly.

"Even worse," Ester says. "It didn't have anyone to maintain its systems."

"Angry?" I still refuse to understand. "Abandoned? How can a sub feel . . . ?"

Dread washes over me. Some things I just do not *want* to realize, even when all the evidence is right there in front of me. "No," I say. "You can't be serious."

"Yes, my dear," Ophelia says. "Nemo created a prototype of what we would call AI, artificial intelligence. The *Nautilus* is alive."

CHAPTER THIRTY-ONE

My whole life has led to this moment.

My parents sacrificed everything. I lost my school and my brother. My classmates risked their lives to cross the Pacific Ocean. Generations of Dakkars, Hardings, and other HP graduates have lifted me onto their shoulders, living and dying in the expectation that someday a descendant of Nemo might once again board his submarine.

And all I want to do is run away.

When you dive, you learn to equalize pressure in your ear canals by pinching your nose and gently puffing air into your sinuses. The deeper you go, the more you need to do it. Otherwise your head starts to feel like a can of soda in the freezer. (Hint: Never put a can of soda in the freezer.)

I wish there was a way to equalize my brain emotionally. I keep getting deeper and deeper. The pressure keeps getting worse. I can't just pinch my nose and adapt to each new level of misery.

First, I believed my parents died in an accident. Then I was told they died recovering a priceless scientific artifact. Now I'm informed that this artifact is a living thing, and it killed my parents—maybe on purpose, maybe not. Gee, we really don't know.

Oh, and by the way, it's right through this door. Would I like to meet it?

I'm not fully aware when I cross the bank-vault threshold. My mind is too busy seesawing between rage and terror. I hear Ophelia saying, "Come."

Nelinha takes me by the elbow. "I got you, babe. Let's go."

Then we are inside the dormant central vent of the volcano. Sheer stone walls soar upward, forming a cone-shaped cathedral of glistening black rock. I feel like I'm standing inside a gigantic hollowed-out chocolate drop. There is no floor—just a pier jutting into a wide circular lake.

Above us, dozens of dragonfly drones buzz through the air, their metal wings flickering in the glow of their jeweled eyes. Are they there for surveillance, or to provide light? Maybe this is just where the robo-bugs hang out when they aren't piloting boats into the atoll or escorting lost freshmen through the base.

The lake is illuminated, too, from below. Clouds of what look like phytoplankton shimmer in the depths. I've seen bioluminescent blooms before, but they are usually blue. These tiny creatures, whatever they are, form thousands of constellations of orange, green, red, and yellow, as if the lake's entire biome has decided to hold a Holi festival. I wonder if my parents saw this, and if they had the same thought. Did they die surrounded by these bewildering nebulae?

Next to me, Ester makes small whimpering noises. Top goes on high alert, sitting in front of Ester and giving her a quick yip that says, *Hey, it's fine. Cute dog right here.* Nelinha whistles under her breath. "Vixe Maria."

I force my eyes to follow her gaze along the length of the pier to the vessel moored at the far end.

The *Nautilus* is like nothing I've ever seen. It's difficult for me to even think of it as a submarine.

Granted, I've never been on an actual sub. That training doesn't start at HP until the second half of our sophomore year. But I *have* seen and studied submarines. Most modern ones look like sleek black tubes with barely any surface profile—just the gentle curve of their topside and a single con tower or "sail." The largest ones in the US Navy can be over six hundred feet from nose to rudder, about the length of two football fields.

The *Nautilus* is about half that size, though that still makes it a big ship. It appears to be tube-shaped—I remember Jules Verne described it as a giant cigar—but it is neither black nor low-profile. Its hull is made from interlocking panels of nemonium, glistening like abalone shell. Intricate coils run along its sides, interspersed with bristly clusters of filaments and rows of indentations that remind me of the vibrissal crypts on Socrates's skin—electroreceptors that allow him to sense his environment.

I can't imagine how a hull so complicated and delicate-looking could have survived intact since the 1800s. It looks like the skin of a sea creature—something between a lionfish and a dolphin.

Even more unsettling are the *Nautilus*'s eyes. I can't think of what else to call them. Set in the ship's bow are two transparent convex ovals latticed with metal girders, like the compound eyes of an insect.

My mind rebels at this design flaw. Windows on a sub? Especially big domed windows? The hydrodynamic drag would make navigation sluggish. The ship's profile would make it easy to spot on sonar. Worst of all, as soon as the sub reached any kind of depth, those windows would implode, flooding the interior and killing everyone inside. And if you went into battle against modern ships with explosive weapons? Forget it. You might as well go to war inside a big glass bottle.

"This should not exist," I say. "It definitely shouldn't be seaworthy."

Ophelia shrugs. "And yet . . ."

And yet here it is: a high-tech, century-and-a-half-old work of nautical art, docked in the middle of a volcano. I remember one of the creepier passages from *20,000 Leagues Under the Sea*, where survivors of the *Nautilus*'s attacks reported seeing giant glowing eyes under the water—the eyes of a sea monster.

I have to admit, if I were a sailor on a three-masted, wooden-hulled merchant ship and I saw this crazy vessel barreling toward me underwater at ramming speed, I would've wet my nineteenth-century knickers.

"But it's in perfect condition," Nelinha says. "You repaired it in just two years, just you and Luca?"

Ophelia snorts. "Hardly. The exterior needed a lot of cleaning and many minor repairs, but the hull is self-maintaining. When Nemo died, the sub sat at the bottom of this lake, buried in silt, and went into a state of estivation."

"Like an African lungfish," Ester says. Suddenly, she is back in familiar territory. "They can stay underground in suspended animation for years."

Ophelia looks pleased. "Exactly so, Ester. The *Nautilus* went into self-preservation mode. It was mostly dormant, using electrical currents and water circulation around the hull to maintain its integrity. But that doesn't mean there wasn't damage. There were leaks. The inside of the ship wasn't flooded, but . . ." She puts her hand in front of her nose, as if remembering the smell.

I sway back and forth, though I don't think the boards are moving under my feet. My gaze wanders across the pier. The opposite side of the dock is lined with workstations and supply sheds that remind me, weirdly, of the shops on the Santa Monica Pier. I feel a hysterical giggle building in my chest. I wonder if we can get an ice-cream cone or some cotton candy before we go aboard the *Nautilus*.

"And Luca is . . . already on board?" I ask.

Ophelia nods. "He starts work every day at four a.m. He would sleep on the *Nautilus* if I let him." She studies me with concern. I imagine I look pretty shell-shocked. "We do not have to board the ship today, Ana. Seeing it from a distance may be enough for your first visit."

Nelinha faces me like, *Yeah, that would be totally fine. Also, please, please, please can we go aboard?*

I don't want to get any closer to the submarine that killed my parents. How can Luca tolerate being inside it, alone, at four in the morning? I'd rather sleep in a haunted house with an ax murderer.

But at the same time, knowing Luca is on board gives me courage. It makes me feel a little ridiculous. If he can do it, why can't I?

"How did it kill my parents?" I ask. My mouth feels full of sand. "What happened, exactly?"

Ophelia exhales through her nostrils. "We successfully raised the ship. We moored it just where you see it now, though at the time it looked more like an island of mud. Your father wanted to open the main hatch immediately. He was . . . perhaps incautious. The door began to open for him. He pushed his way inside. He was just over the threshold when . . ."

Ophelia's voice falters. I realize I am asking her to relive one of her most traumatic moments. But I need to know.

"When what?" I ask.

"There was an electrical charge," she says. "He died instantly, Ana. I doubt he even knew what hit him. Your mother, however . . ." Ophelia's gaze matches her steely eyewear. "She rushed in to try to help him. She grabbed him while . . ."

Oh, god. My poor mother. Despite all her training, *of course* her instinct would have been to grab my father and pull him out of danger. The electricity would have coursed through her body, too . . . maybe not killing her instantly, but causing massive internal damage.

"We could not save her," Ophelia says. The weariness in her voice tells me that she tried everything, with all of her Orca training, and that my mother's death was neither instant nor peaceful.

"I am so sorry, dear," Ophelia says. "Her last wish . . ."

"Cremation," I guess. The black pearl at my neck feels warm. I remember a comment Luca made the night before. "The underwater gardens of Nemo . . . You scattered their ashes there?"

Ophelia lowers her head. "I wish we could have given you and Dev more closure. The circumstances . . . were complicated." She points to the black-pearl necklace. "Sita left that on board our research boat. She never dived with it. That's why it survived, why we could send it to you."

I expect my anger to become a tsunami. I imagine myself raging across this pier, throwing things at Ophelia and the submarine, screaming at the entire world.

Somehow that doesn't happen. I look at the *Nautilus*. I feel smoldering resentment, even hatred, but I also feel more certain than ever that this weird submarine and I are connected by fate. I have to make my parents' sacrifice mean something.

"All right," I say. "Where's the entrance?"

It isn't obvious.

There is no conn tower, no visible hatch, no rails. There isn't even a gangplank.

Ophelia leads us to the middle of the ship. Ester takes my hand, which is completely unlike her. Her palm is warm and moist. I'm not sure who is comforting whom, but I'm glad to have her with me. It occurs to me that this is the first time a

Harding and a Dakkar have been in this cavern together since the day Captain Nemo died.

After a moment, narrow slits like gills open in the side of the ship. Metal tendrils unfold, weaving themselves into a stairway. At the top of the ramp, a circular section of the hull irises open.

My ears roar. It takes me a moment to realize Ophelia has just asked me a question.

"What?" I ask.

"Would you like me to go first?" she says again. "It might be safer if—"

"No, I'll do it," I say.

Nelinha shifts uncomfortably. "Ana, you sure?"

I step to the edge of the stairwell.

Every nerve in my body is telling me to run. I'm so awash with emotions I could drown just fine without water. But I think I know what went wrong for my parents. I think I know what to do.

My father was a Shark. Ophelia is an Orca and a Shark. Luca is a Cephalopod. All of them would have seen the *Nautilus* as a prize to be opened and explored. My mother Sita was the only Dolphin in the group. I doubt she had time to think or act like one when they raised the *Nautilus*. My father was too impulsive. He rushed in and died. My mother died trying to save him.

"Hello, *Nautilus*." I speak in Bundeli.

That was Nemo's native tongue. He would have grown up speaking it, along with English, back when India was under British subjugation. If Nemo spoke any language to his creation, I'm guessing he would have chosen the language he dreamed in.

"I am Ana Dakkar." I try not to feel self-conscious about addressing an open hatchway. I have talked to dolphins, dogs, orangutans, and even students from Land Institute. Talking to an antique submarine shouldn't be any sillier.

"I know you lashed out when my father woke you up." I worry that the *Nautilus* will hear the rage in my voice, but I decide I have to be honest. "You killed my parents. I don't think I can ever forgive that. But I understand you were probably confused, scared, and angry."

The submarine does not respond. Obviously.

"My ancestor," I continue, "the one who called himself Nemo, he left you alone for a very long time. I am sorry for that. The thing is . . . I'm the last of the Dakkars. I'm alone and unique, just like you. We're kind of each other's last chance. I'd like your permission to come aboard. I promise I'll do my best to respect you and listen to you, if you'll do the same for me. And if you could refrain from killing me, that would be great."

There is no way to tell whether the sub has heard me or understood.

Does it have little coppery ears somewhere on that hull? Does its artificial intelligence even recognize voices?

Only one way to find out.

I step onto the ramp.

I am not immediately electrocuted. I decide this is a good sign.

"Thank you," I tell the *Nautilus*. "I am coming aboard."

And I step over the last threshold my parents ever crossed.

CHAPTER THIRTY-TWO

Two things I do not associate with submarines: elegance and air freshener.

From the main hatch, a circular stairwell descends into a grand foyer that looks more like part of a cruise ship than a working sub. I half expect a steward in a white uniform to offer me a tropical beverage.

The black walls gleam like polished ebony, bordered with golden nemonium beams. On the other side of the room, a second spiral staircase leads down to a lower level. In the center of the marble floor (at least, it *looks* like marble) is a mosaic crest: a large golden cursive *N* in a circle of black, wreathed by golden squid. Underneath is the motto MOBILIS IN MOBILE.

Latin. Difficult to translate. Something like *moving through the moveable* or *movement in motion*, neither of which makes much sense.

Seeing that motto in person gives me a punch in the gut. I remember reading it in *20,000 Leagues Under the Sea* the summer before eighth grade, just after my parents left home for the last time . . . before I got the news that I was an orphan. My life was moving through the moveable, and I didn't even know it.

Now I'm standing in the actual *Nautilus*. Cyrus Harding and Bonaventure Pencroft passed through this room. So did Ned Land and Pierre Aronnax. Not just as characters in Jules Verne's novels, but as *real people*.

My head spins. The smell from the air fresheners doesn't help. They are the cheap kind you might buy at a car wash— cardboard cutouts shaped like Christmas trees. Some dangle from the stair railing. Others are taped to the nemonium wall beams. The cloying fragrances of pine and vanilla wage a war for dominance in my nostrils.

Behind those scents, I catch a whiff of mold and decay. Luca and Ophelia have tried their best, but the *Nautilus* still smells like a mixture between a rotted-out fishing wharf and somebody's great-aunt's house. It's going to do a number on Robbie Barr's allergies.

Top seems to think the foyer smells marvelous. He sniffs the air like he's balancing a ball on his nose. Nelinha studies the walls without touching them, her eyes tracing the path of the air ducts. Ester stands in the middle of the coat of arms and turns in a full circle. Then she turns in reverse, as if unwinding herself.

"This ship is angry," she decides. "It feels angry to you, doesn't it?"

I'm not sure how to answer. My senses are overloaded. I do feel a heaviness in the air, like just before a thunderstorm. I may have bought a temporary truce with the *Nautilus*, but I suspect it is watching me, waiting for my next move. We are not friends yet. Not by a long shot.

"It's beautiful," I say. "Scary. Overwhelming."

"And angry," Ester insists. "Please be careful, Ana."

Ophelia is the last one down the stairs. The hatch rises shut behind her.

"So far, so good." She gives me an encouraging smile, but she looks tense. Every muscle in her body seems coiled for action. I imagine if a firecracker went off behind her, she'd jump so high we'd have to pry her off the ceiling. "Let's find my husband."

That, at least, shouldn't be hard.

From the aft region of the ship, I hear the distant echo of someone whistling, punctuated by the whir of a power drill.

"Luca!" Ophelia's shout almost makes *me* jump to the ceiling.

His voice reverberates back as if from the bottom of a well. "Yes, mio cuore! Engine room! It is quite safe!"

Ophelia raises an eyebrow at us. "So he says. I hope he's right this time."

Nelinha frowns. "I thought you said there hadn't been any more, what did you call them, mishaps."

"No serious ones, no," Ophelia says. "But the *Nautilus* can be . . . grumpy. This way."

Oh, hooray. Deeper into a grumpy submarine.

Ophelia leads us aft, down a central corridor.

Paintings in gilded frames hang along the walls. At least I assume they *used* to be paintings. Now they are canvases of black mold. The tile floor is marked with smudge lines where it looks like someone pulled up a rotten carpet. Along the ceiling, bronze oval light fixtures flicker a dim Halloween orange.

As we pass open doorways, it's difficult not to stop and gawk.

To port: A formal dining room with a mahogany table and eight matching high-backed chairs. China and silverware gleam in the sideboard cabinet. Under the table lies a tattered and moldy oriental rug.

To starboard: A library with floor-to-ceiling bookshelves. It hurts my heart to see so many mildewed books, swollen and ruined from water damage. Two cracked leather armchairs sit on either side of a wood-burning fireplace. (Seriously? Where does the smoke go?) Against the far wall, a long oval window provides an underwater view of the phytoplankton constellations outside.

It strikes me that the "bones" of the ship are pretty much intact. Everything Nemo brought on board for furnishing and decoration, however, has not fared so well. The submarine reminds me of an ancient statue, adorned with paint, flowers, and fine clothing that are slowly rotting away until only the stone will remain.

We pass what must have been the crew's quarters. Instead of tiny coffin-size berths stacked one on top of another like I'd expect in a modern sub, there are four full-size bunk beds in each room—much more space per person than what we have on the *Varuna*. For a submarine, this is pure decadence.

Nelinha points to one of the bunks. "I'm sleeping there."

Ophelia snorts. "You're as bad as Luca."

"I heard that!" Luca appears, grinning, at the far end of the corridor. He wears greasy coveralls and holds a pipe wrench in his hand. "Ana, perfect timing! Perhaps you can help me convince the *Nautilus* not to be quite such a prima donna this morning, eh? There is a secret door I have been dying to open!"

CHAPTER THIRTY-THREE

Considering my family's history with this ship, I wish Luca hadn't used the phrase *dying to open*.

Then again, I've spent enough time with Nelinha to know that Cephalopods get tunnel vision when they're working on things that intrigue them. And nothing could be more intriguing than the *Nautilus*.

Luca leads us down another stairwell into what I assume is engineering. Aboard most subs, the engine room would be a hot, cramped space with more equipment than air. No surprise: The *Nautilus* is a different story.

The chamber is paneled floor-to-ceiling in reflective nemonium, which makes it look even bigger than it is. Endlessly mirrored Anas stare back at me from the gleaming metal. I have a vague memory of a scene like this in *Willy Wonka and the Chocolate Factory* (my father loved that movie a bit too much). I feel like I should be wearing sunglasses and a hazmat suit and walking along with Grandpa Joe.

Stacked against the port and starboard walls are rows of large cylinders. At first glance, I guess they're torpedo tubes. Then I sense their gentle synchronized thrum. They must be part of the power system—pistons of some kind.

In the middle of the room stands an island with four control stations. The gauges, readouts, and levers are so intricately designed they remind me of an open-faced Swiss watch. A few displays are lit up, their needles quivering. Most look dark and dead.

Nelinha squeals as she reads the descriptions on various brass plates. I'm afraid she might explode from happiness.

Luca chuckles. "I know. I had the same reaction when I first stepped into this room."

"This one." Nelinha points to an ominous-looking red button. "*Super-Cavitation Drive.* You can't be serious?"

Ophelia crosses her arms. "If only we could get it to work. But yes, it appears Nemo succeeded."

"Super-cavitation . . . ?" I know I've heard that term in Dr. Hewett's class. I start to hum "Supercalifragilisticexpialidocious" in my head, but I'm pretty sure that's a different concept. I probably would have paid closer attention if Hewett had said, *By the way, this technology is real, and your life may depend on it.*

"Cav-drive is next-level propulsion," Nelinha explains. "The world's best navies are researching it now, but no one has gotten it to work yet. You create a sheath of air around the nose of the sub, so you have zero water resistance. Then BANG. You hit the engines and . . . well, in theory, you could shoot across the ocean at any depth at extreme velocity, more like a bullet than a boat."

Ester shivers. "That explains how Nemo covered so much distance in the books. He kept popping up all around the globe. They could never catch him. Don't you guys feel cold?"

It feels really warm to me. Maybe that's because I'm thinking about how much power is coursing through this engine room, and how easy it would be for the *Nautilus* to end its Dakkar problems once and for all with one big *zap.*

"Through there"—Luca gestures to a riveted oval door

with a small porthole window at the back of the room—"is the cold-fusion reactor. It takes hydrogen directly from the ocean. Eternal combustion power with no waste. In case that breaks down for some reason . . ." He points to an identical door on the right. "Nelinha, you will not believe this . . . the backup generator is coal-burning."

Nelinha coughs. "What?"

"That's right!" Luca laughs with delight. "Nemo skipped a century of science. He leap-frogged from steam engines to cold fusion! I've thought about replacing the coal-burner with something less Victorian, but—"

A creaking groan echoes through the ship.

Top barks.

I turn to Ophelia with what may or may not be an expression of sheer terror. "Was that . . . ?"

"The *Nautilus* acting grumpy," she confirms.

"She doesn't like talk about modifications." Ester studies the ceiling like she's discovered hidden zodiac signs.

It's customary to call any ship *she*, but I get the feeling Ester has picked up on something more fundamental about the *Nautilus*. I decide I'll keep Ester at my side whenever I'm on board, and I'll take her warnings seriously.

"What *does* the *Nautilus* like?" I ask.

Ester runs her hand across the console. "She appreciates being cleaned and fixed up. She likes that."

"Ah, you see?" Luca raises his eyebrows at Ophelia. "This is why she enjoys my company so much."

"She tolerates you, anyway," Ophelia says. "She knows you are useful."

"Now, dear. Don't be jealous."

Nelinha continues her inspection of the control panels. She reads aloud the fancy calligraphy on each engraved bronze label:

"Vector thrusters. Dynamic positioning. Recursive ballast control? Oh, this is incredible! *Nautilus*, I love you!"

The ship does not respond, but I imagine she's thinking, *Yes, I know. I am rather marvelous.*

I have trouble sharing Nelinha's enthusiasm. This is still the ship that killed my parents. I try to control my feelings. I'm doing my best to understand my ancestor's strange, ancient, apparently living creation. But part of me wants to grab Luca's pipe wrench and start smashing things.

I try to refocus. "Luca, you said there was a secret door?"

"Yes, just here!" Luca leads me to a hatch that's tucked in a corner behind the giant pistons. It's not so much a door as a service panel, maybe big enough for a child to squeeze through. There is no visible lock or handle.

"Do you know what's inside?" I ask.

Luca hesitates, so Ophelia answers. "We've found several panels like this throughout the ship," she says. "We suspect they allow access to the *Nautilus*'s core processor . . . her brain, if you will. After a century and a half under the sea, her other systems required quite a lot of cleaning and repair. We suspect her core does, too, but . . ."

"She is reluctant to let someone fool around in her brain," Luca says. "Understandable, of course. And I will not try to force the panels."

"No," Ester agrees. "That would be bad."

"But if we *could* clean out these hatches"—Luca gives me a meaningful glance—"I suspect it might help all of us, especially the *Nautilus*."

I get his point. For all we know, the submarine's higher reasoning could be severely impaired. That might be why the *Nautilus* lashed out at my parents when they woke her up. Fixing the sub's brain could make her friendlier and easier to deal with.

On the other hand, it could make her angrier and more dangerous. . . .

Top sniffs the hatch. He, at least, looks eager to smell a submarine brain.

"Ester, any advice?" I ask.

"Be careful," she suggests.

"That's very helpful. Thank you."

"You're welcome."

One of Ester's many superpowers: She is impervious to sarcasm.

I place my hand on the hatch. "*Nautilus*, we would like to clean inside here," I say in Bundeli. "We will be extremely careful not to damage you. Would that be all right?"

The panel clicks.

"Wonderful!" Luca beams. "May I?"

I move aside. Luca pulls open the hatch, which unleashes a hideous stench like Davy Jones's gym locker. Top wags his tail deliriously.

Luca reaches inside. He pulls out a large wad of gunk—algae, seaweed, crustacean poop? I don't know.

"You see?" Luca holds up his prize like it's a golden goose's egg. Black slime coats his arm up to his elbow. "It's a miracle the *Nautilus* still functions at all! Oh, Ana, imagine what she'll be able to do once we get her cleaned up properly. You are the key to—"

FOOOOOOM!

The sound shakes the floor and rattles my eye sockets: a deep, resonant low E-flat, held for a whole note. Luca drops his goo. Top hides behind Ester's legs. Nelinha widens her stance like she's expecting a tidal wave. Ophelia braces herself against the wall.

The noise dies. I wait, but it does not repeat. "That sounded like—"

"The pipe organ," Luca says in alarm.

"It's never done that before," Ophelia murmurs.

"The *what*?" I ask.

Luca and Ophelia look at each other. They seem to have a silent, anxious debate about what to do next.

"I think," Ophelia says at last, "it is time to show Ana the bridge."

CHAPTER THIRTY-FOUR

The first thing you want to install in your high-tech super sub?

A pipe organ, of course.

The wonders of the *Nautilus* have already waged war on my sense of reality. When we reach the bridge, my mind simply runs up the white flag and surrenders. A pipe organ—now silent—does, in fact, take up the entire starboard side of the room, but that's only one of the bridge's oddities.

The prow's "eyes" dominate the front of the bridge. The bulging metal-laced domes provide a wide view of the cavern outside, making me feel like I'm in an aquatic conservatory . . . or maybe a fish tank.

"The windows aren't really glass," Luca assures me. "As near as we can figure out, the material is a transparent iron polymer created at extreme temperature and pressure."

"Like at the bottom of the sea," Nelinha guesses. "Near a volcanic vent."

Luca taps his nose. "Just so, my dear. Perhaps Nemo forged his hull plating using a similar process. We're not sure how he would have managed that. It's yet another mystery to unravel. Of course, when Jules Verne wrote his novels, he didn't know what to call that material, so he called it iron." He plinks a knuckle against the nearest nemonium girder. "Clearly not iron."

Four control stations make a horseshoe curve along the front of the bridge. As in the engine room, each panel is Swiss-watch intricate, with dials and switches labeled in engraved calligraphy. LOCUS nodes, dormant, are mounted on top of each station. Artistic flourishes decorate the borders of the controls: dolphins, whales, and flying fish.

The entire ship is a handcrafted, bespoke work of art. She could never be reproduced, much less mass-produced. I start to appreciate just how unique the *Nautilus* is and why her recovery was so important to HP and to Land Institute. Already on this tour, I have seen half a dozen technological advances that could change the world—if the *Nautilus* would let us take her apart and study her inner workings, which I don't think she would agree to.

"And here," Luca says, gripping the back of what is clearly the captain's chair, "is where we found Nemo."

"Aah!" Ophelia swats his arm. "They did not need to hear that!"

"Well, I thought Ana might want to know he died at his station. We considered trying to extract some of his DNA, but, ah, ethical considerations aside, it soon became clear that the *Nautilus* would not tolerate any clever tricks to bypass her systems. She must *choose* her captain, and it must be a living Dakkar."

Ophelia pinches her nose. "Ana, my dear, I am sorry. My husband has no sense of propriety."

I look at the captain's seat. It's a monstrous metal L on a swivel pedestal, like an old-fashioned barber's chair. Nested in each armrest is a hemispherical hand grip, like the DNA-reader on the *Varuna*. The seat's upholstery appears to be gleaming black leather.

For some reason, the idea of my fourth great-grandfather's body being found here doesn't disturb me as much as I might have thought. In a way, the whole submarine already feels like his crypt, his earthly remains.

I trace my fingers across the supple leather seatback. "This material is new."

"Yes, indeed," Luca agrees. "The metal survived. The original leather was damaged beyond repair. Also, well, the remains of your ancestor had been sitting there for over a century. . . ." He glances at Ophelia to see if she will swat him again. "We committed Nemo to the sea. Then I re-covered the chair. The material itself is seaweed-based. Fortunately I have an excellent leatherworker friend in Firenze. Italian workmanship is the best, as everyone knows."

Ophelia rolls her eyes. "We have, of course, tried to activate more of the ship's systems. But the captain's chair seems to govern access to everything critical: propulsion, weapons, navigation, communications."

She points to each of the four control stations in turn. Then she faces me again, as if waiting. . . .

Of course. She'd like me to sit in the chair. She doesn't want to push, but she's dying to see what will happen if I put my hands on those control spheres. Even for Luca and Ophelia, who have been so kind and welcoming, it's hard for them to see me as a person and not as an all-purpose miracle tool.

I take a deep breath. I don't want to sit in that chair. It isn't mine. I haven't earned it. I'm trying to figure out the politest way to decline when Ester saves me.

"You shouldn't start there," she says. She's been quiet so far, standing in the middle of the bridge, taking in every detail, maybe listening to the mood of the ship. "You should start *there*."

She points to the pipe organ. I've been trying not to think about the huge musical contraption and why it suddenly decided to play a single blast all by itself.

Something about its presence on the bridge creeps me out, even more so than the dead captain's chair. Trying the pipe organ before the bridge controls doesn't sound logical. But then again, Ester seems to understand the ship in a way that goes deeper than logic.

I approach the forest of gleaming metal pipes.

The four-tiered keyboard has seen better days, but it is still beautiful. The major keys look like abalone. The minor keys have the same dark luster as my mother's black pearl. Like the pipes, the pull-stop levers and pedals are of gleaming nemonium, etched with decorative fish leaping through waves.

The bench's velvet cushion is black with mold. Its wooden legs look ready to collapse.

Luca coughs. "I'm afraid I don't know much about pipe organs," he says sheepishly. "I cleaned it as best I could, but its more delicate pieces are still in bad shape. I'm sure it needs tuning . . . however one tunes an organ."

"I have no idea," I admit. "I took piano lessons, but . . ."

The memory takes me back to elementary school.

I recall Dev complaining bitterly whenever Mrs. Flannigan arrived at our house for twice-weekly lessons. He hated playing the piano. It wasn't a sport. It wasn't outside. He couldn't kick it, shoot it, or tackle it.

Still, our parents insisted.

Your future depends on many skills, I remember my father saying, *including the keyboard.*

I'd never understood that. I just chalked it up as yet another of our parents' strange and inscrutable commandments. Like so many things that involved Dev, my own piano lessons were an afterthought. Mrs. Flannigan was coming over anyway. She might as well give us a two-for-one deal.

Dev was always better. Despite his complaints, he had a natural ear. He never practiced. He just stormed up to the keyboard, listened to Mrs. Flannigan play, then imitated her perfectly. His sloppiness and impatience drove her crazy, especially since it didn't stop him from mastering whatever she put in front of him.

As for me, I plodded along, carefully and mathematically, treating the keyboard like another language, learning each song like a sentence to be diagrammed.

Now I wonder if my parents knew about Nemo's pipe organ. Verne mentioned it in *20,000 Leagues*, didn't he? Were they preparing Dev for something more specific than just playing a few nice tunes at a dinner party?

"Did Dev ever come here?" I ask.

Ophelia looks shocked. "Of course not. It would've been much too risky."

Luca adds hastily, "You would not be here, either, my dear, if not for the dire situation."

I still shouldn't be here, I think. I'm a consolation prize. A last-ditch, third-string quarterback for Harding-Pencroft.

"Dev wanted to see the *Nautilus*, of course," Luca continues. "When he was your age . . . Well, the staff at HP had a difficult time convincing him to wait, once he was told the truth. He wanted to come here immediately. Then he argued that he should come right after his graduation from HP. Eventually, he listened to reason. He agreed to go to college first, giving us four more years to restore the ship and understand how it worked. That would also have given him four more years to learn and mature."

I try to process this information. I can recall several times over the last two years when Dev seemed inexplicably angry.

Then again, we'd lost our parents. I wasn't a happy camper, either.

I have no trouble imagining Dev being impatient to see the *Nautilus*. The idea that he would listen to reason and go quietly off to college, though . . . that's a little harder to picture. Sure, he acted excited about graduating. He was looking forward to college. But now that I know about the *Nautilus*, I wonder if Dev was secretly chafing about those extra four years of waiting.

I wish I could have talked to him about it. Now it's too late.

"You should play," Ester suggests. "I think the ship would like that."

Like another language . . .

Still standing, I place my fingers on the lowest keyboard. The keys are as cold as air-conditioner vents.

It's been years since I played . . . since just after my parents died, when our house was sold, and the old piano was rolled away. Do I even remember any songs?

I decide to try Bach's Fugue in D Minor. That was written for the organ. I used to play it every Halloween, because it was so creepy. Played at a slow pace, it's also plaintive and sad, and the composition is so old Nemo might have known it. He might have even played it on this organ.

I peck out the first measure. The notes sound flat, but they resonate through the ship.

Second measure: I miss a beat, hit a D-natural by mistake, but I keep playing. The arpeggio brings me to the first full chord. I let it play out, shaking the floor. I lift my hands. I am trying to recall the next measure when Nelinha says, "Ana."

I turn. Luca and Ophelia are staring in amazement at the lights that have come to life on the bridge. The control panels are all illuminated. Four LOCUS holographic displays float above the control stations like a line of ghostly planets. The great eyes of the prow are lit purple around the borders. The captain's chair has similar mood lighting around the base.

The *Nautilus*, it seems, likes Bach.

"Ana Dakkar," Luca says in a reverent tone, "today is going to be a wonderful day."

CHAPTER THIRTY-FIVE

When Luca says *wonderful*, he means *so busy you will never sit down*.

The rest of the morning, I lead tours of the *Nautilus* for my classmates, taking only a few at a time. Before each visit, I talk to the *Nautilus* to let her know what's up. Ester serves as submarine interpreter, warning everyone to be considerate of the ship's feelings. I'm not sure what our classmates think of this, but they are willing to humor us. Top tags along, sniffing everything.

By lunchtime, the entire freshman class has been on board at least once. We're all left smelling faintly of mildew and vanilla air freshener. On the plus side, no one has been killed by electrical discharges or mold allergies. I consider that a win.

We all gather to eat in the dining room of Lincoln Base, but I'm so frazzled I can barely enjoy Jupiter's excellent macroalgae-cheese soufflé. Most of my classmates seem to be in great spirits, though. They feel safe, shielded from the outside world by our HP mentors and lots of alt-tech gadgetry. They've had a few good meals. The *Nautilus* woke up more easily than anyone anticipated. What's not to feel happy about?

The crew even feels excited about Luca's plans to put us to work after lunch. Twenty people can clean a lot faster than one or two. If the *Nautilus* lets us, we will immediately start hauling out the moldy furniture, un-gooping the internal wiring and ductwork, and scrubbing . . . well, everything. To me, it feels like that scene in *Tom Sawyer* where Tom convinces all his friends to pay him for the fun and privilege of painting his fence, but I guess it'll get the job done.

The news from the sick bay is also encouraging. Though Dr. Hewett remains comatose, his condition has stabilized thanks to experimental medicines Ophelia reverse-engineered from the *Nautilus*'s own laboratory.

I ask her privately if she has anything for menstrual cramps. Mine have passed for now, but periods are like General Douglas MacArthur in World War II: *They shall return.*

Ophelia sighs. "If Nemo had been a woman? That would have been the *first* thing he invented. But, alas, no. Just general pain relief medication. Once the submarine is back to full operations, we will ask her to help us engineer something more specific, yes?"

During lunch, the only person who looks unhappy is Gemini Twain. He sits across from me at the dining table, glumly poking his soufflé with a fork.

"Okay, there, Spidey?" Nelinha asks him.

Gem frowns. "You all shouldn't have gone on board the sub without me this morning. What if something bad had happened?"

"Well," Nelinha says, "I'm sure you would have shot the submarine right between the eyes like a true hero! Fortunately, we survived fine without you."

Gem stares at the table, as if he's saying a prayer for patience. "I'm going to check on Dr. Hewett."

He stands and marches off.

I put a hand on Nelinha's wrist. "We don't need to be sniping at one another."

She looks surprised. "What *sniping*?"

I sigh, get up, and follow Gem.

I find him in the sick bay, leaning against the wall with his arms crossed, staring at Dr. Hewett's unconscious form. Franklin Couch putters around, checking the professor's monitors and fluid levels, but when he sees the serious expression on my face, he says, "If you two will watch my patient for a sec, I'm going to grab some lunch."

He beats a hasty retreat.

"I'm sorry, Gem," I say. "I should've waited for you this morning. I'll make sure you're in the loop from now on."

The frown lines around his eyes soften a bit. "I'd appreciate that. I don't know, Ana. . . . Something doesn't feel right. We shouldn't relax."

I wish I could brush off his concerns as easily as Nelinha does, but I feel unsettled, too, as though I've missed an important warning—like the significance of the security grid flickering the morning Harding-Pencroft was destroyed.

I study Dr. Hewett's face. . . . He still looks too pale, his skin almost translucent, but some of the jaundiced yellow seems to have faded around his neck and cheekbones. His hair has been washed and combed so it looks almost majestic—like the mane of an ancient lion.

"He was my advisor," Gem murmurs. "Also the closest person I ever had to a father."

I feel as if we've stepped out onto opposite sides of a quivering tightrope. Gem's voice is full of pain. I never would have considered Dr. Hewett a surrogate father figure—for Gem, or for Dev—but apparently he'd tried to guide them both. Hewett's condition must be worrying Gem much more than he's let on.

I'm not sure how to ask my next question. I'm not sure I should ask it at all, but Gem seems to be inviting me to take the risk. "Did you know your dad?"

He exhales—a humorless laugh. "My mom and dad are alive and well. Last I heard, they were living in Oregon."

My first thought is *Oh, that's not so far from HP*, but the way Gem says *Oregon*, he might as well be talking about Saturn.

"They weren't in your life," I guess.

He unfolds his spindly arms, then clasps his hands behind his back as if he's not sure what to do with them. As usual, he's wearing no-nonsense commando black: jeans and T-shirt, even his belt and gun holsters—a cowboy on his way to a funeral.

"Do you know how I got the name Gemini?"

"Because of your twin guns, right? I heard your real name is James—Jim—so Gemini . . ."

He shakes his head. "I didn't make up that story, but I don't correct people when they tell it. My legal name is Gemini Twain. My parents are . . . modern-day hippies, I guess you'd call them. They're into horoscopes, crystals, tarot cards, all that. What they weren't into was being parents. When I was little, they left my brother and me with our grandmother in Provo. Gran raised us, brought us into the church. My brother is six years older than me. When he left for his missionary work in Brazil . . ."

He watches the blips on Dr. Hewett's heart monitor. "I guess what I'm saying is, I don't have many connections. So the ones I *do* have are important. I've apologized to Nelinha several times about embarrassing her that day in the cafeteria. I was just . . . I was missing my brother, and looking to make new friends. But I get why she hates me."

The air in my lungs feels raw, as if I'm breathing from a contaminated tank. Nelinha is my bestie. When she hurts, I hurt. But it's terrible that I never considered Gem's side of the story. And I had no idea he'd apologized to her about the *scholarship kid* incident.

"*Hate* may be a little strong," I offer. "Nelinha has agreed with you twice just this week. Miracles can happen."

Gem shrugs. "I suppose. It's just . . . I *need* this team to stay together, Ana. I need HP. Dr. Hewett told me . . . he believed the school could rise from the ashes. He gave me the job of protecting you because you're the only one who can make that happen."

My heart feels as delicate as one of Jupiter's soufflés. "Gem . . . I know we're in an emergency situation, but just because I'm a Dakkar doesn't mean I'm a full-time leader."

He stares at me. "You're kidding, right? Ana, I was on the bridge of the *Varuna* when you cracked that code. You focused your team, got results. I watched you manage the crew for three days. You organized us, deployed everyone's talents, kept us from killing one another. You gave us a purpose when we were falling apart. That's not about your DNA. That's about *you*. I'm glad you're in charge."

I imagine my ears are as bright red as Lee-Ann's, and it's not because I'm about to tell a lie. I have trouble taking compliments. I tend to assume the other person is just trying to be nice or sparing my feelings. But Gem isn't like that. He's a straight shooter. And he's just hit my body center mass with some praise I never expected. "Well . . . thank you."

In the doorway, Franklin coughs. "Didn't mean to eavesdrop, but Gemini is right. Now, if you'll excuse me, I need to change my patient's catheter, unless you two want to stay and help."

Franklin knows how to clear a room. I head back to the dining hall with Gem right behind me, and for the first time, I'm glad to have him at my shoulder.

CHAPTER THIRTY-SIX

That afternoon, we take the entire crew aboard the *Nautilus* for the first time.

I'm worried about the submarine's reaction. The sounds of power tools, vacuums, and kids yelling back and forth is probably the most noise this sub has heard since before Queen Victoria was crowned Empress of India. The Sharks form a bucket brigade to remove goop, along with ruined furniture and moldy artwork. After a few hours, the pile of gross stuff on the pier looks like a garage sale barfed up from the belly of a whale.

Despite all the noise and activity, Ester assures me that the *Nautilus* is content.

"She likes having a crew again," Ester tells me. "She likes being cared for."

I'm glad for that. I don't want to put my friends in any more danger. On the other hand, I struggle to contain my resentment and worry. Do we really *want* to care for this submarine? Do I trust her after what she did to my parents? I wonder what Nemo would tell me. Did he die aboard his ship because he loved it so much, or because it became his personal prison?

Thankfully, I don't get much time to brood. The crew keeps

me busy whenever they find something that needs opening, which happens roughly every six seconds. Among our finds: the weapons bay, with a complement of four very old but probably still dangerous alt-tech torpedoes. We decide to leave those alone for now and hope they don't blow up.

The dive chamber has a dozen sets of nemonium-mesh dive suits, helmets, and tanks. Just cleaning these, figuring out how they work, and testing them for usability could take another month.

On the bottom level of the sub (there are three levels total), we find a shuttle bay with a smaller mini sub nested inside.

"That's the skiff," Ophelia informs me. "And no, we haven't tried it yet."

She shrugs and blows a strand of gray hair from her eyes. I'm starting to appreciate just how much work she and Luca have done on the *Nautilus*, and how much remains to be done.

The skiff itself is fascinating. It has seats for two, under a transparent dome that is sleeker in profile than the eyes on the bridge. The body construction is likewise smooth and hydrodynamic, with small pectoral stabilizers and a tapered serrated tail. It looks like it was modeled after a bluefin tuna, one of the fastest fish in the world. How it moves, though, I can't imagine. I see no room for any kind of engine.

On an external inspection of the hull, scuba divers Kay and Tia discover a large hollow sheath on the underbelly of the sub, like a cross between the open mouth of a baleen whale and the air intake on a fighter jet, but no one can figure out what it's for. Like most of our other discoveries, we don't mess with it.

By the evening, the crew is exhausted but still buzzing with excitement. They can imagine a future for HP again, at Lincoln Base. We'll work on the *Nautilus* all summer, or longer if need be, taking our time to learn the submarine's secrets. We can put its technology to use, building up an unbeatable edge against Land Institute. Then . . . Well, then we will have options. We can come out of hiding, let our loved ones know we survived. We can rebuild our school and hold LI accountable for their attack.

I don't trust these dreams any more than I trust the *Nautilus*. But I smile and nod and let the others talk. I think about what Gem told me—how he's glad I'm in charge. Why, then, do I feel like such a fraud?

For dinner, our orangutan chef feeds us homemade seaweed gnocchi in creamy lemon garlic sauce, followed by a delicious tiramisu cake. Because clearly, we all need more caffeine and sugar.

Afterward, Jupiter is in such a generous mood he lets some of the crew switch off *The Great British Bake Off* so they can play retro games on the PlayStation and GameCube. Others volunteer to return to the *Nautilus* with Luca for some night-time "detail work." I'm not sure what that means. I'm afraid tomorrow morning I'll find the *Nautilus*'s hull decorated with airbrushed flames.

I don't even see Nelinha until bedtime. Ester is already snoring when my Cephalopod friend arrives, grinning and covered in machine grease.

"Luca says we'll take the *Nautilus* for a short spin tomorrow," she whispers to me, "if you can convince it to move!"

I suppose I should be thrilled. I might achieve what every Dakkar since the 1800s has dreamed of: getting the *Nautilus* back into action.

"Yeah." I try to sound enthusiastic for Nelinha's sake. "That would be amazing!"

But I go to sleep more unsettled than ever.

I feel like someone has opened *my* brain's access panels and started cleaning out all the excess goop. I'm not sure I want them in there, removing the residue and debris of my life. Who will I be when they've finished their repairs?

While I sleep, I have more nightmares about being trapped and drowning. Only this time, my underwater tomb looks like the bridge of the *Nautilus*.

CHAPTER THIRTY-SEVEN

The next morning, I'm up early again to dive.

Socrates is nowhere to be seen. In fact, the lagoon seems devoid of any dolphins. This doesn't help my sense of foreboding.

At breakfast, my classmates are in good spirits. Trying to sail the *Nautilus* will be the most challenging thing we've ever done, and I can practically smell the adrenaline in the air, along with the scent of Jupiter's blueberry muffins.

Linzi Huang reports that last night in the sick bay, Dr. Hewett farted in his sleep. Apparently, this means his bodily systems are working better. She jokes that he'll be lecturing us again in no time. Cooper Dunne claims he had a dream about how to fix the *Nautilus*'s torpedoes. His fellow Sharks tease him about doing his best thinking while he's unconscious. Kay Ramsay, who hasn't smiled since she lost her sister in the attack on HP, actually laughs at one of Robbie Barr's corny jokes—something about how many nuclear engineers it takes to change a light bulb. Cephalopod humor—I don't get it.

Some of the crew are whispering about how creepy the old sub is, which just makes them more excited. A few gossip about where Captain Nemo's body was found, and how exactly my parents were killed. They try to have these conversations out of my earshot, so as not to upset me. Unfortunately, I can read lips.

Everybody seems to think that our first spin in the *Nautilus* will be a great success.

"You've got the Nemo touch!" Kiya Jensen tells me, as if she wasn't questioning my taking command of the *Varuna* just a few days ago.

Even Nelinha, who knows how tricky advanced tech can be, seems perfectly at ease. "We are about to operate the oldest, most complicated submarine on the planet," she says. "Aren't you even a little excited?"

I don't know how to answer her. These days, I'm having trouble distinguishing between excitement and terror.

After cleaning up from breakfast (because time, tide, and dirty dishes wait for no one), we gather on the *Nautilus*'s dock for a predive briefing. The Cephalopods have brought their tool kits. The Sharks have brought their weapons. Gemini Twain has so many guns and other dangerous objects strapped to his body he looks like he's expecting to fight off a mermaid apocalypse.

He catches me looking and shrugs like, *You never know.*

The *Nautilus* herself appears unchanged since yesterday. No flames have been painted on her prow, thank goodness. Her giant insect eyes glint in the dim light of the cavern. In the water around her, the multicolored phytoplankton are still putting on their Holi festival.

The submarine looks timeless—as if she *literally* exists outside of time. She doesn't belong in the twenty-first century any more than she belonged in the nineteenth. I try to imagine how lonely that would feel, especially if my creator scuttled me at the bottom of a volcanic grotto for over a century. Would I even be *sane* after all that time?

I don't realize I've zoned out from Luca's lecture until he says, "As I'm sure Ana would agree."

Everybody looks at me.

"Sorry, what?"

My classmates laugh.

"Ana is simply proving my point," Luca says, giving me a good-natured smile. "We must stay focused at all times and take things slow. For today, our task is simple. If we can submerge the *Nautilus* and resurface, that will be a triumph!"

"Aww, but, Dad," Halimah jokes, "can't we just take a short spin around the lake?"

"I want to see what she can do in the open sea!" Dru counters.

The others clap and whoop in approval.

"Hold on," I whisper to Ester. "How does the sub get from here to the open sea?"

"Luca was just saying there's an underwater tunnel that leads out past the atoll." She madly jots down this information on her note cards. "It's probably an old lava vent. Do you think I should write *lava vent* or just *tunnel*?"

Ophelia claps twice, loud and sharp, to get our attention. "Freshmen!"

The group falls silent. For the first time, I appreciate that Ophelia is an HP teacher as well as a scientist. I bet her classes would've been hard. Super interesting, but hard.

"So, then," she continues. "We will take this assignment *seriously*. The *Nautilus* has not been operated in almost two hundred years. We must give Ana, and the rest of us, time to acclimatize. It will be a bit like learning to ride a horse."

Meadow Newman frowns. "The sub is still a machine, right? You make it sound like a wild animal!"

The *Nautilus* is not amused. The whole ship begins to hum.

Ester yells, "Look out!"

She hits the deck as water blasts from either side of the *Nautilus*'s prow, arcing backward over the top of the ship. The starboard deluge falls harmlessly into the lake, but the port-side spray soaks all of us from head to foot.

There's a moment of stunned silence.

Meadow looks flabbergasted. "I'm sorry, *Nautilus*! You are a magnificent creature!"

The crew starts laughing. Top barks and shakes himself off. I can't help but crack a smile. Now we know that the submarine has pride, good hearing, and maybe even a sense of humor, given the fact that it didn't try to kill us.

I'm starting to think my fears were overblown. We're among friends. We're safe. The *Nautilus* just wants some respect. All we have to do is try one quick dive. Then we can fix whatever leaks occur, come back tomorrow, and try again. We have plenty of time.

That's when Socrates breaches in the middle of the lake. He splashes down sideways, making as much noise as possible. A moment later, his head pops up at the base of the pier. He chatters, clicks, and whistles at me urgently.

"Whoa," Gem says. "How did he find us?"

But that's not the right question. The question is *why.*

"Something's wrong," Ester says, her water-blotted note cards forgotten in her hands.

Socrates bucks his head backward—a signal I remember well. *Let's go! Hurry!*

My insides feel like they're plunging into the Mariana Trench. My foreboding starts to make terrible sense.

"Everybody!" I yell. "Hey!"

I don't have Ophelia's skill at getting the class's attention, but the alarm in my voice makes an impression. The others turn toward me.

Nelinha frowns at the dolphin, then at me.

"What's going on?" she asks. "You okay?"

My hands are shaking. "None of us are okay. I think the *Aronnax* has found us."

CHAPTER THIRTY-EIGHT

My announcement douses the class's spirits more effectively than the *Nautilus*'s hose-down.

For a few chaotic moments, the entire class mills around asking "What? What?" while I try to explain why I'm so sure we've been found. For some reason, "The dolphin is telling me so" doesn't clear up the confusion. Meanwhile, Ester and Top try to interview Socrates, but that isn't going well. The dolphin is highly agitated. Judging from his body language, his only message is *Leave now*.

Finally, Ophelia restores order. She gives each house a different assignment: Sharks to check the island's defensive grid; Cephalopods to send out drone reconnaissance; Orcas to monitor communications and LOCUS; Dolphins to sweep the *Varuna* one more time for tracking devices.

"And the four prefects," Ophelia says, "stay with Luca and me."

Our hosts lead Franklin, Tia, Gem, and me aboard the *Nautilus*.

This time, the bridge controls light up as soon as I step into the room. Luca strides over to the comm station and manipulates the LOCUS sphere. He's able to turn it just by holding his hands on either side. Three days using LOCUS aboard the *Varuna* and I never even thought to try that.

"I see nothing," he announces.

"Check again," Ophelia says. "Set the LOCUS to maximum radius."

"Of course I have set the LOCUS to . . ." Luca falters. He adjusts a dial on the control console. "There. I have set the LOCUS to maximum radius. Still nothing."

"We're in the middle of a mountain," Gem says. "That's got to affect the *Nautilus*'s sensors."

Luca smiles thinly. "Not as much as you might think. Even through hundreds of meters of solid rock, these instruments are still more sensitive than anything else in the base."

"But if the *Aronnax* has dynamic camouflage," I say, "which it probably does—"

"We should see thermal variations, nevertheless." Ophelia frowns. "But perhaps not until it gets closer. *Too* close. Tia, are the drones online yet? You should be able to check with the nav console."

"Uh . . ." Tia fiddles with a few knobs. She spins the LOCUS sphere. Even for a brilliant Cephalopod, it takes a few seconds to learn a new interface. "I don't . . . Wait."

She hits a toggle. A swarm of purple dots appears on the holosphere. "Yeah. They're fanning out in a search perimeter. But if the *Aronnax* is out there, won't the drones give away our position?"

"If the *Aronnax* is out there," Luca says grimly, "they already know we're here, and we have much bigger problems."

I clench my fists. I hate the idea that we might have led our enemies to this sanctuary. "How could they have tracked us? We swept the *Varuna*. We were camouflaged and silent. We did everything Dr. Hewett told us. . . ."

Even as I say that, my conviction evaporates. Hewett could've been working for Land Institute after all and set us up to fail. Or maybe somebody else on board was the traitor, and they sent a communication we didn't detect. Just thinking about it makes me nauseated.

"We can't know," Luca says. "Clearly, LI has managed to keep a lot of their advances secret. Theodosius warned us of his designs for the *Aronnax* when he first came to HP. He claimed his sub would rival the *Nautilus*, but he didn't believe LI would actually be able to build it for at least another decade or two. If they've done it so quickly, without us even being aware . . ."

Gem shoulders his collection of rifles. "But Lincoln Base is well-defended, right? We saw the turrets on the way in."

"We have defenses, yes," Ophelia says. "We can fend off almost anything a regular navy could throw at us. But we can't be sure what the *Aronnax*'s capabilities are. We have to assume the worst."

Franklin laces his fingers nervously. The blue streak in his hair has turned violet in the glow of the bridge lights. "We saw what the *Aronnax* did to HP. What happens if one of those warheads hits this island?"

"Wait," Tia says. "Drones six and seven just went dark."

Ophelia hurries to her side. "Did you try rerouting—?"

"Yeah. Sending drones five and eight to sweep that grid . . . Now *they've* gone dark, too."

"EMP weapon, maybe?" Gem asks.

"Perhaps," Luca says. "Four drones malfunctioning at once is unlikely. Something in that grid does not wish to be seen."

"Relative location?" I ask.

"Roughly three kilometers north by northwest," Tia reports.

"That gives us minutes at best," Ophelia says.

She and Luca lock eyes. They seem to come to a silent agreement.

"Ana," Luca says, "you have to take the *Nautilus* away from here, out to open sea. She *cannot* fall into LI's possession."

Gem steps back as if pushed. "Hold on. We don't even know if the sub will *move*."

"You were just lecturing us on taking things slowly!" Franklin agrees.

"And now we have no time," Ophelia says, her voice strained. "If the *Aronnax* put a tracker on the *Varuna*, they will be focused on Lincoln Base, not the *Nautilus* herself. We have enough defenses to keep them occupied while you escape."

"We can help you fight them off!" I say. "Why take the risk of leaving?"

I know my real motive for saying this. It's not about the sub.

I left Dev and HP collapsed around him. I can't watch the same thing happen to Lincoln Base. I can't run away and again watch people I care about die.

"My dear," Luca says, "the greatest risk is that Land Institute acquires this submarine. That is a risk to the entire world. The *Nautilus* will listen to you. I am confident in her seaworthiness. She should have basic propulsion. Her camouflage is operational."

"That's true," Tia says. "We checked it yesterday."

"She can run and hide," Ophelia concludes, "but her long-range weapons are nonfunctional. In a fight, she'd be helpless."

"Also true," Gem says. "We don't know how half her weapons systems work. And those torpedoes . . ." He shakes his head sadly.

"Sitting here," Ophelia says, "the *Nautilus* is simply a prize waiting to be taken. On the open sea, at least she has a chance."

The lights briefly dim. There is a clunking sound somewhere in the lower decks. I can't help but feel that the *Nautilus* is coughing to get my attention. *Um, yeah, get me out of here.*

The idea of the open sea must be appealing to her after sitting in this cavern for so long. Still, my heart flops around in my chest. I wish I could let Luca and Ophelia command the ship, or Gem. . . . But I am the only Dakkar. It has to be me.

I hate my DNA.

"If we do this . . ." I say. "*If*—then what about Dr. Hewett? We can't move him."

"Oh, I'm staying behind," Franklin says, like that should be obvious. "I'm not leaving my patient in the middle of treatment. Ester can be acting prefect."

"But—"

"I'm staying, too," Tia says. "Ophelia and Luca will need help with the island's defensive systems. Besides, Nelinha is your best combat engineer."

Tears well in my eyes. "Tia, I never—"

"Hey, it's fine." She squeezes my arm. "We all have different strengths. Working on this sub . . ." She glances around nervously. "Beautiful as she is, that's not one of mine."

"We would welcome your help in the base," Luca says. Then he turns to me. "Ana, the tunnel from this cavern emerges south of the atoll, directly opposite the *Aronnax*'s approach vector. That should put the island between you and our enemies. We will do our best to draw their attention and buy you time."

I remember Hewett's words to the guards on the docks in San Alejandro: *Buy us time.*

"But if they take the island," I say, "or destroy it . . ."

The memory of Harding-Pencroft crumbling into the Pacific floats in the back of my vision like an old-fashioned photograph resolving in a bath of silver nitrate.

Luca gives me a sad smile. "My dear, do not worry. I have no intention of getting myself killed."

"Or getting *me* killed," Ophelia adds dryly.

"Of course," Luca agrees. "You can take Jupiter on board,

however. He will enjoy the adventure, and he's quite familiar with the sub's galley. Besides, who knows? Perhaps all this is a false alarm! Or perhaps Lincoln Base will destroy the *Aronnax* and save the day!"

I can tell he doesn't believe either scenario, but he wants to keep my spirits up.

Everyone looks at me, waiting for my decision. In the end, it has to be my call. The *Nautilus* will only move for me.

I turn to Gem. I wait for him to tell me that he, too, is staying behind. He will want to be where the fight is.

"Oh, no," he says, reading my expression. "My orders are to keep you safe. Where you go, I go."

Three days ago, this response would have irritated me. I can imagine myself saying, *No, really, that's okay. Go shoot some things. I'll be fine.*

Now I'm grateful to have his support. To my surprise, he's starting to feel like someone I *want* at my side, like Ester and Nelinha, and I'm not sure how to process what that means.

"All right," I say, before I can change my mind. "Luca, I will hold you to your promise. You do *not* get yourselves killed." I take a deep breath and face Gem. "Gather the crew. Get the orangutan. I'm taking command of the *Nautilus*."

CHAPTER THIRTY-NINE

Within fifteen minutes, we're all aboard.

Nelinha gives me a high five before leading the Cephalopods to the engine room. The Orcas lug in crates of food and medical supplies, along with an impressive collection of Jupiter's cookware, while the orangutan waddles along next to them, signing, *Careful with that.*

Gem sends his Sharks to the weapons room to make sure our antique torpedoes are secured. Then he follows me and the other Dolphins to the bridge.

Lee-Ann takes dive control. Virgil takes communications. Halimah takes navigation. That's a no-brainer, since she's our best pilot. Gem takes the weapons console, though we don't have many weapons to speak of. Jack stands by as my runner in case ship-wide communication goes down. (Do we even *have* ship-wide communication?)

I study the captain's chair.

I'm sure the new Florentine seaweed-leather upholstery will be comfortable. The purple mood lighting around the base is a nice touch. The armrest controls seem simple enough: place hands on globes, hope the *Nautilus* responds.

But this chair is still where my ancestor died. His body sat there withering for 150 years. This is the central altar in the Dakkar family mausoleum.

I have to make it more than that. I have to make this a living, working ship again.

I take my post. The chair's padding sighs as it presses against my back.

The flurry of bridge activity dies down. Everyone turns, waiting for my commands. I feel like a little girl playing pretend, the way Dev and I used to do when we were small.

"*Nautilus*," I say in Bundeli. (In case you're wondering, the word is *notilas*. Huge surprise.) "I need access to all systems, please. Our crew is on board. We're ready to get underway."

From the organ comes a soft middle C. Then an octave up, another C joins in, and then an octave below, until it sounds like an entire orchestra tuning itself. The volume crescendos. The hull rumbles. Floor plating vibrates under my feet. Around the bridge, previously dark dials and gauges blink to life.

The organ falls silent.

"Okay," Lee-Ann mutters nervously. "That was different."

Nelinha's voice crackles overhead from a metal speaker shaped like a daffodil. "Ana, you did it! Looks like we've got full power. And that red button for super cavitation? It's glowing now!" There's interference on the line as she has a hasty debate with her colleagues. "Yeah, I know, I know. We won't push it."

"Stand by," I say. "All we need are basic thrust and depth control."

I realize I'm not even sure Nelinha can hear me. I grip my armrest control. "Is this thing on?"

My words boom from speakers across the bridge, reverberating through the ship. Thanks a lot, *Nautilus*.

"Engineering?" I try again. This time, there's no Voice of God echo.

"Oh, yeah," Nelinha says. I can hear the smile in her voice. "We're all awake down here now."

I try to remember my commands and operation procedures. I really wish I had paid more attention to Colonel Apesh's one lecture on submarine protocol last fall.

"Helm?"

"Aye," says Halimah.

"Dive?"

"Aye," says Lee-Ann.

"Comm?"

"Aye, Captain." Virgil uses the title without a trace of irony.

"Weapons?" I ask Gem.

"Uh . . ." He stares at his console. "I mean . . . aye? Short-range Leyden guns, maybe. And this button apparently electrifies the outer hull, but whether it works or not—"

The panel sparks, shocking his fingers. "Ow! Okay, sorry, *Nautilus*. Weapons, aye."

"Right." I can't believe I'm doing this. "Lines free. Hatches sealed . . . Helm, take us out. Ahead slow."

"Ahead slow, aye," Halimah says.

The floor shudders. A wake swells over the great domed windows. We begin to move.

"Yes!" Virgil cheers.

Halimah and Lee-Ann give each other a fist bump.

I can't celebrate quite so easily. I'm afraid my next command will expose thousands of leaks in the sub and get us all drowned.

"Engine room," I say, "rig for dive."

"Engine room," Nelinha responds, "rig for dive, aye."

"Weapons room," Dru Cardenas reports. "We are secured, Captain."

"LIBRARY," Ester's voice announces. "DITTO."

"Library?" I look around, realizing for the first time that

Ester is not on the bridge. I guess I just assumed she would follow me.

"Well, I have to be somewhere," Ester says. "Besides, Jupiter brought maple scones."

Top barks, rattling the speakers. He's probably saying, *Yay for orangutans!*

"Ester, to the bridge, please," I say. "I need your help reading the ship."

"Aye, Captain." She sighs.

"And bring me a scone?"

"Me, too, please," says Virgil.

Halimah, Lee-Ann, Jack, and Gem all raise their hands.

"Six scones," I say.

"Six scones, aye," Ester says. "Would you like any espresso drinks with that today?"

I can't tell if she's kidding. "We're good, thanks."

Though a café au lait would be . . . No.

Wait. What am I doing?

"Dive control." I take a deep breath, then turn to Lee-Ann. "Set depth to ten meters. Here goes nothing."

Lee-Ann grins. "Aye, Captain. Here goes nothing."

The water rises outside, engulfing the bow windows. The *Nautilus* submerges. For the first time in a century and a half, she sails out under her own power.

And then we hit something.

CHAPTER FORTY

The sub shudders and screeches.

"All stop!" I yell.

The screeching continues like nails on a chalkboard until we lose our forward momentum. I take a shaky breath, wondering if we've just ruined the world's most important invention.

"What was that?" I ask.

"Ah, that's on me." Halimah grimaces. "The LOCUS was set for long-range scans. . . ."

She toggles a switch. Her console's holosphere expands to the size of a medicine ball. A glowing purple dot still marks our position in the center, but now I can see our immediate surroundings. Lacey nets of green light define the cavern walls. Rising from the lake bottom are half a dozen spires of rock. The tip of one is right underneath us—a poke-y finger of death touching the *Nautilus*'s belly.

I grit my teeth. Luca and Ophelia might have warned us about the forest of giant stalagmites we'd be navigating through. At least they could've set the LOCUS back to short-range. Then again, our departure was a bit rushed.

"No, that's my fault," I tell Halimah. "I gave the order. Damage report?"

She tries to make sense of her readouts. Given the *Nautilus*'s style, I'm half expecting a brass plaque to pop up from the console with the word *OUCH* written in fancy calligraphy.

Meanwhile the other bridge crew readjust their LOCUS displays.

"Oh, yeah, look at that," Lee-Ann mutters. "Giant rocks."

Ester rushes onto the bridge with a plate of scones. At her feet, Top goes into a play bow, like, *Where's the party?*

"DID WE HIT A ROCK?" Ester demands.

From the overhead speaker, Nelinha's voice announces, "I think we hit a rock."

"Thanks, we got that," I say. "Can anybody tell if we took damage?"

"Not that I see," Nelinha says. "But let's not do it again."

"Agreed. Helm, ease us off of the poke-y finger of death, please."

"Aye, Captain." Halimah sounds relieved.

"I have the tunnel entrance," Virgil says at the comm station. "Fifteen degrees starboard, range ninety meters, depth twenty meters."

I try not to shudder. One of the first things you learn in dive school is how dangerous underwater caves can be. They're the places most likely to kill you.

Being in a sub does not make me feel any better about our chances. We're barely out of the driveway and we've already almost impaled ourselves. Nevertheless, I decide that it wouldn't be good form for the captain to scream *We're all going to die!*

"Make fifteen degrees starboard," I say. "Make depth twenty meters. Ahead slow. Let's get to the exit without hitting anything else, folks."

Gem laughs.

I scowl at him.

"Right, that wasn't funny," he agrees.

We start to move again. I study the LOCUS displays. The tunnel entrance looms closer, like the mouth of a whale.

"Range forty meters," Halimah announces. "Depth is steady at twenty meters."

I glance at Ester, who's standing on my right with her plate of baked goods. "How does the *Nautilus* seem to you?"

"Calm," she says. "Want a scone?"

Calm is good. And, yes, I want a scone.

I hear no groans or creaks, no cries of alarm from the corridors. Still, I imagine a thousand little leaks springing up all along the sub's ancient hull plating.

"Jack," I say, "make a pass through the ship, would you? Check on all hands."

"Aye." He looks relieved to have a job. He grabs a scone and runs off.

"Tunnel entrance ten meters," Halimah says. "This'll be tight."

"You understand how to steer this thing?" Virgil asks.

The pipe organ plays a diminished chord, making us all flinch.

"I mean . . . do you know how to steer this beautiful vessel?" Virgil corrects himself.

"I think so," Halimah says. "*Nautilus*, help me out here. Captain?"

It takes me a second to realize she's asking me a question. I'm still not used to being called Captain.

"Ahead slow," I say. "Course corrections at your discretion."

"Aye." Halimah turns a lever ever so slightly.

As soon as we reach the tunnel, a tremor rattles the bridge. Bubbles cascade over the forward windows.

I grip my armrests. "What was—?"

"Explosion!" Gem yells, a little louder than necessary. "N-not close, though. That was about . . ." He fiddles with his controls and his holosphere changes to a deep purple color. "Whoa, that's cool."

"Something about an explosion?" I prompt.

"Right, sorry. There was a detonation against the north rim of the atoll, about a kilometer away. Torpedo, maybe?"

"Massive shock wave for a torpedo," Virgil says.

"The *Aronnax*," Ester says.

That name is more unsettling than the organ's diminished chord.

I want to believe that Luca and Ophelia blew our enemies out of the water, but I know we couldn't be that lucky. More likely the *Aronnax* was sending a warning shot, letting Lincoln Base know they mean business. At least the cave hasn't collapsed on top of us yet.

"Steady as she goes," I say.

Halimah takes us into the tunnel.

Outside the windows, the constellations of phytoplankton disappear. Only a meter above our heads, the ceiling of the lava tube slithers past, glistening in the purple glow of the bridge. Of course Nemo would make his lighting purple, I realize. The shortest light waves, blue and purple, are the last colors to disappear underwater. I wonder if the *Nautilus* has purple headlights. Or ye olde windshield wipers.

The holospheres at all the stations suddenly flicker and die.

"Halimah?" I ask, alarmed.

"It's okay." Her left hand stays steady on the lever. Her right flits from control to control as if she's used this console her whole life. "I was anticipating that."

"The walls of the lava tube have an exceptionally dense metal content," Lee-Ann tells me. "They're messing with our LOCUS. We'll have to use physical readouts until we reach the other side."

Halimah doesn't reply. She's a little busy trying to keep us in one piece.

"Tactical is down, too," Gem says. "I can't tell what's going on out there."

"Did you get a position on the *Aronnax*?" I ask.

"Nothing. Maybe they're camouflaged."

"That could be good," Ester says, feeding a bit of scone to Top. "Maybe they won't be able to see us, either."

Speaking of which . . .

"Engine room, report," I say. "How are we looking?"

"Well," Nelinha says, "the glowing things are still glowing. The humming things are still humming. I think we're good."

"If we have dynamic camouflage, now would be a good time to activate it."

"Uh . . . yeah. Stand by."

Our passage through the tunnel seems to take forever. Sweat trickles down my back. My shirt sticks to the fine Italian seaweed leather.

No one speaks. Even Top is quiet, sitting patiently at Ester's side, waiting for more pastry bites.

Ester rests her hand on the back of my chair. "The Nautilus feels good," she tells me. "I think she's excited."

That makes one of us.

Jack returns, out of breath from his run through the ship. "No problems," he reports.

Nelinha announces over the intercom: "Camouflage active, babe. I mean Captain. Captain babe."

A moment later, the LOCUS displays flicker to life again.

"We're out," Halimah sighs.

"Yes!" Lee-Ann gives her a round of applause. Jack whoops and pumps his fist. From the hallway behind us, I hear the echoes of cheers from the rest of the crew.

Our enthusiasm doesn't last.

"Ana!" Gem shouts, forgetting the whole "Captain" thing. "I've pinpointed the *Aronnax*." He turns, his expression grim. "That explosion? It didn't just *hit* the north side of the atoll. The north side of the atoll is gone."

CHAPTER FORTY-ONE

Gem flips a switch. His tactical holosphere expands, showing us a 3-D view of Lincoln Base. The main island rises from the lagoon, ringed by the atoll that used to be an almost perfect concentric circle. Now, in addition to the channel the *Varuna* navigated through a few days ago, there's a much larger break in the northern rim. A section of beach and brambles the size of a soccer field has simply disappeared into the sea.

The purple blip of the *Nautilus* glows at the southern edge of the display. Directly opposite us, to the north of the broken atoll, floats a second purple dot: the *Aronnax*.

Weapons fire traces like shooting stars across the holosphere, back and forth between the *Aronnax* and the turrets along what's left of the atoll. One after another, the island's defenses go dark.

My mouth feels full of wet sand. "Gem, can you zoom in on the attacker?"

He fiddles with another knob. Suddenly, I am seeing the *Aronnax* up close and personal—or at least her holographic image.

As we saw on Dr. Hewett's fuzzy drone footage, the ship is shaped like an arrowhead—as if Land Institute retrofitted a stealth bomber for underwater use. Surrounding its hull is a fuzzy violet halo that seems to be soaking up the discharges from the base's defenses.

"What is that?" I ask. "Some kind of shield?"

No one has an answer. We stare in horror as the *Aronnax* continues its slow and steady advance toward the island.

Virgil turns. "Ana . . . Captain . . . if they hit the main base with one of those seismic torpedoes—"

"They wouldn't," Ester says. "Not if they think their prize is inside."

Their prize.

I clutch my armrests. I have never hated anything as much as I hate the *Aronnax*, but Ester is right. The *Nautilus* and I are prizes in a game of keep-away. We can't be combatants in this fight.

"Orders, Captain?" Halimah sounds composed, but her hands tremble over the nav controls—usually not a good thing for a pilot.

I imagine Dr. Hewett lying in his medical bed, Franklin shielding him as debris rains from the ceiling. I picture Lincoln Base's corridors shaking, its lights flickering, Tia, Luca, and Ophelia running desperately from one control panel to another, trying to maintain power as their weapons systems are systematically destroyed.

I wish I could help, but that's not our mission. There's nothing we can do for Lincoln Base.

"Helm, set course due south," I say. "Full speed. Whatever that is."

"Course due south, full speed, aye."

"Dive, make our depth . . ." I blink, trying to clear my head. I check the holosphere above Lee-Ann's console. "Make depth twenty-five meters."

"Twenty-five meters, aye," Lee-Ann says.

In the pit of my stomach, I feel the sub start to accelerate and descend.

"Captain," Nelinha's voice crackles over the loudspeaker. "I think maybe we should back off the speed. I'm getting some weird readings from— OH, THAT'S NOT GOOD."

The *Nautilus* shudders. Over the intercom, I hear the Cephalopods yelling. Behind us, down the corridor, more crew members shout with alarm.

"Weapons room!" Dru's voice comes over the comm. "I've got green slime coming out of the ductwork!"

"Galley!" The voice is Brigid Salter's. Behind her, I can hear an upset orangutan whooping and grunting. "There's some of kind of sludge pouring from the air vents. It's spraying all over Jupiter's pots and pans, and he is NOT okay with it!"

"Engine room!" Nelinha yells. "Main engines are down! We've got goo! I repeat, we've got goo!"

Halimah bangs her fist against the nav console. "Captain, we're dead in the water."

I curse under my breath. I remember the wad of putrefied seaweed that Luca pulled from the wiring compartment my first time on board. I imagine a flood of that foul-smelling Victorian-era sewage spewing from every duct and crevice around the ship, forced into circulation by the demands we're putting on this old bucket of nemonium. What was I thinking, treating the *Nautilus* like a functioning submarine?

"Nelinha," I call through the comm, "we *need* propulsion. Can you repair?"

The only answer is static and garbled shouting in the background.

"I'll go." Jack Wu charges off again.

"Oh . . ." Gem steps away from his console. "No, no, no."

I assume goo must be leaking out of his console, but that's not the problem. On Gem's tactical display, the *Aronnax* has changed course. The base's remaining turrets continue to fire on her, but the *Aronnax* doesn't bother to shoot back. She veers east, making her way around the edge of the atoll.

"What is she doing?" Lee-Ann mutters.

"They've spotted us," I say.

"How?" Halimah demands. "Our camouflage reads as operational."

"Maybe it isn't," Virgil says. "It could've gone down with propulsion. Or maybe the *Aronnax* is picking up our thermal variations, like Ophelia said—"

"It doesn't matter right now," I say. "In less than a minute, they'll have a direct line of fire. I need options."

"There's the skiff," Gem says. "I could pilot it out, maybe draw their fire and buy you time. If I can get close enough to the *Aronnax* with conventional weapons—"

"No, that's suicide," I tell him. "Do we have any shieldy things?"

"Shieldy things . . ." Gem frowns at his console. "Um, I don't—"

"*NAUTILUS.*" The voice booms from our speakers so loudly I jump. "THIS IS THE *ARONNAX*. SURRENDER OR BE DESTROYED."

I recognize that voice. It's our old friend/interrogation subject Caleb South.

"How is this guy back?" Gem grumbles. "I thought Land Institute punished failure."

"He must have come up with a really good lie," Lee-Ann speculates. "Maybe put all the blame on his classmates."

"Bah," Gem says. "I should've poked holes in his pink-ducky water wings."

"YOU'RE MOTIONLESS AND DEFENSELESS IN THAT PIECE OF JUNK," Caleb continues. "GIVE UP NOW, AND WE'LL SPARE YOUR BASE."

The *Nautilus* shudders. I don't think she likes being called junk.

"Can we turn off his voice?" I ask. "How is he even broadcasting over our comm?"

"I—I'm looking," Virgil says, frantically turning dials.

Caleb's tirade continues at a lower volume: "All we want is the *Nautilus* and Ana Dakkar. None of you will be harmed. We'll treat you better than you treated me."

"They're closing," Gem tells me. "One kilometer out now."

The island's defenses continue to fire, trying to draw the *Aronnax*'s attention. Our enemy ignores the barrage. They are locked on us, almost as if . . .

A cramp hits my gut, folding my insides into various origami shapes.

"They were never tracking the *Varuna*," I realize. "They were tracking *me*."

"How?" asks Lee-Ann. "Is your DNA radioactive or something?"

Over the comm, Nelinha says, "Captain, we've got an idea. You're going to hate it, but—"

"If you don't trust me," Caleb South interrupts, "listen to our captain."

I shoot to my feet. "Shut off that stupid transmission!" I yell at Virgil.

Then the enemy captain's voice comes over the intercom and knocks me right back into my chair.

"Hey, sis," says Dev. "You did a great job. But now it's time to give up."

CHAPTER FORTY-TWO

I remember the first time I got nitrogen narcosis.

My instructor took me below a hundred feet with regular air tanks, just to show me what "rapture of the deep" felt like. My vision started to tunnel. I couldn't do simple calculations on my dive computer. I was filled with a strange mixture of euphoria and terror. I knew the beautiful blue void would kill me if I swam any deeper, but that's exactly what I wanted to do.

Hearing Dev's voice makes me feel the same way.

My thoughts turn to syrup. My brother is alive. My brother is a traitor.

I'm relieved. I'm horrified. I'm spiraling into a blue abyss.

"This is impossible," I say.

The bridge crew stares back at me. They look shocked, confused . . . hurt. They need answers. Once again, I have none.

"It—it has to be a fake," I say. "A voice synthesizer—"

"That's his voice, Ana." Ester frowns at the floor. "He's alive."

"But—"

"*NAUTILUS*," Dev says. "Ana, you're out of time. I need to hear that you surrender. Otherwise, we fire."

"He wouldn't," says Lee-Ann.

"He did," Halimah counters. "He's the one who destroyed HP."

No, I think. *Not my brother.*

Then I remember what Dev said on our last day, when he gave me my early birthday present. *You're leaving for your freshman trials today.*

He knew I would be off campus when the attack happened. He played down my concerns about the grid. Land Institute had to have inside help to sabotage the security system. All this time, I've been suspecting my classmates, or Dr. Hewett. . . .

The intercom crackles. Nelinha's voice breaks through my stupor. "Uh, did everyone else hear that? Orders, Captain?"

Orders . . . I almost want to laugh. Why would anyone take orders from me? I'm a stupid little girl who has been duped by her own brother.

"You okay, Ana?" Gem asks. His expression is concerned, expectant, like he's waiting for me to grab a lifeline.

I force myself to breathe. I can't spiral into this emotional vacuum right now . . . not when it would mean abandoning my friends. "Engine room, stand by." I turn to Virgil. "Can they hear us?"

"No," he says. "One-way transmission. Pretty sure. Almost positive."

"Their position?"

Gem checks his panels. "Half a kilometer out. Holding at our six o'clock."

How did they find us, despite all our precautions? They were never following the *Varuna.* They were following *me.* . . .

I wanted you to have the pearl for luck, Dev said, *just in case, you know, you fail spectacularly or something.*

I stand. My fingers close around my mother's black-pearl pendant. I yank it from my neck, breaking the chain. Dev had it reset, just for me. The pearl comes away easily from its new setting. Underneath, glued to the silver base, is a tiny alt-tech receptor.

"Ana, I'm so sorry." Ester's lower lip quivers. She understands how I feel. She knows about being used, being treated like a commodity even by her own family.

"Can I borrow your Leyden gun?" I ask.

She doesn't hesitate. She hands me her pistol.

I set the broken pieces of the necklace on the floor—chain, setting, even the pearl. I can't take any chances. I step back and fire.

Blue tendrils of electricity arc down the length of the chain. The alt-tech receptor pops and burns like a tiny emergency flare. White curlicues of smoke wreath my mother's pearl.

An acrid tang fills the back of my mouth. I'm not sure if it's from the melting tracker or the bitterness welling up in my throat.

Back on the *Varuna*, Land Institute's assault team went out of their way not to hit me with a Leyden gun. They used poison instead. They were hoping to take the whole ship: me, Dr. Hewett's map, the DNA-reader, everything. But if something went wrong, they didn't want to risk damaging their tracking device. I was their insurance policy. I led them—I led *Dev* right to the *Nautilus*.

My brother's voice booms through the ship. His tone is intimate and pleading, just for me. "I warned the school, Ana. I told them to evacuate. I didn't want them to die. I don't want anyone else to die now, especially you."

Oh, god. That garbled audio recording of Dev hadn't come from the school's intercom. He'd been broadcasting from on board the *Aronnax*.

I want to scream at him. I want to demand explanations. But there is no way I will open communications.

An hour ago, I would have traded the *Nautilus* and the

entire world to talk to Dev again. Now I want to be as far away from him as possible.

"Engine room," I say. "You were talking about options?"

A moment of static, then Nelinha responds, "Yes, but you're not going to like—"

"I don't like *anything* right now. Talk to me."

"The cav-drive," she says. "It might still be operational. It uses a different starter system to communicate with the engines—"

Dev's voice overrides hers. "Harding-Pencroft are not our friends, Ana. They've been hoarding our family's inheritance for generations. Their stupidity got our parents killed. They're using you. Land Institute gave me command of their prize ship. They want to use our tech to make the world better. Harding-Pencroft would never. They refused to let me even see the *Nautilus*. This was the only way to force their hand. I'm sorry, but it had to be done. Now we can take what is ours. Yours and mine."

"N-Nelinha, this cav-drive . . ." I try to tune out Dev's words, but I feel like I've been gargling with sea-snake venom. "Are you sure it will work?"

"Absolutely not," she says. "If I push this red button, maybe nothing happens. Maybe we explode right here. Or maybe we shoot halfway across the Pacific and smash straight into the side of an underwater mountain. But that's all I've got, unless you can keep Dev talking for another six or seven hours while we make repairs."

I'd rather explode.

"If we manage to get away," Gem warns, "the *Aronnax* will turn on Lincoln Base."

I know that. Ophelia, Luca, Dr. Hewett, Tia, Franklin . . . How can we leave them at the mercy of that sub . . . of Dev? What has my brother become? On the other hand, I can't surrender this crew. The defenders in Lincoln Base gave me a mission. They stayed behind to make it possible.

"*Nautilus*, listen to me," I tell the sub in Bundeli. "We need to leave immediately. We need to find somewhere safe. If we don't—"

"All right, then." Dev's pained voice reminds me so much of our father's. Dad's disappointed sigh whenever we misbehaved was always the worst punishment. "Ana, we're launching an EMP tornado. It won't destroy you. It'll just knock out your remaining systems. Then we'll board you. You can't stop us. You're a bunch of freshmen on a derelict ship you don't understand. Please don't make us kill your crew."

Gem yells, "Torpedo in the water! Ten seconds to impact!"

"Engine room!" I shout. "Punch the cav-drive *now*!"

For three heartbeats—nothing.

Then sheets of aerated water blast over the front windows like we've plunged into the world's most powerful carwash. The ship shoots forward so violently I am thrown backward across the bridge. I feel a dull *crack* as my head hits metal, and everything goes dark.

CHAPTER FORTY-THREE

When I wake, Ester is standing over me, wearing surgeon's scrubs. My temples throb. The back of my skull feels like it's encased in ice.

"You're in the sick bay," Ester says. "You've been out for four hours. You need to rest—"

I roll sideways out of the bed, trying to find my feet. I step on Top, who yelps in protest. Ester grabs my arm to steady me.

"This is not resting," she observes.

"I have to . . . the ship. Are we safe?"

From somewhere nearby, Nelinha answers, "For now."

I try to focus. Multiple da Silvas swirl in the doorway. She's wearing combat boots, a black-and-white plaid kilt, and a black hoodie, with black lipstick to match so she looks like a highlander commando. On her forehead is a puffy white bandage the size of a dollar bill.

I point unsteadily at her patch. "Are you okay?"

"Who, me? I'm peachy. When we went to cav-drive, my face had a disagreement with a crankshaft. How are *you* feeling?"

That's a good question. My headache is generating an explosive yield of about fifty megatons. I've been unconscious for four hours. At least that saved me from four hours of ugly crying. My brother is alive, and a traitor, and a mass murderer.

"I'll live," I decide. "Who's piloting the ship?"

"Well, Gem has the bridge," Nelinha says, with less distaste than I would have expected, "but nobody's piloting at the moment. We're stationary."

I struggle to process that. "How is the crew?"

"We had seventeen injuries," Ester says. "Mostly minor."

"With Franklin and Tia gone, we only have a crew of eighteen."

"I know," she agrees. "I was lucky. I have good balance. Also, Jupiter is fine. And Top is fine."

Top wags his tail. *Can confirm.*

Ester prods my scalp with her fingers. Maybe she's looking for holes in my head. She hates physical contact, but when I'm just a patient, she has no problem mercilessly poking.

"Your ancestor invented super-cavitation drive," she says, "but he didn't invent seat belts. We have three people with broken arms, two concussions, and one second-degree burn."

"Who got burned?"

"Kay Ramsay." Nelinha points behind me.

Kay is lying fast asleep in the next bed over. Her arm is bandaged from shoulder to fingertips. Poor Kay . . . I hope this med bay has some kind of skin-grafting technology.

I lower my voice. "What happened?"

"She got thrown against a cold-fusion coil." Nelinha's face tightens. "Those things get *hot*. Who knew?"

"We might want to install body harnesses," Ester says. "Or at least give a little warning next time before we punch to cav-drive."

I nod sheepishly. Even that motion hurts. "I need to get back to the bridge."

"Not recommended," Ester says. "You banged your head pretty good. I tried a scanner-type thingy on you, like a LOCUS for bodies—"

"So Nemo invented MRIs and CAT scans, too?" I shiver, hoping Ester hasn't dosed me with ancient alt-tech radiation that will turn me into a fish.

"I didn't see any inflammation," she says. "Still, I'm using equipment and medicine I don't really understand."

I get it. She wants me to rest, which is the main thing I can't do.

I turn to Nelinha. "Damage report?"

She spreads her hands. "I mean . . . we're in one piece? Propulsion is down. The cav-drive blew a fuse or something. We're still digging ourselves out from the Great Goo Explosion. On the other hand, we have internal power. We have air. Our depth is stable at twenty meters. The hull is intact. So we're okay. We just won't be going anywhere for a while."

"What's our position?"

She laughs. "You won't believe it. We're in the Philippine Sea, roughly four hundred miles east of Davao."

I blink, trying to process that. "You mean one punch of the cav-drive shot us—"

"About five thousand miles," she confirms. "It took a couple of hours, mind you. You were unconscious for the whole thing, but still . . ."

"That would take—what, twelve hours in a commercial flight? Six days by sea?"

"I said you wouldn't believe it."

The problem is, I *do* believe it. I add *super-cavitation drive* to the list of reasons why Land Institute wants this "piece of junk" submarine so badly. That kind of proprietary technology could turn the world upside down.

"The *Aronnax*," I remember, my nerves crackling. "Any sign of them?"

"None," Nelinha says. "Our course and bearing were pretty obvious. If the *Aronnax* has a cav-drive, they should have been able to follow us. Since they haven't shown up yet, I think we can assume we have the advantage there."

I exhale. We need all the advantages we can get.

On the other hand, we've left Lincoln Base at the mercy of the *Aronnax*. We're stuck in the middle of the ocean with no propulsion, no allies, and no friendly ports.

At least, I assume so. . . .

I remember asking the *Nautilus* to take us somewhere safe. Did she pick this spot to drop out of cav-drive on purpose, or did she simply run out of steam?

"Is there anything close to us?" I ask.

Nelinha shrugs. "No secret bases that we can detect, if that's what you mean. The Palau Trench is right underneath us—six thousand meters straight down. I wouldn't want to lose dive control here."

I feel like I already have. My brain is developing stress fractures. Why here? What now? How can I face my crew when my brother is the cause of all our problems and I led him right to us at Lincoln Base?

My knees give out. Ester grabs my arm to keep me from falling.

"Ana, you have to sit down, at least," she insists.

"I will," I promise. "In the main dining room." I look at Nelinha. "Gather the crew, will you? And, Ester, I'd appreciate some super-alt-tech aspirin if you've got any. This is going to be a tough conversation."

CHAPTER FORTY-FOUR

A tough conversation, and also the world's strangest brunch.

The table only has seating for eight. We bring in as many other chairs as we can find and put them around the walls. The furniture creaks and smells like mold, but the crew has done their best to clean up the space. The old mahogany tabletop gleams. The abalone chandelier glitters overhead. The silverware, each piece engraved with Captain's Nemo's crest, has been polished like new.

Jupiter has prepared a delicious selection of macroalgae sandwiches. He's also baked several dozen chocolate-chip cookies, which reinforces my belief that he is the most essential member of this crew.

Ester wasn't kidding about the number of injuries. Between us, we have enough bandages, splints, casts, and slings to build a first-aid man.

Once everyone has had something to eat—it's a very quiet meal—I finally speak.

"Guys, I had no idea about Dev." I've practiced what to say, but still I can hardly form the words. "I thought he was dead. What Dev did—I don't even *know* the person who could do that to our school and our friends."

I brush away a tear. I've known my classmates for two years, but right now I can't read their expressions. Their blurry faces swim in front of my eyes. I wonder if this is how Ester feels all the time.

"If you think I was involved somehow," I say, "I don't blame you. At this point, *I* don't trust me, either. I don't own this ship. You deserve another vote about who will be in charge. Gem can take over, or anyone you choose. . . . I guess I'm trying to say I'm sorry."

The only sound is the distant hum of the air circulators.

"Ana," Gem says at last, "nobody blames you."

I stare at him. I'd be less surprised if he told me the ocean was purple.

"You're not your brother," he continues. "What he did doesn't reflect on you. You've brought us this far and kept us alive." He looks around the group. "Anybody disagree? If so, speak up."

No one does.

I wonder if this is just peer pressure. Gem is a hard person to contradict. But I sense no discomfort in the crew: no furtive glances, no squirming in seats.

A feeling of gratitude wraps around me like a warm quilt. I want to thank my friends, but that seems insufficient. The best way I can thank them is by living up to their trust.

"If you're sure," I say, brushing away another tear, "then we have a lot of work to do. Where are we on repairs?"

Their reports do not help my headache. Our to-do list is as long as the submarine. On top of cleaning goop and repairing the systems we broke when we made our escape, there are still a thousand things about the *Nautilus* we don't understand.

Luca and Ophelia spent two years trying to comprehend this ship. They were HP's best. If we ever want to get underway again, we'll have to complete their work without the benefit of their experience—or their base or any other kind of repair facilities. And we don't have two years in which to do it.

Nelinha says what I'm thinking: "We have to help Lincoln Base."

Kiya Jensen shifts her broken arm in her sling. I can tell she doesn't like what she's about to say.

"I'm just going to put this out there," she says. "Our duty is to make sure the *Nautilus* doesn't fall into anyone else's hands, right? Wouldn't Luca and Ophelia tell us *not* to try helping them if there's any chance LI could capture the sub?"

She's right, of course. We're riding in the most destabilizing technological breakthrough ever: a leap forward as dramatic as iron weapons or gunpowder were. And hearing a Shark like Kiya suggest running away hits me like ice water in the face.

"Plus," she continues, "we're outmatched. Dev wasn't wrong about that. We've got a very old, not fully functional sub . . . beautiful and amazing though she is . . ." She says this last part loudly, addressing the chandelier. "And we're not trained to operate her. Land Institute sent their senior class. They were foolish not to send alumni, or their adult staff, but still . . . they've got Dev. They must have been planning this operation for a long time."

I wonder again why LI sent only students, even if they sent their best. Maybe it was school culture—fostering self-reliance, like Caleb said—but I have a feeling it had more to do with Dev. I can imagine him putting conditions on his cooperation—that he and only he would be in charge of the *Aronnax*, that LI had to trust him with command to prove they were different than HP. Maybe, in the back of his mind, he was even trying to level the playing field, to give HP a fighting chance. . . .

No. I can't think like that. I can't be Dev's apologist. He made his choices. *Vile* choices. And now, if he fails to deliver the *Nautilus*, I imagine his new friends will turn unfriendly fast.

Nelinha scowls at her sandwich. "Land Institute killed our friends. They destroyed HP. Now they're holding Lincoln Base. We can't run away from that."

Brigid Salter glumly pushes away her plate. She lost her brother at HP. She knows exactly what Land Institute has done. "They want the *Nautilus*, not the island. Maybe the *Aronnax* left Lincoln Base to follow us."

Judging from her tone, she desperately wants that to be true. She wants her chance at a fight.

"Or," Dru suggests, "sorry to say this, but they could have already destroyed the base."

I shake my head. "They destroyed HP because it was part of their plan. It spurred us into leading them to the *Nautilus*. Lincoln Base is different. It was Nemo's final resting place. They'll want to explore it. They'll expect to find clues to our location, information about the ship. . . ."

"They'll take the island," Gem decides. "Which means they'll take prisoners."

I think about those we left behind: Luca, Ophelia, Dr. Hewett, Franklin, Tia. Even Socrates, though I'm not so worried about him being caught.

"They'll keep our people alive," I say, forcing myself to believe it. "Dev will want to interrogate them."

I'm thinking of him as our enemy now. Not some faceless group of rival students. My own brother. I've fallen into a universe I don't understand and don't want to.

"How long do we have?" Gem asks. I understand his implication: *until the prisoners are no longer useful.*

I defer to Lee-Ann. She's our best interrogator. I can no longer tell if her ears turn red, though, because they're gift-wrapped by a ribbon of gauze around her head.

"Depends on the captors' patience level," she says. "Could be weeks. I imagine Dev—Land Institute is *hoping* we'll come back. They'll be waiting. It'll be useful for them to have live captives."

I think about the interrogation methods I learned at HP. We were always taught to avoid cruelty. That's not our way. Still, some psychological techniques can be devastating, and I doubt Land Institute will take a light hand. Every day in captivity will feel like an eternity.

"We can't take weeks," I decide.

"Also," Ester says, "we can't stay here forever. As long as the reactor is online, we have limitless power, water, and air. But in about seven days, we'll run out of food."

Top rests his head on her thigh. I think he is reminding her that food is important and also it tastes good.

"One week." Nelinha scratches the bandage on her forehead. "To do the impossible. Get engines back up and running."

"Get some of those torpedoes functioning," Dru adds.

"Clean the slime out of the vents." Gem shudders. "So is that the plan, Captain? Return to Lincoln Base?"

I stand, trying not to wobble. "If anyone thinks we should do the sensible thing—running and hiding—speak now."

No one advocates for the sensible thing.

I love my crew.

"Okay, then," I say. "It's a good thing we're the best class Harding-Pencroft has ever seen. We get the *Nautilus* operational in one week. Then we return to Lincoln Base. And we show Land Institute they've messed with the wrong bunch of freshmen."

CHAPTER FORTY-FIVE

After this inspiring speech, I eat cookies in the library.

Ester has ordered me to rest for at least one hour while the aspirin she found on board kicks in. (I think she wants to observe me to see if I actually turn into a fish.) While the rest of the crew scurries around, cleaning and repairing, carrying toolboxes and buckets of goop, I try to relax in a musty armchair, an original French copy of *20,000 Leagues Under the Sea* in my lap.

It feels very meta to be reading a fictional book about the *Nautilus* on board the actual *Nautilus*. I wonder if Nemo read the book before his death, and if the inaccuracies annoyed him. At any rate, it isn't autographed *To Nemo, Love, Jules*. I checked.

Ester sits across from me in a love seat. Top snuggles next to her. Ester uses a library book as a lap desk, jotting down information on each note card, then tossing it onto Top before starting a new one. Judging from Top's contented snoring, he does not mind being buried in information.

The fireplace glows cheerfully. I don't know who started it, and I still don't know how it works, or where the smoke goes, but it does take some of the damp chill out of the air. I wouldn't even know we were underwater except for the window looking out on the blue void, with the occasional silvertip shark swimming past.

I'm grateful for Ester's company. I'm sure she has a million other things to do, but I imagine she also realizes that if she wasn't watching me, I'd jump out of my chair and start working.

"Relax," she chides me again.

It's difficult to relax when someone keeps telling you to relax.

Only a few days ago, Ester and I sat in a different library, on board the *Varuna*, and I was trying to look after *her*. Now we've switched roles.

I flip the pages of the novel. I stop on an illustration of an underwater funeral. A dozen people in old-fashioned dive suits gather solemnly around a grave. I remember the scene—one of Captain Nemo's crew members had died—but I don't remember the details. I hope finding this picture isn't an omen.

"Why did Dev do it?" I murmur. "How could he have . . . ?"

I can't even put his betrayal into words. He lied to me, put a tracker on me, collaborated with our enemies. He destroyed our school, killed our teachers and fellow students . . . all for the sake of a submarine.

Ester puts down her pen. She stares at a spot just above my head. "Why do you think he did it?"

Oof. I forgot Orcas train in psychology. Still, her question is a good one.

I trace my fingers across the funeral illustration. "Our parents' death. He blamed Harding-Pencroft."

"Did he ever tell you that?" she asks. "I mean, before he broadcast it from the *Aronnax*?"

I shake my head. "He always tried to stay positive for me. He was the perfect big brother. I guess I never thought about what might be going on behind that smile. . . ."

It's disturbing to think how little I knew about Dev. It's even more disturbing to realize that he was holding together his positive facade for my sake, while inside he was stewing in bitterness.

I never saw it. Or at least, I never *let* myself see it. Land Institute obviously did. They used it to turn him against HP, and me.

"Captain Nemo had a lot of anger, too." Ester speaks in a monotone, as if recalling a dream from years ago. "When Ned Land and Professor Aronnax met him, he terrified them. The British had killed Nemo's wife and oldest child. He hated the European powers. He wanted to dismantle their empires. He destroyed their ships, funded rebellions. If Nemo was around today, the world governments would probably call him—"

"A terrorist." I remember Caleb South's accusation about Harding-Pencroft: *You were protecting the legacy of an outlaw.*

Ester nods. "Land Institute has always been motivated by fear and anger. They want to destroy Nemo's legacy. But they also want to *be* Nemo."

I study the book's illustration. It's hard to reconcile the idea of Nemo the terrorist with Nemo the brilliant inventor. Then again, our labels always depend on who's doing the labeling. Patriot, freedom fighter, terrorist, thug. Prince Dakkar was a brown man fighting the colonizers. I'm pretty sure that wouldn't have helped his reputation in Europe.

"Wait . . ." I refocus on Ester. "Are you saying I shouldn't judge Dev too harshly? Or . . . ?"

Ester picks up a new index card. She frowns at it, as if the lines aren't quite parallel. "I'm just saying that people are complicated. Nemo was a different man by the time Harding and Pencroft met him: older, bitter, disillusioned. That's why he wanted his technology hidden away and guarded. HP was motivated by Nemo's caution—paranoia, even. So you've got two completely different schools, Land Institute and Harding-Pencroft, inspired by different sides of the same person."

My head throbs. The alt-tech aspirin seems to be stitching my skull back together in the most painful way possible. "Those are my two choices of which Nemo I want to be? The angry one or the paranoid one?"

"No." Ester jots something down—hopefully not therapy notes. "Maybe Dev fell into that trap. He thought he had to choose. Maybe you don't have to. You both have some Dakkar personality traits, sure. But you can decide to be a different kind of Captain Nemo."

I stare at Ester, amazed by how obvious she makes it all sound.

"I just want to do the right thing," I say.

"So does Dev, I bet," Ester says. "The difference is, you have the sub. You have Nemo's resources. You could build an entirely new Harding-Pencroft, if you wanted to. I'd like to help."

"Nemo's resources?" I get the feeling she's not just talking about his cold-fusion engine, or his cav-drive, or his copious reservoir of seaweed slime.

Ester checks her watch. "Hasn't been an hour yet, but I guess you've rested long enough. Come on. There's one more door I want you to unlock."

CHAPTER FORTY-SIX

Every time I think the *Nautilus* can't surprise me anymore, I find out I'm wrong.

On the sub's lowest level, in the back of the main storeroom, crates have been moved aside to reveal a large metal vault door like the one that leads to the subterranean lake in Lincoln Base.

"Rhys and Linzi found it while doing inventory," Ester says. "I think I know what's inside, but there's only one way to be sure."

In other words, she needs the magic Nemo hands.

I study the lock. I trust Ester's instincts, but still . . . I'm hesitant about opening a door someone took the trouble to hide. If Nemo had any skeletons in his closet (literal or otherwise), this seems like the kind of closet he'd keep them in.

"*Nautilus*," I say in Bundeli, "would it be okay if I opened this door?"

All by itself, the lock spins. Bolts click and release. I guess that's a yes.

I pull the door open. Inside . . .

Oh.

Normally, I'm not a material girl. *Stuff* doesn't impress me.

But for a moment, I forget how to breathe. I relive one of my earliest memories, when Dev, who must've been pretty much a baby himself, blew in my nostrils, his stronger lungs overwhelming my own, leaving me gasping in shock.

I can't believe what I'm seeing.

"Nemo's treasury," Ester says, remarkably calm. "I thought so."

Now I understand the old saying *all that glitters is not gold.* Because in Nemo's treasury room, a lot of the glitter comes from silver, diamonds, rubies, pearls, and crazy fancy jewelry. The shelves are lined with wooden chests, each overflowing with carefully sorted loot. Nemo was apparently obsessed with order. He has all the diamonds grouped together, all the rubies, all the pearls sorted by color and size. Against the far wall is a pallet of gold bricks. There's even a shelf with half a dozen crowns, each of which looks like it might have been ripped from the head of some nineteenth-century monarch. All in all, the room reminds me of a bizarre supply store.

Excuse me, sir, where can I find sapphires?

Yes, those would be on aisle three, just past the silver-ingot display.

"Wow," I say, which seems insufficient.

Ester looks around in awe. "This room was organized by a genius."

Top sniffs around the treasure, wagging his tail half-heartedly as if to say, *Well, I guess it's all right, but it ain't doggy treats.*

Ester picks up a shoebox-size chest of white pearls. "Nemo gave Harding and Pencroft a box like this. It was enough to build the academy."

"There must be twenty boxes like that in here," I say.

Ester scans the room, probably running estimates. "Nemo gathered some of it from the merchant vessels he plundered, some from older shipwrecks he discovered. In *20,000 Leagues,* he boasted that he could pay off the national debt of France and it wouldn't make a dent in his fortune. This room may be just *one* of his stashes. Harding family legends say Nemo had supply bases hidden all over the world."

I wonder if this is what Land Institute wanted, too, along with the technology: money. Such a common thing to want, but with this much wealth, they could probably build three more *Aronnax*es and topple several world governments. Given the potential payoff, risking their brand-new sub and their senior class starts to sound like a solid gamble.

Thinking about it in those terms makes me want to take a shower.

My eyes fix on a strange-looking instrument propped in the corner. It's about the size of a guitar, but with a keyboard instead of strings, alt-tech gears and levers where the fret board should be, even a dial that looks like a color wheel, maybe for special visual effects?

"What in the—?" I pick it up gingerly. "Captain Nemo invented the keytar?"

Ester laughs. It's a rare, adorable sound, like a piglet being tickled. She doesn't often find my jokes amusing (which keeps me humble), but absurdities get her every time. "He took his music seriously."

"I guess so." I study the intricate controls. I remember the way the *Nautilus* reacted the first time I played the organ on the bridge. This keytar was important enough to hold in the treasury, so it must have a purpose beyond entertainment. I decide to come back later and figure it out. For now, though, I can't shake the image of Captain Nemo dancing through the corridors of the *Nautilus* with his keytar, jamming to "Little Red Corvette."

Did that song come out during the Victorian era? Close enough.

I look at Ester, still cradling the box of pearls like it's a litter of kittens.

The sight gives me a warm sense of satisfaction. "At least something good came out of our troubles," I tell her. "You don't need your trustees anymore. You can rebuild Harding-Pencroft all on your own."

Ester stiffens. "No, I wasn't . . ." She hastily offers me the box of pearls. "It's not my treasure. I would never . . . I would only do that if you decided—"

"Ester." I push the box gently back to her. "I trust you. We'll figure out the details later, but I can't imagine a world without Harding-Pencroft Academy. As Prince Dakkar's descendant and captain of the *Nautilus*, I ask you to please take this gift. I know you'll make HP even better than it was. *We* will, together."

Her mouth quivers. She blinks back tears. For a moment, I worry I may have misjudged her wishes and given her a burden she didn't really want.

Then she says, "I love you. I'm going to put this under my bunk."

And off she goes with Top at her heels.

As I stand alone in the treasury, I wonder if Nemo ever worried about his crew walking off with a few hundred million in gold and jewels. I guess not. What would it have mattered to him if they did? The sea gave him everything he needed.

Yet with all his wealth and advanced tech, he still ended his life bitter and defeated. He was so alone he had to trust his legacy to shipwrecked strangers.

He didn't believe in humanity. He didn't believe in himself. He tried and failed to change the world—and ended up being written off as a fictional character.

I think about Dev aboard the *Aronnax*. I remember him telling me he *had* to destroy HP because it was the only way to take what was rightfully ours: this ship, Nemo's legacy.

I wish he were here now. I would punch him. Then I would give him a hug. Next I would force him to look at all this wealth and see how pointless it was for Nemo. Absolute power can corrupt anyone. Nemo knew that. In the end, all he could do was bury himself with his sub and his riches and hope that maybe someday human nature would improve to the point where we could handle his power.

And yet here we are, more than a century and a half later, still fighting over the *Nautilus* like it's a prized toy in the sandbox.

Someone grunts behind me, breaking me out of my thoughts.

I turn to find Jupiter waiting for my attention. He looks past me at the room full of treasure. Then he signs, *Where did your crew put my muffin pans?*

I have to smile. At least orangutans have their priorities straight.

"Let's go look," I tell him.

We head off in search of real treasure. We can't use billions in the middle of the Palau Trench, but we can definitely use Jupiter's blueberry muffins.

CHAPTER FORTY-SEVEN

Day and night don't mean much underwater, but I spend the hours until dinnertime checking on my crew around the ship, helping out where I can.

The *Nautilus* is acting cranky. I suppose she didn't like being called an antique piece of junk by the crew of a newer submarine, then running from a fight by shooting halfway across the Pacific. I soothe her with compliments and promises that we will get her back in fighting shape, if she'll just let us work without shocking us or spewing gunk in our faces.

I guess she understands at least some of my submarine-whispering. By day's end, the Cephalopods have restored basic propulsion. The cav-drive will take longer, but that's fine by me. I'm not anxious for another test run until we've figured out the seat-belt situation.

When we reconvene for our evening meal, everyone seems in a better mood. At this point, each day we stay alive is a win, but we're also making progress on repairs. Jupiter's food continues to make our bellies happy. And word has gotten around about Nemo's treasury.

I left the vault door open so all the crew members could take a look. I made it clear that if anyone wanted to walk away after we've finished repairs, they could do so and become an instant billionaire.

So far, there haven't been any takers. Everyone seems determined to get the *Nautilus* in order, return to Lincoln Base, save our friends, and defeat the *Aronnax*. Afterward (if there *is* an afterward) we can figure out how to rebuild HP with our new-found shiny pretties. This doesn't stop the crew from calling one another billionaires, however. Nelinha is now Billionaire Engineer da Silva, I am Billionaire Captain Dakkar, and Jupiter is the Billionaire Gourmet Orangutan.

I think Nemo might have been wrong about human nature. There are good people in the world. Despite what happened with Dev and Land Institute, despite Harding-Pencroft's own failures, this crew is made up of people I trust.

I go to sleep that night in my ancestor's stateroom, staring at the conch-patterned bas-relief on the ceiling. I wonder what the *Nautilus* thinks of her new crew. I hope, as we continue to clean her ancient brain, she doesn't start remembering the downsides of working with humans.

The next day is my fifteenth birthday. Ester and Nelinha bring me a cupcake for breakfast and sing to me quietly, but they understand I don't want any other recognition. We have so much else going on, and so little to celebrate. . . . Also, I do *not* want to spend this day reflecting on how much has changed in the past year, or even the past week. And as for blowing out candles and making wishes, I'm not sure I could express any of my wishes without breaking into tears. Better to just keep moving forward.

We've given ourselves a week to repair the ship, which isn't nearly enough time, but we also know that every day we spend here is another day our friends are prisoners of Land Institute.

I wish I could believe the *Aronnax* had left Lincoln Base alone. I'd feel relieved if I knew they were following the *Nautilus*, hoping to catch us. But I suspect Lee-Ann was right about Dev taking hostages and waiting to see if we would come back. I just have to hope this old submarine still has some surprises up her torpedo tubes. We have to figure out a way not to cav-drive ourselves right into a trap. Otherwise, all our tech and all that treasure in the hold isn't going to do us any good.

The day after my birthday, we finish de-gunking the innards of the *Nautilus*. As near as Nelinha can tell, the cav-drive is back online. The Sharks repair the forward and aft Leyden cannons. They also manage to piece together two working torpedoes by cannibalizing parts from the others on board.

"They would have exploded in the bay if we'd tried to fire them at the *Aronnax*," Gem assures me. "So it's a good thing we didn't."

The next day, Halimah and Jack get the skiff operational and take it out for a spin. They manage not to crash or drown. Robbie figures out how to run Jupiter's *Great British Bake Off* Blu-rays through the LOCUS display in the galley, so our chef can watch Mary Berry in holographic purple 3-D (which is just as terrifying as it sounds). I discover that Captain Nemo's keytar can be synched with the bridge's pipe organ, so I can play music from anywhere in the ship.

"Or even outside the ship," Ester guesses. "That keytar thing looks waterproof. I bet you could broadcast music while you're in the deep."

Nelinha frowns. "Why would she want to do that?"

"I don't know," Ester says. "Because it's cool?"

That afternoon, I spend most of my time on the pipe organ. I don't plan it that way. I run through one Bach fugue just because the crew is curious. Most of them have never heard me play.

When I finish, I realize everyone on the bridge is staring at me.

"That was beautiful," Virgil says.

From the overhead speaker, Meadow Newman says, "Engine room. Hey, Ana? Keep doing that. Panels lit up down here that we haven't been able to get working before."

So I play another Bach piece. After that I play "Imagine" by John Lennon. A few tunes later, I get wild and play my favorite, Adele's "Someone Like You."

The bridge lights brighten. The keyboard seems to warm under my fingers. The notes come more easily, as if the organ is anticipating the tune.

Then the *Nautilus* joins in. She begins to play her own countermelodies. The song becomes even richer and sadder. I feel the submarine start to dive.

"Whoa," says Lee-Ann. "Depth now forty meters . . . fifty. Is it supposed to be doing this?"

My ears ring. The hull creaks, but I don't stop the song.

I have a feeling that the *Nautilus* and I are really talking for the first time. She's sharing her grief. . . . Maybe apologizing for what happened to my parents. We've both lost so many people.

When the song finally ends, my face is wet with tears.

At the helm, Halimah exhales. "We've leveled off at one hundred meters. Captain, I think the *Nautilus* likes Adele a little too much."

A shadow falls across the keyboard. I wonder how long Gem has been standing next to me. "That was amazing, Ana. You keep surprising me."

He offers me a linen handkerchief. Where did *that* come from? I wonder if he always keeps it handy, which seems like a very old-fashioned *Gem* sort of thing to do. Or maybe he just uses it to clean his gun barrels.

A few days ago, if he'd offered me a hankie, I would've laughed at him. Now, I take it and dab my eyes, grateful that my back is turned to the rest of the bridge crew. "Thanks."

He nods. "It's okay to be emotional."

I sniffle. Why is he being nice to me? And why is it only making me feel worse?

"I—" I get to my feet shakily, then set the handkerchief across the keyboard. "I'll be in my quarters."

Ester finds me there an hour later. I suspect she's allowed me that much time to pull myself back together after my emotional-wreckage mini concert.

Top jumps onto my bed. He knows the drill. When Ana plays sad music, the only remedy is dog-cuddling.

"That must have been hard," Ester tells me, picking at her thumb. "But it was important."

I nod glumly, though I'm not sure I understand her meaning. "The *Nautilus* and I were communicating, I think."

"Mm." Ester crosses to the far side of the stateroom. She presses her hand against the wall as if checking for hot spots. "It was more than talking. The *Nautilus* heals better when you play."

"Heals. Like . . . physically?"

Ester tilts her head. "Maybe that's the wrong word. But the pipe organ wasn't just made for show. The music—"

"It's a programming language," I realize.

Why didn't I see that sooner? I'm a Dolphin, specializing in languages. Yet I've completely missed the connection between language, music, and AI. Every time I play, I'm teaching the *Nautilus* new cognitive pathways, altering her operating system based on my input. Dread sinks into my gut like a bowling ball. "Have I messed up?"

Ester considers this question long enough to make me really worried.

"You've changed the *Nautilus*," she decides. "You've heard of imprinting?"

"Like when a baby duck imprints on its mother," I say. "They form an attachment."

"Or when another species of animal attaches to humans," she says. "Dogs, for instance."

Top thumps his tail. He knows the word *dog.*

"You're saying the *Nautilus* is my baby duck?" I ask.

"Or maybe you're the *Nautilus*'s baby duck," Ester muses. "Either way, you're connecting to each other. I think that's good. I guess we'll find out tomorrow."

"Tomorrow?"

Ester looks puzzled. "Nelinha didn't tell you? She wants you to go outside the ship and try something with the hull."

CHAPTER FORTY-EIGHT

"Leidenfrost," Gem says as we're suiting up.

He actually says it twice. The first time I don't respond, because I'm obsessing about my most recent nightmare. I was glued to Captain Nemo's chair while the bridge filled with green slime. . . .

"Sorry, what?" I ask.

"It's a kind of shielding," Gem says. "Different than Leyden guns. Leidenfrost would create a near-freezing sheath of water around the hull."

He sits on the bench across from me, connecting hoses to his antique dive suit. On the other side of the interior airlock door, Nelinha raps her knuckles on the window. "Red hose in the red valve, Twain," she says over the intercom. "We marked them for you. And Leidenfrost shielding wasn't meant for combat."

"I know, I know." Gem rolls his eyes at me. "Ever since she became a billionaire engineer, she's impossible."

"I can hear you, billionaire gunslinger," Nelinha says.

Gem grins. Among the many things I never thought I would see in this life: Gem and Nelinha joking good-naturedly with each other.

"Anyway," he says, picking up his helmet, "Leidenfrost was

designed so the *Nautilus* could dive in extreme temperatures. Like, she could theoretically plunge through an active volcanic vent, straight through lava, and suffer no damage."

"Wow." I stare at the exterior door that will lead us into the abyss. "*Nautilus*, what kind of adventures did you get up to back in the day?"

The sub does not answer, but I imagine her feeling smug. *Yeah, kid, if you only knew.*

"If we can get our Leidenfrost shield working," Gem says, "it might disperse energy weapons. Obviously, Nemo didn't use it that way. No other ships in his time had Leyden cannons. But I have a theory the *Aronnax* is using Leidenfrost and that's why it was impervious to Lincoln Base's electrical turrets."

I remember the fuzzy aura around the enemy sub on our LOCUS displays. "Okay. So how do we get it working?"

"I'll guide you," Nelinha says over the comm. "There's a damaged conduit just past the starboard aft bulkhead. I have a feeling it'll need that special Nemo touch, which is why we've gotta send you, but otherwise, it should be a simple fix."

"If we weren't doing it a hundred meters underwater," I say.

The *Nautilus* has stubbornly refused to budge from this depth, for reasons none of us understand. I can't shake the sense that she wants us to be in this particular spot, though there is nothing around us on the LOCUS but the yawning canyon of the Palau Trench.

"You'll be fine," Nelinha says. If I didn't know her so well, I might miss the nervousness in her voice. "We've pressure-tested the suits. They're better than anything modern navies could design."

Still, we'll be the first people to use them since the 1800s, at a depth where only the best modern technical divers with nitrox tanks should work.

The suit's mesh material doesn't cling like a wetsuit. It also isn't bulky like a typical drysuit. It's so light and flexible I can't imagine how it will provide any thermal protection. Nelinha tells me it's a nemonium weave. The texture feels more like a cashmere sweater than metal.

The air tanks are impossibly small and compact, no larger than a school backpack. Instead of fins, we have boots with squid-inspired jet propulsion (naturally).

The helmets are the most disconcerting part of the gear. The transparent spheres are made of the same pseudo-glass as the windows on the bridge. When I put mine on, I can breathe just fine. I have a great range of vision. But I feel like my head's in a fishbowl that smells like . . . well, a fishbowl.

Gem stands. He looks strange without his holsters, like his hips have suddenly gotten narrower. "May I?"

His voice comes through loud and clear in my stereophonic fishbowl. We check each other's gear, looking for tears, snags, loose connectors. We shoulder the toolkits Nelinha gave us. Finally, there's no more reason for delay.

"Okay, Nelinha," I say. "Flood the airlock."

It happens in the time it takes Gem to hum one chorus of "Someone Like You," which he seems to do unironically. We stand in the murky green water, waiting to see if our gear malfunctions. Better here than once we open the exterior lock and get exposed to the pressure of ten atmospheres.

Nothing leaks. I can breathe normally. The suit feels warm, dry, and comfy—so much so that I resent all the hours I spent training in uncomfortable neoprene.

Gem gives me the *okay* sign—the universal diver's signal that means, you guessed it, okay.

The moment of truth.

"*Nautilus,*" I say. "I'm going to leave the ship for a while. We need to inspect the hull."

I half expect her to respond like an overprotective parent. *And what time will you be home, young lady?*

I pull the release latch. The exterior door irises open with no problem.

I barely feel the pressure equalize: a tightening in the fabric of my suit, a soft pop in my ears. I curl my toes, the way Nelinha instructed us, and my jet-boots shoot me into the deep.

"Hey, wait up!" Gem's voice rings in my helmet.

The sound that escapes my throat is somewhere between a laugh and a roller-coaster scream. I've gone diving hundreds of times, but it's never been this exhilarating. I can move effortlessly. There's no breathing apparatus stuck in my mouth. I turn and rocket in a different direction, scattering a school of bluefin tuna. "This is incredible!"

Gem is laughing, too. He jets past on my left, his helmet glowing like a phosphorescent jellyfish. He tucks his knees and somersaults into the dark.

"Okay, you two," Nelinha's voice chides. "You've got work to do out there."

"Aw, but, Mom . . ." Gem says.

"Don't start with me, Twain," she warns, "or I'll take away your SIG Sauers. Now, if you'll both please make your way toward the aft of the sub."

We do as she asks, though it's difficult not to just float and admire the *Nautilus*.

She's breathtaking from the outside: elegant and stately with her frills, barbs, and vine-like wiring. Her nemonium hull catches the 1 percent of sunlight able to filter down to this depth, turning her a dim purple color that matches her great domed eyes. Unlike the hatchet-shaped *Aronnax*, the *Nautilus* looks like she belongs here—a gentle giant, a queen of the deep. I wonder if that strange sheath along her belly really does scoop up krill like the mouth of a blue whale to keep her fed.

We find the damaged conduit with no problem. As near as we can figure, the *Nautilus* must have been lying against a rock at that spot while she was on the bottom of the lake. Her self-healing hull wasn't able to do its job, so over the last 150 years she developed a kind of bedsore. I apply some thick healing paste to the area—a concoction the Cephalopods and Orcas came up with together—while Gem runs a new section of wiring to bypass the break.

"I am so sorry," I tell the *Nautilus*. I don't know if she can feel pain the way people do, but the longer I spend with the submarine, the worse I feel for her, having spent so much time alone, wounded, neglected. If humans had woken me up after all those years, I probably would have lashed out, too.

When we're done with the repair, we float back to what we hope is a safe distance, about twenty meters.

"Okay, Nelinha," I say. "You want to give it a try?"

"We're going to run two tests," she tells me. "First, we're going to electrify the hull. Then, if it goes okay, we'll try the Leidenfrost shield. Ready?"

The entire ship lights up like a carnival. The hull glows in a thousand different places—brilliant white, blue, and gold spots adding to the purple. Search beams arc through the water fore and aft, top and bottom.

One sweeps right across my face, momentarily blinding me.

"Gah!" I yelp. "Nelinha, is that supposed to be happening?"

"No!" she says. "Hang on . . . I don't . . . Bridge, did somebody hit the wrong button? Are we having a grand opening nobody told me about? Electricity! Not floodlights!"

Next to me, Gem whistles appreciatively. "It is kind of beautiful."

But something doesn't feel right. This much brilliance in the dark . . . What is *Nautilus* doing?

"Guys," I say over the comm. "I really think you should kill those lights."

"We're trying to!" Cooper Dunne says from the bridge. "I don't get it. We didn't even—"

The connection breaks into a garble of static and voices yelling at once.

"Contact on LOCUS!" Cooper yells.

Hairs rise on the back of my neck. "Where? A ship?"

"No, too big—Ana, Gem, you need to—" Cooper's voice becomes a shriek. "Below!"

I look down and see a gargantuan shadow rising from the depths, unfolding like the wings of death.

CHAPTER FORTY-NINE

Gem tackles me and jets me out of the way, but the creature isn't interested in us.

Eight tentacles the size of bridge cables wrap themselves around the *Nautilus*.

The submarine tilts aft. My helmet's comm fills with the crew's screams. As the monster's head emerges from the dark—I'm not going to lie—the interior of my nice, warm nemonium dive suit gets wet for the first time as I pee myself in terror.

I have been in the water with great white sharks and killer whales. I've seen big, dangerous sea animals up close, and I've never panicked. But the thing in front of us should not exist. It's a giant Pacific octopus, or closely related to one, except ten times larger than the biggest specimen I've ever heard of. Its full tentacle span must be fifty meters, half the length of the *Nautilus*. It must weigh close to a ton.

I am paralyzed by the thought of what those powerful arms could do to our ship. At the same time, I am awestruck by the octopus's beauty.

Its bulbous head makes it look like a supervillain with an overdeveloped brain. Its dark eyes are alert and curious. When it breathes, the siphons on the sides of its face plume to the size of jumbo jet engines. Each tentacle ripples with white-ringed suckers. Its skin is perfectly textured for blending into rocks and coral, though I can't imagine any coral reef big enough to hide this leviathan. In the dark water, it appears a muddy brown, but where the ship's searchlights hit it, the octopus's hue turns a brilliant red. It appears to be mottling, too, as if trying to camouflage itself with the multicolored glow of the *Nautilus*.

At last, my brain unfreezes. "*Nautilus*, status!"

"Octopus!" Cooper's voice crackles through the static. "On the ship!"

If we live through this experience, I will have to rename him Acting Captain Obvious.

Nelinha breaks in. "It's squeezing us. Hull integrity . . . I don't know if—"

"Electricity!" Gem yells. "That story about the giant squid!"

I know the one he means. In *20,000 Leagues*, the *Nautilus* gave a cranky squid some shock therapy to get it off the ship. Something about that account always seemed off to me, but before I can say anything, Cooper gives the order: "Electrify the hull!"

The sub's grand-opening lights go dark. A moment later, green tendrils of lightning flash through the deep. They dance across the octopus's skin, illuminating its membranes and backlighting its eyes. I expect the creature to loosen its grip. That *had* to hurt. Instead, it wraps its arms even tighter around the *Nautilus*. I can't see its beak, but I imagine it snapping, looking for purchase on the side of the hull.

"Gah!" Nelinha shouts. "Get off us, you creep!"

"Cooper, try another charge!" Gem says. "More power—!"

"No, wait!" My mental gears start to spin. "Cooper, belay that order!"

Gem's face is ghostly purple in his gumball-machine helmet. "You have a better idea?"

His tone isn't sarcastic. He genuinely *wants* a better idea.

"It likes the electricity," I say, silently cursing my own stupidity.

"SHE'S RIGHT," Ester joins the conversation at maximum volume. "Octopuses communicate with electrical currents. That probably felt *good* to it. To *him*."

Him?

Oh . . . right. Now I see that one of the octopus's arms doesn't have suckers all the way to the tip. Instead, it's tapered with flat, dark circular designs—the creature's reproductive arm.

"He's not attacking," I realize. "He's being affectionate."

"EEEEWWWW!" someone shrieks on board.

"Nelinha!" I call. "We need to tell Romeo to respect our personal space. That Leidenfrost shielding—give it one strong blast."

"But—" Her voice breaks. "Oh, I see."

"Right," I say. "Romeo needs a cold shower."

A moment later, white jets of aerated water erupt from the prow, sheathing the Nautilus and crashing into the octopus's tentacles like an avalanche.

Romeo shudders. His bulbous head pulses, probably from serious brain freeze.

"Once more!" I say.

Another blast, and Romeo lets go of the ship. He lurches away, spewing a cloud of ink so vast that it engulfs everything. I can't see Gem, or the *Nautilus*, or the octopus. The only sound in my helmet is my own ragged breathing.

"Cooper?" I call. "Anyone?"

Static.

"We're here," Cooper says at last. "We're okay. That was intense."

"Is the octopus gone?" Gem asks.

"Uh . . ." Cooper hesitates, perhaps checking his LOCUS displays. "Actually, guys . . . ?"

Before he can finish, the ink cloud dissipates and gives me my answer. Romeo has not left. He is, in fact, floating right in front of me, his giant eye reflecting my entire form like a full-length mirror.

Maybe it's my imagination, but his gaze seems hurt, offended, as if he's thinking, *Why did you do that to me?*

"Hey, Ana?" Gem's voice sounds unusually high. "How 'bout we don't make any sudden moves?"

I try to stay calm. This is surprisingly hard to do with a one-ton octopus in my face. If Romeo wanted to kill me, though, I would already be dead. He just keeps looking at me as if waiting for something. I consider the way he showed up as soon as the *Nautilus* put on her light show. I think about colors, and lights, and the electrical impulses octopuses use to communicate.

An idea comes to me—probably the worst one I've ever had. "Ester, can you hear me?"

"I'M HERE," she says in my helmet. "Ana, that octopus is really close to you."

"I noticed. How would you feel about suiting up and joining us?"

"Is that a joke?" Ester asks. "I have trouble telling with your jokes."

"No," I assure her. "I need my animal specialist. And bring the keytar, will you? I think I understand why the *Nautilus* brought us here."

CHAPTER FIFTY

As we wait, I try to keep Romeo engaged (probably a bad choice of words) by showing him sign language. I don't expect him to understand, but octopuses are intelligent and highly curious. I hope I can at least give him something to think about besides making another pass at our ship.

Meanwhile, I'm also talking on the comm, explaining my idea to the crew—that maybe, just maybe, our submarine *brought* us here so we could find Romeo.

Gem is the only one whose face I can see. He does not look convinced. "It's a stretch, Ana. How could the *Nautilus* know Romeo would be here? How long would an octopus this size live, anyway?"

It's a good question. From what I remember about giant octopuses, they only live a few years. Then again, no octopus this large has ever been discovered.

"I don't know," I admit. "Romeo could be ancient, or a descendant of octopuses who have always lived here. . . . At any rate, I don't think the *Nautilus* would have brought us here just to get us killed. I think, in her own way, she's trying to help us."

Romeo gives me no indication of how he's feeling. He could crush me easily, or chop me in half with his giant beak, but I try not to think about that. I still have his full attention. I want to keep it that way.

A-N-A, I sign for the tenth time. *I am Ana.*

I show him the name sign I've created for *Romeo*: the letter R, palm out, fingers crossed—a sign that could easily be made with two tentacles if he ever chooses to use it in a social situation with his monstrous octopus friends.

Gem checks the antique displays on his wrist control. "We have twenty minutes of air left, if I'm reading this gauge correctly."

That's not great news. At this depth, using unfamiliar equipment, we could easily find twenty minutes of air turning into ten, or five, or none, with no warning. We should be heading for the airlock right now, but I have a lot more work to do if I'm going to test my theory, plus there's this giant octopus staring me down.

At last, the ship's exterior lock irises open. Ester jets into the void with the keytar, like she's about to take the strangest rock solo in history. She must have put unequal pressure in her boots, because she ends up spinning head over heels.

"I HATE THIS," she announces.

"Relax your feet," Gem advises. "Okay . . . now, left and right boots at the same time, one quick burst."

She follows Gem's directions. Slowly, awkwardly, she lurches toward us. Her face looks even more shocked than usual, floating in its purple glass fishbowl.

"Oh, wow," she says. "Romeo's big. He's really pretty."

I'm thankful she likes animals, even huge scary ones. We don't need any more bladder accidents.

Ester floats closer and hands me the keytar. "Do you think I can touch him?" she asks.

"Well, I mean . . ."

She puts her hand gently on Romeo's forehead. His skin quivers and pales, but his muscles seem to relax.

"Okay." I shoulder the keytar. "Ester, I need you to watch Romeo's responses. If I do something wrong, help me change course."

"What if things go *really* wrong?" Gem asks.

His tone warns me how on edge he is. He has no weapons (thankfully), but he looks ready to drag me back to the ship or punch the octopus in the eye to give me time to escape.

"It'll work," I say.

I never realized how much of leadership is learning to sound confident when you're actually terrified.

In truth, I have no idea whether my plan will work. I don't know if I'm about to make a breakthrough in octopus–human communication or infuriate a one-ton lovesick cephalopod that could snap me like a twig.

"*Nautilus*, I need your help," I say in Bundeli. "I think you brought us here to meet your . . . your friend. If that's the case, help me talk to him."

As I'm explaining to the *Nautilus* what I want to ask Romeo, I realize how many things could go wrong. Just translating from one language to another is hard enough. I'm trying to talk to a Victorian-era AI in a rare Indo-Aryan dialect, hoping she can help me accurately relay a message to a creature from another species. But I have to try. I'm a Dolphin. I believe that communication can solve any problem if the parties have the will and the intelligence to learn to understand each other.

I turn on the keyboard. I test a few notes. As Ester suspected, the instrument works just fine underwater. Over my comm, I can hear the notes resonating throughout the ship. I can also feel the vibrations rippling outward from the hull, as if the *Nautilus* is acting as one massive amplifier.

I turn the keytar's color wheel. Romeo seems to find this fascinating. The lights reflect in his great dark eye like Christmas decorations through a rain-streaked window.

I hold a C chord. The notes synchronize with the ship's lights, turning the dark water an intense shade of indigo. Romeo's coloration begins to change, matching the blue. The sound waves are strong enough to rattle the seal of my helmet.

"Is it working?" Gem asks.

"Hold on," I tell him. "I'm still saying hello."

I play a verse of Adele, just to see how it goes. The *Nautilus* puts on her light show. Romeo watches my hands on the keyboard. His skin ripples with different colors, as if he's trying to absorb a new spectrum of information.

"I think he likes puzzles," Ester decides. "Try the Bach, something intricate."

Organ Sonata Number 4 is about as intricate as I can get without tying my fingers in knots. I turn the color wheel, setting it to brighter hues that normally wouldn't be visible this deep, then I start to play. The *Nautilus* obliges with bursts of red and yellow, more like Romeo's natural pigmentation. About halfway through the song, the *Nautilus* starts adding harmonic riffs.

Romeo responds with his own palette of colors. His enormous head pulses. Maybe I'm crazy, but I think the *Nautilus* is using my song to send a message.

I hope that message is not *Hi, buddy! I brought you lunch!*

"Ana," Gem says urgently, "we're almost out of air."

I end the song. The ship's lights fade to a gentle purple glow.

I float eye to eye with the octopus. I can feel my air supply thinning, starting to smell like hot metal.

At last, Romeo's tentacles undulate. His entire boneless mass compresses into a flattened lozenge shape, much smaller than should be possible for a creature his size. But octopuses can do such things. They are amazing creatures.

I laugh. My message has been received.

"Okay," I tell Ester and Gem. "Let's get back on board."

As we jet to the ship, Romeo returns to his regular form.

He floats there, apparently content just to be near the *Nautilus*, though he still looks a bit lovelorn.

The airlock drains quickly. That's good, since I'm sucking the last molecules of oxygen from my helmet. Thankfully, the nemonium suits are self-regulating, so we won't have to spend hours decompressing.

I'm just removing my helmet when Nelinha opens the interior door. She marches in, Top right behind her. The dog sniffs my suit, letting me know I smell like pee. Nelinha glares at me angrily. "Are you crazy, risking yourself like that?"

I give her a big wet hug.

"I love cephalopods," I tell her. "You, the rest of your team, and the giant one outside. You're all wonderful."

Nelinha scowls at Gem. "Does she have nitrogen narcosis? Did you break my Ana?"

"I don't think so," Gem says. "She was like that when I found her."

"That octopus is amazing," Ester says.

Top barks.

"Not as amazing as you," Ester assures the dog.

"Get the crew ready," I tell Nelinha. "I'll explain my plan. Then we're going to war."

CHAPTER FIFTY-ONE

The best lesson I ever got in military-tactics class wasn't even from a naval officer. It was an army saying attributed to Dwight D. Eisenhower, Supreme Allied Commander during World War II: *Plans are worthless, but planning is everything.*

That's how I feel, talking to my crew. We go over every possible scenario. I tell them what I *think* Dev will do. We come up with Plans A, B, and C, knowing we'll probably throw all of them out in the heat of combat. But at least the discussion helps us wrap our minds around the challenges we're facing. They are considerable.

Finally, I explain my ace-in-the-hole strategy, or more specifically, *octopus*-in-the-hole. After a full week of crazy stuff, the idea takes us to a whole new level of bonkers.

But the crew agrees that it's worth a try. If we can do it without breaking into a million pieces, all the better.

Three hours later, I'm on the bridge. All stations are manned. We've repaired our systems as best we can without dock facilities. We've got working dynamic camouflage, electrifiable hull plating, Leidenfrost shielding, and some really cool mood lighting. The fore and aft Leyden cannons are operational, along with two somewhat questionable torpedoes.

Best of all, our special cargo has been loaded into the sheath along the ship's belly.

Ester and Robbie return to the bridge after a visual inspection, both of their dive suits still dripping wet.

Robbie looks shell-shocked. "That was the most disturbing thing I've ever seen."

"You mean amazing," Ester says.

I can't believe it actually worked. I find myself grinning.

"Don't celebrate yet," Gem warns. "The extra weight may make it impossible for us to use the cav-drive."

"I heard that," Nelinha says from the engine room. "Don't bad-mouth my engines, Spider-Man. They'll do just fine. Captain, waiting on your orders."

I take my chair. I strap myself in with a newly installed alt-tech modification the Cephalopods call a "seat belt" (patent pending).

I open ship-wide communications. "All hands, this is the captain." As if they don't know me. "We've worked hard for this moment. You all know your jobs. We can do this. Assuming our course is plotted correctly—"

"It is," Halimah assures me.

"Our cavitation shot will be two hours forty-six minutes, exit point-two kilometers south-southeast of Lincoln Base. Brace for cav-drive. Stand by battle stations. We have to expect the *Aronnax* will see us when we arrive."

"They will," Gem mutters. "The cav-drive will make us light up like an explosion."

"Let's not talk about explosions," I say. "I'll need quick targeting resolution when we arrive, Mr. Twain. Watch that LOCUS."

He gives me a faint smile, then puts one fist on his chest and bows slightly. "Aye, Captain." He turns back to his console.

Not long ago, I would have assumed Gem was making fun

of me. Now, I realize he's offering me a genuine show of respect and deference. The rest of the bridge crew smiles in turn and looks to me for orders. It's time to go to work.

I square my shoulders. "Helm," I say, "set course."

"Course set, aye," says Halimah.

"Engine room." I take a deep breath. "Punch to cav-drive."

FOOOM!

This time I remain conscious, so I can appreciate the display. Torrents of air sheet over the prow, whiting out the windows like a blizzard. The extra g-force pushes me into my seat. The lights dim. The hull creaks and shivers, but the ship stays together.

"Engine room, status," I say, gritting my teeth. "Any injuries?"

"Status nominal," Nelinha says. "No injuries down here. Told you she could handle it."

The wait that follows is the hardest part. Almost three hours at heavy g-force is not fun. I feel like I have a walrus sitting on my chest. We can't move around or do much of anything except watch our control panels. It doesn't help that LOCUS displays don't work during a cav-shot, so we're essentially blind.

"Stay with me," I whisper to the *Nautilus*. "We're going to show our enemies what you can do."

I have to believe the *Nautilus* understands. She's attuned to my voice now. She's ready to fight. I just hope she has enough tricks in her arsenal to go up against a much newer sub. We're going to need every advantage we can get.

After a long while, the scent of oatmeal-raisin cookies wafts from the kitchen. How is Jupiter making cookies right now? And why can't I have one?

I make a mental note that in the future, cookies will be distributed *before* punching to cav-drive. Then I start thinking about ways to install drink holders for glasses of milk. . . .

Finally, Halimah gives me the news I've been waiting for: "Five minutes to termination."

"Can we please not call it that?" Ester asks. She's sitting at the back of the bridge next to Top, who wears a special harness in his doggy bed.

"Destination?" Lee-Ann suggests.

"Good," Ester says. "Destinations are good."

Top sighs heavily. He seems to agree that a destination would be great, because cav-drive is worse than being stuck in a kennel.

I open the comm. "All hands, battle stations."

As if I need to tell them that. They've been stuck at their battle stations for hours. I just hope we don't have an immediate line for the bathrooms as soon as we drop out of cav-drive.

"One minute to—uh, destination," Halimah says.

I drum my fingers against the armrest controls. I imagine us overshooting our goal and slamming into the Hawaiian coast like an alt-tech bug against a windshield.

"Five, four . . ." Halimah grips her controls. "One."

The blizzard of air disappears from the windows, and I'm looking at blue ocean.

The LOCUS holospheres flicker to life.

"Weapons online," Gem says. "Scanning for targets."

"Evasive course," I say. "Activate camouflage. Thirty degrees starboard. Make depth—"

The ship shudders as if we've passed over a speed bump.

"That was our payload deploying." Lee-Ann sounds relieved.

"Is the payload okay?" Ester asks.

I understand her concern. That was a long time at a lot of g's, but I can see the large blip on Lee-Ann's LOCUS, descending at a diagonal under his own power. I have to hope our large hitchhiker isn't carsick now as well as lovesick.

If we're lucky, the *Aronnax* will be moored in the lagoon or even the cavern. That will give us time to get away from our payload and the exit point of our cav-shot—using camouflage to obscure our position.

If we're unlucky . . .

"Contact!" yells Virgil. "One kilometer, twelve o'clock, depth ten meters. It's the *Aronnax*. They're right between us and Lincoln Base."

I curse. I didn't really expect Dev to let his guard down, even after a week. Still, the sight of that awful purple arrowhead on Gem's tactical display makes me hesitate a millisecond too long. The second smaller blip comes out of nowhere—right in front of our prow.

"Torpedo in the water!" Gem shouts.

I start to yell, "Leidenfrost—!"

The *Nautilus* lurches forward, almost jolting my head from my neck.

CHAPTER FIFTY-TWO

"Power is down!" Halimah yells. "EMP blast!"

I blink spots from my eyes. The bridge is dark.

Dev's voice comes over our loudspeaker: "Welcome back, *Nautilus*. Stand down and prepare to be boarded."

I hate how smug he sounds. He's been waiting to pull exactly this trick: disable us, then take us without a fight. The fact that I anticipated the scenario doesn't make it any better. I was hoping to have a few more seconds for evasive maneuvers. Now I have to pray for Plan C to work.

"Come on, *Nautilus*," I murmur. "Engine room, how is Plan C?"

"Little busy down here, Captain!" Nelinha says. "I managed to hit the kill switch before impact. Reactor is down, but hopefully our circuits aren't fried. If we can just— Aha!"

The engines hum. The bridge lights flicker back to life. LOCUS spheres reform over the control consoles.

"Yes, querida!" Nelinha laughs. "We have auxiliary power! Eat coal, *Aronnax*!"

The bridge crew whoops and hollers. Plan C is for *coal*. Our Victorian backup generator won't give us nearly as much power as cold fusion, but it's better than nothing.

"Da Silva," I say, "you are one brilliant Cephalopod!"

"Well, I'm a Cephalopod, so *brilliant* is redundant, but thanks, Captain. Now, if you'll excuse me, we have coal to shovel!"

In the background, Robbie Barr sneezes. "I'm the one shoveling, and I think I'm allergic!"

Gem's hands fly across his controls. "Captain, *Aronnax* is stationary, still one klick dead ahead. But I have secondary contact—a small submersible. Boarding party, probably. Five hundred meters and closing."

"As expected," I say. "Let's send them a message. Make ready torpedo one."

"Torpedo one ready."

"Target the *Aronnax* amidships. Fire!"

Our hull shudders as the antique missile speeds into the deep.

"Helm, hard to port, ahead full!" I grip my armrests as the ship tilts. "Dive, make depth thirty meters!"

The *Nautilus* seems to execute my commands before Lee-Ann and Halimah even touch their controls. We plunge and veer toward Lincoln Base, keeping the enemy skiff between us and the *Aronnax*. On Gem's LOCUS, our torpedo explodes off the *Aronnax*'s port side in a beautiful purple starburst.

"They weren't expecting that!" Virgil says. "I'm getting enemy chatter on the comm."

He puts it on loudspeaker: Dev shouting orders, six or seven other voices replying all at once. I hear enough to understand that Dev is on the skiff, demanding status reports from the *Aronnax*'s bridge. Then someone on their end cuts the transmission.

I allow myself a grim smile. Dev got overconfident. He figured he would just putter over on his skiff and take command of our dead ship. Now he's caught between the *Aronnax* and us, and we're very much alive.

I love their confusion, but I know it won't last.

"Make ready torpedo two."

"That's our last one," Gem reminds me.

"Yes, but they don't know that. Helm, thirty degrees port, full ahead. Keep that skiff between us and the *Aronnax*."

"Trying, Captain," Halimah says. "They're taking evasive action."

"The skiff is within cannon range," Gem offers.

"No." As much as I hate my brother right now, I don't relish the idea of possibly cooking him alive in a tin can. "Stay focused on the *Aronnax*. If we can target their propulsion—"

A *CLUNK* echoes through the corridors. The bridge lights suddenly dim.

"Hey, Captain," Nelinha breaks in. "We're stressing the old choo-choo engine. Maybe take it easy on the fancy maneuvers?"

"Just a little longer," I tell her, hoping it's true.

Our octopus-in-the-hole gamble has not paid off yet. Romeo is nowhere to be seen. I'm disappointed, but not surprised. I knew I was playing with things I didn't understand.

On Halimah's LOCUS, the enemy skiff is pulling away from us. The *Aronnax* turns her prow in our direction, trying to keep us in her sights. She seems to be moving sluggishly—or maybe that's just my wishful thinking.

"Captain, torpedo in the water!" Gem yells.

"Fire second tube! Rig for depth charge!"

The floor shudders as our last working missile leaves the tube. This time, out the bridge windows, I can actually see the white wake line cutting through the blue. I hold my breath. I watch Gem's LOCUS as two purple blips—our torpedo and theirs—hurtle toward each other. I don't need the LOCUS to tell me when they collide. The explosion rolls the *Nautilus* on her starboard side, her hull groaning like she's got intestinal distress. Only my newfangled seat belt keeps me from flying into the pipe organ.

Gem glances back, his eyes wide. "That was a seismic charge. If it had hit us . . ."

He doesn't need to spell it out. Somebody on the bridge of the *Aronnax* is getting angry—or possibly panicked. With or without Dev's permission, they are shooting to kill.

I make a fist. This time, the military maxim that comes to mind isn't from Eisenhower—it's from the Chinese general Sun Tzu: *Appear weak when you are strong, and strong when you are weak.*

"Helm, turn us about," I say. "Take us directly toward the *Aronnax.*"

Halimah and Lee-Ann both look at me like maybe they misheard.

"Captain—" Halimah stops herself, apparently tamping down her misgivings. "Aye, Captain. Bringing us about."

The ship groans louder as we level off and turn.

"Engine room," Nelinha says. "Captain, about that stress on the choo-choo—"

"I know, Nelinha," I say. "Just keep her together a little longer, please. Weapons, power up the forward Leyden cannon. Stand by for Leidenfrost shielding. Comm, can you open a channel to the *Aronnax* and its skiff?"

"Aye, Captain," Virgil says. "Channel open."

I press my hand against the armrest's control sphere, as if it can reassure me that I do in fact have Nemo's DNA. This is the first time I've spoken to Dev since his betrayal. It's the first time I've announced myself to our enemies. I can't have my voice trembling.

"*Aronnax,*" I say. "This is Captain Ana Dakkar of the *Nautilus.* Stand down or you will be destroyed."

Silence.

The hardest thing about making a stupid bluff is reminding yourself that your opponent doesn't *know* it's a stupid bluff. The *Aronnax* has seen us recover from an EMP blast. They've seen us fire two torpedoes. They won't know if we have any more. They won't know what other capabilities we might have.

I also have to assume they took some damage from our first shot. I don't expect them to surrender. Dev would never do that. But he might stall for time, giving his skiff a chance to return to the *Aronnax*. Until our cold-fusion reactor is back online, I'll take all the time I can get.

When Dev speaks, he sounds ready to snap. "Nice try, sis. But right now, I'm the only one over here trying to keep you alive. The next shot won't be to cripple. It'll send you all to the bottom. *Nautilus* crew, you know who I am. I'm the senior Dakkar family member. That ship belongs to me. *Stand down.*"

The bridge crew looks to me.

"Gearr an líne," I tell Virgil. *Cut the line.*

Gem turns. "They're opening forward tubes. Four of them."

My heart sinks into my gut. A spread of four torpedoes at this range—

"Leidenfrost shields," I order. "Fire forward Leyden cannon. Helm, evasive maneuvers—"

But it's too much to ask of the old choo-choo engine. A *CLANG* echoes through the ship like we've broken a crankshaft. The LOCUS displays flicker like candle flames in a breeze.

"Helm unresponsive!" Halimah says.

"Leidenfrost inoperative!" Gem adds.

"NO!" Nelinha comes on the comm, sharing a few choice curses in Portuguese. "I told you, Ana! I need more time!"

"We need more power!" I yell back.

But we don't have either.

On Gem's display, the purple triangle of the *Aronnax* looms closer. Dev's skiff hovers a few hundred meters off our port side, waiting to loot the carcass of our ship. Then a string of four smaller blips appears from the *Aronnax*'s prow.

We are about to be dead in the water. Literally.

CHAPTER FIFTY-THREE

I have one last desperation play. I slam my hand against the armrest console and yell, "*Nautilus*, emergency dive! Forward vents!"

The ship must hear the urgency in my voice. With her final gasp of coal-powered energy, she spews aerated water over the prow, whiting out the windows.

An emergency descent is one thing submarines do very well. Rather like giving up and collapsing, it doesn't take much energy. We sink like a rock.

On Gem's LOCUS, the *Aronnax*'s four torpedoes sail straight over our heads—their guidance systems confused by the cloud of air and ballast.

I start to say, "Rig for—" when the chain explosion detonates a hundred meters beyond our stern.

I black out from the shock wave.

When my senses start working again, the bridge is dark except for an electrical fire at Virgil's comm station. The LOCUS displays are dead. An acrid haze hangs in the air. Top is barking indignantly, still restrained in his doggy bed. Ester stumbles around, checking the bridge crew for injuries. Virgil sits dazed on the floor, his seat belt broken, a wisp of smoke curling from his hair. Gem has a trickle of blood glistening on the side of his face.

"All weapons offline," Gem says. "No shielding."

"No helm control," says Halimah.

"Depth forty-two meters," Lee-Ann reports. "I've only got analog readings, but the *Aronnax* . . . Oh." Her voice shrinks. "There she is."

She's not looking at her controls. She's looking out the windows.

For the first time, I see the enemy sub in person.

About fifty meters away through the clear blue water, the *Aronnax* looms over us. She appears smaller than the *Nautilus*, though much more sinister—a black triangle of death with zero sonar profile. Disappointingly, I see no damage on her hull from our torpedo. I doubt we look as intact or dangerous to them.

"Comm, can you pick up anything?" I ask. Then I remember Virgil is on the floor and his station is on fire.

The *Nautilus* responds to my request instead. The loudspeaker crackles. Garbled voices come over the line—Dev yelling from the skiff; a young woman's voice yelling back from the *Aronnax*'s bridge. Apparently, Dev is miffed about her decision to fire a full complement of torpedoes at near point-blank range. His prize could've been destroyed. *He* could have been destroyed.

My mouth tastes like the bottom of a barbecue pit. Dev isn't worried about me or any of the other lives on the *Nautilus*. He really *is* someone I don't know.

"Engine room," I say. "Nelinha, status?"

No answer. I can't even be sure the engine room is still in one piece.

Over the comm, Dev snaps at his comrade on the *Aronnax*'s bridge. "Boarding party on our approach again. Now back off, Karen!"

Karen's exasperated sigh could ignite kindling. "If the *Nautilus* tries any more tricks, I will blast her to pieces, whether or not you're on board!"

My bridge crew looks at me with a mix of desperation and hope. I must have another idea, another ace to play. Except I don't.

My heart compresses into a lump of nemonium. "Prepare for boarding. Issue Leyden guns to any of the crew still willing and able to fight. We'll have to"—I gaze out the window—"wait."

"Wait?" Ester asks, confused.

I fumble to unlatch my seat belt. I run to the giant bug's-eye dome to get a front-row view as our payload returns from the deep.

Why he chose this exact moment to emerge, I don't know, but the ways of lovesick giant octopuses are mysterious. Romeo's enormous tentacles wrap around the *Aronnax*, pulling her into an embrace. Our comm fills with screams from the enemy sub. I imagine her entire crew tumbling sideways into the starboard walls.

Romeo's bulbous head pulses with excitement as he shows his new friend some affection. *I've heard all about you,* he seems to be thinking. *You need a hug.*

At the same time, as if the *Nautilus* has a sense of humor, our cold-fusion reactor decides to come back online. The purple bridge lights glow. LOCUS displays flicker to life.

Nelinha's voice says, "Sorry, Captain. Still not at full power, but . . ." She falters, probably checking her external displays. "VIXE MARIA what—? Oh, YES, BABY! That's my cephalopod!"

Cheers echo through the corridors of the *Nautilus.* The bridge crew gathers around me to watch as Romeo drags the *Aronnax* down.

"I bet they'll try electrifying their hull," Gem says, "right about now."

The *Aronnax* does not disappoint. Green lightning dances across their hull, putting the glow of romance in Romeo's eyes. Our octopus friend squeezes even tighter.

"*Nautilus*," I say, "open a channel?"

She responds with a cheerful triangle *ding*. She's clearly pleased with herself.

"*Aronnax*, this is Ana Dakkar," I announce. "You need to abandon ship immediately."

"Ana!" Dev shrieks. "What is that? What have you—?"

I feel the implosion in my gut. Romeo snaps the *Aronnax* like gingerbread. Fire and sea churn together. Giant silvery air bubbles, some with people inside, billow toward the surface. Romeo has broken the submarine's heart.

My crew hoots and hollers, but I don't feel like celebrating. We haven't won anything if we take more lives.

"Ester," I say. "Gather the Orcas. Suit up and get out there for rescue operations. See if you can get Romeo to stand down."

She nods. "I can do that."

"They're Land Institute," Lee-Ann points out. "The people who destroyed our entire school."

"Yes," I agree. "And we're going to save them because we're *not* Land Institute. Lee-Ann, go with them to help."

She gulps. "Aye, Captain."

On their way out, they get Virgil to his feet and escort him from the bridge. Halimah and Gem return to their stations.

"Captain," Halimah says, "the enemy skiff has veered off."

"Picking up survivors?"

"No . . ." Halimah frowns. "They're heading for the mouth of the underwater tunnel."

I curse. I've been so focused on the *Aronnax*, I'd forgotten about Lincoln Base. I'd hoped that watching a monster octopus crush his ship would stun Dev into submission, but he's as stubborn as ever. He hasn't *completely* changed.

Knowing the way he thinks, I imagine Ophelia, Luca, Tia, Franklin, and Dr. Hewett are still being held prisoner on the island. Dev is racing to take charge of his hostages personally so he can use their lives as leverage.

I check Gem's readout. "Can we disable them—?"

"Cannons are still offline," Gem says. "Besides, it's too late."

The purple blip of the skiff disappears into the tunnel.

"Our people will be guarded," Halimah warns. "When Dev arrives, he'll dig in for a stand-off."

"Which is why we'll attack now," I decide, "before he has time to regroup."

Gem frowns. "Ana, the *Nautilus* is in no condition—"

"The *Nautilus* stays here." I put my hand on the console and continue in Bundeli. "*Nautilus*, I've got to try to save our people. If anything happens to me, protect your crew. They're your family now, whether they are Dakkar or not."

Halimah raises an eyebrow. Aside from me, she's the Dolphin on board who's most fluent in South Asian languages, so she understands Bundeli well. "You think the *Nautilus* will listen to us?"

"Absolutely." I hope I sound more confident than I feel. "Halimah, you have the bridge. Gem, you and I are taking the skiff. We're going after Dev. We're going to end this. Get all the guns you can carry."

Gem's smile makes me glad he's on my side. "I thought you'd never ask."

CHAPTER FIFTY-FOUR

Gem packs light.

He only brings his regular sidearms, a Leyden pistol, a Leyden rifle, and a bandolier of high-tech grenades he found who-knows-where. No flamethrower, and he hasn't dismantled the forward cannon to lug it along, either. For him, this shows great restraint.

I bring only a Leyden pistol and my dive knife. Still, the skiff is a snug fit, especially since we're wearing dive suits and helmets. We're not sure what we'll be facing. The skiff has no weapons or defenses. We may need to ditch it at a moment's notice. I suppose we could take the top off and make it a convertible, but this doesn't seem like the right occasion for a joyride.

Strapped in and sealed up, we flood the docking bay. The floor irises open and we drop into the blue. I ease forward on the throttle. The skiff responds like a Maserati. (Full disclosure: I have never driven a Maserati.) We zip toward Lincoln Base, following the LOCUS sphere's guidance system.

"They've had a week to set up new defenses," Gem muses. "Could be contact mines in the tunnel. Lasers."

"Maybe," I say. "But at the speed Dev raced through it—"

"Yeah," Gem agrees. "Dev tends to play an offensive game. Let's keep our eyes peeled anyway."

I glance over. I forget that Dev was Gem's house captain. Over the last two years, they've probably spent more time together than Dev and I have.

On the side of Gem's face, the trickle of blood has dried in a grim serpentine design. In the faint glow of his fishbowl helmet, his countenance reminds me of the bronze Shiva statue my dad used to keep in our family shrine: serene and vigilant, ready to smite evildoers by any means necessary. Maybe I can see some similarity between Gem, Dev, and Dr. Hewett after all—they all have the same aura of latent ferocity.

"When we get there," I say, "our first priority is saving the hostages."

"If they're alive."

"They will be." I force myself to believe it. "Otherwise, Dev wouldn't be racing back to the base. We do whatever's needed to free them, but we don't use lethal force unless we have to."

Gem scowls. "Define 'have to.'"

"Gem . . ."

"I'm kidding. Mostly."

We plunge into the mouth of the cave.

I wish I had time to appreciate how well the skiff handles. The adventures I could have in this thing! I wonder what Socrates would think if I showed up in the skiff to give him dance lessons and squid.

The thought of my dolphin friend brings me back to the present. Socrates is probably in the *least* danger of anyone at Lincoln Base. Still . . . I roll forward on the control sphere, pushing us faster through the tunnel.

As soon as we emerge from the lava tube, our LOCUS display flickers back to life.

"EJECT!" I yell, before I have time to process why.

Dev's skiff is waiting for us. A millisecond after I register it on the LOCUS, I see it with my own eyes: a black wedge bristling with weapons like the spines of a porcupine fish. It faces us from only fifty feet away, and behind its transparent front view shield, in the pilot's seat, is my brother.

Maybe it's something in his face, or just my instincts. I punch the emergency eject: simultaneously killing our engine, blowing the roof, and launching Gem and me out of our seats. It's a good thing we're already in dive suits. We hurtle forward, driven by momentum and our jet boots over the top of Dev's submersible as he fires a projectile at our now-abandoned skiff. The silver harpoon impales the seat where I was sitting a moment before, discharging a fractal lacework of blue lightning.

We sail over Dev's stern. Before Dev can turn to face us, Gem shoulders his Leyden rifle and fires two rounds straight into the submersible's propulsion system. Green flashes illuminate the engine casing. The propeller freezes. Deprived of power, Dev's sub lists to port and begins to sink.

"Should we pull out the crew?" Gem asks.

I am shaking with rage and adrenaline. Part of me wants to pry my brother from that heavily armed shoebox just so I can kick him in the groin. He wasn't wearing a dive suit when I glimpsed him through the window of his sub. It will take him and his boarding party time to either restore power or gear up and abandon ship, but I'm sure they'll survive. Dev is resourceful.

"The hostages are more important," I say. "We keep going."

We jet through the lagoon, stirring up clouds of luminous phytoplankton in our wake. As the dock's pylons come into view, gunfire rains down from above, the bullets punching white funnel clouds into the water before the drag and density stop them cold.

At five meters deep, we're safe from just about any kind of conventional ammo fired from the dock. Neither can we fire up at them with any success. Land Institute must know this. They're just sending us a message. *We're here, we know you're there, and if you try to surface, you're dead.*

"Under the dock," I suggest. "Come up behind them."

"Got it," Gem says.

But Land Institute saves us the trouble. Apparently, they're feeling like kids on Christmas morning. We're their presents, and they want to open us *right now.* The gunfire stops. Two divers plunge feet-first into the water, right on top of us, engulfing us in a tornado of bubbles.

CHAPTER FIFTY-FIVE

Underwater hand-to-hand combat is the worst.

It's like trying to fight someone to the death while wearing one of those inflatable sumo-wrestler costumes. Your movements are slow, cumbersome, and ridiculous. You can't get any muscle behind your punches and kicks. But since we can't zap our enemies point-blank underwater without zapping ourselves, Gem and I don't have much choice.

The nearest diver jabs me with his knife.

If I were wearing a regular wetsuit, I'd be dead. As it is, my nemonium weave deflects the point, but it doesn't spare me completely. The razor-sharp edge rips the fabric and grazes my ribs.

Salt water and open wounds are a painful combination. My left side seizes up. White spots swim in my eyes. Nevertheless, I use my boots to wrestle my attacker, pushing him backward into one of the pier's pylons. His air tank hits the post with a dull *clink*. I grab his wrist, stopping his blade an inch from my face.

To my left, the sounds of bubbles and angry grunts tell me Gem is fighting the second diver. I can't risk a glance to see how he's doing.

My opponent glares at me through his scuba mask, his eyes

full of hate. I imagine he's heard about the destruction of the *Aronnax*. He wants revenge.

I'm not going win a contest of strength against him, especially with my left side in agony. My Leyden gun is useless in close quarters, so while my enemy is focused on trying to stab me in the face, I grope for my knife instead. Before the diver realizes what's happening, I unsheathe my blade and stab him in the BC vest.

I don't have the strength to wound him seriously, but that's not my goal. With his vest's air bladder punctured, my opponent is blinded by bubbles. He starts to sink, instinctively releasing my wrist and flailing for balance. On his way down, I kick him in the face for good measure.

I imagine he'll be back, but in the meantime, I turn toward Gem.

Despite all his guns, Mr. Twain has gotten himself into a bit of a jam. The second LI diver apparently landed in the water *behind* him and has managed to wrap one arm around Gem's neck. He's now attempting to pop Gem's helmet to get at the tasty prizes inside. Gem struggles to free himself, firing one of his SIG Sauers next to his attacker's ear, but even for Gem, it's not easy to blast someone who's strangling him from behind.

I squeeze a burst of speed from my boots and zip toward them. Unfortunately, I slam right into the diver's steel air tank, which hurts me more than it does him.

At least I get his attention. The diver turns to face me.

I have time to register his blue eyes and the dark hair billowing around his face before he disappears as if ripped from the universe. A large silver blur slams into him with such force he seems to teleport sixty feet away in the blink of an eye.

Socrates has entered the chat.

He's brought friends, too. While he headbutts the blue-eyed diver into submission, three of the local bottlenose dolphins descend on the other guy, who has picked the wrong moment to reappear. It must be terrifying to have three large marine animals jump you all at once. The dolphins welcome him to the neighborhood with an extreme tail-fin smackdown.

Gem's voice speaks in my helmet. "I really love those dolphins."

"Dolphins are the best," I agree. "Much better than Sharks."

"I didn't say *that*."

I laugh, which sends hot needles jabbing into my side.

"You're hurt," Gem notes.

"I'm fine."

"That cloud of blood pluming from your suit says otherwise."

"Don't worry about it. We need to keep going." I give Socrates a quick *thank you* in sign language. Whether he notices or not, I can't tell, since he's still playing with his new diver toy.

Gem and I jet to the back of the dock. We surface cautiously, scanning above us, but as far as we can tell, there are no other hostiles waiting. Even the dragonfly drones seem to have abandoned the cavern. I hope they escaped on their own and weren't captured or destroyed.

Gem draws his Leyden gun. He guards me while I climb the nearest ladder. The effort is excruciating, but I make it to the top without passing out or getting attacked. I gesture for Gem to follow.

Once he's joined me, we take off our helmets.

"We really need to bandage that," he says, pointing to my ribs.

The bleeding looks a lot worse out of the water. I don't want to know how bad the wound is. "There's no time—"

"No time for you to pass out in combat, either." Gem peels off the top of his dive suit.

My face starts to burn. "Gem, what are you—?"

"It'll just take a sec." He strips off his T-shirt.

"But—"

He rips his shirt in half. "We can wrap this around—"

"Gem, not to kill your 'gallant knight' vibe or anything, but there's a first-aid kit in the cabinet right there." I point to one of Luca's many supply lockers.

Gem frowns at his ruined T-shirt. "I knew that."

We take cover as best we can between two of the supply sheds. Gem bandages me up with gauze while I keep watch. I do not at all feel awkward or distracted by the fact that Gem is shirtless while he's tending my wound. It's totally fine. Business as usual.

My eyes flit from the lagoon's calm waters to the vault door at the end of the pier. I'm waiting for Dev's damaged skiff to surface, or for more guards to pour onto the dock from the base. It's not a question of whether someone else will attack us—it's a question of how soon and from which direction.

"Good enough," I tell Gem at last. "Tie off the bandages and let's go."

CHAPTER FIFTY-SIX

The lagoon's vault door opens for my handprint. You can't keep a good Dakkar out, I guess. Or a bad one, since Dev was probably the last one to use it.

Pistols drawn, Gem peeks into the corridor. It's empty. I see no one standing guard at the other end, but that doesn't mean anything. Hostiles could be waiting in the room just beyond. The straight cylindrical passage will offer us no cover for fifty feet. Any sound we make will reverberate. Unfortunately, from where we are, this is the only way back into the base.

"Wait here, please," Gem whispers.

Crouching like a cat, he inches into the corridor. He's about twenty feet in when two LI students pop out from either side of the tunnel's far exit and fire their Leyden guns. They must have been lying in ambush, but Gem is ready. A nanosecond before they pull their triggers, Gem fires his SIG Sauers. Both guards drop like sandbags. Their miniature harpoon projectiles scrape trails of sparks as they skitter harmlessly across the walls of the corridor.

I have to remind myself to breathe. I can't decide whether I'm relieved or horrified. Did Gem just . . . ? No, those couldn't have been lethal rounds. I glance behind me, but the lagoon grotto is still empty. If Gem's gunfire didn't alert every hostile in the base, I'm pretty sure my pounding heartbeat will.

Gem crouches lower. He moves to his left, keeping his eyes on the far exit. No one else appears from the room. He creeps forward. When he reaches the opposite end, he sweeps the area with his gun sights, then kicks the fallen guards to make sure they're no threat.

"Clear," he calls to me, his voice low.

I limp down the hall, my side on fire. Blood is already soaking through the bandages. When I join Gem, I look down at the guards, both of whom have nasty red welts in the middle of their foreheads. I take the name of a certain Nazarene carpenter in vain.

"Please don't blaspheme," Gem says automatically. "I used rubber ammo. They might have nasty headaches when they wake up, but they won't die."

"How are you not in shock?" I ask.

"I've been in shock for days," he whispers, then points to the next corridor. "Aren't the security monitors in the room just ahead?"

Without further challenges, we reach the monitors in question. Why the surveillance room is not guarded, I don't know, but I suspect it's because Gem just shot the guards in the head. Gem stands watch at the door while I cycle through views from the various cameras.

The base is mostly empty . . . *very* empty. The armory has been stripped. Luca's gold-level boxes and alt-tech experiments have disappeared from his workshop. In the server room, Ophelia's computers are either gone or disassembled, their hard drives probably pulled. And in the sick bay . . .

An ice cube lodges in my throat. The patient's bed is empty.

"Where's Hewett?" I wonder.

Gem starts. "What?"

"Hold on. . . ." I toggle through more cameras, my fingers trembling. If I was wrong about the hostages, if they and Dr. Hewett were on board the *Aronnax* . . . I switch to the view of the front dock, and my shoulders relax just a little.

"There he is," I tell Gem. "Two hostiles are bringing his stretcher aboard the *Varuna*."

Gem frowns. "Why would they—?"

"Insurance," I guess. "They've stripped all the information and tech they can from the base. With the *Aronnax* gone, the *Varuna* is their only way out."

Gem's expression hardens. "And with Hewett on board, they figure we're less likely to attack the ship. What about the other hostages?"

"Not sure . . ." I toggle through more live feeds. "Oh." The ice cube slides farther down my esophagus. "Dining room. The good news is they're still alive. . . ."

Gem risks a look at the screen.

The bad news is our friends are being held at gunpoint. In the middle of the dining room, Luca, Ophelia, Franklin, and Tia are on their knees with their hands tied behind their backs. Two hostiles stand behind them with Leyden guns trained on their heads. Two more hostiles, also armed with zappy mini harpoons, pace the room restlessly, like they're waiting for orders. . . .

"Human shields," Gem mutters. "They take Hewett on the ship, leave the rest of our people here under guard. More insurance to let the *Varuna* get away safely. We have to take the dining hall, then reach the boat before it casts off."

"But if we go charging in there—"

Above our heads, the ceiling vent rattles. I almost leap out of my squid boots. Gem trains his guns on the levered slates. The head of a small metal insect pokes out, his glittery eyes like Fabergé eggs.

I laugh with relief. *"Pilot Bug?"*

I can't be sure if it's the same drone who guided our ship into the lagoon days ago, but it spits a festive electrical spark as if it's happy to see us. Then it buzzes out of its hiding place, followed by half a dozen of its shiny emerald insect friends.

"Oh, you beautiful bots!" I run a finger down Pilot Bug's back, making his wings flutter. "I'm so glad you guys are safe."

The bugs snap their mandibles and spit sparks, letting me know how they feel about LI taking over their base.

Gem shakes his head in amazement. "They must've been hiding in the ducts this whole time."

The ductwork.

An idea starts to tingle at the base of my brain. I look at the bugs, then the monitor, then the AC vent. "Gem, do you have any nonlethal grenades?"

"Sure, but why . . . ?" His eyes gleam. "Oh, I get you." He pulls one of his alt-tech baubles from his bandolier. "Pilot Bug, could you fly with this much weight?"

Pilot Bug's wings buzz indignantly. He spools out his copper tongue and coils it around the grenade.

"Perfect," Gem says. "One bug can carry; another can pull the pin. That's a short-burst EMP. It won't hurt people, but it should knock out anything electronic in an enclosed room. Pilot Bug, as soon as you drop it, you need to get away from there *quick*."

"Hold on," I say. "Will it work on their Leyden guns?"

Gem tilts his head. "I *think* so. Usually a thin metal sheath is enough to protect a piece of electronics. Our Leyden bullets are encased in carbonite inside a nemonium magazine. If we're outside the room when the blast goes off, our weapons might be okay. But theirs . . . those harpoons carry the charge on the outside of the projectile. An EMP blast should at least short-circuit them, make them less dangerous. It might even make the weapons malfunction altogether."

"*Might.*"

He spreads his hands. "I can't promise."

"We'll need something more, then. Something to disorient the guards . . ." It's difficult to think with my side throbbing and adrenaline jackhammering in my temples, but I recall how the LI commandos attacked the *Varuna* when we were leaving San Alejandro. "Gem, you wouldn't happen to have . . ."

Apparently, his mind is working along the same lines. "A Nemo version of a flash-bang?" He pulls another grenade from his bandolier and grins a very Shark-like grin. "Why, yes I do. And payback is my favorite dessert."

CHAPTER FIFTY-SEVEN

"WE GIVE UP!" I yell.

This seems like a good way to open negotiations.

Gem and I have pressed ourselves against either wall of the corridor, just outside the dining room. The door is closed, and it's a good thing I'm not standing in front of it, since the tip of a Leyden harpoon punches through the wood the moment I speak. The guards inside must be getting jumpy. Being left behind on an enemy base to watch hostages so their classmates can make a break for it probably isn't doing wonders for their morale.

"STOP FIRING!" I shout. "THIS IS ANA DAKKAR! I WANT TO SURRENDER!"

Silence from the dining room. No more harpoons pierce the door.

"Miei amici!" Luca yells from inside. "Run! Do not—"

"Shut up!" barks another voice, followed by an ugly *smack*.

"Leave my husband alone!" Ophelia shouts.

"HEY!" I yell. "HEY, LI, LISTEN TO ME! Or don't you want the credit for capturing me alive?"

There's a tense exchange of words among the guards. Apparently, this scenario was not covered in their senior-project playbook.

One of them shouts, "Open the door slowly. Show us your hands."

Gem meets my eyes and nods. It's not because he heard the guard. Unlike me, Gem has first-aid cotton balls stuffed in his ears, so he can't hear much of anything. But enough time should have gone by for our commando dragonflies to get into position.

"Okay, I'm opening the door!" I yell to the guards. "Don't kill me! I'm no good to you dead!"

This is the tricky part. Well . . . the whole thing is tricky, but I want the guards focused on my grand entrance, not on the hostages. I grip the door handle. I turn it slowly and start to pull the door toward me.

"I'm going to show you my hands now!" I lie. "Chiudete gli occhi!"

I say this in the same tone as everything else, so it sounds like just another concession I'm about to make. Even if the LI guards speak Italian, I'm gambling that the order *Close your eyes* won't make any sense to them in context, but Luca might get the message. And the robo-bugs will hear our agreed-upon code phrase.

It happens fast. From inside, I hear the *plunk, plunk* of two metal objects hitting the floor, followed by a confused "WHAT THE—?" because grenades do not normally fall from ventilation ducts. Then a tsunami of color and sound blasts from the dining room.

I think I'm mentally prepared for the alt-tech flash-bang, but I'm really not. Even shielded by a half-closed door, I feel like a three-day psychedelic music festival is being stuffed down my ears over the course of a millisecond. Fluorescent jellyfish dance in my eyes. I have just enough presence of mind to stagger out of the way as Gem pushes past me and bursts into the dining room, his guns blazing.

I stumble in after him, my Leyden pistol raised, but there's no one left to shoot at.

Our friends are still alive, though they've looked better. They're curled on their sides now, groaning and squinting. Luca has a black eye. Ophelia has a busted lip. Blood trickles from Tia's left ear. Franklin has just finished throwing up.

All four hostiles are out cold, spread-eagled on the floor, goofy grins frozen on their faces like they really enjoyed that millisecond concert before Gem shot them in the heads with rubber bullets. Their Leyden harpoon guns are all burning and smoking.

"Well, that worked," I note.

"WHAT?" Gem asks.

I point at his ears, reminding him about the cotton. Then I rush to untie our friends.

"Hello, there," Ophelia grumbles. "Lovely to see you again. Thank you so much for the grenades."

"Sorry about that." I pull my dive knife and saw through her zip tie.

"Quite all right," she assures me. "The *Nautilus*? The crew?"

I give them the brief version: The *Aronnax* has been destroyed, the *Nautilus* is banged up but okay, and the base has been cleared (for now), thanks to our robot dragonfly freedom fighters.

Luca giggles, his tone slightly hysterical. "Oh. Chiudete gli occhi! Now I get it! I think I may be blind!"

"It should pass," I tell him, hoping I'm right.

Franklin retches. "I can taste the color turquoise. Is that normal?"

"Ana, are you okay?" Tia asks. "Your bandages are soaked with blood."

"You should see the other guy." I don't mention that Tia, Franklin, Luca, and Ophelia also look like they've been worked over by the local gang of dolphins. "I'm sorry we couldn't get here sooner."

"You kidding?" Tia winces as I snap her restraints. "We were prepared to hold out for at least a month."

"Well, we could come back later. . . ."

"Now is good. Thanks, Captain."

"We need to get to the *Varuna*," Gem says, clipping Franklin's zip tie.

"Yeah." Franklin smacks his lips, probably trying to clear the taste of bile and turquoise. "They took Dr. Hewett. He was responding well to treatment, but he's in *no* shape to be moved."

"They've also taken our best research and tech," Ophelia adds. Without her steel-framed glasses, she looks a bit like a mole dragged blinking and disoriented from a nice dark tunnel. "They must be stopped. Go!"

"None of you are in any shape to fight," I fret. "And Dev could be coming in from the lagoon any minute."

"Are your Leyden guns still functional?" Ophelia asks. "Leave us some of those."

Gem donates his Leyden rifle to Tia, his Leyden pistol to Franklin, and his remaining grenades to Luca.

Luca beams. "I love grenades! Thank you!"

I hand Ophelia my pistol. This leaves me with just my dive knife and Gem with his SIG Sauers, but that will have to do.

"What about our friends here?" Gem gestures at the four unconscious guards.

"Oh, not to worry." Tia gets a wicked glint in her eyes. "I'm personally going to give them the pink-ducky treatment. Now get going!"

CHAPTER FIFTY-EIGHT

As Gem and I race through the front corridor, I try the comm on my drysuit collar. "Dakkar to *Nautilus*, do you read?"

The line hisses. "*Nautilus* here," Halimah says. "Are you okay?"

"More or less. Hostiles have the *Varuna*. They're making a run for it. They have Dr. Hewett on board. Gem and I will try to intercept. Do you copy?"

"We— Say again—?" The comm goes dead.

"Mine is out, too," Gem says.

With the amount of abuse our suits have taken today, I guess I shouldn't be surprised. Even if Halimah got the gist of my message, the *Nautilus* is in no shape to give us any assistance. We're on our own.

We burst onto the dock of the lagoon. The sunlight blinds me. I haven't been outside in the surface world for over a week. There's too much sky. The horizons are too wide. The colors are too bright.

The rev of a boat's engines shakes me from my paralysis. The *Varuna* is pulling away from the dock.

Gem sprints after it. He takes a flying leap and lands on the transom. My jump is not as graceful. I slam into the aft railing, which doesn't do wonders for my wounded side. Gem grabs my arm to keep me from falling overboard.

"Thanks," I grumble.

"Take a gun." He offers me one of his SIG Sauers. I have never seen him let anyone touch one of his precious twins before.

I start to protest. "Gem—"

"Please," he says. "Just do it for me."

I take the gun.

The *Varuna* picks up speed, heading north for the wide new gap that the *Aronnax*'s weapons blasted in the atoll's ring. From where we stand, I can't see anyone else on board. I hope that means the boat is lightly manned. I like small numbers, like one or two.

"Split up?" Gem asks, gesturing to port and starboard.

"That's always a mistake in the movies," I say.

"Fair enough."

Together, we make our way forward along the port gunwale, me leading, Gem guarding my six.

We reach the middeck. Still no one in sight. This feels wrong. The roar of the engines is deafening. I'd forgotten how loud the upper world can be.

I turn . . . and my question to Gem devolves into a scream when I see a familiar figure looming behind him.

Too late, Gem pivots. My brother smacks him across the head with a ratchet.

Gem collapses. Dev kicks his gun across the deck.

I step back, my heart in my throat. Gem's second P226 quivers in my hand like a dowsing rod.

My brother glares at me. His hair has its usual cowlick crest along the front, but I don't find it endearing anymore. It looks like something dark and menacing is trying to push its way out of his skull. Somehow, he must have repaired the skiff well enough to intercept the *Varuna*. Where the rest of his boarding party went, I have no idea, but Dev by himself is enough of a problem. Water trickles down the black neoprene of his wetsuit. It's the same one he wore the last morning we dove together—emblazoned with the logo of the HP Shark captain. I tighten my grip on the gun.

Dev sneers, tossing aside his wrench. "You're really going to shoot me? Go ahead."

God, I want to. I know the bullets are nonlethal. I hate that my trigger finger is rebelling against me. But Dev is still my brother. No matter what he's done, I find shooting him at point-blank range very difficult to manage.

"I thought so," he growls. "Stupid little girl, you've ruined everything."

Then he charges at me.

CHAPTER FIFTY-NINE

The two of us have had the same combat training, but Dev has had years more practice.

He grabs my wrist, slapping the gun from my hand, then steps in and twists, attempting to throw me over his shoulder. I use the "boneless toddler" defense, collapsing so my entire body weight works against him. He shuffles, off-balance, and I turn my fall into a backward roll, leveraging Dev's own grip to pull him with me. He sails over my head and crashes into the starboard gunwale.

One point for Ana.

My wounded side is on fire. I can feel warm blood trickling down my belly. I struggle to my feet. Dev rises, looking unperturbed.

"You're wounded," he notes.

He has the audacity to sound concerned. His earlier words still drip in my mind like hydrochloric acid. *Stupid little girl.*

"You've already lost, Dev."

"I don't think so. We've got enough tech and data now to make our next *Aronnax* a *Nautilus*-killer. And I don't think your friends will be bothering this boat with your poor sick professor on board."

He attacks with a flurry of punches that forces me back to the port railing.

I block, parry, and dodge, but my limbs are growing heavy. My head feels like it's floating on my neck.

I sidestep and trap Dev's arm, hoping to dislocate his elbow. But he knows that move too well. He sinks on one leg and sweep-kicks me off my feet. I roll out of the way and come up just in time to block his next kick.

He backs away, giving me time to breathe. "We don't have to fight, Ana. We're still family."

My weakness is making him calmer, kinder. I hate this about him. He likes me being his needy little sister—the junior Dakkar.

"Yes, we're family." I wince as I regain my footing. "Which is why your betrayal hurts so much."

I push him across the deck, determined to wipe that smug smile from his face, but he easily parries my attacks.

The *Varuna* speeds through the break in the atoll. The midday sun bakes my shoulders. My nemonium drysuit is light and flexible, but it was not designed for surface hand-to-hand combat. I am breathing hard, slowing down, wearing myself out. Dev knows it.

Anger gives me momentum.

I feint with a jab step, then land a punch to Dev's gut. My gym teacher, Dr. Kind, would have been proud. Unfortunately, I'm too dizzy to follow through. I stagger away, wheezing, while Dev cradles his sore stomach.

"I'm not the traitor, Ana," he says through gritted teeth. "Harding-Pencroft got our parents killed. HP could've used Nemo's tech a hundred times to save the world. Instead they kept it locked up. They shut us out of our inheritance."

I glance over at Gem, still lying facedown on the deck. His fingers are twitching, but there's no way he'll be battle-ready anytime soon. At least no Land Institute upperclassmen are running onto the deck to help Dev.

It's just me and my brother. Like old times. Except completely different.

"The *Nautilus* isn't our inheritance," I say. "The *Nautilus* belongs to herself."

"*Herself?*" Dev scoffs. "Come on, Ana. It's a machine made by Prince Dakkar. It belongs to us!"

He lunges, trying for a full-body tackle. I dance out of his path, though my "dance" is more of a clumsy stumble. My chest wound throbs. The inside of my drysuit is lacquered with warm, sticky blood.

"I thought about telling you," Dev continues, as if we're having a casual conversation, "but you weren't ready. You didn't know about alt-tech. You didn't understand what HP had done to our family. They still have you fooled. It's time to wake up."

I scream and charge. It's not my smartest move. I feint a punch, try to knee him in the groin, but he's expecting that. He blocks, then tosses me aside like a practice dummy. I land hard on my butt. Pain flares up my spine.

"Give it up," Dev snaps. "Don't be stupid."

Stupid little girl.

Behind me, my fingers close around textured metal. One of Gem's pistols.

"I'll admit, I underestimated you," Dev says. "That giant octopus . . ." He shakes his head. "You'll have to explain how you pulled *that* off. But you don't belong at HP any more than I do. We're going to board the *Nautilus* together, and you're going to surrender command to me. I *will* take what's rightfully mine."

Somehow, I get to my feet.

Dev frowns at the gun in my hand. "Come on, Ana, you had your chance to kill me. You couldn't do it, remember?"

Kill him?

Suddenly, I realize why Dev has been so uninterested in Gem's weapons. He assumes they are loaded with standard rounds. A laugh bubbles up in my throat. Dev has no intention of killing me. And he knows I won't kill him, so the guns are useless. It would never occur to my brother to use anything less than lethal ammunition. *Dev tends to play an offensive game.*

My hysterical giggle seems to unsettle him.

"Ana, you've lost a lot of blood." His tone is so caring, so brotherly. "Put that down—"

"You don't get it, Dev." I raise the gun. "What's *rightfully yours* isn't the sub. It's your family. Your friends. And you destroyed it all."

I shoot him three times. The last rubber bullet snaps his head back, raising an ugly red spot right between his eyes. He falls backward, crashing spread-eagled on the deck.

My hysteria turns to despair. I sob and drop the gun.

I'm not sure how long I spend weeping at my brother's side. He'll live. His pulse is strong. Still . . . I'm mourning. Something between us has died.

Nearby, Gem groans. "Ana?"

I wipe my face. "Hey . . ." Still wobbly, I straggle to Gem's side. He looks groggy and cross-eyed, but otherwise not too bad for somebody who was recently smacked with a ratchet.

I hold up two fingers. "How many fingers?"

He squints. "Twenty-five?"

"Yeah, you'll be fine."

"Is Dev—?"

"Taken care of," I say, trying to keep my voice from breaking. "I shot him with rubber bullets."

Gem's eyes widen. "That couldn't have been easy, Ana. Are you—?"

"I'm okay," I lie. "I'll be okay."

I try to help him sit up, but he groans and lies down again. "I think maybe I should just . . . stay here for a minute. Why has the boat stopped?"

I hadn't even noticed. The engines have gone silent. We're dead in the water. This means someone stopped the boat. Which means there are more enemies on board.

"I'll check the bridge," I say.

"You look terrible."

"Thanks. Don't worry, I've got this gun."

"It's a nice gun," Gem agrees. "Be careful."

I totter off. I imagine I'll be defeated if I have to fight anything more dangerous than a three-year-old with a pool noodle, but I have to secure the ship.

In the bridge, I get another surprise. Standing over the unconscious body of an LI upperclassman is a frizzy-haired girl in a nemonium dive suit, a Leyden gun in her hand.

"Ester?" I croak.

She turns, looking embarrassed. "So I got your comm message. It turns out dolphins aren't the only ones who can fit through that chute that leads to the tank in your cabin."

"I love you so much right now," I say.

"I know. I think you're about to pass out."

As usual, Ester is right. My knees buckle. She catches me as I collapse, and my consciousness sinks deeper than my body has ever gone.

CHAPTER SIXTY

I've always been better at making messes than cleaning them up.

We have some big messes to deal with at Lincoln Base.

The next two days, I am out of commission. Franklin and Ester hook me up to the machines in the *Nautilus*'s sick bay, which I'm told will slowly rehydrate me, replenish my blood supply, and ensure that my internal organs do not explode.

My roommates are Gem, recovering from his head injury, and Dr. Hewett, who actually looks better than I remember. During the professor's rare moments of semiconsciousness, he grumbles about his students' substandard quiz scores. I never wanted to know what teachers dream about. Now I do.

Franklin tells me that the *Nautilus* seems to have ideas about how to treat pancreatic cancer. He isn't sure what compounds the med-bay machines are producing, but they are slowly flushing the cancer cells out of Hewett's body.

Since Nemo understood DNA 150 years ago, I guess I shouldn't be surprised. But as I lie in bed, I have time to think about what Dev said—about how HP could have used Nemo's technology to save the world a hundred times over.

On the other hand, I've seen what Land Institute's hunger for power did to my brother. Humans are *still* not ready for all of Nemo's advances. I don't know what Land Institute's school motto is, but I want it to be *This is why we can't have nice things*.

As for Gem, he stays in the sick bay with me probably longer than he needs to. Even when Franklin clears him for duty, Gem says, "Maybe I'll rest here a bit longer. Head injuries can be tricky, right?"

Franklin frowns at him, then at me. "Yeah. Sure. Tricky."

I laugh, which hurts my newly stitched side. "Gem, you don't have to be on bodyguard duty anymore. I'm fine."

He glances toward the corridor, which may be the first time I've ever seen him take his eyes off a target. "Not a bodyguard. Maybe I could just, you know, stay as a friend."

A warm feeling spreads out from my sternum. I remember what Gem told me days ago, in Lincoln Base's sick bay: *I don't have many connections. So the ones I do have are important.*

I realize I am now included in that very small group of important connections, and I wouldn't have it any other way.

"Of course," I say. "I'd welcome your company."

Franklin starts to protest, "But Gem's injuries aren't even—"

"Franklin," Gem and I say in unison.

"Right," grumbles the medic. "I'll go get some lunch."

Our other casualties from the battle are, fortunately, minor. There were no deaths on either side, which in itself is a miracle. Thanks to the Orcas' quick efforts, the entire crew of the *Aronnax* was rescued. Many of them were wounded. Some nearly drowned. Most will have chapodiphobia for the rest of their days, but they will all live. Battered and shocked, they offered no resistance as my crew herded them into Lincoln Base's improvised holding cells.

On the fourth day after the battle, I feel good enough to go diving.

I find our giant friend Romeo tucked away in a cozy abyss

just south of the island. He comes up to say hello when I play my keytar. I do my best to convey our gratitude. I also try asking if he wants us to give him a ride back to where we met him, but he seems content to stay with us.

Over the next few days, whenever Ester and Top take a walk around what's left of the atoll, Romeo surfaces and watches them, while Top barks happily and goes into his "play bow." I have nightmares about Romeo learning to play fetch with the dog, throwing a ball all the way to Fiji, and Top trying to swim after it.

As for Socrates, he doesn't seem sure what to make of the giant octopus. Socrates likes his cephalopods small and tasty, not big enough to eat *him*. He and the rest of his adopted dolphin family give Romeo a wide berth, but otherwise they seem happy. I feed them many delicious squid and thank them for their help in the battle.

When Socrates asks about my brother—doing a little flick of his fin that I've learned to translate as *Dev*—I don't know what to tell him. At least underwater I can cry as much as I want. The ocean doesn't care about a few more drops of salt water.

Once the *Nautilus* is back up and running, Tia Romero oversees our recovery efforts on the wreckage of the *Aronnax*. It will take weeks to complete, but we need to understand how far Land Institute has come in their research. Also, we don't want all that junk littering the ocean floor on our front lawn.

On the fifth day, we set our prisoners free—all of them except Dev. It's not a popular decision. They're still our enemies, with too much blood on their hands, but we aren't set up to run a prison camp indefinitely, and there's no easy way to bring Land Institute to justice or to prove what they've done in any court of law. The best bad choice I have is to let them go, knowing that we may face them again in the future. I give them the *Varuna*, though it hurts me to do so. We stock the boat with enough food, water, and fuel to make it to the California coast. We strip the ship of anything dangerous or valuable—weapons, LOCUS, dynamic camouflage. We even remove the books from the library.

Honestly, our hostages shouldn't complain. We've been treating them well and feeding them Jupiter's baked delicacies. They've all put on a few pounds. They'd never admit it, but I suspect they will miss the gâteau mille-feuille d'orang-outan.

Caleb South is indignant when I give him command of the *Varuna*. "Why would you do this? You're just letting us go. And we know where your base is."

"Yes, you do," I say. "You also know what happened when you tried to take us on. Twenty of our freshmen beat your entire senior class. You want a rematch, come on back."

His eye twitches, but he says nothing. A few minutes later, I watch my first command ship motor out of the lagoon.

"You think it was smart to goad him like that?" Gem asks.

Nelinha makes a face. "It was *perfect*. Let them come back if they dare."

I suspect that's mostly bravado on her part. Nobody wants a repeat of what we just went through. But Nelinha has earned the right to boast a little. We won a hard victory. All my friends should feel good about what we've accomplished.

The next day, Dr. Hewett is able to move around with the help of a walker. I take him to the pier in the cavern, which he has never actually seen. We admire the glowing green robo-bugs zipping overhead, and the luminous phytoplankton festival in the water. Most of all, we admire the *Nautilus*.

Hewett is dressed in an old blue bathrobe and pajamas. His face is still haggard. His white hair is like a greasy tuft of cotton just burst from the pod. But he's alive, and he doesn't stink. I take those two things as signs of progress.

"Ana, you've done better than I ever imagined," he tells me.

I study his face. He's never called me Ana before.

"Is that a compliment?" I ask carefully. "I'm not sure how well you imagined me doing."

He wheezes. "Oh, please don't make me laugh. It hurts. No, Prefect . . . *Captain* Dakkar. I always knew you were capable of greatness. I am sorry I did not show you that, or extend you the respect you deserved."

I narrow my eyes. "But?"

"No *but*," he assures me. "It's true that Dev was everyone's focus, including mine. I worried he was too impetuous, too angry, too . . . Well, too much like me, and like the students I taught at Land Institute. That's why I tried so hard to counsel him. Still, I never imagined he would . . ." Hewett shakes his head sadly. "At any rate, *you* were the one we should have been preparing for command. Despite insufficient training, in the midst of utmost tragedy, look what you have accomplished." He gestures at the *Nautilus*. "Have you decided what we will do next?"

My feet feel glued to the dock. "*We?* Is that really my decision?"

Dr. Hewett arches his shaggy eyebrows. "Oh, yes. You are Captain Nemo now. The *Nautilus* has accepted you. The remaining students have accepted you. And the faculty . . . what remains of us . . . we have seen your potential. We will assist you, continue your training if you wish. But you will set our course. Whatever you decide, we are here for you."

I'm grateful to hear this, but I also feel strangely uneasy. I wonder if this is what it means to be a leader, and if the doubts ever go away.

"I have to talk to Ester," I tell him. "And the rest of the class, of course. But, yes, I think I know what happens next. . . ."

CHAPTER SIXTY-ONE

The answer is dinner.

The answer is always dinner.

First, I check with Ester. She is in complete agreement with my plan. Then I run my ideas past Gem and Nelinha. They are both on board. Nelinha's only comment is "Of course. Duh."

Top listens and wags his tail, which either means he loves the way I think, or he wants a treat.

That night, the entire crew gathers around the dining table in the main hall of Lincoln Base. *The Great British Bake Off* is playing in the background—our comfort soundtrack of choice. Jupiter waddles around, handing out plates of crespelle alla fiorentina. The wafer-thin pancakes are made from porphyra flour and buttery-tasting algae oil. The "ricotta-and-spinach" filling is carrageen-moss extract and seaweed. The sauce . . . You know what? I don't care. I'm just going to eat it, because it tastes good.

Luca regales the crew with stories about how he resisted the Land Institute attack on the island. We've already heard them a dozen times, but each time they get more elaborate. Ophelia just shakes her head and smirks, occasionally pulling her husband toward her and kissing him.

"I have married a brilliant man who is also an idiot," she muses. "How is this possible?"

After we've finished our main course, I ask Gem to turn down *The Great British Bake Off*. I clink a fork against my glass to get everyone's attention. I rise, because this feels like something I should stand up for.

"Crew of the *Nautilus*," I say, "freshman class of Harding-Pencroft, we're only alive today because of your brilliance and bravery."

Nelinha raises her glass. "Here's to being alive!"

This gets some laughs. Glasses are clinked.

When the noise dies down, I forge ahead. "Now we have choices to make. I know that many of you . . ." My voice falters. "Many of you have families on the mainland. You'll want to let them know you're still alive, probably spend the summer at home. After what we've been through, some of you may decide you're done with this craziness and you want a normal high school experience."

"*Normal?*" Franklin mutters, like it's the worst insult he can think of.

"If so," I continue, "I support your choice. You can take your share from the *Nautilus*'s treasury and go your own way, no hard feelings."

Halimah leans forward. "Or?"

Except for Mary Berry waxing poetic about oven temperatures in the background, the room is completely silent.

"*Or* we keep working together," I say. "I love this team. I also know that Land Institute isn't done. They'll keep researching. They'll build a new sub. They'll keep coming for the *Nautilus*. They'll be more determined than ever, especially if they think they've destroyed the only other school that stood in their way."

My classmates murmur. Their expressions have turned grim. That tends to happen when anyone mentions Land Institute.

"So Ester and I have been talking," I say. "We considered starting something completely new—a clean slate. We all know that Harding-Pencroft wasn't perfect. Too many secrets. Too little trust in the students."

Luca coughs. "This is awkward."

"She's right, though," Ophelia adds.

"But," I say, "Harding-Pencroft did a lot of things *right*. Nemo chose them to carry on his legacy. I don't want to throw out a hundred and fifty years of tradition. Besides, we're going to need new generations of students to help keep LI at bay. And those students will need training. Also, since the *Aronnax*—since *Dev* sent HP a warning before the attack, it's possible some of our classmates and teachers got out alive. If so, they might be in hiding, afraid for their lives. We need to find them and help them. And we have, well, almost unlimited funds. Because of all that . . . Ester?"

Ester stands. She's gone almost red as the pomodoro sauce. "I want to rebuild Harding-Pencroft."

"Volume, babe," Nelinha says.

"Sorry."

"No." Nelinha grins. "I mean say it LOUDER!"

Ester frowns in consternation, then screams at the top of her lungs, "I WANT TO REBUILD HARDING-PENCROFT!"

The crew cheers. Several Sharks pound their fists on the table, much to the annoyance of Jupiter, who is trying to serve the tiramisu.

"IT WON'T BE EXACTLY THE SAME," Ester continues.

"Now you can bring down the volume," Nelinha advises.

"We'll have better defenses," Ester says. "Maybe we won't build quite so close to the cliffs."

Lots of nodding.

"We'll honor my ancestor's wishes," Ester says. "And Ana's ancestor's, obviously. Our tech has to stay out of the hands of governments and corporations. It *definitely* has to stay out of Land Institute's possession. But from now on, we'll use the *Nautilus* to train. We'll use Lincoln Base, too. We can go back and forth from California easily now."

Tia whistles appreciatively. "Sophomore year is starting to sound interesting."

"We keep training," I say. "We keep fighting LI. We keep learning about Nemo's tech. We know he had at least a dozen secret bases, and Ester thinks there are more still undiscovered. Who knows what we'll find? And we haven't even scratched the surface of what the *Nautilus* can do once we get her in prime shape." I glance around at my crew. "We will be the first class of HP to actually *crew* Captain Nemo's ship. Can you imagine how much we'll have learned by the time we graduate?"

"Enough to scare the holy bejabbers out of Land Institute," Nelinha says.

"But I'm not going to lie," I conclude. "It'll be a tough three years ahead of us. Rebuilding everything. Always looking over our shoulders for another attack. Those who are interested in staying, maybe just a show of hands . . ."

I hope about half of them will stay. For me, and for Ester, it's not really a choice—it's our destiny. But for the others . . . They could walk away and have normal lives, along with a robust chunk of change for their college savings accounts.

Instead, every hand goes up.

Gem makes a show of counting votes. "I think it's unanimous. My only question is what's next, Captain?"

"To Harding-Pencroft!" Nelinha yells.

"To Harding-Pencroft!" the crew responds. "To Captain Nemo!"

I share in the toast and the laughter. I am overwhelmed with love and gratitude for my friends. But in the back of my mind, I'm also pondering Gem's question: *What's next?* Because there's one conversation I still need to have, and it will be the hardest of all.

CHAPTER SIXTY-TWO

Dev paces restlessly in his cell.

I suppose I can't blame him. It's been two weeks. As nice as the former guest room is, he must be getting stir-crazy.

He stops when he sees me. He's wearing khaki shorts and one of Luca's old T-shirts that says UMBRIA JAZZ '09. He's gripping his arms, probably freezing, as usual.

"You're here." He tries to look angry, but his lower lip quivers. I can tell he's on the verge of tears. This hurts even worse than the insults he's thrown at me on my previous visits.

He marches to the grate across the doorway and grips the top of it with his fingers. He hangs there like Jupiter might. The barrier was created by the Cephalopods from nemonium mesh. It's light and flexible, but Dev could never get through it, especially since he has nothing more dangerous in his room than a pillow and a roll of toilet paper.

"You need me, you know."

I was anticipating a lot of things he might say, but that wasn't one of them. "Do I?"

"You're going after them, aren't you? If you attack Land Institute, you'll need somebody who knows their campus, their security, their people."

I stare at him, trying to find the Dev I used to know. "You're offering to *help* us?"

"It's better than staying in here forever." He shakes the grate. I've never known him to be claustrophobic, but now I'm starting to wonder. He seems panicky, lost, scared. "Let's cut a deal. I help you, you let me go. You—you'll never see me again, I swear."

His words are crushing my heart, but I try not to show it. I shake my head. "No deal."

"Ana, please . . . I . . . What do you want? You let the others go. I can't stay in this box forever. You're not that cruel."

"Maybe not. But you'll have to do something else if you want your freedom."

He tilts his head, no doubt anticipating some kind of trap. "What?"

I wave at the security camera in the corridor. The grate slides open.

"I have something to show you," I tell Dev. "Come on."

He laughs incredulously. "You'll just let me walk out of here?"

"For the moment," I say.

"Where are your guards?"

"No guards," I say. "I asked everyone to stay clear. It's just you and me." I raise an eyebrow. "If you want to try to overpower me, go ahead."

Most animals, including humans, can sense fear. They can smell weakness. I am terrified, of course, but I guess I do a good enough job hiding it. Dev steps over the threshold cautiously, as if I might attack *him*.

"This way." I turn and lead him down the corridor.

My shoulder blades tingle. I can sense my brother glaring at my back, thinking about different ways he could knock me unconscious and escape. I'm not at all certain he won't try. But this is something I have to do. It will only work if I act like I'm completely in command—even if that's not how I feel.

We stop at the vault door that leads to the lagoon.

"Go ahead." I gesture to the lock. "It'll still respond to your DNA."

His eyes glitter coldly. "Now I *know* this is a trick. You're letting me near the *Nautilus*? What did you do, program the door to shock me? Teach me a lesson?"

I feel so heavy and sad I can barely shake my head. "No tricks. No shocks. We're not Land Institute, Dev. Neither are you."

He frowns, then places his hand on the panel. The internal mechanisms click and release. The door swings open.

Inside the cavern, green metal dragonflies swirl lazily overhead. Docked at the pier, in the multicolored light of the phytoplankton clouds, the *Nautilus* glimmers like an alt-tech mirage. The bristles, wiring, and complex quilt-work of her hull no longer seem strange to me. She looks like home.

Dev inhales sharply. He's only ever seen the *Nautilus* under-water and from a distance, or as a glowing blip on the *Aronnax*'s readouts. Now, seeing her up close for the first time . . . Well, I remember how that felt.

"She's beautiful," he murmurs. His tone is a mix of envy and wonder.

Near our feet, Socrates breaks the surface of the water. He chatters furiously at Dev.

"Hey, buddy." Dev's voice turns ragged. He crouches at the edge of the pier.

Socrates continues to excoriate him.

Dev looks sheepishly at me. "I can guess what he's saying."

"He's not happy with you," I agree.

Dev nods morosely. I trust him not to hurt Socrates, at least. Even if Dev could convince himself to destroy our entire school, intentionally doing harm to someone who loves you, face-to-face . . . that's much harder. We are not abstract things for Dev to hate. We're his family. I need him to see the difference, to *feel* it.

"I don't have anything for you, Socrates." Dev's hollow expression makes me suspect he doesn't just mean food. He means he doesn't have any explanations, or any apologies that would hold weight.

I open the nearest cabinet, pop Luca's ice chest, and grab a frozen squid. I offer it to Dev.

He looks at the *Loligo opalescens* like it has fallen from another dimension. I imagine, like me, he's remembering the last time we stood together, ready to feed Socrates.

He tosses the squid. Socrates snaps it up, because no matter how angry a dolphin is, he will not turn down food. Socrates lets out another scathing tirade of dolphin insults, then turns tail to leave, splashing us both as he submerges.

Dev lowers his head. "Okay. I get it. This is the punishment. The cell was better."

"No, Dev," I say, my voice turning stern. "We're not done. We're going inside the *Nautilus*."

CHAPTER SIXTY-THREE

Before we even reach the bottom of the staircase, Dev's hands are shaking.

He stands awestruck in the entry chamber, unsure where to focus his gaze.

I address the ship in Bundeli. "*Nautilus*, this is Dev. I told you about him."

The ship hums. The lights brighten.

Dev stares at me. At this point, I am pretty sure any thought he had about attacking me is gone. He's feeling too overwhelmed, too vulnerable.

"The ship is voice-controlled?" he asks. "In Bundeli?"

"No, Dev," I say calmly. "She's not *controlled* at all. She's alive."

"Alive . . . ? No, that's not . . ."

The *Nautilus* shifts under our feet. A subtle message. *Listen to your sister, boy.*

"Come," I tell him.

He follows me to the bridge.

"My god . . ." He runs his hand over the back of the captain's chair. He gawps at the pipe organ, the great eye windows, the

LOCUS orbs glowing over the control consoles. "Why are you letting me see this, Ana? Is this my punishment?"

He sounds bitter, yes, but there's more to it. I think he's starting to realize what he's lost . . . and it isn't just the *Nautilus*. It's HP. His own future. Maybe even me.

"I wanted you to meet her," I say. "And also to show you something. *Nautilus* has heard about you. You're a Dakkar. If you like, you can try to give her an order."

He looks at me skeptically, but his eyes gleam with desire.

"*Nautilus*," he says at last. His Bundeli is rustier than mine, but he gives it a try. "I'm Dev Dakkar. I . . . was supposed to be your captain. Will you dive for me? Set depth at five meters."

Nothing happens.

I think Dev expected this. His shoulders slump, nonetheless. "You've locked me out."

"No," I say. "The *Nautilus* just doesn't trust you. You insulted her, tried to capture her."

He frowns, dismayed. "Ana . . . I know the story. This ship killed our parents."

The bridge's lighting turns a shade of violet.

"This ship," I say, "was left sitting on the bottom of the lagoon for a century and a half. She was angry and only half-functioning. She lashed out. Now she's grieving, just like we are."

"Grieving . . ." Dev sounds like he's trying to remember the word. "Have you really forgiven the ship?"

"I'm working on it," I say, which is the truth. Dev and the *Nautilus* deserve nothing less. With my eyes still locked on my brother, I give the ship a command I've been avoiding since I first stepped on board. "*Nautilus*, take us to the bottom of the lagoon, please. Show us the gardens."

Immediately, the engines hum. The moorings retract. Water laps over the great windows as we submerge.

We sink slowly, almost reverently, into the dark center of the old volcano.

"What are the gardens?" Dev asks warily.

"We'll see," I tell him.

I walk to the prow and stare out the windows. After some hesitation, Dev joins me.

We watch in silence until the *Nautilus* comes to a stop, hovering in the deep. She switches on her forward lights. Before us stretches a seascape of a thousand different marine plants: orchards of kelp that ripple orange in the submarine's light, thick fields of purple moss, rows of bright-green sea-grape bushes. Some of the plants seem to be there only for decoration, dotted with strange flowers that could be anemones, or orchids, or something from another planet, blooming in shades of violet and red.

Dev swallows. "It's beautiful."

"The gardens are where our parents found the *Nautilus*," I say. "It's also where Luca and Ophelia scattered the ashes of the dead. Prince Dakkar is here. Mom and Dad, too." I look at my brother. "We never got to say good-bye properly. I thought you might want to. I know I do."

The trembling becomes too much for him. He falls to his knees. He begins to shake and cry, letting out years of anger and sorrow. I hope he's letting out some of his bitterness, too. I remember a little boy dancing through the botanical gardens with his sparkler on a summer evening. I remember my parents sitting together, looking out contentedly over the sunflowers and baby blue eyes.

I can't trust Dev. I don't know if I'll ever be able to, but I do love him. He's still my brother. Maybe he can start to realize what he has done, and how far he needs to climb to come back to me. I have to be strong for him, as I was for my crew. I stand over him as he cries, and I watch the flowers of the sea changing color in the light of the *Nautilus*.

I say good-bye to my mother and father.

I say a prayer for my brother, and for the future. I will not give up on either of them.

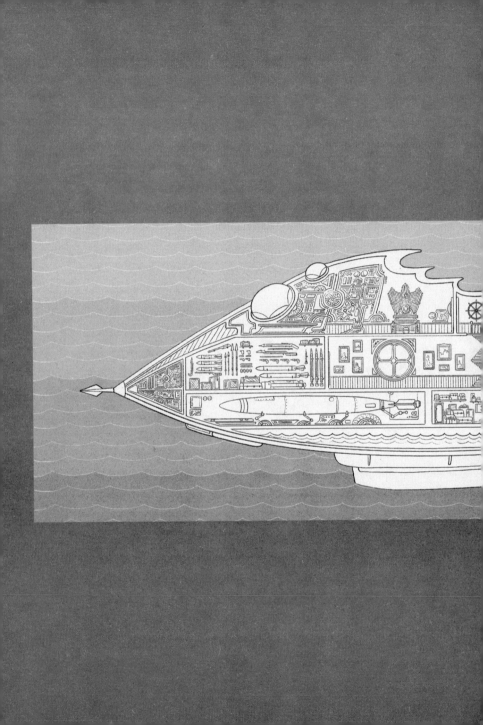

THE GREEKS AREN'T
THE *ONLY* GODS IN TOWN.

Follow @ReadRiordan

thrilled to be doing so. "This whole place feels like my soul," Nico joked to Will. "You know, empty and dark."

Will swallowed down some chicken kebabs. "You're not empty," he said, then pointed the skewer at Nico. "You are definitely dark, though."

"Dark as the pits of the Underworld."

Will looked down, focusing on his food like it was the most interesting thing he'd ever seen.

"We don't have to talk about it if you don't want to," said Nico.

Will managed a smile. His warmth was genuine—like it always was, since he was basically a *literal* ray of sunshine—and it softened Nico just a bit. "We can," he said. "Just maybe not now, Nico. Austin and Kayla just left. The camp is calm. Serene. *Quiet.* Let's just appreciate the break, okay?"

Nico nodded, but he wasn't sure how he was supposed to do what Will had requested. When had he *ever* gotten a break before? If it wasn't dead Roman emperors, it was his father. Or Minos. Or his stepmother, Persephone. It had been years since that particular incident had happened, but he was *still* annoyed about being turned into a dandelion. A *dandelion*! It was an affront to his aesthetic!

And there were other things he didn't want to remember. Darker things. Ghosts that would probably visit him eventually. Nico stuffed it all down—making a grumpy little ball of darkness inside his chest. Then he forced a smile as he listened to Will talk about all the things they could do that fall while they stayed at camp.

It would be fine. Everything would be fine.

"My grumpy little ball of darkness," added Will, poking him in the ribs.

"Ew, gross," said Nico, dancing away from him. "We are *not* making that a thing."

"Did you already forget that I was once your—and I am quoting you here, Nico—'significant annoyance'?"

"Oh, you're *still* that," said Nico, and then Will was chasing him down the hill, back into camp. In that moment, Nico allowed himself to enjoy the sensation. Will was right: there were no threats whatsoever on the horizon. No Big Bads. No lurking demigod traitors, no hidden monsters waiting to destroy Camp Half-Blood.

But then dread prickled across Nico's skin. His body was warning him, wasn't it? *Don't get too comfortable*, it was telling him. *He's waiting for you in Tartarus. Or have you forgotten about him like everyone else did?*

Maybe this period of rest wasn't such a good thing. If Nico didn't have some terrible monster or villain to fight, then what excuse did he have to ignore the voice any longer?

The truth was, he couldn't ignore it even if he wanted to. He'd been visited by so many ghosts over the years. The dead wanted to be heard, and who better to listen to them than the son of Hades?

But *this* voice . . . it did not belong to someone who had passed on. And Nico had never heard someone sound as desperate for help.

So his mood was muted by the time he and Will made it to the dining pavilion after stopping by their cabins to freshen up first. It felt strange to be in this place that was normally so alive. Now, there were only a few staff dryads and harpies spread unevenly around the various tables. The camp director, Dionysus—Mr. D to all of them—was lounging at the head table with Chiron, who had somehow beaten them to dinner. The two administrators were so deep in conversation that they barely acknowledged Will when he waved.

Even the satyrs who served Nico and Will didn't seem all that

Her words were lost as the taxi jerked forward and disappeared in a blur of gray.

Yep. Nico loved the sisters.

"So, that's it," said Will. "They were the last, weren't they?"

"Indeed," said Chiron. "Aside from some of the staff, the satyrs, and the dryads, Camp Half-Blood is actually . . . empty."

The old centaur sounded a bit lost. As far as Nico could recall since he'd started coming here, this was the first time that there were no demigods present. Aside from him and Will, that is.

"This is weird," said Nico. "*Really* weird."

"A lot has happened over the past few years," said Chiron wistfully. "I understand more than ever why campers would want to go home to be with their families, or to see the world."

"I guess . . ." said Nico.

"Now, gentlemen," said Chiron, dusting off the front of his vest, "I've got a meeting with Juniper and the dryads about tree rot. Exciting stuff, I assure you. I'll see you at dinner?"

They nodded, then waved as Chiron galloped off.

"So," said Nico, "what do we do next?"

Will, still holding Nico's hand, guided him back up the hill. "Well, we don't have any monsters to slay."

"Boo. I could raise a skeleton army to perform a choreographed dance. I bet I could teach them 'Single Ladies,' if you like."

Will chuckled. "We don't have any Roman emperors to locate and dethrone, either."

Nico flinched. "Ugh. Don't remind me. If I could go the rest of my life without even thinking Nero's name again, I'd be happy."

"That's a funny joke," said Will as they reached the summit. "What is?"

"You," said Will. "Being happy."

Nico rolled his eyes.

"I think we are," said Will, taking Nico's hand. "Mom's touring for her new album this fall, and I don't know if I want to bounce around the country in the back of a van."

"Could be fun," said Austin. "I hope I get to travel because of my music one day."

Kayla nodded. "I wonder what it would be like to see other places without worrying whether some murderous statue is going to kill you."

"Oh, come on," said Nico. "Where's the fun in that?"

"Are you going to get in the car?" Tempest growled. "Or are you paying us to listen to your boring conversation?"

She was hanging out the window with an open palm extended toward them. Austin paid her with three drachmas, tipping her heavily as Chiron had suggested. Tempest examined the coins for a moment—Nico didn't know how, as she had no eyes behind that thick gray curtain of hair—then grunted. She pulled herself back into the car.

"Get in," she said.

There were quick hugs and cheek kisses, and then Austin and Kayla climbed into the backseat of the Gray Sisters' taxi. All the while, the sisters continued to argue.

Kayla looked around the cab. "We've been on worse adventures," she said to those outside the car.

"*Have* we?" asked Austin.

"Anyway, hope to see you soon," said Kayla. "And don't get into any trouble, you two."

Austin leaned across Kayla to poke his head out the window, a mischievous excitement on his face. "But if there *is* trouble . . ."

Will waved at them. "You'll know. Promise."

"Be safe yourselves!" Chiron called out.

"Drive, Anger! Drive!" screamed Wasp. "Isn't that what you *do*? Honestly, why do you even sit in that seat if you don't—"

Still, he sympathized with Kayla and Austin. As Chiron worked to open the trunk, both demigods looked more frightened than they ever had in the last year.

"You sure you don't want me to shadow-travel you to Manhattan?" Nico offered.

Will sighed. "Nico, you can't use shadow-travel like public transportation. It'll drain you dry."

"It's okay, Nico," Kayla said, sounding like she was trying hard to believe it. "We'll be fine."

"Plus, we're going to different places," said Austin. "My mom's meeting me uptown. I actually got into an academy up in Harlem, and she found an apartment for us close by!"

"Sounds like a good place to end up," said Will. "Not too far from here."

"And there's so much history in Harlem to explore," added Austin. "Apparently, one of the clubs where Miles Davis used to play has reopened!"

Nico nodded halfheartedly. He tried to remember who Miles Davis was. . . . Had he scored the soundtrack for *Star Wars?*

"What about you, Kayla?" asked Chiron, loading her archery gear into the trunk.

"Back to Toronto," she said. "Dad wanted me to come home, and it's actually been a while. I'm pretty excited, to be honest." Her eyes glinted. "Especially to prove that I'm now better than him at archery!"

Austin turned to Nico and Will. "So . . . you two are really staying here?"

Nico hoped Will would answer first. The sun falling behind the western hills made Will's curly blond hair look like it was aflame. For a moment, Nico wondered if Will was using his glow-in-the-dark power.

Either way, it made Nico a little annoyed. Why did Will have to be so beautiful all the time?

shadow-travel to the bumpy, vomit-inducing nightmare that was riding in that car. The Gray Sisters had a long history of detesting heroes, and at this point they viewed *every* inhabitant of Camp Half-Blood as a potential hero to be detested.

Nico didn't want to admit it to the others, but he had met the sisters several times on his own, and he kind of liked them. They were thorny. Difficult. Stuck in their ways. Chaotic, yet weirdly dependable. They wore their darkness on their sleeves. For Styx's sake, they all shared a single *eye*. How could Nico *not* appreciate them?

The sisters were in the midst of an argument as one of the rear doors swung open.

"I know exactly what I'm doing, Wasp," said the old lady sitting shotgun, her stringy gray hair swaying over her face. "When have I ever *not* known what I'm doing?"

"Oh, *oh!*" screeched Wasp, who sat up front in the middle. "That's lush. That's a real *lush* opinion, Tempest!"

"Do you even know what *lush* means?" Tempest shot back.

The driver groaned dramatically. "Are you two *children*? Will you please stop talking?"

Tempest threw her hands up and put on her best imitation of the driver (which confused Nico, since they all sounded identical). "Oh, my name is Anger, and I'm *sooooo* mature."

"I will eat the eye," warned Anger. "I'll do it."

"You *wouldn't*," said Wasp.

"With salt and pepper and a little paprika!" Anger threatened. "I'll do it."

"Hi," said Austin, hoisting his saxophone case. "Is there any way you could pop the trunk? We have some luggage."

All three Gray Sisters spun toward Austin and spoke in unison: "NO!"

Then they fell back into arguing. Nico decided right then and there that these were his favorite people in the whole world.

heard what the Oracle had prophesied a few weeks ago, and Nico hadn't shared it with anyone else yet, not even the other counselors. Why should he? It hadn't warned of any doomsday threats to Camp Half-Blood. The world was—as far as he knew—safe for now from angry gods or rebellious Titans. Resurrected maniacal Roman emperors were no longer a thing to worry about.

The prophecy merely concerned that lone voice in his dreams, begging for help.

Specifically, *Nico's* help.

"Some of the satyrs collected your things," said Chiron as the four demigods joined him at the road. "They wish you well on your journey."

"We might need it," Kayla grumbled. "Chiron, just tell us the truth. The Gray Sisters aren't going to kill us, are they?"

"What? No!" He looked aghast. "At least, they haven't killed anyone so far."

"You and Nico!" cried Austin, throwing up his hands. "Both of you think that's an acceptable thing to tell us?"

Chiron's smile lines crinkled around his eyes. "Now, now, you're demigods. You'll be fine. Try tipping them a few extra drachmas at the start of the trip, though. I've heard that helps make the experience less . . . intense?"

He fished in the pocket of his archery vest, pulled out a golden coin, and threw it into the road. "*Stop, O Chariot of Damnation!*"

No sooner had Chiron finished speaking than the taxi arrived.

It did not putter or cruise up to the group. It *appeared*. The coin sank into the pavement, tendrils of dark smoke curled upward, the asphalt twisted, and the Gray Sisters' taxi erupted into being. It *looked* like a taxi, all right, but its edges swirled and wafted if you stared at it too long. Nico had heard all about Percy's, Meg's, and Apollo's experiences with this particular mode of transportation. They'd repeatedly told him that they even preferred his times exhausting to be one of their counselors. He especially didn't want to say good-bye to Kayla and Austin.

As they passed through the strawberry fields, Nico sensed Kayla's and Austin's tension growing. They'd had to make a difficult decision about their travel arrangements earlier that day, and as the four of them climbed Half-Blood Hill, Kayla and Austin slowed.

"I'm thinking that maybe we should have chosen differently," said Kayla.

"You sure we'll be fine, Nico?" asked Austin.

"Yeah," he said. "I mean . . . no one has ever *died* or anything."

"That's not nearly as comforting as you think it is!" said Kayla.

"You'll be okay," said Will, and he put his hand on Austin's shoulder. "I've heard it's chaotic, maybe a bit nauseating, but you'll make it home safely."

They reached the summit of the hill, where the Golden Fleece glittered on the lowest branch of the pine tree. Below, Farm Road 3.141 curved around the base of the hill, defining the outer border of camp. On the gravel shoulder, next to a pile of boxes and duffel bags stood Chiron, the Camp Half-Blood activities director, his equine lower half gleaming white in the afternoon light.

"There you are!" the centaur called out. "Come along, then."

None of them hurried. It was obvious to Nico that Kayla and Austin weren't in a rush to leave camp. Most everyone else had already returned to their "normal" lives, except . . . well, what was normal for someone like Nico?

Epic battles.

Constantly facing the threat of defeat and death.

The dead talking to him.

Prophecies.

The voice from his dreams bubbled up inside him again now, calling out for help.

Rachel Dare's words haunted him, too. Only he and Will had

"I'm considering all the reasons why you'd give that answer," he said. "You might be onto something."

"He's powerful," said Nico.

"And decisive," added Will. "He'd always know exactly where to go for your date. No arguing about that."

"Does he take off his helmet to eat?" said Kayla.

Nico laid his hand over his heart. "Imagine Darth Vader removing his helmet over dinner and then staring longingly into your eyes over the table. Now *that* is romance."

Will laughed hard, then flashed that brilliant smile of his.

Why, oh why, did it feel like such a victory to make Will laugh? For a long time, Nico had assumed he himself did not have a heart. He was the son of Hades, after all. Love didn't find people like him. But then came . . . Will. Will, who could melt Nico's iciness with a smile. Anyone could have guessed which god was Will's father—he radiated energy and light. Sometimes *literally*, as they had learned in the troglodytes' caverns earlier that year. Will was Apollo's son, through and through.

Maybe that whole saying about opposites attracting was true, because Nico didn't know a single person who was more his opposite. Despite that, they were coming up on a year. A year *together*. Nico had an actual boyfriend.

He still wasn't sure he believed it was real.

The four demigods continued their walk through Camp Half-Blood. There was no fire burning in the amphitheater. Maybe, since it was starting to cool down on Long Island, Nico and Will would light one tonight. No campers were rushing off to the armory or the forge; no one was visiting the Cave of the Oracle. The cabins were empty (aside from Hades's and Apollo's), and that was the clearest sign summer was over.

Nico didn't want to admit it out loud, but he was going to miss . . . well, pretty much all the campers, even though it was at

What did I ever do to deserve him? Nico wondered. He asked himself that question a lot.

"Okay, I've made my decision," said Nico.

"I might explode," said Austin.

"The world might end," said Kayla, now holding the lollipop at her side, her eyes bright with anxiety. "Like, *actually* end this time."

"So," said Nico, "if I had to choose . . ."

"Yes?" prompted Will. "You would choose . . . ?"

Nico took a deep breath.

"Darth Vader."

Will and Kayla groaned, but Austin looked like Nico had just given him a Ferrari as a birthday present.

"Dude!" Austin screamed. "That is the best answer!"

"It is the *worst* answer!" said Kayla. "Why would you choose Vader when Kylo Ren is *right there?*"

"*I* was hoping for a deep cut," Will mused. "Maybe someone like General Grievous or Dryden Vos."

"Hold on," said Nico. "I just finished watching all those movies *yesterday.* I can barely remember what happened in the prequels at this point." He paused. "Were those all actual characters in Star Wars, or are you joking?"

"Don't distract from your truth, Nico," said Kayla. "*Darth Vader?* You'd go on a date with *Darth Vader?*" She crunched on her lollipop. "I've lost all joy, Nico. All of it."

"Welcome to my world," Nico joked. He caught Will grimacing—a brief flicker of one, but he still caught it.

"This is a safe space," said Austin. "No judgment allowed for our answers, remember?"

"I take it back," said Kayla. "It's an all-judgment space."

"You're very quiet, Will," said Nico. "Especially as *the* number one Star Wars fan in the group."

CHAPTER

Nico faced the worst decision of his life, and he was certain he was going to mess it up.

"I can't do this," he said to Will Solace, the stunningly beautiful son of Apollo, who stood across from him. But it was Austin Lake—one of Will's half-siblings—who Nico chose to focus on. He was pacing behind Will, which only made Nico more nervous.

"Stop moving, Austin," said Nico. "I can't concentrate."

"Sorry, dude," said Austin. "This is just so stressful."

"You gotta choose," Will said to Nico. "Those are the rules."

Nico frowned. "I'm the son of Hades. I don't live by most rules."

"But you *did* agree to these," said Kayla Knowles, another child of Apollo. She twirled a cherry lollipop in her mouth. "Are you a demigod without honor, Nico di Angelo?"

Austin kept pacing. "To be fair, I don't think this task requires any *actual* honor."

"Quiet!" said Nico, running his hands through his hair. What if he made the wrong choice? Would Will be disappointed in him?

But studying Will's face, Nico saw only anticipation. The good kind. Will was ready for whatever Nico would say, and no matter how this ended, Will would still think just as highly of him.

COMING NEXT FROM RICK RIORDAN

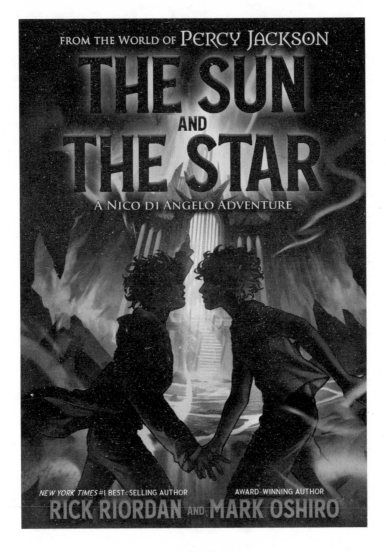

MAY 2023

ACKNOWLEDGMENTS

I'd like to thank my advance readers for their help with this book: Roshani Chokshi, author of the best-selling Aru Shah quintet; sensitivity readers Riddhi Kamal Parekh and Lizzie Huxley-Jones; and Dr. Robert Ballard, a retired United States Navy officer and professor of oceanography who is now a full-time deep-sea explorer. If you want to read about his amazing real-life underwater adventures, check out his book *Into the Deep: A Memoir from the Man Who Found the* Titanic.